She Followed He...
Heartbreak an...

When she was sixteen her father married her off to a drunken neighbor in return for a tract of land. Her motherless childhood had already been hard as a farm girl on the desolate prairies of North Dakota. Abused and helpless, Marge Garrity seemed destined for a tragic fate.

But Marge is determined to make her life count, no matter what. Her escape from her brutal marriage takes her to California, where she struggles to survive the Great Depression and soon answers the lure of the state's untamed northern half. There, embraced by the rough-and-ready people who built the great Ruck-a-chucky Dam on the American River, she begins to find her true mission in life and the possibility for love and happiness with an Army Corp engineer of Cherokee Indian descent.

This vivid saga of one woman's life in the early decades of a turbulent century is told from the heart of a true storyteller.

Author Dolores Durando knows Marge's world very well. She grew up ninety years ago on the plains of North Dakota.

Beyond the Bougainvillea

DOLORES DURANDO

Bell Bridge Books

This is a work of fiction. Names, characters, places and incidents are either the products of the author's imagination or are used fictitiously. Any resemblance to actual persons (living or dead,) events or locations is entirely coincidental.

Bell Bridge Books
PO BOX 300921
Memphis, TN 38130
ISBN: 978-1-61194-004-6

Bell Bridge Books is an Imprint of BelleBooks, Inc.

We at BelleBooks enjoy hearing from readers.
Visit our websites – www.BelleBooks.com and www.BellBridgeBooks.com.

10 9 8 7 6 5 4 3 2

Cover design: Debra Dixon
Interior design: Hank Smith
Photo credits: Flowers © Irina Magrelo | Dreamstime.com
Woman (manipulated) © Jpaget Rfphotos | Dreamstime.com

Author photo: Marilane Jorgenson

:Ltbb:01:

For my children

DoriAnne, who took two years of her life to decipher my handwritten pages, and who lit the lamp when it got dark.

Marilane, who mothers me and whose love covers me like a warm blanket, whose faith in me never falters.

My steadfast son, Bill; my pride knows no bounds! A man among men. Hats off to his devoted wife, Cathy.

My son Michael; hand in hand we've raced down the "road less traveled." His spirit is ever with me.

My love and gratitude to my other son Matthew; who is always there for me, who shows me such love, both in word and deed.

ACKNOWLEDGEMENTS

The author wishes to acknowledge the invaluable assistance of the following people:

This book would still be at rest under my bed had it not been for the determined efforts of my friend, Elaine Baack; thank you seems so inadequate.

My heartfelt gratitude to a fine editor, Barbara Holiday, whose friendship I treasure and whose patience I envy.

Last, but not least, I am grateful for the support of the Rogue River Writer's Group, who has pushed me when I lingered!

Chapter 1

1924

Trembling against the onslaught of the punishing wind that drove the swirling snow into every crevice, the old house stood. A house, not far removed from the sod shanty it had once been, forlorn, on a half section of the frozen, desolate North Dakota prairie.

The girl stood at the upstairs window of her mother's bedroom to watch the sleigh that bucked and struggled on the road. Only the snow-covered fence posts marked the way that was little more than a cow path, even in the best of times.

Her mother's casket, although wrapped tightly in the sleigh, slid and bounced as the horses plunged through the deep snow.

She watched until the sleigh became just a tiny speck, then blurred into the horizon.

A small girl for her age, just eleven, with long red hair that curled around the shoulders of her slight body, her gray eyes, now red and swollen, seemed far too big for the tear-stained little face. The sobs had dissipated into hiccups when Aunt Kate's voice called from the kitchen.

"Mary Margaret. Please come down. You can't stay up there another minute. Please, I want to talk to you."

The child held tight to the worn railing as she slowly descended the stairs, then sat silently as Aunt Kate stirred up the fire in the old cookstove.

"My dear, I've been here two weeks, now I must go home," she paused as she added water to the battered coffeepot, then added the coffee grounds.

"I've tried so hard to convince your Pa to let you come home with me, but he won't hear of it." Pulling a chair close, she encircled the girl in her arms.

"My sister will never rest if I have to leave you here. When your mother and I found the opportunity to come to America, we endured the long frightening journey to what we believed would be a better life.

Well, I found mine; your mother found Cormac. He was a hard man then and I don't see that time has changed him for the better." Her tears fell on the curls that covered the child's face.

Sometime during the night the girl was awakened by the sound of the sleigh on the icy snow and the closing of the barn door. She knew the team would still be harnessed in the morning but at least they were in the barn. The sound of a kitchen door slamming, a chair knocked over, a slurred curse, and she knew Pa was looking in the dark for his Seagram's Seven Crown bottle, trying to remember where he had hidden it.

The next morning, Pa was hunched over his coffee cup in the same clothes in which he had slept. Aunt Kate pulled up a chair beside him. With a soft voice she pleaded, "Cormac, won't you please let Mary Margaret come home with me? She needs a mother."

"Hell no. I've told ya a dozen times. How many more times do I have to say NO? She's eleven years old now, time to learn some responsibility. Her mother spoiled her rotten. It was 'school' this and 'school' that. Why can't ya call me Mac like everybody else does? Every time ya say 'Cormac,' I know yer gonna say sumpthin' I don't wanna hear."

"Promise me you won't take her out of school. Her mother was so proud of her; she always stood at the head of her class. Promise me, Cormac," she begged.

"Yeah, sure, I promise. As long as she gets her work done first."

Four years later she was taller and thinner. Her fair skin was chapped. Her hands were always rough, fingernails broken, her hair long and unkempt. She dreaded Mondays the most, the day she scrubbed the dirty clothes, rubbing them on a tin washboard. Boiling them on the stove and hanging them on a rope stretched between two large trees. In the winter the clothes would freeze on the line.

What she hated the most was Pa and Ed hanging about, spitting Copenhagen in an old rusty tomato can, passing the bottle back and forth. Sometimes a halfhearted shoving match would ensue between the two of them. Ed was a farmer who lived on the adjoining half section of land, and whose friendship Pa had acquired, or the other way around. The two men found they had a mutual interest in Seagram's Seven, politics and cards. Ed was often too drunk to go home at night and slept on the couch, rousing himself in the mornings to grumble loudly, "Get some coal for that there fire…colder'n hell in here."

She struggled to keep up with her schoolwork, bringing her books home to study by the light of the smoky lamp until her Pa would yell, "Will ya blow that damn lamp out? Kerosene costs money and money don't grow on trees. Ya hear me girl?" Once she had dared ask him if whiskey was free. "Yer a gettin' too damn sassy. I think you better forget about school fer a couple weeks," he slurred.

One night Ed looked up from his cards, leaned across the table to Pa and breathed out, "Ya know, Mac, that girl of your'n is beginning to look like a woman, pretty, all that red hair. She's a good worker, too."

Later that same week, Pa looked at the girl as though it was the first time he'd ever seen her. "I'm gonna take ya to town and get ya some new work boots and maybe a dress. We get tired of look'n at ya in them overalls."

She had just finished her chores in the barn the morning she saw Ed coming down the path. She was surprised and asked, "For gracious sake, are you lost?" "No, but I want to talk to you," he said. "You know, Marge, you and I should get married. Your Pa says you're almost sixteen. We could combine the farms and we'd own a full section. Why we'd even be able to hire some help and you'd never have to do outside chores again. I'd buy you lots of pretty dresses and you could go to school every day. You could even graduate with your class next year."

Marge looked at him in amazement and laughed. "Ed, you're as old as Pa. I don't want to ever get married." Ed was stung by her reference to his age.

"I'm still the man I was at twenty, don't you worry about that." Then he added, "You'd better think about it because your Pa has made all the plans. Just think…you'd get to finish school and never have to milk these miserable cows again."

In June, on her sixteenth birthday, the Justice of the Peace pronounced her Mrs. Ed Garrity. On the way home Ed leaned close to her, his stale breath wet on the side of her face, "Do ya feel any different, Mrs. Garrity?"

"No," she whispered.

"Well, cheer up, you will," he said with a sidelong glance.

That night when she went upstairs to bed she heard Pa and Ed laughing loudly as they chinked glasses and celebrated the marriage with a joke not meant for a lady's ears. She propped a chair against the door and lay rigid in her mother's bed, afraid to close her eyes. Hours later she heard him pushing and swearing at the door.

"Marge. Open this damn door," he demanded.

"Go to bed, you're drunk." Her terrified answer.

"Yer damn right I'm drunk, but not too drunk," he chuckled. "I'm your husband now and I'm a comin' in."

"Pa." she screamed. "Pa, make Ed go away, make him go to the couch."

"Open that door, Marge. He's your husband and he has the right." yelled her Pa from downstairs.

The door flew open as the chair splintered and Ed lurched into the room, falling onto the bed. She was on her feet in an instant, screaming "Pa. Pa." She stumbled over the chair; Ed knocked her back over the bed and shook her until she thought her neck would break.

"Listen here you damn little heifer, yer my wife and I have the right. Got that? Don't you try that again."

Fear and shock ran through her as she smothered under his sweaty body. The pain came, agonizing pain, unlike any she had ever known. His sweat and her blood mingled as it stained her body and left its indelible scar forever.

"Pa." She shrieked until her throat felt raw and Ed's huge beefy hand covered her mouth.

When he finished, he chuckled, "Now Mrs. Garrity, do you feel any different?" As she crawled to the edge of the bed and vomited, he turned, snoring beside her.

The next morning Ed slept in. The girl made coffee. Listlessly, through dry cracked lips, she asked, "Pa, why didn't you help me when I called out to you?"

"It was your party," he shrugged. The coffeepot slipped out of her hand and the steaming brew ran through his hair and down his face. Pa leaped to his feet screaming, "Ya little bitch, ya did that on purpose."

Hesitating in the kitchen doorway, the milk pail in her hand, she called back bitterly, "Sorry, Pa, I thought it was a party." A small line fought to carve a smile on her lips as his curses bellowed after her all the way to the barn. She sat on the three-legged stool and sobbed. Her head bent against the old cow's warm flank, the milk and tears flowing together. *If only Aunt Kate were still alive…where can I go? I'm worse than a slave to those drunken old men; surely it can't get any worse than this*, she thought.

Later that day when both men had gone into town to play poker at the local tavern, Marge bridled the big draft mare and rode bareback fifteen miles to the Gunderson farm. They were not only the nearest, but the only neighbors that Marge knew. Ruth Gunderson was a loving and kind woman who had suspected something wasn't right when she heard the young neighbor girl had married the old man. She knew Ed's previous wife had left him; rumor had it for very good reasons.

The moment Ruth put her arms around her, the thin, quivering girl broke into hysterical tears, sobbing out her fear and outrage. Ruth sat with her arms around Marge and rocked her. She listened to Marge's story with tears in her eyes and frustration rising in her heart. It seemed there was nothing she could do to help this young girl. "I've been lucky … married to a good man for forty-five years. I don't know what to tell you except that I am here for you." As Marge rode away, Ruth waved and called, "Try to take care of yourself; God's knows I'd help you if I could."

Pa and Ed came home late that night, laughing about Ed's foul boasts to his poker buddies. "Yep, I'm a better man now than I was at twenty. There's a party every night at our house," he bragged.

From her mother's bed, Marge heard their drunken laughter; she heard the springs in the worn old couch creak and knew that Ed couldn't make it up the stairs.

"Thank God … I hope they both die in their sleep."

By August the heat and humidity was unbearable, with no reprieve at night. There was an endless battle with mosquitoes, flies and grasshoppers. The insects clung to her sweat-drenched body as she rode the bull rake to gather up the winter hay; after that, there were always the evening chores. Finally her body rebelled. One evening she fell asleep in the fragrant hay. Not much later she was rudely awakened by Ed coming down the path in the dark yelling, "Where the hell is supper?"

The very thought of food revolted her, especially in the mornings when she cooked breakfast; the smell of unwashed bodies, sour whiskey breath and greasy side pork frying sickened her. This morning she stumbled to the porch, clung to the railing as wave after wave of nausea convulsed her slender body. Everything turned black and she fell to the floor.

Pa shoved back his chair and grumbled, "Damn it, Ed, pick her up, I guess Dr. Tom will have to see what in the hell is wrong with her; probably the same thing her mother died from."

"You sure as hell sold me a bill of goods, damn you, Mac. You said she was strong as a horse and by God it's you that's go'n to pay the doctor bill when we get her into town."

Dr. Tom was thorough and minced no words. "She is seriously underweight, bordering on anemia, and almost three months pregnant. Sixteen years old is too damn young to be carrying a baby and taking care of you two old drunks. I doubt she will carry it to term. She needs bed rest and lots of it. A good diet and . . . here, take these pills for her."

On the way home, Ed and Pa quarreled furiously. "You can pay for those damn pills, too. Doc thinks money grows on trees."

"The hell I will, she's your wife. It wasn't me partyin' upstairs every night," Pa jeered. "You used to sleep on the couch with your boots on and now you can't find your rubbers?"

Ed was nearly speechless with rage. "It sure as hell has never been a party. She's as cold as a stone and I have to fight her every time. Sign my half section over to me and you can have your damn daughter back. Did you remember to pick up a bottle?"

Marge curled up on the backseat with her hands over her ears and she prayed, *"Please, God, not his baby. Let me lose it or let me die … not his baby."*

Marge lay upstairs in her mother's bed. She could hear the men bickering constantly.

"It's your turn to milk, I'll cook."

"No, I'll cook, here's the pail."

"Hire some help you lazy old skinflint, I'm takin' care of the hay at my place."

"Your place? You mean 'our' place don't ya?"

"Go to hell." The screen door slammed hard enough to make the windows rattle.

Ruth tried to come over every week and bring good home-cooked food and other basic necessities. Marge foraged in the kitchen at night when both men were asleep; she kept her own clean dishes upstairs.

Ed attempted to get into the bedroom one night and banged on the door. "You been rest'n long enough, I'm a'comin on in. You hear me, girl?"

"I'll tell Dr. Tom. I'll tell Dr. Tom," she screamed. He cursed both her and Dr. Tom all the way down the stairs.

Pa woke up and said, "Leave her alone, Ed. For God's sake, she's sick and pregnant."

"You can go to hell, too," Ed said as he sat on the squeaky old couch and pulled off his boots. The couch groaned as Ed's big body settled into the lumps of cotton padding.

"It's your turn to do chores in the morning."

"Are you say'n your prayers, Ed?" Pa snickered.

The months passed slowly. The hot summer days faded into fall, then came the bitter cold that ushered in winter. Marge's slender body thickened and became clumsy. She averted her eyes when she passed the mirror on her mother's dresser. Her brain kept up a steady chant, *I don't want it. I don't want this baby. Please God, let me lose it or let me die.*

Her eyes were huge in her thin face. She lost any desire for food. Ruth tried in vain to get her to eat. "Honey, you must eat something or you'll lose your strength."

"I want to die, Ruth, please let me be."

"Oh honey, please don't say that; you're so young, just try this. I just took it out of the oven. You'll feel better if you eat."

"No, no, no. I'm not hungry. My back hurts so bad I can hardly stand it."

"Let me take you in to see Dr. Tom," Ruth coaxed.

"No, he can't help me now. There's only one way for me to feel better. I've got six weeks to go and then I'll be free of this thing."

Ruth shook her head sadly and replied, "Honey, I have to go home now. Be sure to have Marianne call if you need me." Marge heard the door close, then the sound of the car sputter to a start. She was alone, wrapped in her mother's threadbare robe. She paced back and forth holding her belly with both hands, her pain worsening with every step. *This can't be happening; it's not due for six weeks.*

Her pain intensified as did her fear, and finally she faced the grim reality that the baby was coming ... now. She wanted to scream but all that came through her tight lips was a moan. In desperation, she dragged herself to the head of the stairs and screamed, "Pa, Pa." After what seemed a century, Pa shoved his head out the doorway of his room.

"What in hell is going on?" he barked. "Do you know what time it is?"

"Oh Pa, I'm so sick. I think the baby is coming now. Please help me."

"What the hell do you want me to do about it?"

"Call Ruth, Pa, please."

"You tell Ed. And tell him to blow that goddamn lamp out before he goes to bed. That kerosene costs money."

"Please, Pa, please get Dr. Tom." Her voice faltered as the agonizing pain held her speechless.

"Alright, alright. I'll go first thing in the morning." With that he closed the door.

Clinging to the handrail, she started downstairs, pausing every other step when her body convulsed. *God is punishing me for wishing it dead.*

At last she reached the phone and dialed the operator. "Marianne, call Ruth and tell her the baby's coming and I'm alone." She dropped the receiver as she felt a great flood of warm water rush down her legs, then she crumpled to the freezing old wooden floor.

Pain like a butcher knife sliced through her. It seemed as though a giant hand was squeezing the very life from her body. Just when Marge thought she had no strength left, her body wrenched and she gave a violent, agonizing push. Reaching down, she felt the head, then a shoulder slide out. With another push, "it" fully emerged. She lay panting in a pool of blood and mucus. The room was silent, broken only by her ragged breathing. Marge lay there for a moment then raised herself on her elbows and looked down at the bloody thing between her legs. It didn't move. *At last I'm rid of it, thank God it's dead.*

Marge lay back exhausted, but now fully aware of the cold. Something moved against her leg. She again raised herself on her elbows and was horrified to see a tiny hand flutter upward as though pleading. Then a thin mewing sound came from the still attached bloody baby, breaking the silence, exploding into her newly found peace.

Dear God, what should I do, what should I do? Again she heard the pitiful mewing, almost a whisper cry. She tugged at a corner of the robe and bent to wipe the mucus from its face; as she did, her brain cried out, *Dear God, this baby has my mother's face and my red hair. It is no part of him—it's mine, it's mine.*

She lifted the slippery baby and held it tightly against her. Pain, shock, and fear blurred through her brain like a fog. She knew they would freeze if she didn't get upstairs and under the blankets. She crawled to a chair, one arm holding the baby close to her body and struggled to her feet, pushed the chair ahead of her to the stairs. She grasped the handrail and realized she was too weak to take the first step up. *Oh, please, God help me,* she sobbed. *We'll die if we don't get warm. I've got to get into bed.*

Step by torturous step, she pulled herself up. With one last desperate effort, she collapsed on the bed. The baby, now wet and cold, lay quiet against her belly under the blankets. Marge felt its tiny doll-like hands and feet and tried to warm them with her own chilled body.

A few hours later the men were up. Marge heard Ed growl, "What the hell is this mess all over the floor?"

"I think you've got a baby upstairs, DADDY," Pa gibed.

"I sure as hell never wanted any kids. Why in the hell did she have to go and get herself pregnant anyhow?" Ed stormed in his outrage. Marge turned her face to the wall when she heard him clumping up the stairs. He jerked the blanket back, looked down at the baby and snorted, "Looks like you got yourself a red-headed girl. Sure is ugly, don't look like any a my kin." The baby moved its head and nuzzled against her making little sucking sounds. As in a living nightmare where there is no waking, she whispered, "This isn't real; I have no baby because I have no milk." The blackness crowded in.

Sometime later, Marge woke up to the furious voice of Dr. Tom. "Get the hell out of here and stay out."

"Lookie here, Doc, I got the right," Ed whined.

Dr. Tom, his face contorted with rage, advanced on him. "I said, get the hell out of here before I knock you down those stairs. You got NO RIGHTS, you son of a bitch."

Ed threw up his hands. "Alright, alright," he muttered, "I'm leavin'." Ruth entered the room and stood silently as Dr. Tom pulled back the blanket. He turned a horrified face to Ruth. "God in heaven. How could you let her get like this? What time was the baby born?"

"Sometime around two, I think, on the kitchen floor by the phone. I just got here myself," Ruth answered.

"Sorry. I'm sorry, Ruth," Dr. Tom spoke softly, apologetically. "Those two old bastards ought to be hanged. I'd like to be the one to slap the horse."

He examined the baby and turning to Ruth asked, "Can this girl go home with you? She will die if she stays here. The baby's lungs are full of fluid and the heartbeat is completely off."

"Of course. I brought some clean towels and blankets to wrap her in".

Dr. Tom gathered up the semiconscious Marge, who clung to her baby, and carefully carried them to Ruth's car. His voice shook as he gave Ruth instructions.

"We'll have to make a sugar-tit and try to get some milk into this baby if it is to survive at all."

Marge awoke to find that she was warm in a feather-tick bed with clean bedding wrapped snugly around her. The smell of baking bread told her she was ravenously hungry. She turned her head and saw Ruth beside her rocking the baby, pausing at intervals to dip a cloth into a dish of sweetened milk, then attempting to squeeze a drop or two into the baby's mouth. The milk dribbled quickly down her chin. Ruth tenderly wiped the tiny face and tried again and again.

"What are you going to name this girl?" Ruth asked, not taking her eyes away from the task at hand.

"I will name her for my mother, Margaret. There is no Dugan or Garrity blood in my baby. We will be Marge and Margaret Reagan. Would you help me up, Ruth? I want to rock my baby."

Ruth helped Marge to the rocker and gently handed her the baby girl.

"See if you can get her to swallow. She is the tiniest baby I've ever seen. I doubt she weighs three pounds." Ruth stepped back and gazed at mother and daughter embraced by the soft rays of the late afternoon sun.

Over the next few days, Marge slowly began to regain her strength, tempted by the nourishing food Ruth so lovingly prepared.

Her baby lay listless and silent, only the wheezing sound with each breath indicated that there was still a flickering of life. Marge rocked her constantly, pausing only to drip the sweetened milk into her little mouth, then to wipe off her small, soft chin.

That night Ruth wrapped the heavy quilt around Marge and her dying baby. The colorful squares were suddenly obscene. Marge shivered as a chill ran up her back. When the morning dawned, she was still rocking the baby.

On the sixth day, Dr. Tom drove out, shook the snow from his boots and handed his jacket to Ruth. He sat in a straight-back chair next to the rocker and took hold of Marge's hand. "Marge, I need to tell you," his voice kind and gentle. "This baby cannot survive. You must accept that and go on with your life."

Marge kept on rocking.

Dr. Tom sighed, and with eyes clouded with compassion, continued: "You are a woman now, you must come to terms with life. You must leave here and go as far away as possible. I will help you financially as long as you need it."

Marge rocked. She listened, but was silent. A part of her mind wondered, *when did I become a woman? Was it when Ed broke the door down or was it when I lay on the kitchen floor with a baby between my legs?*

Early the next morning, Marge called out, "Ruth, would you warm the milk? Mother is rocking her now and says that the baby will eat." Ruth's eyes blurred as she pulled the blanket back and saw the tiny face at peace.

It was not long before Dr. Tom arrived. He went to Marge and leaned in close to her. "May I hold the baby, Marge?" She continued to rock without answering, her eyes closed softly as she held the child tightly.

"Please let me hold her," Dr. Tom continued. Again, there was no response. He pulled up a chair and sat close, in silence. Ruth appeared, handing him a cup of steaming coffee.

"She doesn't talk to me either nor has she eaten for almost two days."

Dr. Tom blew on the coffee and drank it quickly. He handed the empty cup to Ruth.

"Marge, please give me the baby now," Dr. Tom coaxed. Marge held the baby tighter.

"I gave her to mother, Dr. Tom." She opened her eyes and stared ahead unblinking. He reached to take the child from Marge, but she held her baby close.

"I don't have her, she's with my mother now. Mother says the baby has dimples when she smiles."

The doctor filled a syringe, gently positioned it against Marge's bare arm and released the plunger. Her eyes slowly closed and her body relaxed. Dr. Tom bent and gently took the small bundle and turned to Ruth.

"The ground is too frozen to dig. I will build a little box and keep her in my shed until spring." His body seemed to shrink under the sadness he felt. "We will tell Marge we have buried her baby next to her mother. That is probably the only comfort we can give her. She must get away as soon as her body mends. I doubt her spirit ever will. I will support her until she can support herself; you know I have no children of my own." Ruth nodded in understanding, feeling compassion for both Marge and Dr. Tom.

It was almost twenty-four hours later when Marge woke up. She turned her head to see the snow drifting down, coating the window with a soft translucent curtain. She lay there quietly, her eyes closed, and attempted to sort out the fuzzy events of the past weeks. She had lost all sense of time and place. She heard her mother's voice speak her name. *Mary Margaret, you know the baby is safe with me. Don't grieve for her. You must get out of that bed and build a life for yourself, far away. I will always be with you, but you must do it yourself. Only you can do it.*

Marge pushed the blankets back and lifted her legs to the side of the bed. She sat there shaking and felt her mother's arms around her. Slowly, her mind cleared. She opened her eyes to see Ruth beside her with tears streaming down her face.

"Honey, Dr. Tom said to tell you he has buried little Margaret beside your mother. He knows that is what you would have wanted. He left something for you and told me to give it to you as soon as you are well." Marge wiped the tears from Ruth's face with the sleeve of her nightgown and smoothed back the gray hair from her brow.

"Ruth, don't cry anymore. You and Dr. Tom have done the right thing. You have saved my life." Marge looked tenderly at Ruth and continued, "To know there are people like you and Dr. Tom has given me hope. Mother told me to do something with my life and now I'm ready. That other life does not exist for me anymore, starting right now." Ruth stood and helped Marge up. She hugged her tightly and thanked the good Lord under her breath.

"I love you, little Marge."

"I am so hungry I could eat a loaf of that wonderful bread with butter and chokecherry jelly…I love you, too."

"I love you both, now let's eat," Ruth's husband boomed.

The nourishing food, the magic feather bed, combined with a stress-free, loving environment, began to show results in the weeks to come. Marge's hair, once so dull and lifeless, regained its natural curl and grew long and luxurious. The heartbreaking past slowly receded into her subconscious. Her body began to fill out, no longer that of an undernourished seventeen-year-old girl, but that of a fully endowed woman.

"You look just like your mother when she first came over from County Cork. She was the most beautiful woman any of us had ever seen…and she was as good as she was beautiful." Ruth gazed upon the lovely young woman standing before her and continued. "Dr. Tom has left a valise for you and a train ticket for Los Angeles. He thinks it is time for you to start over. You have been like a daughter to me, Marge. I love you dearly…but you must do what is best for you. My sister Annie lives in Los Angeles and I have written to her about you. She writes back that you can stay with her family for as long as you like and she will meet you at the station. Annie has a sixteen-year-old daughter, Sue Anne. Perhaps you can finish school with her. Dr. Tom says he will pay your three-dollars-a-week room and board." Ruth let out a deep sigh of relief now that Marge's immediate future was secure.

That night when Marge blew out the smoky lamp and pulled the clean, warm blankets around her, she tossed and turned unable to sleep. She had promised herself she would never think of the past again, but was unable to escape the vivid images that crowded into the very fiber of her being. Her rage and hurt, so long suppressed, flared like a prairie fire gone out of control. Her mind raced around every possibility, discarding this plan or that plan. The night seemed forever, but when the dawn broke and the sun appeared, she laughed out loud. *That's it. That's it. They take the cream to town every Friday, then stay to play poker. The Great Northern train stops at the depot at three forty-five in the afternoon. It's perfect.* As her eyes closed, she smiled. It was not the smile of a girl nearing seventeen, but the smile of a woman who had made a decision … one that would influence the rest of her life.

Marge spoke softly as she cleared the breakfast dishes. "Ruth, let's have another cup of coffee and talk. I have decided you and Dr. Tom know what is best for me. I'd like to leave for California next Friday if you are sure your sister will want me. You know that I will always love you, Ruth. I will never forget you or Dr. Tom; both of you saved my

life and made it possible for me to do something with the rest of it."
Ruth's face crumpled into tears.

"Of course, I will take you, my dear." Ruth's eyes brimmed over
once again. "The men will be in town, won't they? The cream goes in
on Fridays, doesn't it?"

The following week passed slowly now that Marge had made a
plan. There was not much to pack: two heavy, dark dresses that Ruth
had altered to fit Marge's slender body, a flannel nightgown, and a new
cotton dress that Ruth had ordered straight from the Sears & Roebuck
catalogue. Marge never forgot her first store-bought dress, a blue
dirndl with a square-neck and big puffy sleeves. She would never wear
overalls again in her life.

It was early April, but the cold leaden sky didn't seem to care. The
wind pushed the drifted snow back and forth across the road, the
tumbleweeds hanging on the fence like lonely sentinels. As Ruth
neared the dilapidated old house, Marge felt the icy fingers of revulsion
running hand-in-hand with a wild exhilaration that made her heart
thud against her ribs so hard it left her breathless. "Ruth, you'll have to
wait, just a little while. I won't be long."

Marge walked up the narrow dirt path, her courage almost
deserting her as she pushed open the door and hurried through the
house that held such horrible memories.

At the foot of the stairs she paused a moment and remembered
back to the day when she believed her torment would never end;
willing herself to move, she climbed up to the room she had once
thought was her refuge. She faltered beside the threshold, then quickly
made her way across the room. She dropped to her knees and reached
under the bed as far as she could until her fingers found all she had left
of her mother—a round, battered hatbox. The red rose images faded
into the cardboard and the worn gold braid clung by a thread. If the
hatbox could have spoken, it would have told of the long, weary trip
from the Emerald Isle to this godforsaken farm and the crushing
disappointment upon arrival.

Carefully, the lid was lifted. Trembling hands picked up the
beautiful Irish lace shawl. Now yellow with age, her mother had
brought this with her from County Cork to wear as a bride. With great
tenderness, Marge draped the shawl around her shoulders, closed her
eyes and felt her mother's presence; the soft caress of the lace seemed

to embrace her as in years gone by when her mother held her. She felt a gentle urging, a nudge to go on, move forward, let go, and the tears flooded down her cheeks as she reached for the rosary, remembering the many times she had witnessed the beads slip through her mother's reddened, work-worn hands.

On the very bottom of the box lay the wedding photo. It was of her mother only. On one side of the photo, the ragged edges hinted at the rage Marge felt the morning after her own marriage when she had ripped her father's image into shreds, adding them to the fire she built to make his coffee. Carefully, she replaced the photo and lifted the shawl from her shoulders; with love and gentleness, she returned it to the confines of the box and laid the rosary within its folds. With the hatbox under her arm, she quickly made her way down the stairs, placed the articles outside the front door and waved to Ruth.

Marge hurriedly closed the door and ran through the kitchen and out to the rickety shed. There in the corner were two large containers of kerosene. Half carrying and half dragging, she pushed them into the kitchen. She pulled one container upstairs and spilled the contents on the bed, the floor, and the tired yellowed curtains, saving just enough to soak each stair-step behind her. Downstairs she moved into her father's bedroom and pulled back the dirty blankets. She grabbed his greasy pillow, pushed her hand to the bottom of the covering. She laughed as she pulled out his stash of poker money neatly tied in a brown paper bag. Back in the living room she stepped over to the old couch where Ed slept; the couch seemed to permanently hold the imprint of his big body. Leaning over, she lifted the middle cushion and found the dirty cloth bag closed with a large safety pin. She stuffed it in the pocket of her coat next to Pa's stash.

Quickly now, she walked through the kitchen gathering everything burnable, including the wooden chairs. Next, the drawers from the timeworn cabinets, the dirty clothes of both men, all heaped on Pa's bed. She soaked the mattress and all that was piled upon it. She soaked the couch and everything she could reach, using the last remaining drops on the floor. Pulling off her apron she threw it on Ed's couch, lit the match and watched it burst into flames. The fire ran on the line of fuel to the left and jumped on Pa's bed. Instantly it torched the greasy clothes, then ran straight ahead and danced up the stairs. Both rooms began to burn furiously when she stepped out the door, tucked the hatbox under her arm and ran to the car. Pulling open the door she said breathlessly, "Ruth, hurry. I don't want to miss that train."

"You sure do smell like kerosene, child, how did you get that all over you?"

"I'll tell you later, let's go." Ruth stepped on the gas and drove the long straight stretch of road. Marge looked back and clapped her hands, exploding into hysterical laughter.

"What's so funny?" Ruth asked.

"Look back," Marge yelled between gulps of laughter. Reaching for the sky, the flames seemed to crackle and pop in an ecstasy of joy. The black oily smoke boiled furiously, then dissipated into the gray horizon.

"Oh honey. You didn't," Ruth gasped in horror.

"I did, I did."

Ruth slowed the car with a look of disbelief and then, laughing without restraint, she fumbled for the lever on the steering column of her husband's pride and joy.

"We better not miss that train. I'm glad it's starting to snow, our tracks will be covered." They both doubled over in a fit of laughter.

The Great Northern stood like a bull ready to charge, spewing steam and fuming with anticipation. The engineer blew the whistle and shouted, "ALL ABOARD." Marge got on the train and found her way to a seat covered in red velour, next to the window. Moments later the train snorted, spilled a cloud of steam across the platform and jolted her forward. She watched Ruth out of the window as she ran beside the slow-moving train, waving and laughing. The train picked up speed and Ruth, still waving, disappeared in the distance. Marge tucked her valise beneath the seat and sat quietly, though her thoughts were running rampant. Apprehensive of the future, her hands trembled, but soon the exciting promise of a new life in the magical golden state dried the tears on her cheeks and she smiled.

It was late in the afternoon when Ruth drove in the driveway. Her husband met her at the gate.

"Hurry," he urged. "Give me the keys, there's smoke over at Mac's place. I suppose the miserable old drunk has set himself on fire with those damn cigarettes. I'll be back as soon as I can." Ruth handed him the keys without a word and hurried through the new-fallen snow into the haven of her kitchen.

She stoked up the fire and put the coffeepot on. Her knees shook as she grabbed for a chair and sat down heavily. With head in hands she rocked back and forth. *What am I going to tell John?* Suddenly the consequences of her actions were knocking on her door. *I've never lied to him in forty-five years and I don't want to lie to him now. He's never raised his voice to me, he's never needed to. I've always been a good wife, but knowing Marge burned that house…how is he going to feel about that? I can't say I'm sorry, I'd do it again. Marge had every reason and they deserved what they got. I hope they sleep in the snow tonight.*

If I have to lie, God will forgive me. So will John, eventually, especially if he has to sleep on the sofa. If that doesn't work, what am I going to do? But what I've done, I'd do again. Maybe Marge and I baked cookies all day for the Ladies Aid at the Lutheran Church. I hope he doesn't want a cookie with his coffee.

Ruth was still sitting at the table in the kitchen when she heard the car drive up, the door slam, and then the stomping of his feet as John kicked the snow from his boots. He seemed ten feet tall as he loomed in the doorway. Her heart beat so loudly she thought he must surely hear. Silently he pulled off his heavy jacket and hung it over the back of a chair. He poured a cup of coffee for her, then filled one for himself. He sat in his usual place at the kitchen table, slowly stirring the sugar cubes as they melted. He did not speak. Ruth waited in an agony of suspense. Then looking directly at her, he said, "It's been an interesting afternoon."

She tried to meet his eyes but found herself looking over his shoulder at the clock on the wall, as though she had never seen it before. Her voice quivered when she spoke, "Tell me."

"Well, the house was burned to the ground. There wasn't a board left standing. There were a few bricks where the stove had stood and two charred kerosene cans in the ashes, burned pretty bad, but you could tell they were kerosene cans." He paused and poured himself another cup of coffee. Ruth fretted over a hangnail she had just discovered.

"Those two old drunks had been fighting. Garrity's eyes were nearly swollen shut and they will be beauts tomorrow," John continued, taking a swig of coffee. "Mac had his jacket off, lying in the snow. Ed had blood all over him; Mac had taken a swing at him and got lucky I guess, broke his nose for sure. Both of 'em cussin' and stompin' around. Mac said Ed was digging through the snow and ashes like a dog. Ed said Mac was blubbering like a baby, cussin' Marge, say'n he knew she'd done it. Said she knew where they kept the kerosene.

He was waving an apron, burned pretty bad, with one tie dangling. Said it was evidence for the sheriff tomorrow.

"Ed grabbed Mac by the throat and threatened, 'If you don't sign over that half section you ain't gonna live 'til tomorrow, you crooked old SOB.' After I pulled Ed off, I asked Mac what the land had to do with it. Of course I knew, but I wanted to hear him say it. He said, 'Mind your own business. You and Ruth have meddled enough in my affairs, and when I get done with Marge I'll settle with the both of you.' He got so ugly I thought I might have to smack him myself, so I let Ed have another go at him.

"Cryin' and cussin' he said he'd be here in the morning for her with the sheriff."

THERE IT WAS. THEY KNEW. Ruth's mind screamed. Her fear erupted into white-hot fury in an instant. She slammed her coffee cup to the floor, quickly followed by the sugar bowl. She sprang to her feet and grabbed the broom. "Never known Marge to do a bad thing," she raged. "Whatever happened to those damned old bastards, they had it coming. Too bad their dirty old hides didn't get scorched, too. I'd say, toast 'em like a marshmallow. If Garrity shows his ugly face over here, he'd better have more than that weak-kneed sheriff with him, he better bring the whole damn National Guard 'cause that's what it's gonna take."

"Ruth. Ruthie," John gasped. "In forty-five years of married life I've never seen you in such a temper. Please don't use that kind of language. It ain't lady-like. What would your mother say? Please stop waving that broom around, you're gonna hurt somebody. Ruthie, let me finish. When Garrity said he and the sheriff would be over in the morning, I told him, 'That'll be fine with me, 'cause I been cleaning the spark plugs on the old John Deere all day and I can tell you Marge didn't leave the house. No way could she have done it. The girls have been working on a patchwork quilt since breakfast.' Ruth, it was a quilt, wasn't it?"

Speechless, Ruth could only nod. She dropped the broom, collapsed in her chair, and watched with disbelieving eyes as he roared with laughter, his big shoulders shaking with unrestrained glee. Wiping her tears, her laughter echoed his. "Fooled you, didn't I, Ruthie?"

Her staid, respectable, always-truthful husband suddenly took on the proportions of a knight in shining armor. Stumbling from her chair she flung her arms around him and kissed him fervently.

"Now Ruth, Ruthie. You know what happens when you kiss me

like that?."

"Of course I do."

Getting up from his chair and taking her by the hand, he looked at the clock. "It's only seven o'clock," he whispered in her ear, "but we old folks need to get our rest, especially if you're gonna whip that weak-kneed sheriff and the whole damn National Guard tomorrow."

Ruth was still smiling the next morning when she swept up pieces of the broken coffee cup and heard the crunch of sugar beneath her shoes.

Chapter 2

Marge sat rigid in the corner of the seat, every muscle tense, the collar of her mother's coat pulled high over her chin nearly covering her ears. She imagined every eye was on her and her guilty secret lay draped about her like a red flag. The train kept up a steady tempo over the snow-covered prairie, the miles sliding by. Various passengers rearranged their belongings for convenience, laughed and chatted with their nearest seatmates. Marge slowly relaxed. The car was warm and she slipped the heavy coat from her shoulders, breathing a trace of her mother's delicate scent that seemed to cling within the woolen material.

The train rattled on, a door opening and the porter emerging. He was the first Negro Marge had ever seen. "Tickets, have your tickets ready," he called as he came down the aisle. She quickly retrieved her valise from under the seat to produce the ticket Dr. Tom had given her just two days ago. She tried not to stare, but was fascinated by the porter's wide white smile and the pink of his palms as he validated her ticket and moved on. She returned her ticket to its hiding place in the valise and saw the crumpled dirty bags that held what had once been her tormenter's poker stash. Their faces flashed before her, and the smell. It was then she realized the odor was escaping from the bags themselves. Swiftly she closed the valise and was on her feet. She carried it toward the room marked "Ladies," moving carefully down the narrow aisle, balancing herself as the train swayed.

Marge had never seen a flush toilet before. She examined it with interest, read the directions, pulled the chain and with a smothered scream fell back against the basin as the water rose, swirled and emptied with a loud bang. She laughed at herself as she saw her reflection in the mirror. It will take more courage to sit on that thing than it took to strike the first match.

The plug was placed tightly in the basin as she lined it with paper towels. The contents of the paper bag and the old cloth bag secured by the safety pin were spilled into it with only a hint of sound from the clinking silver coins among the bills. Marge wiped each bill with a damp handkerchief, stacking them neatly. Removing the paper towels, she washed the silver with hot soapy water, carefully drying each one. When the deed was completed, she counted her bounty: forty dollars in paper money, seven dollars in silver. Now they all smelled like Ivory soap.

Secreting the money, she tossed the empty bags into the toilet and pulled the chain. *There goes my old life.* Marge laughed as she watched the empty bags twist and disappear with a bang somewhere along the lonely railroad tracks.

The rattling of the door told her she needed to hurry as she washed her hands. She grabbed her valise, opened the door and brushed past a young woman leading a small boy. It was obvious from the stain spreading on the front of his trousers there was no need to hurry now.

Marge settled into the soft velour of her seat and leaned back with a sigh. Relief swept over her. With eyes closed, still holding the valise, her thoughts reached back into her childhood. She remembered the fifty-cent piece her mother said the leprechauns had hidden under her pillow when she lost her tooth, but Pa had taken it straight away. *Now I have forty-seven dollars plus the ten dollars that Dr. Tom gave me. A total of fifty-seven dollars. I feel rich—what will I do with all this money?*

The porter entered the car calling out, "The dining car is now open for dinner, the dining car is now open for dinner." Marge was too tired to move. She opened the sack lunch Ruth had so lovingly prepared. She ate and reflected on the flames devouring the old house. With the last bite of chocolate cake she wondered where Ed and her Pa might be sleeping tonight. *I really don't care where they lay their heads.* She laid her own head on the valise, covering herself with her mother's heavy wool coat, smiling to herself. Marge slept the sleep of the innocent.

She was awakened by the voice of the porter who called, "The dining car is now open for breakfast."

It was early morning and the tantalizing aroma of bacon and fresh-brewed coffee seemed to have followed the porter into the car. She hurried to the ladies' room and scrubbed her face. When she looked into the mirror it was a different girl who looked back at her. Those large gray eyes sparkled with expectation, her face was free of worry and fear, and every red curl danced in defiance of the brush. Her smile made you know she was Irish to the core and one day would be a woman to be reckoned with.

Marge timidly followed the other passengers to the dining car and was seated opposite a middle-aged man and his beautifully dressed wife. They introduced themselves as Lillian and George Hardy from Chicago. "Margaret Reagan," she almost whispered. She surveyed the beautifully laid table covered with white linen, sparkling crystal goblets and elaborate silverware. *What am I supposed to do with all these knives and forks?*

Her newfound self-confidence evaporated in an instant when the waiter presented the menu and she sat in an agony of embarrassment. Mrs. Hardy sensed the young girl's obvious distress and said kindly, "Would you like me to help you with that menu? It can be so confusing. May I sit beside you?"

Marge could only nod. Mr. Hardy, with a broad smile, said "Now I can look at two pretty girls at the same time."

As Marge looked at the menu, it seemed to her it was almost written in another language. She was grateful for the suggestion offered by Mrs. Hardy who ordered for both of them.

"Shirred eggs." "Eggs Benedict." "Eggs Florentine." The selections went on and on. Marge wondered, *whatever happened to "fried eggs over easy?"* She ate heartily and after the third cup of coffee, leaned back saying to Mrs. Hardy, "I thank you for your kindness."

Mr. Hardy laughed and said, "You girls can surely put it away—I thought I was the hungry one. I suppose you'll want ice cream now?"

Marge looked up and asked, "What's ice cream?"

He looked at her with surprise and then asked, gently, "You've never eaten ice cream?"

When Marge shook her head, he signaled the waiter. "Bring us three vanilla ice creams, please." The waiter looked surprised, but he smiled as he turned away.

Mrs. Hardy almost giggled, looked at her husband in amazement. "George, George. Surely I didn't hear you order ice cream for breakfast."

He looked at her as he wiped his lips with his napkin, then said calmly but with a twinkle in his eye, "I don't know what's come over me after that big breakfast, but I have this uncontrollable desire for vanilla ice cream."

"Waiter, check please."

As they arose from the table to go back to their compartment, Mrs. Hardy slipped her arm around Marge, giving her a loving hug. "My dear, Mr. Hardy and I will be stopping in Denver. We've come to see our first grandbaby, so we probably won't be seeing you again. Take good care of yourself. You can tell your friends that you had breakfast with the Senator from Illinois."

Mr. Hardy reached for Marge's hand and added, "May all your dreams come true in California, good-bye little girl."

Marge's eyes blurred, she wondered why she always seemed to be saying good-bye?

Marge walked back to her seat and leaned forward to watch the always different scenery as it flashed by. The snow-covered prairies now another world behind her. The rolling hills and valleys turning from soft shades of browns to pink buds and green, promising spring to come, the beginning of a new life, not only for the fields and trees, but for her as well.

As they neared Denver she was awed by her first sight of the majestic Rocky Mountains. The jagged snow-covered peaks pushed their way into the sky White, fleecy clouds wrapped around their lofty summits as though to hide them from the eyes of a mere mortal. It seemed she could hear her mother's voice, *"The firmaments declare the glory of God and the heavens display His handiwork."*

She had become accustomed to the train's noisy stops and starts as it paused at the small towns just long enough for a passenger to get on or off; but the miles of twists and turns through the mountains seemed to have taken their toll as the powerful engine pulled slowly into the Denver station steam billowing, coming to a grinding halt.

Like bees to a honeycomb, the maintenance men swarmed over the stationary giant. Soon the big engine started its rhythmic throbbing and began to move again.

The last whistle shrilled as the porter held the door for a bedraggled young boy who climbed the steps breathlessly and collapsed on the seat opposite Marge.

He covered his face behind a battered cardboard suitcase tied with twine, then with a convulsive sob, choked, "I didn't think I was gonna to make it."

Later, the boy curled up on the seat, feet that seemed miles too big for his long, skinny legs, extending into the aisle; one sock had disappeared into his shoe, only a ragged edge betrayed its existence. The hole in the toe of the other shoe showed a sock of a different color. One hand between his knees, the other under his head, he slept.

Marge looked at him curiously. He was tall, taller than she, and pitifully thin. His lank brown hair fell over his face that showed only downy fuzz, the shadow of whiskers yet to come. The wrinkled black suit folded over him, almost like a blanket, the sleeves rolled up to show the bony, reddened wrists and hands with their broken dirty fingernails.

He awoke with a start, as the porter came through calling that the dining car was open for supper. Marge tidied her hair and arranged her clothing in anticipation of a good supper. The dining car was the highlight of her day. She had absorbed Mrs. Hardy's instructions and, with her newfound confidence, thought she could cope with any amount of knives and forks. As she stood, she glanced at the boy across the aisle. His suitcase was open and she was shocked to see chunks of bread in a torn paper wrapper and several shriveled apples mixed among some miscellaneous clutter.

Impulsively she asked, "Is that your supper?" His face reddened with embarrassment as he looked up from a partly eaten apple, "Yes, ma'am, I guess it is." Looking down at him, she hesitated for a moment, then asked softly, "I wonder if I might ask a favor of you?"

He scrambled to his feet, "Of course, ma'am, I'll be pleased to help you any way I can."

She explained, "I am embarrassed to go into the dining car alone and I'd like you to join me for supper."

He stepped back, disbelief and frustration racing across his face. "Ah, ma'am, you don't know how I would love to do that, it doesn't seem as though I've ever et anything but potato soup and stale bread. Eighty cents is all I have left to my name and it's got to last until I get to Long Beach, Californy."

Marge tugged him along, saying, "My Pa and his friend gave me more than enough money to buy food until I get to Los Angeles and I know they'd want me to share with you. Go wash your face and comb your hair and I'll wait for you." She laughed and he laughed, too, but he didn't know what was funny.

The travelers at the next table looked surprised when they saw the beautiful red-haired girl who had breakfasted with the Senator from Illinois now dining with a ragged, unkempt young boy who devoured his food as though he was starving. When the last bite was gone, Marge motioned the waiter, "Please bring us two vanilla ice creams and put it in the stemmed compote goblets. Thank you." She turned to the boy and said, "Please take your elbows off the table and don't call me "ma'am," my name is Marge."

"Yes ma'am. I mean, yes, Miss Marge. Wisht I could sit on these here elbows; they're always in the way. My name is Ben Olson."

With the beautiful goblets heaped with the creamy dessert set in front of him, Ben whispered, "It's too purty to eat," as his hand shook picking up his spoon. "How can I ever thank you? I've been on the road almost a week, hitching rides from Newville, Kansas. Folks were good to pick me up, but that last fellow got lost, I was sure I'd miss this train. I've never been so far from home and I've never been so scared and hungry. I doubt I'll ever eat like this again; Gramaw would say, 'God Bless you' and that's what I'll say."

When they returned to their seats, he paused as she seated herself. His face flushed as he asked hesitantly, "Would you mind if I set a spell with you?

"How old are you, Ben?"

"Well, in a year and a half I'll be seventeen."

Marge laughed and said, "Come and sit awhile, neighbor, and tell me where you're going."

"Well, I'm going to Californy to work for my uncle in Long Beach."

"Won't you miss your family? That's a long way from home."

"Well, sure. Pa wanted to come but he couldn't leave Gramaw; she's old and crazy in the head and won't leave the land. Ma died about four years ago with the dropsy, so there's not much left of us. Awful hard times in Kansas. The dust storms were turrible bad, didn't have rain for years. The land just dried up and then the wind just blew the dirt until the dust storms made the sky dark. We had to light the lamp in the middle of the day. It was so dark we couldn't see the barn. Pa wouldn't give up, he planted wheat and the wind just blew the seed out of the ground; then he planted corn. It wasn't but an inch high when the grasshoppers came. The sky was black with 'em too; ate it right to the ground. I never saw my Pa cry, not even when Ma died, but he stood in that bare field and cried out loud. I never let on I seen him.

"Then the government wanted the farmers to kill their livestock, never did understand all that, what with people starvin' in the big cities. I herded the hogs out to a big trench Pa had dug and he shot 'em. Just as well, we didn't have nothin' to feed 'em. Seemed like a turrible waste to me, people so hungry. I don't doubt it, we ate an awful lot of potato soup.

"Guess Pa had to mortgage the farm and the bank foreclosed. Lot of farms foreclosed on, don't know where all them people went.

"The big bulldozers and tractors came and just knocked the

houses over. When they came to our place, Gramaw took her bible in one hand and an old shotgun with the firing pin all busted, and laid down on the front steps and hollered, 'Now you thieven' sons of bitches come and knock it down. I was a borned here and I'm a gonna die here. What are ya waitin' for, ya damned vultures?'

"You shoulda' seen Pa's face. He started to laugh, like to have busted a gut, so we went over and sat beside her. She got up and jumped around wavin' that old busted gun and talkin' bad and had me holdin' the Bible." Ben grinned as he continued.

"The man stopped the tractor and said, real ugly like, 'Missus. I hope I don't hafta come down from this rig.' And my Pa said, 'I sincerely hope you don't either, 'cause you'll never go back up.' I looked at Pa and his eyes scared me, black and cold.

"The guy on the bulldozer cussed but turned that thing around and pushed over the barn; wasn't nothing' in it, no how.

"Then he took a run at the grainery and knocked it down, tore all the fences up, too.

"I said to Gramaw, 'That was turrible language you was sayin' and with the Bible in yer hand, too.' I didn't dast say much to her, she was still pretty feisty. She said, 'I didn't take the Lord's name in vain, so it wasn't cursin', just cussin.'"

Ben looked apologetically at Marge and said, "I hope my Gramaw's language didn't offend you, Miss Marge, but that's how it was."

Marge smiled and patted his arm, "No, it didn't offend me, I respect her for standing up and fighting for what she believed to be right. You should'a got the firing pin on that gun fixed."

"Pa said there wasn't any future for me here, so he sold the best team of mules in the county, the harness and wagon, too, for the ticket money from Denver. I cried when them mules left, I raised old Maude on a bottle after her mother died.

"But now I'm goin' to Californy where the sun always shines and you can reach out your window and pick an orange right off the tree. A big ocean where you can swim or fish anytime of the year, lots of work. No more farmin' for me, no more grasshoppers. People are friendly. I'd like to go back to school, too, never got past sixth grade.

"I'm gonna save my money and send for my Pa just as soon as he can come and we'll be a family again."

An older man who sat nearby had been listening quietly and when Ben paused, the man spoke.

"Well, son, I hope you won't be disappointed. This country is in a worldwide depression. Over eight million men out of work, begging to work for fifteen cents an hour. A man ain't too proud to beg when his family is starving. That terrible draught and dust storms you talked about in Kansas, also hit Oklahoma, Texas, Arkansas and up into the Dakotas, too. Thousands of people migrated to California and the California people are hostile.

"I'm from Oakland myself, that's near San Francisco, and conditions are horrible there. Just on the outskirts of Oakland, over two hundred homeless living in huge concrete pipes stored above ground. Every six foot a family, ends closed with burlap and cardboard. Living on anything they can scrounge, call it 'Pipe City,' some call it 'Misery Ville.'"

"Well," Ben said confidently, "where I'm goin' ain't none of that stuff goin' on."

The man answered, "I just went back to bury my Dad, and I'm glad to be coming home, but, facts are facts and you'll find out, I'm afraid. The bread lines stretch for a mile in Los Angeles and ten thousand people fed in New York on Christmas day and now the President has slashed the relief fund. How can a man feed his family on three dollars a week?

"The vets were promised a cash bonus and then the government never paid. The vets and their families marched to Washington, D.C., and camped in shacks on the Anacastin Flats. That embarrassed the President. That damn Hoover, I'm glad I never voted for him.

"Ordered out the regular troops, MacArthur headed that up, burned their shacks, run 'em off with their women and children, no place to go. That's how our veterans got treated, and that's a shame to our country.

"Terrible hard times boy, terrible hard times," and his voice shook as he turned his face to the window.

Marge listened silently, as her thoughts flashed back to a *skinny eleven-year-old girl who got up in the dark, built a fire with wood she'd carried in the night before, then pulled on her boots and grabbed her Pa's ragged, cast-off jacket, the milk pail and lantern, and struggled through the snowdrifts to the barn. Her fingers were so cold and stiff she could hardly milk the pitifully thin cow she had to kick out of the frozen manure. Then she had to feed the hogs before she made breakfast.*

Then Pa would get up scratchin' and yawnin' and make policy. Marge thought, *I got a five-year start on "hard times." I know about "hard times."*

For a long time, the boy and Marge sat in silence, each engrossed in their own thoughts. At last, Ben stood and self-consciously patted her on the shoulder. "Miss Marge, don't let anybody discourage you. You and me are gonna be alright, don't worry." Marge was touched by his concern.

"Yes, we will, Ben," she smiled. "Good night."

That night Marge lay awake, her scattered thoughts put her emotions on a roller-coaster ride. She worried . . . *What if Annie didn't meet the train? What if Annie didn't like her? But, of course, she would. Hadn't Ruth said so? What if I don't like California? But, of course, I will since Dr. Tom sent me here. I hope that boy will find a better life in California. He is so young . . .* Marge smiled to herself. *I feel like his big sister and I'm only a year older.* Finally, she slept. She felt she'd just gotten to sleep when the porter called out for breakfast. She looked across the aisle and met the eyes of the boy.

"Mornin,' Miss Marge. Will you be comfortable goin' into breakfast alone or will you want me to take you?"

"Of course, I'll need you. Comb your hair." She found it easy to talk to Ben. He seemed like a little brother—despite the fact that he was at least six inches taller—rather than a boy who was on the verge of becoming a man. He had already changed into his only other shirt, but the black suit still hug on his thin frame.

"Where in the world did you get that black suit?"

Ben blushed as he looked down at himself.

"I know it's miles too big, but it was all I had to wear. I didn't want to wear my overalls. This here was Pa's wedding suit. Of course, it fit him better."

Marge looked at her own dress—a dress that Ruth had altered with love in every stitch—and she knew it wasn't a dress that a young girl would wear.

"I think we are a matched pair, Ben."

"My Grandma always said, 'God made the man and the tailor made the clothes.' And I'm still waitin' on the tailor, but some day I'll have a suit that fits and I know you'd be purty in whatever you wore."

They both blushed with embarrassment—Ben not knowing he was giving a compliment and Marge not knowing how to accept one.

Marge watched in amazement as Ben gobbled down eggs benedict, eggs florentine, a double order of bacon, toast heaped high with marmalade, and a stack of hotcakes with real maple syrup.

She couldn't hold back her laughter. "Ben, if you eat the plates, your grandma will be looking for the castor oil."

Blushing, he grinned goodnaturedly. "I ain't never et so good and I don't 'spect I ever will again. And if I do, I'll always think of a purty red-haired girl. Not that I'll ever forget you." Now the blush mounted his ears.

"It isn't 'et,' it is *eaten*. When you get that suit, you will need to use better English, Ben."

"Yes, ma'am . . . I mean, Miss Marge. Will you pass that last piece of toast? Grandma always said, 'Waste not, want not,' but she was wrong bout that 'cause we wanted and we never wasted. We used everything on the hog but the squeal. Will we be having ice cream?"

"Of course . . . this is our last meal together before my final stop, so let's celebrate and order double helpings."

"I was hoping for that, Miss Marge."

Marge knew Pa had never enjoyed his poker money as much as she was enjoying it now. She looked across the table at the young boy, his plate finally so empty that the Great Northern insignia showed plainly. Ben's face was flushed with happiness, his belly full, his dream waiting on the horizon. He seemed to her so young, so innocent. She prayed life would be kind to him.

The train was nearing Marge's final destination and she was almost dizzy with anticipation. Ben sensed her excitement.

"Are you going to be okay, Miss Marge?"

"Of course, I'll be fine. It's just that the train is so slow; I could walk faster."

She sat on the edge of her seat, her heavy winter coat over her arm, her heart pounding in near agony with suspense. Her mind whirled . . . *the moment this train stops, I will be the first one off.*

At last the brakes screeched, the steam blew and the train shuddered to a stop. Marge looked out the window and, to her surprise, she was terrified. There were more people on the platform than she had ever dreamed existed. How would Annie ever find her? She shrunk back, too frightened to move as the hurrying passengers crowded past her seat. Ben saw the fear slide across her face like a dark shadow.

"Don't be afraid, Miss Marge," he comforted. "This is where our new life begins. I'll go with you."

He reached for her valise and, taking her hand, he walked her to the door. His voice trembled. "Good-bye, Miss Marge, I'll miss you."

Impulsively she stood on tip-toe to kiss his nearly hairless cheek and murmured, "Good-bye, Ben, take care."

He handed her the valise and turned away, his eyes blurred by tears he hoped she hadn't seen.

Desperately clinging to the safety bar, she froze in the doorway. The impatient passengers behind her urging her to step down . . . *step down.*

Standing on the threshold, she looked down into the crowd, her eyes frantically searching for a woman she had never seen. From miles way it seemed, she heard her name called, and then she saw a blue umbrella dancing wildly up and down. The umbrella was held by a woman who was vigorously pushing her way through the crowd. It was a woman who was the spitting image of Ruth.

Marge stumbled down the steps into the arms of Annie, who hugged her tightly, then released her and stepped back, exclaiming, "Ruth told me to look for the prettiest red-haired girl I would ever see and here you are."

Annie turned to the smiling girl beside her and added, "This is my daughter, Sue Anne."

Marge extended her hand but Sue Anne laughed and flung her arms around Marge. "Hey. I've waited a long time for a sister and here you are at last. What fun we'll have."

Marge, having had so little interaction with anyone her own age, instinctively turned to Annie. Recognizing Marge's uncertainty, she stepped between the two girls and put an arm around each. Annie led the way through the crowded terminal into the bright California sunshine.

Thoughts hopscotched in Marge's head. *Was it only four days ago I was on the snowbound North Dakota prairie carrying kerosene into the house I was born in and subsequently reduced to ashes? Is it possible that I am really, truly at my destination? Am I really on the sidewalk that will lead to such a different life?* Her heart exalted . . . *I'm here. Thank God, I'm here.* And with that thought, she felt her knees tremble in anticipation with every step she took.

Sue Anne dropped Marge's hand and danced ahead to the streetcar station, her hair hanging long and golden in the rays of the warm sun. "Hurry or we'll miss this one."

Marge stared at her retreating back and was shocked to see so much of Sue Anne's long legs showing beneath the hem of her pretty blue dress. The skirt patterned with pink rosebuds scattered haphazardly as though tossed by an errant hand. Marge looked down at herself. *I look like a drab gray mouse in this heavy wool dress and old-lady shoes.* Simultaneously, other thoughts flashed through her mind, but not for long. *I've still got Pa's stash.*

The streetcar arrived and they mounted the steps. Annie jingled three nickels into the coin box as they quickly seated themselves before the streetcar jerked away from the stop.

Annie gazed thoughtfully at the two girls as they sat directly across from her on a well-worn bench. What a study in contrasts. Her vivacious daughter, blond hair swinging with every turn of the head, nonstop chatter radiated the self-confidence acquired by the loving care she and her husband had given Sue Anne for nearly seventeen years. Marge, her long red hair fighting the hairpins holding captive each curl as it struggled to escape the tightly coiled bun, sat quietly, listening and looking. Her heavy long skirt was pulled modestly to her shoe tops.

It was then that Annie sensed the truth. *This is a woman. A woman . . . no longer a girl. I don't think she has ever been young; she lost her childhood years somewhere along the way. And I'd guess she has known hurts and responsibilities in a life barren of the loving care our daughter has had. Thank God she had the courage to break away and make her own life. The potential is there. She is a beautiful young woman but she doesn't know it yet.*

Sue Anne peeked sideways at Marge. *She sure is pretty, even in those awful clothes. Poor thing, she's scared to death. Mom will sew her something beautiful. I don't suppose she knows how to dance—the prom is in two weeks. I will teach her all the latest dance steps and fix her hair. Maybe I can even get her a date.*

Marge, trying not to stare, looked around discreetly at people she had only read about. Tears hid behind lids as she witnessed a large Negro woman sitting in the back and nursing her equally dark-skinned baby cocooned in a fuzzy pink blanket. Nearby, an oriental man with a long black pigtail was wrestling with several large packages. A Mexican mother with three small children, all replicas of her, endeavored to keep the peace as the children struggled for control of a brightly colored toy.

Marge was intrigued by the large painted ads that lined the walls of the streetcar.

Lydia Pinkham's Tonic for women's ailments—
A baby in every bottle
Now playing at the Orpheum Theater: "The Sheik"

starring Rudolph Valentino and Pola Negri. The best show in town.
Burlesque at the Gaiety ... Girls. Girls. Girls. Adults only.
Spade Cooley and his famous band at the Pier.

The sound of the streetcar's warning signal clanged loudly as it slowed at every intersection and every time a passenger reached up to pull the cord to exit. Competing with the noisy car was the din of the great city, bursting in each time the folding doors opened. As the vehicle traveled down the long curving tracks, Sue Anne pointed excitedly to places of interest.

"Oh, look. Right there ... that's where I got these wedgies. And there is the store that sells movie stars' old clothes. Do you like to shop?" Not waiting for an answer ... "Right there. That's Union High School. Seven-hundred fifty students attend and, oh, the fellows there." Sue Anne rolled her eyes.

"Susy, hush for a moment, dear, and let Marge catch her breath." Annie smiled indulgently.

"We're almost there." Sue Anne exclaimed and reached to pull the cord that halted the car. As the streetcar slowed, there was a sign on the corner that read, "Melrose & N. Orange Dr." Jumping to her feet, Sue Anne was the first one down the steps and out of the car. Annie and Marge followed quickly and hurried to keep up with the exuberant teenager who seemed never to run out of words or energy.

"Mom? Mom. Let's have a party for Marge. It's almost my birthday." Turning to Marge, Susy exclaimed, "I'll be seventeen. How old are you?"

"I'll be seventeen, too. Next week." Marge smiled, thinking, *This must be what it's like to be seventeen.*

"How wonderful—we could be twins. I'll invite all my friends and you can meet them. Can we, Mom?"

Annie smiled, "Of course. I'll put thirty-four candles on the cake."

Marge turned her head. The quick sting of tears surfaced as she remembered her own mother's attempts to make her birthday special and Pa's rough voice, "No. That costs money and money don't grow on trees." An unbidden thought crept into Marge's mind ... *I wonder where you're sleeping tonight, Pa.* She smiled.

The bungalows lining the street were a rainbow of color. Bougainvillea crawled over red tile roofs and formed a halo of purple as it crawled down the sides and over the fences that separated the narrow space between. Exotic flowers bloomed in every yard and the stately palm trees seemed to stand guard as they pushed against the sky. Marge felt as though she was floating through a sea of color. They walked the few remaining blocks and stopped at a neat little yellow house set back on an emerald-green lawn. The house was fronted by a jasmine hedge that released a fragrance so sweet, so subtle . . . it hung in the air like smoke.

The door opened and a great bear of a man stood with his arms outstretched. It was Annie's husband, Boots.

"What a lucky man I am," his voice boomed. "Two beautiful women and, of course, my ugly duckling, Susy."

Despite her outraged "Daddy," Susy giggled as he lifted her up and whirled her around, set her gently down and depositing a loud smack in the vicinity of her ear. Spying her shoes . . . "Don't tell me I spent my money on those ugly shoes."

"These are the very latest style and all the movie stars wear them. They're called wedgies, Dad."

Still smiling, Boots turned to Marge and enveloped her in a giant bear hug. Swinging her off her feet as he had Susy, he whirled her, then put her down and kissed her gently on the cheek. "Welcome to our home. We are so happy to have you. Susy needs a sister."

"Boots. Now look what you've done," Annie scolded. "You've scared her half to death and made her cry."

"No, no. I'm crying because I'm happy." Marge laughed through her tears. "Oh. I don't know why I'm crying."

Then the tears that Marge had withheld for so many years flooded between her fingers as though they would never stop. While Susy stood in wide-eyed amazement, speechless for once, Annie wrapped her arms around the sobbing girl and wiped her tears with a corner of her apron. Boots watched helplessly.

"Margie, Margie . . . I didn't mean to frighten you. I'm so sorry. Please don't cry." Boots stammered, his face red with embarrassment.

Annie looked over her shoulder at her husband. "Go water the garden, Dad. This isn't about you."

Boots needed no further urging. The screen door slammed against his hasty retreat. Annie gently mopped up the tears as they continued to flow from the near hysterical girl. *My guess is,* thought Annie, *this is seventeen years of accumulated tears.*

Sobs turned to hiccups as tears dried salty on her cheeks. Annie turned to Susy. "I think Marge would enjoy a nice warm bath. She's had a long hard trip. See if you can find her one of your cotton robes until she gets unpacked."

"Thank you." Marge nodded toward Annie and followed Susy down a short hallway where family photos were randomly hung, competing with the rose-patterned wallpaper.

"The bath is just across the hall from our bedroom. Mom and Dad's room is on the other side. Wait a moment, I'll find something cool for you to wear." Susy quickly returned with a big soft towel thrown over her arm and handed Marge a colorful robe as they entered the bathroom. Marge looked curiously at the first bathtub she had ever seen as Susy adjusted the faucets and a steady rush of water filled the tub. This accomplishment fascinated Marge as did the bubbles that covered the rising water and floated above in the air. Susy laughed at Marge's surprised expression.

"Bubble Bath," she explained. "I love them and you will, too. It smells soooo good."

She handed Marge the shampoo. "Just relax, don't hurry. I'll tidy up our messy room: The door closed behind her and Marge was alone as she relished her first glimpse of heaven.

Marge felt her legs would not support her another moment. She sank down on the commode and watched the iridescent bubbles rise into the air. She quickly peeled off her heavy winter clothing, pulled pins from her hair and stepped into the tub. In her mind she floated with the bubbles that now surrounded her young body. *I am out of my cocoon forever . . . now I can fly.*

An hour later, revived, renewed and snuggled tightly in Susy's robe, Marge crossed the hall into the bedroom. Susy looked up, her eyes widened in admiration. *Who is this beautiful stranger in my robe? Who is that girl with red-gold hair curling about her face, hanging so long and heavy down her back?*

Marge smiled and surveyed the cluttered room that smelled strongly of singed hair. A lamp with a curling iron stuck in the chimney gave silent declaration of Susy's determination for curls, at any cost. Clothing was strewn everywhere.

"I've been cleaning out the closet." Susy laughed and nodded toward a chair where several brightly colored dresses lay. "If you like any of those, you may have them. Mom loves to sew, but she makes all my dresses too long. That green dress would look really nice on you. Mom and Dad are so old-fashioned. If Dad thinks my skirts are too short, he makes me change. When I'm out I just tuck the skirts up under my belt and then they can be as short as I like," she giggled.

"No face paint, either, as Dad calls it. I just carry my make-up in my purse until I'm out of the house."

Is this how it is to be young? Marge wondered.

Susy pointed to the dresser with a large ornate mirror. Mom just bought that for three dollars from a woman down the street. They are awfully poor and last week she sold the family dining-room set. Her husband has been out of work for months. Mom says 'Thank God Dad has a good job with the City.' The stupid depression is all anyone talks about. Dad won't let us go downtown anymore. It's all so boring."

Preening herself in the mirror, she struck a pose and giggled. "Don't you think I look just like Mary Pickford?"

"Who is Mary Pickford?"

"Why, she's my favorite movie star."

"I've never seen a movie."

"You've never seen a movie? Marge, you're joking. Don't they have theaters in North Dakota?"

Marge removed clothing from a chair and sat down, her smile tight with embarrassment.

"Well, they might, but I didn't get to town much. What a pretty dress. Where shall I hang it? "There . . . right there," Susy said. "That will be your half of the closet, and these two drawers."

"I don't need much room. I brought only a few things."

She walked to the window and pulled back the pink ruffled curtain. A fence, barely visible, appeared captured beneath the crush of the climbing purple flowers, their tendrils already reaching for the birdhouse perched precariously on a post. Marge murmured, "This must be the most beautiful place in the world."

Susy looked puzzled. "What are you looking at? I don't see anything but an old rickety fence, all overgrown with those purple flowers that grow everywhere and that orange tree is older than I am."

"Girls, will you come and set the table for dinner? Dad's starving," Annie called.

Dinner? It's 'supper' in North Dakota, Marge pondered.

The table, covered by a hand-embroidered cloth, was soon readied for the meal that was created mostly from their own garden. Marge was seated next to Susy. Dad sat at the head of the table with his napkin already tucked in his collar and flowing across his ample belly. Annie sat in the chair next to the kitchen. Steam was rising from the mashed potatoes and the aroma from the gravy boat was making Marge's mouth water.

"Dad, will you say the blessing?"

Dad bobbed his head for a brief moment. "Praise the Lord and pass the potatoes."

"Dad," Annie exclaimed. "The Lord would have to be pretty quick to have caught that. Can't you do better?"

"Of course, He is quick . . . didn't He create the world in seven days? Susy, will you PLEASE save some of those potatoes for the rest of us? Annie, I thank God every day for my family, our home, our health and a good joy that puts food on the table. If you could go downtown and see the pitiful people that pour in every day—driving their dilapidated cars loaded up with everything they own—hungry, dirty and broke. They look for a job that has been taken already by one of a hundred other men just as desperate, begging for work for twenty cents an hour. How in hell can a man feed his family on that? And their kids. Why, your heart would break . . . "

"Daddy, why don't they stay home? Why are they coming here?" Susy interrupted.

"If you would get your pretty nose out of those *True Confession* magazines and read the newspaper, you would know that the Midwest has been devastated by the worst drought in history. Dust storms have blown the farmers' crops right out of the ground and what survived, the grasshoppers ate. Those poor farmers couldn't make the payments on their land so the bank foreclosed and forced them out of their homes—many of them homesteaded that land. It's a damn tragedy. They have migrated to California by the thousands praying to find work and better living conditions. This is the worst depression the world has ever known. Damn those crooked politicians. Hoover is the worst of the lot. Thank God I never voted for him."

"Dad, you promised not to talk politics at the table. Shame on you for swearing in front of the girls."

"Sorry, girls. Annie, I'd feel better if I had a piece of that pie—a big piece."

Marge now understood what the man on the train was talking about . . . "All those poor people. Thank God we're safe here."

"Dad? Dad, can Marge and I go to the beach tomorrow? I want to show her the ocean—we'd have such fun. The Santa Monica streetcar will take us almost to the pier. Please, Dad?"

"Well . . . maybe, if your mother goes with you."

"Mom, can we? Can we, please?"

"Maybe. I'll think about it when the dishes are done."

As they pushed back their chairs, Susy was already pouring soap in the dishpan.

It seemed to Marge like forever since she stepped from the train into the waiting arms of this loving family. When the lights went out that night, she relaxed into an exhausted sleep.

The memories that she kept at bay in her waking hours escaped her subconscious as she slept. Marge felt the baby move against her, cuddled in the curve of her arm, smelling of baby oil and talcum powder. The hungry little mouth was open and moved in blind anticipation for the nipple dripping with milk; then, the baby girl was nursing vigorously, making soft little cooing sounds, her tiny pink fingers wrapped tightly around a strand of her mother's hair. Marge gazed down adoringly and with the tip of her finger traced the perfect tiny ears, the small nib of a nose, and the closed eyes with lashes tipped with gold. Her heart exploded with love. "Thank God. Thank you, God. I knew you wouldn't take my baby."

Susy sat up in bed. "Marge . . . Marge . . . you alright? You're talking in your sleep. Go back to sleep, it's only a dream."

Her empty arms dropped limply to her sides as she lay her head down on the pillow. *Yes, it was only a dream.*

Marge was awakened by the sunlight that had slowly crept through the curtains and burst forth into the room, lighting it as though the Almighty had thrown a switch. *How grateful I am to be here, away from the pain and despair that has been my life. It is all behind me now, and I feel clean and new.* She dressed quickly and followed the happy aroma of perking coffee. She found Annie sitting at the kitchen table making toast.

"Good morning, dear. I see you're an early riser. Boots has already left for work and Susy will sleep late, as usual. Will you tend to the toast and I'll pour you a cup of fresh-perked coffee?"

Seated in Annie's cheerful kitchen, eating a double helping of jam on homemade toast, Marge thought of Ruth—her eyes filled with tears. How similar the sisters were, both in appearance and personality.

The warm California sunshine on her back danced through the red-gold of her hair and reflected her image in the glass cupboard door. Having never known a scissor on the farm, Marge's hair had always hung in a long braid. Later Annie would show her how to pin it up. This morning, however, she had given it only a quick brush and it hung over her shoulders, the curling tendrils framing her face.

She is the most beautiful girl I have ever seen—except for Susy, of course, Annie thought as she stared at Marge.

Leaning back in her chair, sated with toast and coffee and insulated in Annie's love and concern, Marge sat quietly. Both she and Annie were lost in their thoughts. Annie broke the silence.

"Have you had time to think of what you plan to do in the future, dear?"

"More than anything, I want to finish school. I haven't been able to study much. How wonderful if I could catch up and graduate with Susy next year. Ruth thought perhaps there might be a summer school. I wonder if Susy would know"

"I wish Susy had some of your enthusiasm for school. I think we may have spoiled her, so you will be a good influence," Annie laughed. "Susy had a favorite teacher, Mrs. Lowenstein, who had to leave school in the second semester." Annie looked thoughtful and spoke slowly, thinking out loud . . . "She left school because her husband became very sick. I understand he is bedridden now. I know she struggles to keep their deli open but, even in these hard times, it has done well. The well-to-do Jewish people patronize it because the food is very good. And kosher, of course."

"Kosher? What's that?" Marge looked puzzled.

"That is the way Jewish people prepare their food. They have traditional rituals in their religious beliefs, which are quite different from our own." Annie paused and, instead of explaining kosher in detail as Marge had hoped, she thought out loud once again. "I wonder if Mrs. Lowenstein could find time to help you . . . perhaps in exchange for your work in the deli. We could surely ask."

"Oh, Annie, that would be a dream come true." Marge's face was radiant. "When can we see her?"

"Not today." Susy pouted, standing in the doorway. "Mom, you promised we could go to the beach today. I want to wear my new bathing suit. You promised . . . Mom?"

"Susy, we can do both. The deli is only a few blocks from the streetcar stop. If we leave soon, Mrs. Lowenstein won't be too busy this early; maybe she'll have time to talk to Marge. This is important to her."

"Oh, alright. But let's hurry."

"I'll tidy up the kitchen, you girls get ready. It won't take me long."

"I'll help," Marge answers as she started to sweep.

Susy scampered to the bedroom, but in a moment she danced into the kitchen in a bright red bathing suit. Twirling in front of her mother, "What do you think, Mom?" Her mother's shocked face said it all.

"Susy, you are not going anywhere in that. It is about two sizes too small for you. The one we agreed upon in the store fit properly and was black. You will have to take it back."

Susy burst into tears. "Mom, how can you be so forgetful, the one we bought was red. You know I hate black. I can't take it back after I've worn it. All the girls are wearing this very same style. Do you want everyone to make fun of me?"

"You've only worn that about five minutes and I don't care what the other girls are wearing. We'd both be in such trouble if Dad saw you. Take it back," Annie ordered.

Susy sobbed loudly, "Well then, go without me. I just won't go to the beach this summer, you just don't want me to be happy."

Her mother instantly capitulated. "Now baby, don't cry. You know we want you to be happy. Stand still and let me see what I can do. Maybe I can make this fit properly when we get home." With a pinch of material between her fingers, she speculated, "If I took this seam out it would lengthen at least two inches in the back; perhaps a bit of lace at the bosom..." Her voice trailed off, but rallied momentarily, "You must wear something over this today."

Susy's sobs stopped abruptly, "Oh, Mom, you're so old fashioned. Hurry up and get ready."

Marge kept her indignant thoughts to herself.

The streetcar seemed to take forever. Marge sat on the edge of her seat, tense, almost dizzy with anticipation, praying that Mrs. Lowenstein would be receptive to their proposal.

Annie was thoughtful and quiet, hopeful that her plan would work for this girl of whom she had become so fond.

Susy fidgeted, her mind overflowing with thoughts of the handsome lifeguard she was determined to meet today—one way or another.

As the streetcar's door clanged shut behind them, Susy pleaded again, "Mom, do we have to stop at the deli today?"

"Yes, we do. We won't be long, now hush."

The deli, painted a pristine white, identified only as "Lowenstein's" by a sign that hung above the door, stood in stark contrast to the adjacent building, a forlorn appearing structure with two broken windows that stared with unseeing eyes at an uncaring world. The faded sign read "Closed."

Marge shivered as she hurried by another derelict house that looked as though the door had never opened to a happier time—a "Notice of Foreclosure" was nailed to the broken porch railing.

Only a few more steps and breathless from the hurried walk, they paused momentarily to admire the red geraniums that bloomed so abundantly in the window boxes beneath the green-and-white-striped awning that protected the doorway of the deli.

Annie opened the door and, as they stepped over the threshold, the tinkling of a little bell announced their arrival.

Marge looked with disbelieving eyes at the numerous rows of mouthwatering pastries decorated so beautifully. A long glass-enclosed case held meat, chicken, salads and other perishable items on a sparkling bed of ice. On top of the counter stood a large glass container that held captive the oversized green pickles that pushed against the garlic and dill. Susy whispered, "Everybody knows about kosher pickles." The yeasty smell of freshly baked bread betrayed the location of the crusty loaves—the sign read "Five cents." Bagels heaped high on a platter would have tempted the devil himself.

The swinging door behind the counter parted, nudged by the hip of a small woman wrapped in an oversized flour-covered apron. With both hands, she carried a tray heaped high. As she carefully deposited her burden on the counter, she looked up, surprised to see Annie smiling at her. "Annie, how nice to see you. Susy, too." Wiping her hands on her apron, she walked quickly around the counter and hugged each one.

"You haven't been in for ages, Susy. Have you been keeping your studies up? How I miss you all. I'm trying to keep this deli going and it doesn't appear as though I'll ever get back to teaching. You perhaps know, my husband is very ill.

"Who is this pretty young lady?"

Quickly Annie introduced Marge, who was nearly speechless. "Mrs. Lowenstein, it is about this young lady that we've come. Have you time to talk to us?"

Susy shifted foot to foot and whined, "Mom." Annie silenced her with a look.

Mrs. Lowenstein looked puzzled, but quickly answered, "Of course. I have some bread in the oven, but it won't be ready for awhile. How can I help you?"

"Well, actually, we want to help you," Annie laughed.

"Let's sit at the counter and be comfortable," the dark-haired little woman invited. "I'm not very busy this morning."

Annie nervously presented her plan. "Marge has just arrived from North Dakota and has been unable to attend school for awhile. She is so eager to learn and to graduate next year is her dream, but she needs some assistance to catch up. We are hoping you could use her help here. In return, she would be so grateful for any time you could give her with her studies."

Mrs. Lowenstein listened attentively, interrupting momentarily to ask a quick question as she glanced at Marge. The pleading expression on Marge's easily read face did not escape her sharp eyes. She turned to Marge, "You understand the work is hard and I am very particular. It would include clean-up and waiting on customers. Do you know how to work a cash register?" Marge shook her head. "Never mind, I could teach you. I need help in the kitchen, too, and there are many other duties. This is a lot of responsibility for so young a girl."

As she looked into Marge's eyes, she recognized the intelligence there. A thought flashed through her mind. *It would be such a pleasure for me to teach this young girl who is so determined to learn, and I miss teaching. I am so tired, God knows I need the help. The nurse comes in for four hours every day, and I could work with this girl then.*

She spoke. "You understand there would be no money involved?"

Marge blinked to keep back the tears. "Oh yes, this would be so much better than money. Please let me try."

"Can you come Sunday morning at six-thirty? Then we can talk about your schoolwork and familiarize you with the routine. Don't be late."

"Yes, oh yes, I thank you." Annie's happy face was only a faint reflection of the ecstatic look that Marge wore during her waking hours.

"Mom, will you hurry? It's already ten-thirty."

"Sue Anne, I don't want to hear another 'hurry up' from you. Remember that streetcar runs both ways."

"Well, we'd better hurry 'cause here comes one right now, going our way." Susy laughed as she sprinted to stand first in line.

A thirty-minute ride took them to Pacific Palisades. A short walk on a winding path led them to the safety rail that marked the steep descent to the beach.

Nothing Marge had ever dreamed of was comparable to the scene below. The brilliant blue of the foamed-topped waves pushed at the shore, then retreated into an equally blue horizon that seemed to stretch forever. The roar of the mighty ocean muted the noisy revelers that crowded the beach. Umbrellas stood like giant, brightly colored mushrooms, almost side by side, covering the more cautious sun enthusiasts. Adding still more color were beach towels held stationary by the sun lovers' tanned bodies glistening with oil. People, young and old alike, shrieked with laughter as they frolicked in the waves. Vendors hawked their wares as the tantalizing smell of hot dogs wafted upward on a stray current of air. The faint sound of music emanated from somewhere—"Probably an organ grinder with his monkey," Annie explained. It was a kaleidoscope of color.

Marge felt as though someone had waved a magic wand that carried her to a fairytale world where there was happiness, music, and laughter. It seemed as though the whole world was celebrating.

Overwhelmed, Marge sank down on a nearby bench. Annie stood silently beside her, remembering her first view of the ocean. Marge sat, lost in her own thoughts—*Mother must have felt like this the first time we saw the Northern lights.* It seemed a lifetime ago.

"Mom, I didn't come here to enjoy the view. The steps are right here. Me first." Susy pushed ahead.

Annie and Marge trailed behind her, cautious of the steep footing that led to the sandy beach.

"Susy, we're going to stay together. I don't want you out of my sight."

"But Mom, can't I at least get my suit wet? I won't go out any farther than the surf. I promise. Anyhow, the lifeguard is right there." She pointed to a handsome young man tilted precariously on a beach chair, his feet propped on a railing of the platform, his binoculars trained on a noisy group of young people playing in the waves.

"I want to ask him something, Mom. I'll be right back."

She escaped before Annie could answer, but returned almost at once, her face flushed with embarrassment and anger.

"I asked him a simple question and he was so rude. He laughed at me and said 'run and play little girl.' I told him I was not a little girl, I was seventeen. He just laughed at me. He said, 'Call me when you grow up.' Just wait, I'll get even with him."

"For goodness sake, Susy. You are a little girl, you're only seventeen. What did you ask him?"

"I asked him about the surf." As she turned her head she winked at Marge and ran gleefully into the foam-topped surf.

"Marge, take your shoes 'n stockings off and follow me. Then you can tell your friends in North Dakota you waded in the Pacific Ocean. Mom can put your stuff in the beach bag. C'mon, let's have some fun."

Annie smiled, "Marge, go have fun. Stay with Susy. I'm going to walk ahead. I want to find that hot dog stand. We've only had toast for breakfast and I'm starved. Be right back, meet you right here by the lifeguard stand. Isn't this a wonderful day?" She tucked Marge's shoes in her bag.

As she walked, a disturbing thought that crept into her mind was instantly dismissed. *Susy wouldn't. She promised me. She's a good girl, although sometimes she just forgets. I'm glad Marge is with her.*

The hot-dog stand was farther than she thought. She waited impatiently at the end of the line until finally her order was taken. Three hot dogs complete with pickles, ketchup, relish, onions—all the buns could hold—wrapped in paper napkins and tucked in a paper sack.

As she turned to leave, her attention was taken by the organ grinder's wheezy music. The sad, tired little monkey danced listlessly, then scampered about to pick up the few pennies that were thrown for him. *Poor little thing*, Annie thought, *he's tired. Me, too. What a day this has been.* She rested a moment on the bench before starting back.

Marge stood barefoot in the sand, holding her skirt up with one hand, shading her eyes with the other, transfixed at the perpetual motion of the ocean and listening to the raucous squeals of the gulls as they swooped effortlessly, fearlessly, among the revelers—close enough to touch.

Can this be me? Can this be real? I've got a job with a teacher and now I'm going to wade in the Pacific Ocean—all in one day. Can this really be happening to me?

"C'mon, fraidy cat. Get your feet wet," Susy called, already surrounded by a group of noisy teenage boys, all vying for her attention.

"Aren't you too far out?" Marge called. "Doesn't look like surf to me. Remember your promise?"

"Don't you dare tell Mom." Susy answered. "I'm only going out a little farther. At least I want to get my suit wet.

Marge's hair, free from the pins, curled loosely around her face as the damp ocean air enveloped her. Attentively she stepped into the swirling white-capped surf. She gasped as the cold blue-green water tugged at her knees. She felt with awe the push-pull of the mighty ocean. She stood mesmerized, shifting from foot to foot striving to keep her balance, her skirt now forgotten, soaked, clinging to her legs. Her heart beating wildly, breathless with excitement she walked slowly along the shoreline looking down to see her feet, so white in the translucent water, the small rosy-colored shells, the seaweed that washed up with the changing tides. *I will never forget this day, this wonderful day.*

She walked on, slowly enjoying each moment, but the worrisome picture of Susy kept pushing into her mind. Reluctantly, she turned back.

Walking more quickly, soon she was able to identify the small group and faintly she heard Susy's taunting voice.

"C'mon, you fraidy cats, what are you scared of? The lifeguard is right there. C'mon." She threw the big beach ball out as far as she could. "I dare you. Double dare you. What a bunch of babies." She turned and pushed back through the waves. "I'll get it myself."

They shouted, "Don't do it. The waves are getting rougher."

"Count me out, I'm not going any farther."

"Me, neither, let's go in and get a hot dog."

"C'mon, Blondie, don't be foolish."

From a distance, Marge saw the boys straggle in, but Susy, conspicuous in her red suit, was not among them.

This has been such a perfect day. I wish that foolish girl wouldn't spoil it for us. Annie would be terribly upset if she knew Susy was out so far, especially since she promised. I'm the foolish one to worry. She probably came in and I just didn't see her. Those boys are all standing together, so Susy is probably right in the middle.

But Marge's mind would not be appeased. Walking faster, her wet skirt slapping against her legs, she tried to reason herself apart from the fear that worsened with every step. Finally, she broke into a run as she saw a crowd gathering around the boys and saw the pointing fingers, heard the shouting voices. Breathless, she pressed her way to the front of the now subdued revelers. Her heart seemed to stop as she glimpsed for one heartbreaking moment, the unmistakable red dot, tossing about in the great swelling waves.

Marge closed her eyes at the unbearable sight. *God. Oh, God in heaven,* she prayed. Her eyes opened to see another figure, far out in waves that momentarily claimed both the struggling pair. The devouring ocean seemed reluctant to give up its prey. The onlookers stood silently, almost reverently. With a sudden intake of breath, and barely audible prayers, a muffled scream as the lifeguard surfaced, only to disappear again. The spectators watched, horrified at the life-and-death struggle that played like a bad movie scene. Time seemed to stand still as the exhausted man inched his way toward shore.

The crowd erupted in an ecstasy of joy and relief, clapping and cheering as they parted to let the man with his limp burden stagger over the wet sand to higher ground.

Marge waited, terrified. His labored breathing lessened as he lay Susy down, then swept aside the long blond hair that covered her face like a spider web. He held her as her body retched the sea water from her lungs. Susy wiped her mouth with the back of her hand as she slowly regained her composure and realized she was safe. Not only safe, but the center of attention in the comforting arms of the handsome lifeguard. She smiled and waved to the excited circle of well-wishers.

His voice shook as he asked, "Are you okay? How do you feel? Didn't your folks warn you about going out so far?"

"I didn't mean to go out so far, just far enough that you would have to come and save me." She smiled up at him.

He sputtered, shocked, "You foolish, foolish little girl. Don't you realize we nearly drowned out there? You ought to be spanked."

Her smile vanished as if by magic and was replaced by a furious look. She pushed herself from his arms, then spoke loudly, angrily. "I told you this morning, I'm not a 'little girl' and I told you I'd get even with you, remember? Do you think we're even now?"

A shocked silence fell over the rejoicing well-wishers and spread like wildfire throughout the crowd.

The impact of her words stunned him for a moment. Outrage and disbelief competed on his flushed face as the reality of this pointless brush with death was made very clear. He stood unsteadily to his feet, his face looking down, contorted. "Well, I'll be damned. You spoiled rotten brat. We nearly drowned because of your stupidity. I should have let you drown." He kicked sand on her as he turned, cursing to himself as he walked on unsteady legs back to his station.

The surrounding people slowly dissipated, their disgusted, unfriendly faces and comments frightened the girl who had never known an unkind word.

Marge came forward, sinking to her knees. "Susy, you didn't. You couldn't." Her voice choked.

"Don't you dare tell Mom," Susy cried. Don't you dare tell Mom.

Don't you dare. I'll tell how you weren't here with me."

Annie stood. *For goodness sake. I must have dozed off. These hot dogs will be cold dogs if I don't hurry. The girls will be starved.* She walked quickly, but the deep sand slowed her steps.

Looking ahead, she could see a large group of people who all seemed to be pointing in the same direction. *Probably one of those wild boys hit someone with that big beach ball and started a fight. I'm sure the girls stayed close to the lifeguard station. They are probably wading in the surf, gathering shells.* In the back of her mind the little voice nagged, *Susy forgets sometimes. I know she wouldn't do anything dangerous. Anyway, she's with Marge.*

Annie walked faster, dodging around the hordes of people, almost losing direction. *How could I have gone so far?* She saw a man point and paused to hear him say, "Look honey, it looks like some fool has gone out too far in those rough waves. I think I saw the lifeguard go out. Look at all the people gathering right there."

Annie felt paralyzed with fear and then thought, *Why do I worry myself like this? She promised, yes, but sometimes she forgets.* Unstoppable, the fear flooded through her mind. She dropped the beach bag, then the sack, spilling the hot dogs to the noisy, hungry gulls. She ran until her lungs were begging for air. It seemed forever before she reached the now dispersing group.

Elbowing her way through the last of them, she finally saw the girls. Marge sat with arms around the now blubbering Susy who had slowly come to the reality of her near brush with death and the consequences that followed.

Annie collapsed, dropped to her knees and crawled to the girls.

"Baby, baby. What happened?"

Susy ceased her crying as she answered, "Mom, we were right here in the surf when a huge wave rolled right over me and pulled me way, way out. I was so scared, I screamed and screamed and finally the lifeguard came."

"Yes, and if I hadn't risked my life to save yours, you'd be dead. Not sitting here lying to your mother." They all looked up to see the lifeguard looking down, his anger still obvious.

"Thank God, thank God." Annie's eyes filed with tears. "How can I ever find the words to thank you?"

"The joy on your face has already thanked me, ma'am."

Annie added, "I believe you've misunderstood Susy, she's just confused. I know how quickly those big waves can roll in."

The guard interrupted, "Was she confused this morning when she asked me for a date? When she said she'd get even with me when I told her to grow up? When, not a half hour ago, she said she'd gone out that far so I would have to come and get her? Ask your other girl and see if she will tell the truth."

Annie turned a horrified gaze toward Marge, who reluctantly met the unblinking eyes of the guard. "Yes, he is telling the truth."

She heard Susy's quick intake of breath behind her.

"Thank you, miss." He extended his hand to Annie. "May I help you up, ma'am? Would this be your beach bag? I found it near here." He smiled at Annie, nodded to Marge. "Good-bye, ladies." Turning, he waved and walked away.

This time it was Annie who said, "Let's hurry—we need to get home." She pulled a large towel from the beach bag and threw it over Susy's shoulders.

"Mom, you're not going to tell Dad, are you, Mom?"

"No, of course I'm not going to tell Dad . . . but you are. And right after supper, make no mistake about that. I cannot begin to tell you how ashamed I am to know you are so quick to lie. You do it so well it seems to me you have had a lot of practice."

"Mom, that's the first time I've ever lied to you."

"And . . . that is the second lie today, isn't it, Susy? I'll let Dad take care of it tonight."

It was a long, quiet ride home, broken only by Susy's sniffles. Marge was relieved when the little yellow house came into view.

As the three of them walked up the steps, Annie gave a heavy sigh. "Let's have a cup of coffee before we start dinner. I'm so tired. I just cannot believe this has happened." The tears slid silently down her cheeks as she waited for the coffee to perk. Marge put her arms tenderly around Annie's shoulders, which shook with every sob.

"Don't cry, Annie, she's safe now."

They heard a car door slam as Dad stepped out smiling and shaking hands with the driver. Annie rose to her feet, quickly drying her eyes.

"I'd better get supper started. Dad's always hungry when he gets home."

"Isn't that a police car?" Marge asked curiously.

"Yes," Annie replied. "Sometimes one of the other policemen gives Dad a ride. Ten hours walking a beat is hard work and he has been doing it for eighteen years. Would you please set the table, Marge?"

Boots opened the door, the *Los Angeles Times* tucked under his arm. "I'm home early girls ... hitched me a ride tonight. When's dinner?"

"Read your paper, Dad. Dinner will be on the table shortly."

He sat down heavily in his big worn chair, kicked off his shoes, then shook open the paper. "Don't know why I even read this—certainly there is not much good news. Sure is quiet in here. Where's my Susy?"

Annie shuddered, thinking of Susy's close brush with death. "I think she's taking a nap, but I'll call her. Dinner is almost ready."

Susy quietly opened the door to her room and stepped out. Seeing Dad engrossed in his paper, she walked to Annie and whispered, "Mom, please. You tell him. You know how mad he'll be at me."

"You talk to your father right after dinner, Susy. This time I will not intercede on your behalf."

Dad turned a page and glanced up. "Susy. Come here, girl, and give your old Dad a kiss."

Dinner was over more quickly than usual.

"Why is it so quiet around here? What did you girls do all day?"

Annie looked up from the dish pan. "We went to see Mrs. Lowenstein and she has agreed to teach Marge in exchange for Marge's help in the deli ... "

Boots interrupted, "What a grand idea. Marge, I'm so happy for you. Bring home a kosher pickle for me—I love 'em. Susy, did you have a good time?"

Susy looked imploringly at her mother to no avail.

"Dad, can I talk to you? Promise me you won't get mad at me? Promise?"

"Susy, do I ever get very mad at you?" He chuckled and tousled her hair. "What is this horrible secret? Too much face paint again? You can't fool your old Dad.

Susy slowly approached her father who waited expectantly.

"Well ... ," Susy started, not knowing the best way to present her problem. "Mom bought me this new bathing suit. I told her it was too small, but she liked the color ... "

"Susy." Annie's shocked look was enough to be Boots on alert.

"I'd like to see this bathing suit. I'd guess it's blue since that's your mother's favorite color."

"Oh, Dad, it's just a plain old suit. All the girls are wearing them. I think it's still drying on the line."

"Sue Ann. I want to see that suit right now."

She walked slowly to the bedroom.

"Excuse me, I have some letters to write." Marge quietly left the room. She passed Susy in the hallway and looked apprehensively at the bathing suit hanging from Susy's arm. Even through the closed door Marge could hear Boots roar.

"Annie, I can't believe you allowed my daughter to be seen in public . . . almost naked," he raged. "There isn't enough material in this to make a decent handkerchief. Why in heaven's name did you buy this for her in the first place? I'm ashamed of both of you. Go to your room, Susy. No, wait. Is that the whole story?"

Susy looked pleadingly at her mother.

Still smarting from her husband reprimand, Annie answered, "No, it isn't all there is to the story. Sue Anne, tell your father. Now."

The tears came in a flood, but Dad was not going to be swayed this time. Boots' anger frightened and surprised Marge since Susy could usually sweet-talk her father into a watered-down slap on the wrist.

"Daddy . . . I nearly drowned and now that I'm home safe, you're yelling at me. You should be glad I'm alive. It was horrible, just horrible . . . I was so scared I thought I was going to die, then the lifeguard saved me."

Boots' voice was suddenly very calm and cold. "And where was your mother, may I ask? How many times have you promised me to go no farther than the surf? And how many times have I told your mother to stay with you? Bring me that suit."

Susy handed her father the swimsuit and with one mighty jerk, he tore it from neck to hemline, then held it out in Annie's direction.

"Here, this might do as a cleaning rag. Susy, you won't need to worry about a suit for a very long time unless you plan to drown in the bathtub. You do understand that you will not go to the beach this summer? Now go to your room. We will discuss this further tomorrow."

"Yes, Dad." Susy fled the room, her sobs could still be heard as she reached the end of the hall.

Boots turned to Annie. "Have I not told you never to leave her alone on the beach?"

"Marge was with her. I only . . . "

"Marge is not her mother, is she?"

"Boots, it could have happened if you had been there . . . "

"Do tell me how she nearly drowned the time I took her. Your carelessness has nearly cost me my daughter's life."

Annie turned, tears filled her eyes. "Good night, Boots."

"I'm not done talking to you, Annie. Sit down. I seem to have more control on the streets than I have in my own home. In the future . . . "

"I said good night, Boots." Annie brushed passed him and paused in the doorway, her voice betrayed both sadness and anger. "I think we are speaking of *our* daughter, Boots. I recall playing the lead role about seventeen years ago. *Our* daughter is home safe after a terrible ordeal. I thank God and the lifeguard. Now, if you'll excuse me." She turned back and walked down the hall. He heard the bedroom door close.

Chapter 3

But what will I wear to work tomorrow? Probably that green dress Susy gave me. Shall I pin my hair up or tie it back? I'll ask Annie. These ugly old shoes— they've never been comfortable.

That evening when dinner was finished, Annie sat in her worn old chair, her hands busy with the darning and mending that seemed never finished, Boots engrossed in his newspaper, reading quietly except for an occasional indignant "Well, I'll be damned." Annie's soft response, "Shhh. Dad, the girls." as Susy retrieved her *True Confessions* from its hiding place.

Marge walked down the hall and seated herself on a low stool at Annie's feet. As she retrieved an errant ball of yarn that had rolled under Annie's chair, she spoke "Annie, these are my only shoes, they are so ugly and they have never been comfortable. Do you think we could find a shoe store where I could buy shoes that I can work in?"

Annie quickly replied, "Of course. You should have shoes that fit properly, you'll be on your feet all day. Sears & Roebuck nearly always has a sale on. You'll really enjoy it. I don't suppose you've ever been in a big department store?" Susy, her *True Confessions* quickly hidden once more, appeared as though by magic. "Oh, Mom, what fun. Can we go tomorrow?"

Boots folded his paper, then spoke gruffly, "Girls, I hate to spoil your plans, but Sears & Roebuck is all the way downtown. There are so many strangers from all over the country who are so desperate and hungry that the streets are dangerous. Can't you find some place closer?"

"Oh," Susy coaxed, "Marge can't work in those old shoes. We'll all stay together and be so careful. Sears has a big sale on. Think of all the money we'll save. Please?"

Annie spoke quietly, "Boots, we'll only go to Sears, then right home. I'll take good care of the girls, and Marge really needs shoes."

Reluctantly, Boots gave his consent, but added, "I'm going to give each of you a card with a telephone number that will reach me anywhere. Use it only for emergencies. Put it in your purse and be sure you have it anytime you leave the house. "Don't lose it."

He produced the cards from his billfold, then returned to his chair. As he shook his paper out he muttered, "The best news in this paper is the comics. You can't beat 'Mutt & Jeff' or 'Andy Gump'."

Susy danced down the hallway to the bedroom. Marge followed more sedately, but her face was flushed with the anticipation of tomorrow. Both girls rushed to the closet. In an instant, clothing was scattered about the room, thrown over the bed, draped over a chair, heaped high. "I haven't got a thing to wear." This was the universal cry of women since time began.

In the morning, after Boots' usual hurried breakfast, he left for work. Pausing in the doorway, he sternly admonished Annie not to let the girls out of her sight with the hurtful reminder, "You know what happened at the beach."

Annie sat in the now quiet kitchen, toying with a second cup of coffee. Her thoughts wandered back to the times on the North Dakota farm. *Ruthie and I were young, dreaming of a wonderful life, an exciting future, what would it hold for us? I dreamed of the day when I would be a famous dancer who traveled the world or maybe a great designer since I love to sew. Ruthie dreamed of a Prince Charming, a lovely home and a large family.*

Annie sipped her coffee thinking, *those dreams were just that, dreams.*

Ruth had found her Prince Charming, disguised as the boy who lived on the next farm; never had the children she had wanted so badly, but she was happy in her country home.

I, so anxious for my life to begin, married too young. The great love of my life, I thought. Boots is a good man, but who am I? Just an obedient wife and mother. Is that all there is for me? My life is encompassed by four walls, a beloved headstrong daughter with her life ahead of her, a husband engrossed in his job who makes all the decisions.

Instantly, guilt flooded through her consciousness, but the searching thoughts would not be evaded. *What of my wants? My needs? My dreams? I need to be someone who is not just Boots' wife or Susy's mother.*

The reality of today, like a noxious weed, smothered yesterday's dream, leaving only the sweet scent of flowers after a spring rain.

Why did I let it go? I wish I could start all over again.

Once a month Boots takes me to those stuffy meetings, lots of beer, cigar smoke, and potluck. Then the women do the clean-up and the men retire to another room to talk shop and tell each other about the "big one that got away." After awhile, "it" gets much bigger. The women make small talk about the kids and exchange recipes. I get so bored I could scream. Although, at the last meeting someone brought a gramophone and we women danced together. I learned how to do the two-step and caught on quick to the Charleston.

Boots would have had a heart attack if he had seen my stockings rolled down and my hands on my bare knees. But, oh, wouldn't it be fun to be me in a sparkly, beaded dress with a fringe and ... her thoughts were interrupted by the noisy entrance of Susy.

"Mom, get ready—it's a long ride downtown. Do you think I could get some new shoes, too? Please, Mom?"

"No. You don't need shoes. Call Marge while I fix a quick breakfast. Don't rush me." Nonetheless, breakfast was a hurried affair.

It was a forty-five-minute ride on the jerky streetcar to the downtown station. The ride ended too quickly for Marge as she watched out the window to marvel at the tall buildings, the diversity of the passing people, and the tall, faded, blue mountains in the background.

As they left the streetcar and started the short walk to the big department store, Susy hurried ahead. Marge's steps slowed, her excited, happy mood was disturbed by a creeping sense of uneasiness for no apparent reason that she could identify.

As they turned the corner, Susy's startled look quickly turned to apprehension. Turning, she hurried back to her mother, surprised and frightened by the flood of men who snaked down the sidewalk as far as the eye could see.

The sounds of the great sprawling city seemed to echo the dissonance of the eternal sea. Despite the golden sunshine, it did not seem to bring cheer, but rather cast a spotlight on the struggling humanity below.

Men crowded the sidewalks. A deadly quiet seemed to prevail as though they were conserving their strength to exist another day. They seemed to wander aimlessly without destination, but eventually reached the forlorn end of the line. A long line that stretched like a great river of weary travelers huddled together at the end of their dream. No gold at the end of this rainbow, and worse, no hope. The feeling of despair screamed soundlessly, a pall of desolation hung over the city like a see-through curtain.

"Mom, what are all these men doing here? Is it a parade? There's no music, no fire trucks, it's so quiet. Why are they all on the sidewalks? Is this why Dad said the streets were dangerous? Look, there are policemen walking beside them. Where are they all going? It's scary."

Annie's voice trembled. "Now I know what Dad's been so upset about. He said the soup kitchen fed ten thousand men at Christmastime in New York. It wasn't real to me before, but now that I've seen with my own eyes, it's too horrible. I wish I hadn't seen it. What of their families? Dad said men were grateful for a twelve-hour-a-day job for three dollars a week."

They stood watching as the line moved slowly past the several large receptacles and each man paused holding a container, a cup of soup was ladled in, a slice of bread thrown on top almost as an afterthought. Occasionally a man would drink his portion ravenously, then attempt to push his way back into the line. But he was roughly pushed aside with a curse or a threatening fist. Some men took their portions and walked away.

"Mom, where are they going with it?"

"Probably to take it to their family. I'd guess that soup is mighty thin, no meat, I'm sure. What with the drought in the Midwest, the farmers putting down their starving livestock."

At last Marge fully comprehended what that man on the train had tried to tell her, but his grave account paled into nothingness when compared to the scene before her. "My God, my God. How can God allow this to happen?"

Annie could give her no answer. Annie could almost hear Boots say, "That damned Hoover, I wish he were the last in line, damn Republican."

Annie urged the girls to the store's entrance. Susy stayed close to her mother, but Marge hesitated. She had noticed a man with a small boy standing near the window that displayed men's and boys' clothing. Then she heard the boy's shrill, excited voice as he pressed his nose against the glass. He pointed to a pair of high-topped shoes with yellow and red plaid laces.

"Pa, Pa, can I get them? Can I, Pa? Please? I'll be so good. I'll never sass Ma again." Extending a badly worn and scuffed shoe, he pleaded, "Look, the cardboard keeps wearing out and they pinch my toes. It hurts. Please, Pa?"

"Joey, you know we haven't any money. With the new baby coming, Ma needs extra things, but as soon as I find a job . . . ," he paused, his voice choked, a look of grief and shame flushed his face as he saw the tears slide down the boy's cheeks.

Annie, mindful of her promise to Boots, tugged at Marge's arm. "Let's hurry Marge, I told Boots we wouldn't be long." Even before

Annie finished, Marge had pulled away and moved to the man with the child.

She met his surprised, questioning look with a smile as she extended her hand. Confused, he shook it, wondering if she was someone he should have remembered or someone his wife may have known. As he withdrew his hand, he felt something in his palm. Looking down, he saw the unmistakable five-dollar imprint on the crumpled bill. He hesitated a moment, then stepped toward her and pressed the money back in her hand.

Annie stood as though her feet had grown fast to the sidewalk, never taking her eyes from the ragged man whose face looked angry. She could not hear him say, "I thank you, miss, from the bottom of my heart, but I cannot take money from a woman and call myself a man."

She saw Marge stand a little taller and step forward and then heard her outraged voice clearly.

"Your foolish pride won't buy your son, the son you love, the shoes that he needs. Will your pride keep his feet warm or keep your wife's belly full? Or keep her bed warm tonight?

"Your selfishness would deny both me and your son the happiness that this money would buy. Is selfishness and foolish pride what makes a man? Buy those shoes and get something your wife must need and bring home a chicken for supper."

She bent over the boy and tucked the money into his pocket, then turned to take Annie's arm as they walked into the store.

The boy looked up, "Gee, Pa, that lady sounded real mad. Ma never talks to you like that."

"For sure, she was mad, but she did tell the truth. C'mon, we'd better see about those shoes."

Annie's heartbeat returned to normal and with a sideways glace at Marge said, "Now I've seen the Marge that Ruth told me about. Guess there's more than one way to light a fire."

They giggled like two schoolgirls as they looked for the shoe department.

"What's so funny, Mom? I'm going to tell Dad that Marge talked to a man on the street. He looked mad, too."

A sharp pinch surprised Susy. "You'll do no such thing, young lady. Don't forget it." The imprint of Annie's discipline was clearly evident.

Despite the sale signs everywhere, the aisles were not crowded, although there seemed to be an abundance of salesladies hovering about.

Marge's eyes widened with amazement; the magnitude of the huge store was almost frightening.

Annie walked ahead. Marge stood, looking almost with disbelief at the rows and shelves of merchandise that stretched as far as her eye could see. She watched Susy feel her way through a rack of brightly colored dresses, then hold one up to the front of her as she preened before the floor-length mirror. Susy saw Marge's reflection in the mirror, then hurried back to her, carrying the dress.

"Oh Marge, c'mon. Isn't this just beautiful? Wouldn't it be so perfect for the prom?"

As Marge stepped forward, she accidentally brushed against a mannequin.

"Oh, excuse me, ma'am." Then realizing her mistake, she blushed with embarrassment. Susy giggled uncontrollably until Annie looked back with a stern look. Susy vividly recalled the painful pinch.

"Oh, Mom, look," Susy exclaimed.

"Susy, we are here to buy shoes, not dresses."

"But Mom, just look at this blue one. It's only two dollars, marked down from four." Holding the dress in front of her, Susy pleaded, "Please, Mom? I don't have a thing to wear to the prom."

"Come along, Susy. The shoe department is right over there."

"Mom, it's just my size."

Marge, remembering the joy she had felt the day the mailman delivered the dress that Ruth had ordered for her, said, "Susy, I'll buy it for you. It's your birthday present and you'll be the prettiest girl at the prom."

Susy gave a gleeful whoop and wrapped her arms around Marge. "Oh, thank you, thank you. You can wear my green chiffon, the one with the pink roses on it. Let's look at shoes."

The saleslady appeared, as if by magic, and the transaction was quickly completed. Annie looked resigned, but pleased to see the interaction between the two young women.

Susy, holding her hard-won treasure closely, hurried ahead to the shoe department.

"Did Ruth ever tell you about my inheritance?" Marge asked with a guileless smile.

"I believe she may have mentioned it," Annie answered with a twinkle in her eye. Heads turned to see the cause of their unrestrained laughter.

The clerk led the way to an alcove that seemed to hold all the shoes in the world. Marge was happy to sit down while her foot was measured.

"That's a size five, a difficult size. Perhaps we can find something in the sample shoes. They're much cheaper, too, because there isn't much demand for so small a size."

Marge interjected, "I want something comfortable, not fancy."

"I know the very shoe." The saleslady returned in a moment, her arms heaped high with boxes.

"No, no, not that color." Annie protested.

"These rub my heels," Marge added.

Susy shuddered, "Ugly. Ugly old-lady shoes."

Finally, with only two boxes left, Susy pulled the lid off a box and announced, "Here they are Marge. You'll like these."

The saleslady gave a great sigh of relief as Marge agreed. "You've made a wise choice, my dear. They are marked down to a dollar fifty. Now, shouldn't you have a pair for dress up?"

"Oh no, I couldn't. Two pair of shoes in one day? The very thought is shocking. I've never even bought one pair in my entire life. Pa always bought them. He said, 'Wear 'em—don't mind if they don't fit just right. Money don't grow on trees.' They were always too big and always ugly."

Susy's laughing voice broke in, "Marge, are you Irish or really Scotch?"

The saleslady reappeared and, with a dramatic flourish, held aloft a shoe that was too elegant, too dainty to be a shoe. It was a Cinderella slipper that Marge thought would make a girl cry with envy. A strip of shining black patent across the front, another strip across the back, leaving the instep bare.

The clerk was so enthusiastic, it was as though she really held Cinderella's glass slipper. "This is a D'Orsay pump with a two-inch heel, the very latest style." She knelt to slip them on Marge's feet. "Fits perfectly," she said triumphantly, "and only two dollars and fifty cents."

Susy pulled Marge upright. Nearly speechless, Marge's voice shook. "These aren't *my* feet." She turned to Susy. "I could never walk in these high heels, but, oh, they are so beautiful. Someday . . . "

"Oh, yes, you can. It just takes practice."

What lovely feet and legs she has. What a shame if she doesn't take them, thought the saleslady.

Marge tottered back to her seat to slowly return the shiny slippers to the box. "Not today, but someday."

Annie thought, *she's spent all her money.*

"Marge, it would give us such pleasure for these to be your birthday present. You know, your birthdays are only three days apart." She nodded to the saleslady and added, "We need to look for underwear, too. Wrap them up."

"I will practice what I preach. It will be my pleasure to accept." Marge walked behind them carrying the precious packages, tears running unashamedly down her cheeks.

Susy took her arm. "Happy birthday to us. Shall I sing?"

I will never be this happy again, Marge thought as she wiped her eyes.

Annie, following the saleslady, walked quickly ahead, but Susy and Marge were already there, their packages tucked safely under one arm, looking through the stacks of pastel-colored underclothing, both giggling like the teenagers they are. *Thank God, let them have their girlhoods.* Annie thought.

The D'Orsay pumps had shattered Marge's reserve. Her spontaneous laughter was contagious—heads turned to see the joyful red-haired girl laugh with such exuberance. They had to smile, too.

Annie wandered down the aisle, admiring the displays of lingerie. Smiling to herself at the girls' excited laughter, she remembered how she and Ruthie had found fun and laughter in the simplest things. Ruthie had always said, "Life is just a bowl of cherries."

Marge, her mind still savoring the contents of the box that held her shoes, paid little attention to the underclothes that Susy declared essential.

"Finally, one last thing, Marge. You must have some pretty stockings to go with those shoes." She met with no resistance from the spellbound Marge.

"Where's Mom? Oh, there."

Marge's eyes followed Susy's pointing finger to see Annie standing with her eyes closed, fondling a dainty nightgown with tiny tucks and pleats flowing down the front, lacey inserts on the collar and in the sleeves. And, of course, blue.

"Susy, when is your Mom's birthday?"

"Oh, several months ago. Dad got her a new iron, the handle was so worn on the old one. I gave her some pretty handkerchiefs."

Marge nodded to the ever-present saleslady indicating Susy's accumulated stack, adding, "The nightgown that lady is holding also."

As she paid, she said the magic words triumphantly: "Wrap it up."

When they left the store, she averted her eyes from the long line of men that still endured. Her conscience nagged, but she smothered it with the thought, *I've been that poor, hungry, and hopeless for most of my seventeen years. It's my turn.*

The trip downtown that had taken forty-five minutes seemed to have grown wings as they were homeward bound.

Annie sat silently with closed eyes, remembering when she and Ruth had trekked to town over the frozen snow in a sleigh for thirty miles. Pa had bought them overshoes that buckled almost to the knee. She smiled to herself as she recalled her and Ruthie dancing about in the kitchen, then Pa whirling Ma about. *"Let us show you girls how to do the polka."*

"Why are you trying to dance in those overshoes?"

Then his great booming laugh. I was always his favorite because I was the baby.

A giggle, a rustle of tissue paper and an unintended nudge caused Annie's eyes to open surprising an irrepressible Susy who was opening one end of her box, tissue paper floating to the floor and a shimmering blue peeking out.

"Susy, what on earth are you doing? Don't you dare open that here."

"Oh, Mom, I just wanted to see it again real quick. I can't wait."

Marge, her eyes bright with excitement, red curls tumbling over her shoulder, bent over her shoe box and opened just enough to slip one hand in to caress the soft, shiny blackness of her dainty pumps.

"Susy, I don't think we need to mention your dress tonight. Marge probably will want to show Dad her nice work shoes." They exchanged a knowing look. "Well after I've had it awhile, I can say it's not new—I've had it for ages. What about the fancy nightgown?"

Annie laughed, "I intend to surprise him with that."

Susy was out the door almost before the car stopped. Marge and Annie followed quickly, Susy chattering nonstop.

"Mom, you don't need to have a big birthday party for us. It's only two weeks until the prom, so we can celebrate there."

"Well, if you'd like that better, all your friends would be there. And our house is small. I'll bake a cake though."

Marge interrupted, "Susy, you know I'll be working."

"Not on Saturday you won't. I think Clara has a brother who doesn't have a date, he'd probably love to take you. You'll look gorgeous in that green chiffon dress."

"Susy, I can't. I don't even know him or any of your friends. And the only dancing I've ever done was when I danced down to the barn with a milk pail in one hand and a pitchfork in the other."

Susy looked at Marge as though she were speaking a foreign language. "Mom will teach you how to dance, we've got two weeks."

Annie interceded, "Of course I'll teach you, Marge. You need to make friends with people your own age. You'll have a wonderful time."

That evening Boots congratulated Marge on her sensible work shoes as he unlaced his own and tossed them aside. He shook open the paper, read for a few minutes then threw it to the floor in disgust. "Doesn't look as though there will ever be an end to this depression, all those damned Republicans can do is talk about it."

Annie sat, rocking quietly. She had listened to this same dialogue for so long she could have given it herself, word for word.

The clicking of her knitting needles was interrupted by a burst of laughter coming from the girl's bedroom.

"You'd better check on those girls. Sounds like they're having way too much fun. They're up to some devilment."

Annie walked down the hall and peeked in the door. She laughed to see Marge tottering on her high heels, endeavoring to stay upright, and Susy in her shimmering blue dress, her hair piled high, preening in front of the mirror. Their happiness was contagious.

When she returned, she smiled at Boots. "They're just having fun, like girls do."

"C'mon, its bedtime, I've had a long day," he answered.

The girls made their sleepy appearance the next morning. Susy teased Marge about her attempts to walk gracefully in her new pumps and Marge, laughing, threatened to let down the hem in the blue dress.

Boots' empty breakfast dishes still sat on the kitchen table. He'd eaten early as usual.

Annie sat, sipping a cold cup of coffee, a slice of uneaten toast on her plate. The defeated slope of her shoulders went unnoticed by Susy as she bent over to hug her mother.

"Well, Mom, what did Dad say about the new nightie?"

Annie turned away. She did not want the smoldering rage in her heart to show on her face. "He said, 'Oh, go to bed and act your age.'"

Both girls fell silent at the thought of the hurting words.

"Oh, Mom, what did you say?"

"I said, 'You didn't worry about my age when I was sixteen.'"

Annie didn't add that he had turned his back and gone to sleep.

"Mom." Susy's shocked voice asked, "How old were you when you married Dad?"

"Not quite seventeen."

"How old was Dad?"

"Twenty-nine."

Annie didn't feel the girls needed to know the details of the old-time shotgun wedding. It hurt too much to remember the pain and disappointment in Pa's eyes and how Ma had cried.

Last night, she had never felt so alone in her life.

Chapter 4

Susy lay awake, counting the hours until she could flaunt her conquest. Hal was president of the senior graduating class and captain of the football team. She could envision herself dancing with Hal, her clinging dress shimmering with every step, gloating over the envious stares of the other girls.

"Marge, wake up. The prom is just five days away, you just have to learn to dance." Susy nudged her awake.

Susy, still in her pajamas, burst into the kitchen with Marge following, rubbing her eyes.

"Mom, what's for breakfast? Will you teach Marge the two-step? Mom, the prom is in five days."

Annie smiled as she put down her empty cup. "Make your own breakfast, sweetie, I'm going out to the garden to pull weeds before the sun gets too hot."

"Then it's toast and cold cereal. Marge, make the coffee."

As Susy chattered, Marge interrupted. "I wish I could be as excited about the prom as you are Susy, but I won't know any of your friends, I can't dance, I've never even seen this boy you've coaxed to be my escort, and I'd only be an embarrassment to you. Remember I'm going to work the next morning. That's what I'm excited about."

"Marge, Clara's brother is a tall, skinny boy who is the valedictorian. He is very shy and very quiet, too quiet for my tastes. A few trips to the punch bowl would liven him up. You'll be perfectly safe. All the plans have been made so you can't back out now. Be a good sport, you know Dad won't let me go if you don't go. He thinks you're *Miss Perfect.*"

Marge felt a momentary irritation at Susy's skillful manipulation. "No, I certainly didn't know that. Isn't Clara that friend of yours that Boots doesn't like? Says she wears too much face paint, that she is a bad influence?"

"Marge, do you want to spoil all my plans? Dad doesn't have to know everything. Besides, the prom is chaperoned. C'mon, let's start right now."

"I'll wind up the Victrola. Dad bought it years ago, and Mom said he used to love the waltz. This might cheer her up, she seems so sad lately."

Marge found Annie on her knees in the garden furiously pulling weeds as though she had a personal vendetta against each one.

"Annie, we need you. Susy says she won't let me step on her feet so you will have to teach me. I have to know the two-step by next Saturday."

"That's a good idea; weeding isn't my idea of fun."

The sound of the Victrola grew louder as they approached the house. Annie stopped at the door and kicked off her gardening shoes.

"I'll wash my hands and be right in."

Moments later Annie danced into the kitchen, laughing as she reached for Marge and swung her about. "Here. Put your hands here. When I step forward, you step back. Relax. Count 1 - 2 - 3, 1 - 2 - 3."

Marge's feet seemed to have developed a mind of their own.

Susy danced beside them. "See how easy it is? Move like this."

Annie was a patient teacher and slowly Marge relaxed as her natural sense of rhythm dominated. She learned quickly, surprised to realize how much she was enjoying herself.

The unmade beds, the weeds in the garden, various other duties were forgotten as they wound and re-wound the Victrola. Annie, breathless and laughing, her face flushed, felt as young as she did when she and Ruth practiced years ago, happy in their mother's kitchen.

"Girls, it's almost noon and you're still in your pajamas."

"One more time, only one more time," they pleaded. Laughing hysterically, they collapsed around the table that still held the breakfast dishes.

Then, Marge was shocked as she heard her own words. "I want to learn the Charleston, too. I never dreamed dancing was so much fun."

The irrepressible Susy, for once, was speechless.

Sure knowledge burst upon Annie's consciousness: *This beautiful butterfly is shedding her cocoon and blowing the hinges from Pandora's Box. Her personality, smothered for so many years, has popped like the cork from a champagne bottle. The real Marge is a million miles from North Dakota.*

On her side of the closet Marge arranged and rearranged her work clothes, placing her new work shoes neatly beneath.

Her apprehension grew with each passing day. Her "what if's" were overwhelming. *What shall I do about my hair, tie it back? Pin it up?* She despaired that any ribbon could contain those unruly curls that always seemed to evade both pins and ties for any length of time. Annie's assurances and encouragement momentarily comforted her.

Marge envied Susy's carefree attitude as she danced about her few chores, singing *"Yes Sir, That's My Baby"* without a care in the world.

"Three more days, Mom. It's forever."

"Susy, you'd better be doing something about that dress. You know Dad is not going to let you out of the house with that low neckline. Pin a scarf or something to cover up some skin. Dad wouldn't have let you go at all if Hal hadn't been the precinct captain's son. No kissing good night and you'd better be home on time. You know Dad will be waiting up."

"I suppose he'll be checking on *Miss Perfect*, too."

"He already has, and he also talked to the principal who gave Tim a good reference."

"Oh, for gosh sakes, Mom, I'll be so glad next year when I'm eighteen and I can do what I please. No curfews for me."

"I doubt that," Annie laughed.

At last. The long-awaited dream had become a reality. The girls had been dressing, re-dressing, doing each other's hair or fingernails until their degree of perfection had been achieved. The magical moment had arrived.

They dressed with care, mindful of Dad's critical eye. Susy's concealing scarf was held by Annie's brooch. Only a blush of face powder had been applied; lipstick and mascara would come later. Their hair, pinned high in front, cascaded in heavy curls down the back. Susy's tresses displayed Marge's expertise with the curling iron.

The picture they presented as they walked down the hall for Dad's appraisal was that of two exceptionally lovely young women.

They were unaware that two cars with their youthful escorts had arrived almost simultaneously. Annie guessed that the boys had planned it that way—safety in numbers.

Boots looked up from his paper as the girls stood in the doorway for his inspection. For a long minute he stared wordlessly until Susy started to fidget. His eyes blurred with tears. *A calloused old cop*, he thought. *I'm about to lose it. It was only yesterday she took her first baby steps, hanging on for dear life to my rough old finger. Her little shoes would both fit in my hand with lots of room to spare. Her first words were "da-da" and she followed me everywhere…when did she grow up? God, how I love her.*

His thoughts were interrupted by the ringing of the doorbell and Susy's impatient, "Dad."

He opened the door, inviting the two nervous boys in for inspection. He smiled inwardly, deriving a perverse satisfaction in knowing the effect he had on them.

The greetings and introductions soon over, and Hal expertly pinned on Susy's corsage. Tim tried to follow Hal's example and his sister's instructions but fumbled desperately under Boots' scrutiny.

Red with embarrassment, he was saved by Annie, who quickly accomplished that which Tim had found impossible.

Boots had been thoroughly enjoying himself before Annie appeared.

To everyone's immense relief, he announced, "You boys drive carefully. Have these girls home by eleven-thirty, looking just like they look now. I hope I don't have to come and get them."

The boys, as one, hurriedly assured him the girls would be home before curfew, then gratefully made their escape.

Tim pulled away from the curb, speechless for the first few blocks, vividly aware of the girl beside him. Gone from his mind were the extravagant promises he had made his father as he pleaded for the car.

Suddenly, "Clara said you were pretty, she didn't tell me you were beautiful." He blurted the sentence as though it was one word.

"Well, thank you, I thought you were really brave with that corsage thing, too. Boots can be very scary sometimes." They laughed, the silence broken. She turned toward him. "I hope I won't embarrass you. This is my first prom and I've only just learned to dance. These high heels may be my downfall."

"Don't worry about that. I'll be lucky to get the first or last dance with you," and knew it to be true.

As he drove, she peeked at him. He seemed so familiar. Of whom did he remind her? That hair that obviously had been slicked back, now hung over his forehead; that shy, eager-to-please look, the tall lanky frame ... Of course, it was Ben. And as she looked at the long tapered fingers that held the steering wheel, she saw Ben's broken, dirty fingernails, the calluses, the shy smile of a scared, hungry boy seeking his dream of fame and fortune.

As Tim turned the last corner, he looked for a safe place to park in the already crowded space. Hal rolled his window down, calling, "Hey, wait up. You know we'll have to run the gauntlet. We need to present a united front through that stag line at the door."

They could hear the orchestra tuning up the instruments as they walked up the steps of the brightly lit gym, already crowded with the happy revelers. As they stepped through the door, they were confronted by the rowdy boys without dates; a boisterous group who heckled their more fortunate classmates with long expressive wolf whistles, unheeded advice, and comments just this side of respectability.

"Tim. Is that our very own bookworm? You sneaky devil. Where have you been hiding that gorgeous redhead? Bet you didn't find her in the library."

Tim grinned self-consciously, "Not for the likes of you, you losers." Moving ahead, he waved nonchalantly, but the delight that spread from ear to ear said it all.

Hal nudged his way through, but not before Susy had her moments of bliss. "Ooooh, Blondie. Give me your dance card. Give your feet a break. Hal can't dance, he can only tackle."

"He didn't get my vote."

"I'd be so good to you."

"Me, too. Me, too."

Their voices pleaded.

Susy blew kisses and flirted outrageously until Hal pulled her through. "Enough of this. Find your own dates, you noisy children."

They joined Hal's immediate circle of admirers and introductions were exchanged. Susy excused herself and nudged Marge. "C'mon, let's get our war paint on. When they entered the alcove titled "Girls," it was packed with primping girls who had the same plans.

Although the rainbow-colored lights that swirled from every corner seemed to transform the large gym into a fairyland, the unmistakable odor of dirty socks and sweaty bodies lingered in the atmosphere. No amount of perfume and aftershave could completely eliminate that.

The ceiling was ablaze with brilliantly colored balloons that clung tenaciously, their long tails dangling...an occasional *pop*. Then a shriek and the explosive laughter of some lucky boy who had happened upon a golden opportunity.

The principal was far removed from the snack bar, where the noise was most deafening. The students in all their finery swarmed about the punch bowl like hummingbirds around a feeder.

The band gave a warning roll of the drums and the principal

stood. "Welcome, students. Enjoy yourselves, but no drinking, no smoking, no offensive language and no jazz. Obey the rules."

The chaperones grumbled. "He's such a crank. Why doesn't he let the kids have a little fun? Hasn't he ever been young?"

"No, I think he was born in that ugly suit with a scowl on his face."

Susy emerged with the first sound of music, her lips a vibrant red, the perfect Cupid's bow lips made famous by Clara Bow, the *It* girl.

Susy's mascaraed eyes teased Hal as he held her closer. He felt a tap on his shoulder as she was whirled away.

"Oh damn. Hey, don't forget whose date you are," he called to her retreating back held snugly in his classmate's arms.

Tim put his arms around Marge, but his feet seemed glued to the floor as he desperately tried to remember his sister's instructions. Marge gave a little push, then counted "1 - 2 - 3, 1 - 2 - 3." His face red with embarrassment, he awkwardly danced her to a corner where he hoped to evade any marauding stags. His hopes were dashed almost immediately as a grinning classmate tapped him on the shoulder. Tim reluctantly stepped aside to see Marge disappear into the crowd of whirling teenagers, changing partners frequently.

Well, he grumbled to himself. *I'm glad she's having a wonderful time, but I wish it were with me.*

Finally, he had her in his arms again.

"Oh, Tim, this is just as much fun as Susy said it would be. I'm so glad I learned to dance. Where have you been?"

Her face was flushed, her eyes sparkled, a few stray curls were attempting their escape. "Let's sit this one out, Tim, I'm exhausted. I haven't missed a dance. I'd love another glass of that punch. I've never tasted anything so good. Your friend brought me two glasses, but I'm still so thirsty."

Tim looked surprised. "You'd better go easy on that punch, it's probably spiked."

"No, your friend said it was 7-Up and grape juice."

Tim returned with the drink and Marge drained the glass and stood. "Now I can dance all night. Let's ask the band to play something besides these lullabies."

She walked a bit unsteadily toward the musicians with Tim following. As though her words had been directly transmitted to their ears, they broke into a jazzy "Yes sir, that's my baby, no sir, don't mean maybe . . ."

"Oh, Tim. Let me teach you the Charleston."

Stepping quickly away from him, she slipped off her shoes and stuffed them in his pockets.

"C'mon." Her stockings rolled down, she lifted her dress and the Charleston was in full swing. Tim's shocked look quickly turned to a grin of appreciation, then uncontrollable laughter as he clapped in time to her flying feet.

In a moment, there was a curious ring of onlookers following Tim's example.

"Who wants to learn the Charleston?" Marge called.

A few, then a few more, and then many couples joined the circle. Other dancers were crowding in. A ring of stomping, clapping, dancing teenagers yelling encouragements. "Do it again." "Swing it, Marge" "One more time." The band, caught up in the fun, played on.

Marge's upswept hair lost its pins, tumbled down, swinging in sync with every movement; her dress slipped down revealing one bare ivory-colored shoulder.

The chaperones looked at each other, then laughed as they joined the boisterous circle that enclosed Marge.

The principal seemed petrified. Could this be happening in his school? His gym? His students?

Struggling to his feet, he stalked through the crowd. The band ceased playing but Marge was still dancing as a sudden silence descended, broke only by a few discreet *boos*. Taking the laughing Marge by the arm, he escorted her from the floor.

"Young lady, you better go home and sober up."

"Sober up? I am sober."

"We don't allow drinking or that *hoochie coochie* dancing in this school."

"I haven't drunk anything but punch," Marge retorted indignantly.

The principal raised incredulous eyes. One of the chaperones hurried to the punch bowl, took a sip, rolled his eyes, then drank a full glass. "Boy, that packs a wallop," then hurriedly carried it from the room.

"Who brought this girl?" the principal demanded.

"I did, sir. I'm sure she didn't know the punch was spiked."

"Not in my school."

"Yes sir. C'mon Marge, let's get some fresh air. We'll take a little walk."

She took Tim's hand, then turned, pointing a finger at the irate principal, she sang *"Yes sir, that's my baby,"* then blew him a kiss. The gym rocked with laughter that followed her all the way to the door.

She leaned unsteadily as the room started to whirl.

"How do you feel, Marge? Not going to be sick, are you?" He sent up a silent prayer, *Please God, not in my father's car.* They walked across the parking lot.

"What time is it? My head is whirling. I feel so sick I think I should go home. For goodness sakes, where are my new shoes?"

Quickly Tim produced the shoes. As she bent to put one on, her stomach revolted. Miserable, she said, "Tim, wait for me at the car." Again and again she retched until she felt she could lie right down on the asphalt and die. Tim, who had gone just far enough to give her privacy, returned to help her to the car.

Limping on one shoe and carrying the other, Marge moaned, "Oh, Tim, I am so sorry, so ashamed. What could have been in that punch to make me so sick?"

"Vodka, I'd guess. I thought you knew."

She groaned. "Are we nearly home? What time is it?"

"Only ten. I can't take you home; Boots will kill me. Don't be sick in Dad's car."

"I couldn't be, there's nothing left. Please, I want to go home."

Reluctantly, Tim turned the car. When he neared the house, he turned the lights off, cut the motor and coasted to a stop. He whispered, "Try not to let Boots see you."

He steadied her uncertain steps to the door, rang the bell, then hurried back to the car. Marge slumped against the doorjamb, one shoe off, one in her hand, one stocking hugging her ankle.

Annie opened the door. One horrified look told the story.

"Oh, Annie, I'm so sorry."

Annie put her finger to her lips and hurried Marge's faltering footsteps down the hall.

Boots called from his chair, "What's going on, who is it?"

"It's Marge. I knew she wasn't feeling well. I never should have let her go to that dance. The excitement has been too much; she has a terrible headache. I'll get her some aspirin. She has to work tomorrow so it's just as well she came home early."

She helped Marge undress, washed her face, then pulled the covers over her.

I think I'd better set the alarm for five a.m. She'd be heartsick if she missed her first day of work.

69

Boots grumbled. "I wish Susy had come, too. I don't like her being out so late."

"Boots, it's prom night and it's not even ten-thirty," Annie responded.

But at ten o'clock, Susy was in the backseat of the precinct captain's Model A trying to prevent his son from unbuttoning her dress while she was enthusiastically enjoying his kisses.

At eleven, Boots was looking at the clock and looking out the window at the sound of every passing car.

Despite the icy cold water and the rough paper towels in the unpretentious ladies' room, Susy's face was scrubbed clean and her hair hastily pinned up when Boots opened the door, promptly at eleven-thirty.

"Baby, I'm glad you're home," Boots sighed with relief.

"Good night, Dad, I had a wonderful time."

Boots went to bed, unknowing that he had missed the main event, satisfied his girls were home safe and respectable.

Chapter 5

The little hand pointed to five as the alarm shook the nightstand with its raucous message.

"Make it stop. Make it stop," Susy wailed as she pulled a pillow over her head.

With her eyes closed, Marge reached for the clock, succeeding only in knocking it to the floor where it rolled under the bed, finally whimpering to a stop.

Her sudden movement sent excruciating pain flooding through her head. "I can't. I can't," she groaned, as she fell back.

"Oh, yes, you can. And you will." Annie in her nightgown materialized like a ghost in the semidarkness. "C'mon Marge, you've promised Mrs. Lowenstein and this is your first day——you've got to go."

"Mom, I'm trying to sleep."

"Then hush up and go to sleep," Annie replied as she tugged the blanket from Marge's protesting body. Annie took her hand, pulling her to a sitting position. "Here, take these. You'll feel better," and handed her a glass of water.

Marge's hand trembled as she put the glass down.

Annie helped her stand as Marge cradled her head between two shaking hands, knowing it would explode if she moved.

"Annie, I can't. Honest, I can't."

"I don't want to hear *can't* again. Get your clothes, take a cold shower, and get down to the kitchen in twenty minutes. Hurry up." Annie had never used that tone of voice to Marge before.

Shocked, her pain momentarily forgotten, she staggered to the bathroom, her clothing over her arm. *Never, never again,* she vowed as she shuddered under the stinging ice-cold water.

Twenty minutes later she was in the kitchen.

"Are you feeling better?"

"A little, thank you, Annie. I could never have made it without you."

"I'm going to walk part of the way with you. It's hardly daylight and you don't need to be there till six-thirty, so relax a moment. I'll get Boots' breakfast going. Could you stand a cup of black coffee?"

Marge cringed. It didn't even smell good. Her stomach threatened disaster at the very thought.

Entering the kitchen, Boots nodded, "Good morning." Turning to Marge, "I'm glad you had the good sense to come home early. You look a little pale, are you sure you feel well enough to go to work?"

"Oh, yes, I'm feeling so much better. I don't often have such bad headaches, but I wouldn't miss my first day at work for anything." She felt her face flush as she looked to see Annie turn her head and her shoulders shake.

"That's a wonderful attitude, Marge, never forget it." Finishing his breakfast, he reached for his jacket, "LAPD" prominently displayed on the back; the door closing behind him.

"That's a rare compliment, Marge. No wonder Susy calls you 'Miss Perfect'."

"Well, it's a compliment I'm not deserving of. I'm ashamed of myself. Isn't it time to leave?"

Taking Annie's hand, they walked through the slowly awakening neighborhood. Marge's headache was gradually diminishing.

They walked in silence for several blocks, then Marge stopped abruptly, sobbing as though her heart would break.

"Annie, I'm so ashamed of myself. I'm not who I thought I was. I would never, ever have believed I could get drunk, just like Pa. Make a fool of myself at the prom. Embarrass that nice boy who took me... To think I have to face that principal this fall. Worst of all, to lie. Pa was a liar, too. I should go back where I belong. I don't deserve to be with decent people. What kind of a person am I?"

Her words were almost indistinguishable above the sobs. When Marge's sobs had turned to hiccups, Annie turned her so they were face-to-face.

"Here, here's a dry hanky, blow your nose. Only you can truly know who you really are in your heart. I believe I know what kind of a person you are.

"You are a young woman who has survived some horrible experiences not of your choosing and you have had the courage to change your life. Promise me you'll never again think of going back, especially since you know how different life can be.

"You deserve the best life you can make for yourself. It wasn't your fault that you got drunk, certainly not your fault that you were sick. I don't doubt that young man will be back and if that principal even remembers you, I'd be surprised. If he does, blow him a kiss.

"You are not Mac's daughter. He was never a father to you. He was there for his pleasure when you were conceived.

"Ruthie tells me you are exactly like your mother, who made a hurtful mistake when she left Ireland for what she hoped was a better life. And let me tell you about lies—actually there is only one kind of lie. A real lie is an untruth told to deliberately hurt someone.

"If you were to tell me that I look beautiful in curlers, wearing my old flannel nightgown when I make the morning coffee, I'd know you only said it because you love me and don't want to hurt me with the brutal truth. That's a little white fabrication that cannot be called a lie."

Annie laughed and continued. "Despite the fact that Boots thinks you're Miss Perfect, you're not. You are a good person who will make mistakes and foolish choices throughout your lifetime, just as we all do. That doesn't make you a bad person. It just makes you human. Wipe your nose."

The next morning at roll call, the Captain clapped Boots familiarly on the shoulder and grinned knowingly. "Look what I found in the backseat of my car. Hal said it was your daughter's." He handed Boots the filmy scarf, the broach still attached to the torn corner.

"Hal is pretty fast with the girls, I've heard. I wasn't too slow myself. Like father, like son I always say. Wouldn't it be a joke if we ended up related?"

The surrounding officers snickered. It was obvious the Captain had hit a nerve. It was no secret that Susy was above reproach in her father's eyes.

Boots raged inwardly and left for home an hour early.

Marge had just arrived home, breathless from a fast walk. She kicked off her shoes as she sank down on a chair at the kitchen table where Annie and Susy were still enthusing about the prom.

Annie thought, *strange that Susy had not mentioned Marge's escapade.* Then she felt a glow of pride to know that Susy wasn't going to tattle. She was unaware that Susy had been enjoying the prom in the backseat of a Model A.

When Boots stalked into the kitchen, the angry look on his face left no doubt as to his feelings. An ominous silence quieted Susy's description of the previous night's excitement.

Dangling the scarf by one finger, as though it contained an evil life of its own, Boots demanded, "Whose scarf is this?"

The silence defied him.

"Annie, this is yours. The Captain found it in the backseat of his car this morning. Susy, get that damned dress. You won't wear that again. I'll rip it to shreds. You sure as hell won't see that skirt-chasing Hal again either. Do you understand me clearly?"

Susy's sudden rage matched her father's as she scrambled out of her chair to confront him, her face as contorted as his.

"You'll never get my dress And I will see Hal whenever I want to."

A stinging slap across her face halted her furious words. Susy's head snapped back, her face registering the disbelief she felt as she raised a hand to her smarting cheek.

Boots looked dumbfounded at his hand as though it was not part of him.

Susy stepped forward, the imprint of her father's hand clearly visible. Looking up into his eyes, she spoke furiously, hands on her hips. "You will never slap me again. I will see who I please or I will leave this house and never look back. Do you understand me clearly? And I hate you. Hate you." Susy stormed down the hall.

Tears stood in Boots' eyes, his shoulders slumped as he walked defeated from the room. They heard the front door close behind him. Shocked by the drama that exploded before them, Annie and Marge sat speechless.

"Well," Annie sighed, "that's been coming for awhile. I'm glad it's over. That's the first time Boots has ever raised a hand to her. He has never wanted to let go of his 'baby.'

"Let's have a cup of coffee and relax. I want to hear about your day."

Marge was enthusiastic about her first day at work. No mention was made of the inauspicious beginning.

"Mrs. Lowenstein has taught me how to make bagels already. It's really easy and fun, too. She's borrowed the books I'll need from the school. She says if I really study extra hard, I can catch up. I'm so excited."

The sound of Susy's high-heeled shoes tapping down the hall stopped her in mid-sentence.

"Mom, I'm going out and I expect to be very late, so I'll kiss you good night now. Ooops, don't smear my lipstick. See you later, Marge."

Annie stood at the window and watched Boots' "baby" leave the nest.

"Well, I guess she's earned this. She's got more gumption than I have. She's her father's daughter," Annie sighed.

"Oh, Marge, there's a letter for you. I put it on your night stand; I think it's from Ruthie. I'll start dinner—guess it's just for two."

As Marge returned with the letter, tears glistened in her eyes as the yeast smells of freshly baked bread—the soft scent of Ruthie—seemed to float from the opened envelope. She read aloud:

Margie dear,

It seems you've been gone forever. We miss you, but are so happy that you are with Annie.

How do you like sunny California? Is it as beautiful as I've heard? How do you and Susy get along? Annie tells me Boots has spoiled her but I suppose that happens when she's an only child.

My beloved Annie, what fun we used to have. Remember?

Dad is working in the fields now. I hear even your Pa and Ed are out. They've sold the cows to give them poker money. AND since you aren't there to do the chores, they rented a room from a half-breed Indian woman who Dad says could have whipped Custer by herself. She sure doesn't need any help to collect the three-fifty that she charges for room and board. A sign in her boarding house says "No Drinking," but they came home drunk one night, got into a fight and broke something, so she threw them out. Now they live in an old chicken coop that she let them stay in. After they put a floor in, she raised their rent 50 cents. Boy, were they nasty, but they've met their match. They sure won't be very cozy in the wintertime.

They're still quarreling over the property, of course. Speaking of which, I haven't heard a word from the sheriff. Ha ha.

I keep busy—I'm working on a quilt and put a big garden in earlier.

Met Dr. Tom in town one day. He's enclosing a check, one for Annie and five dollars for your birthday.

He said to tell you to buy something pretty.

Give my love to Annie. I'll write her later.
Love, Ruthie

It was after twelve when Boots opened the door quietly, fumbling his way down the hall in the dark. Annie smelled the potent odor of whiskey and, as he fell heavily into bed, she realized he hadn't undressed.

Sometime later, the door opened to admit Susy, whose hair had tumbled down, evading a few random pins; hair that framed a flushed face devoid of lipstick. She paused in the hallway and sniffed, "Smells like Dad had a few drinks, too. Good night all," she giggled.

Annie was torn between tears and laughter. *Oh yes, she's her father's daughter.*

Boots slept heavily, but instinctively awakened at his usual time with the most excruciating headache he had ever known. He groaned, *I must have been poisoned.* His first thought was, *I can't make it, I'll call in sick.* But the stinging cold shower and the sure knowledge that the girls would know he couldn't hold his liquor forced him out the door.

His conscience berated him. *What the hell is the matter with me? Sure, I like a few drinks, always have, but I've never been so drunk. I don't even know how I got home. Even worse, I slept in my clothes. How can I face Annie? They'll all be laughing at me, all because of a silly little quarrel with Susy.*

But the overwhelming memory of Susy's devastating words, ". . . I hate you. Hate you." forced reality through his heart like a dull knife. Despite his throbbing head and wounded ego, a pride in his daughter comforted him. *At least I've been bested by my own. There's not a man in the precinct who would have dared to challenge Boots Malone as my daughter did. She is her father's daughter, how I love her.*

Dinner was a quiet affair. Susy ate hurriedly, then carrying her plate to the kitchen, called over her shoulder, "I'm going out, see you later." The door closed behind her. Annie exchanged glances with Marge, a smile tugging at the corners of her mouth.

Boots' thick black eyebrows seemed to grow together in a straight line as he glowered into his food. Shoving his plate aside, he retreated with the paper to the solace of his big worn chair.

As the dishes clattered in the soapy water, the girls talked quietly to each other.

"Busted by his own seventeen-year-old 'baby'." They laughed

soundlessly.

Boots could feel his kingdom starting to crumble. His penetrating stare focused over the top of the paper as he rattled it angrily.

"Why don't you two find something to do, and do it somewhere else."

How the mighty hath fallen.

Gradually, the stormy events of the "breakout," as Susy boasted to her friends, dissipated, but the residue hung heavy in the air, unacknowledged but very present. It was no longer "baby," but "Sue Anne," and "Dad" turned into "Boots," which made him cringe anytime she referred to him.

Marge was uneasy about the transition as Susy became bolder, more insolent and thoughtless. It seemed Susy had changed places with Boots.

Despite Marge's repeated, "Susy, please. Please don't wake me when you come in. Five o'clock comes early and I'm so tired, can't you be quiet? Undress in the dark?" But when the door opened, lights came on, dresser drawers opened and closed, Susy sang to herself, or tried the latest dance steps. "Marge, you awake? Oh, we had such a wonderful time. Hal is a marvelous dancer. My dress was just perfect, everyone said."

"Susy, will you be quiet? Turn off that light."

"Oh, I forgot to tell you…"

"SUSY." Marge's irritation came through loud and clear.

Saturday morning, Marge's day to sleep in, Susy reached for Marge's pillow and gave it a yank that sent it flying.

"Marge, wake up. Mom's not in the kitchen, you better get out there and make coffee. Make some toast, too, as long as you're up."

Marge didn't answer. She could feel the rage growing, expanding into every cell of her body.

She turned, planted her feet and with a mighty push sent Susy sprawling on the floor. As Susy scrambled to her feet, Marge grabbed her by the shoulders, whirled her around, then shook her like a rag doll.

"Don't you ever dare wake me again you nasty, inconsiderate, lazy little bully, spoiled rotten brat. I've had more than enough of you."

Marge's angry words scared Susy and she struggled to get free of Marge's punishing hands, yelling, "MOM. MOM."

Annie appeared in the doorway. "I couldn't have said it better myself, Marge. Susy, I want you in the kitchen fifteen minutes from now. Get dressed."

Susy's tearful cry, "MOM."

She stalked into the kitchen in her nightgown, an indignant scowl on her face, reaching for the coffeepot.

Annie gave her a resounding smack on her bottom and turned her around. "I said, get dressed."

Susy stomped down the hall. She was dressed when she returned to the kitchen.

Annie pointed to a chair, Susy sat. Annie stood contemplating, as though uncertain where to start, a variety of emotions crisscrossing her face.

Annie's unusual words and actions made Susy apprehensive as she fidgeted in her chair.

Then it started. "We've had enough of your obnoxious behavior. Now you listen to me and I mean listen. This is NOT your father talking.

"There will be no more of this come-and-go as you please. You have a ten o'clock curfew and I want to know where you are. And I never want to smell liquor on your breath again."

"But MOM."

"Don't interrupt. You will do your share of the chores around here, and you will apologize to Marge. So make up your mind; I've investigated the Holmsby House for Wayward Girls and they will take you on my signature. I have discussed this with your father," Annie lied, "and he has agreed. The first time you disobey, you will have a new address."

"MOM." The tears began to flow.

"Don't waste your tears on me. Find your gloves, the garden needs at least two hours of your valuable time. Oh, if you wake Marge up again, I will personally wake you at the same time and you can get a head start on your chores."

On her way to the garden, Susy mumbled, "Sorry, Marge."

Following Annie's unmovable edict, Susy's brief fling at freedom flickered out. She sulked about, but finding the timeworn approach was ignored, she contented herself with her ten o'clock curfew and dreamed of her eighteenth birthday when her time was her own.

The Malone house had returned to its usual pattern.

Marge continued her enthusiastic learning process that flooded over her scholastic ambitions to the give and take of life in general. Her shyness was replaced by a newly discovered pleasure in expressing herself with confidence as she cajoled the deli's most particular customers, who often debated for fifteen minutes, "Shall it be the cinnamon bagels or the chocolate covered cream puff?"

Mrs. Lowenstein was enthralled as she watched week after week the transformation progress from the frightened girl who had appeared unannounced, literally, on her doorstep. Her heart warmed with a deep feeling of pride and humility as she acknowledged to herself that she had been an important tool that had helped to form the future of this beautiful, self-possessed young woman.

Chapter 6

Summer had passed like a dream—it had been a time of intense study and work at the deli with limited time to join Susy and her fun-loving friends. Picnics, parties and movies were all on hold for Marge.

Then suddenly it was September and the doors of the big, ivy-covered brick high school swung open. Marge became increasingly apprehensive, despite Annie's assurances.

"Aren't you the girl who got drunk and did that hoochie-coochie dance at the prom?"

Marge could visualize the principal's furious face, hear his accusing voice. *Aren't you the girls who got drunk and did that hoochie-koochie dance at the prom?*

"I'll just die if he remembers me, and what of my school records?" she lamented to Mrs. Lowenstein.

"Don't worry so, Marge. I've known Mr. Foster for as long as he's been principal. When I tell him you've been taught at home and how diligent you've been with your studies, he will be delighted to have you.

"Let's sit down and have a cup of coffee."

They seated themselves at the little corner table.

"You are an exceptional young woman, Marge. Never underestimate your own self-worth. In many ways you are wise beyond my understanding, yet you have a childish innocence that intrigues me. You have been such a pleasure to teach, a gold mine of potential. What a joy you have been to me; to see you develop into the lovely young woman that you are. To know that I have contributed to your future has given my life a new meaning. I love you as the daughter I never had. Let's have that cup of coffee before I cry."

Marge sat silently, tears begging to be released pressing against her eyelids. Her thoughts sparked the memory of Ruth, whose love had taken root but could never thrive in the swamp of despair that was Marge's heart. The damage was so great; the hurt too deep.

Ruth, secure in the knowledge that her husband loved her, stood as a buffer between her and the world's careless intrusions.

Annie, on the other hand, was a frustrated woman who had

settled for less at seventeen because of the dictates pushed by the customs of that time. Annie saw herself reflected in Marge's life. That Annie loved her, there was no doubt. Marge prayed that someday Annie would realize her self-worth and love herself.

Marge's voice choked with tears as she leaned across the table and spoke to the intense little Jewish woman with whom she had formed such a deep-rooted bond.

"You have been my guiding light, my confidant, my mentor. These few short months I have spent with you have been a lifetime of learning for me. You have finished what Ruth and Annie started; you have directed my life on a different path. More than you could ever know. Although this is my last day here, you'll see me often. I'll never forget you."

Mrs. Lowenstein wiped her nose. "Let's dry our tears, have a bagel, then close up shop. Speaking of bagels, I suppose my bagel sales will go down now that you're not here. I wonder what that boy's mother did with all those bagels."

"You mean Tim, my little brother?"

"Little brother? He's at least six feet tall. And it's obvious he doesn't love you like a sister; that boy is hearing wedding bells."

"I don't ever want to get married." Her stomach sickened as she remembered the first time she had uttered those words.

Marge's first class was another venture into an uncharted world, but as Mrs. Lowenstein had promised, Marge was easily integrated into the swirling mass of noisy teenagers. Due to her passionate desire to learn, it was soon obvious she was one of the students who stood at the top.

Among the carefree throng whose only ambition seemed to be the pursuit of happiness, Marge discovered a zest for life she had never known before. A laughing, dancing, fun-loving teenager, the center of every party.

Her childhood had been trampled in the ashes of the house in which she had been born, but now, all that misery had dissipated, like smoke, deep into her subconscious; it had happened to another person, in another world.

Her future lay in the here and now.

"She came here just a dumb country girl in those awful clothes; I taught her everything she knows. How to dress, how to dance, introduced her to my friends. Now they are her friends. 'Miss Perfect' must think she's a movie star."

"Oh Susy, you know that isn't true. Marge has just discovered that she is young. Let her enjoy her girlhood as you have always enjoyed yours. Don't be jealous."

"Oh Mom, you just don't understand. Hal even thinks she's putting out."

"Susy, I wish you weren't so involved with Hal. You're too young to be going steady. Give the other fellows a chance."

"Mom, I love him. I love him and I think he loves me. He hasn't said so but I know he does. I want to spend every minute of my life with him."

"Oh Susy, be careful. It's so easy when you're young to make a mistake that will change your life. Be a good girl. Don't let him talk you into anything that can only end in heartbreak for all concerned."

"Mom, you think we're going all the way, don't you? You did it . . . that's how I happened. Didn't you love me?"

Susy's face flushed. She couldn't meet her mother's eyes as she remembered Hal's demanding kisses, his rough hands as he pushed her back, pulling at her clothes. And her own mounting excitement rising to meet his. Suddenly, the shocking light that illuminated the backseat, then the indignant voice, "What the hell are you two kids doing up here at this time of night? Get out."

As they squirmed out of the car in the blaze of light, the officer exclaimed, "Hey, aren't you Boots Malone's girl?"

Turning to Hal, "If you know Boots Malone like I know him, you wouldn't have the guts to be messing around with his daughter."

"Go home before I write you a ticket for loitering. I'll follow you down the hill."

Hal cursed inaudibly as he fumbled with his buttons. So near and yet so far.

"Mom, I promise you I'll wait until I'm married. I want Dad to walk me down the aisle of that little old church where I was baptized. I want to wear a gorgeous white satin dress with lace all down the skirt, carrying a beautiful, really big bouquet of pink orchids. At least six of my very best friends will be bridesmaids and you can sit back and cry."

Laughing, she threw her arms around her mother. Annie, holding back her tears, laughed with her.

Two weeks later, Hal and Susy were parked in a more secluded area. Shining through the trees, the sliver of moon shone on Susy's white skin. Hal's arms holding her tightly, his hands touching, caressing, intruding; his lips pleading his own need. Susy's body responded passionately as the urgency of his body pushed against her. She didn't want anyone in the world but herself and Hal, but her mother's voice cut through her consciousness like a knife. *"Susy, wait, you promised."*

She struggled upright, "Hal, no, no, please. I can't. I promised my mother. You know this isn't right. Don't. I want to go home before anything happens."

"Well, damn you. Keep it then. I'm tired of being put off, you damned little teaser. You want it as bad as I do, but you want me to beg."

"Hal, Hal darling. You know I love you, but . . . "

"Hell, yes, I know how much you love me. If you loved me you'd prove it."

"Hal, I want to be married in a church with six bridesmaids and . . ."

Hal's voice scornfully disbelieving, "ME? Me, get married? Forget it. Why buy the cow when the milk's so cheap. I ought to dump you right here."

Furiously he started the car. "Find yourself another sucker. You aren't the only girl in the world and I intend to have my share."

Her pleas were cut short as he pulled into the driveway. "Get out. See you around sometime, but don't hold your breath."

Sobbing hysterically, she fled into the house. As he gunned the motor, only the echo of his words hung in the air.

Boots dropped his paper as Susy burst in crying hysterically. "Susy, Susy. What's the matter, what's happened, are you alright?"

She sank down on the arm of his chair, her hands covering her tear-streaked face. Trying to restrain her tears, she wailed, "Oh, Dad, Hal and I had such an awful fight. He broke up with me."

Boots pulled her close as she sobbed. "I just think I'll die without him."

Annie in her nightgown hurried down the hall, paused at the door. "Susy, are you alright?"

"Oh Mom, Hal broke up with me. What am I going to do?"

Annie thought, *thank God is what I'm going to do.*

"Well, for starters you can stop that crying and tell me what happened."

"Mom, Hal was flirting and dancing with this girl. On the way home I told him I didn't like it one bit. He said I was just jealous, said he could dance with whoever he wanted to. Then he said he didn't want to go steady anymore. When I got out of the car he said, 'See you around sometime, but don't hold your breath.'"

The murderous look on Boots' face said it all. "I'll kill that son of a bitch."

"No Dad, no. It was all my fault, honest."

Annie continued, "Susy, I think it's for the best. I don't think Hal treated you very well. He never comes to the door for you, he sits out there and honks, doesn't help you in. There are dozens of nice boys who would be delighted to hold the car door for you. Someday you'll meet someone who really loves you, you won't even remember Hal's name."

That bastard. Whistles my daughter out like a dog. How I'd love to lay my nightstick over his knees. I'll bet he'd dance for me.

Susy's tears dried on her angry face as she flounced from the room.

"Dad wants to kill him, you want me to forget the only man I'll ever love. Thanks a lot."

The next morning, her eyes swollen and red, Susy announced, "I'm going to drop out of school. I can't stand to face everybody. They'll laugh at me. I can't bear to see him with another girl."

"You will do no such thing. You think you're old enough to be in love? Can you hear yourself? Whining, acting like a two-year-old. Grow a little backbone."

Annie stormed, "Better yet, grow up."

Boots thundered, "Forget it. You're going to graduate in a few months so hit the books and bring me a decent report card."

Susy, who had never met such combined resistance from her parents before, took Boots' advice.

Walking home from school in late November, she heard the familiar sound of the motor, then the heavenly sound of the horn.

"Hey Blondie. Want a ride?"

"Well, Romeo, you must be desperate. Your other girl stand you up?"

"Still jealous, huh? Stop playin' hard-to-get. You know I'm the only one you love. C'mon, baby, get in, you know you want to."

Wordlessly she walked to the car and opened the door.

It was late when they heard the car door slam. Both Boots and Annie were trying to downplay their anxiety. Marge was suspicious that Hal was the reason for Susy's late appearance.

Boots fumed. "If I could lay my hands on that son of a bitch. But it would mean my job. He's the Captain's son, after all."

Annie sighed. "That would only make Susy more determined. We'll just have to wait and pray she gets tired of him."

One glimpse of Susy's radiant face when she walked in told them it would be a long wait.

It was the same radiant Susy who came to breakfast the next morning.

"He said he loves me, Mom. I knew he did. Can we invite him to dinner? When you get to know him, you will love him, too. Please, Mom? I want you to meet him."

Inwardly Annie's heart sank. "Of course, you know we'd like to get to know him. When would you like to do this? We can plan something special."

Susy's happiness was contagious. Annie smiled; no sacrifice was too great to see her daughter happy.

"Dad's home early on Sunday, that would be a good day. We have something important to tell you. I can't wait."

"You tell your Dad we're having a guest. Sunday would be fine." Inwardly Annie groaned as she visualized Boots' reaction.

That evening as Boots was taking the last bite of his favorite pie after an exceptionally good dinner, Susy slipped her arm around his massive shoulders.

"Dad, listen. Please don't get mad. I want to ask Hal to dinner Sunday night so you can get know each other."

Boots choked on his pie, his face purpled as he fought for breath. Alarmed, Annie hurried around the table and pounded on his back. When he could finally speak his words came out in a constricted croak, directed at his panic-stricken daughter.

"Are you trying to kill me?"

But Susy was not to be deterred. "Please, Dad. Please say yes and promise to be nice or we'll just run away."

"That does it," Boots muttered as he stumbled out of the kitchen and closed the bedroom door behind him.

Later, when Annie opened the door, he exploded, "How could you encourage Susy to ask that asshole to dinner ... in my house? How can I sit there and make small talk when all I want to do is get my hands around his throat. That worthless son of a bitch. Even his own father can't stand him. I'll kill him before I'll see Susy throw her life away on that bum."

"Well, you'd better try to go along with this. We can only wait it out; we can't stop her. When she said they'd run away, she meant it. And will you please watch your language?"

Hal sat on the edge of his father's desk, ignoring the disapproving frown.

"Dad, can you believe this? I've been invited to the Malone's for dinner Sunday night. I guess the old man wants to give me the once-over. I hope that old fire-snorter is on his best behavior."

"You listen here. If it wasn't for his quick temper, it would be his feet under this desk. He's the best man on the force. You keep a respectful tongue in your head and don't you mess with his daughter, IF you value your life."

"Mess with her." Hal shrugged, "She's a holdout. She wants to get married—first. I told her maybe."

"Wipe that smirk off your face. You've been raised better than that. Get your lazy ass off my desk. I'm busy. Go find yourself a job."

Hal grew increasingly uneasy as Sunday neared. *Why in the hell did I let Susy talk me into this? I wonder if this damn dinner will be worth it. Well, the old man can't get too rough with me. When push comes to shove, he'll remember I'm the Captain's son.*

Susy spent a frantic week planning the menu, cleaning the good silver, instructing her mother and Marge, sweet-talking her father. Everything had to be perfect, just perfect.

Sunday evening, Hal, his hat on the back of his head, his finger on the doorbell, thought, *What the hell am I doing here?*

Susy, casting her apron aside, fairly flew to the door, her face flushed with joy and excitement, urged him in along with the mouth-watering aroma of the dinner yet to come. Annie and Marge followed from the kitchen as they came to greet him.

Then taking him by the hand, Susy led him into the living room where Boots was apparently deeply engrossed in his paper.

"Daddy, this is Hal." As he stood and stepped forward, Hal thought, *hell, this man is twelve feet tall.*

"Boots. I think I've seen you around the precinct."

Ignoring Hal's outstretched hand, Boots replied stiffly, "You can call me Mr. Malone and when you're in my house, take off your hat."

Hal got the message. *That's how he wants to play.*

"Sure, Pops, hang it up for me would you?"

Susy gave her father an imploring look as she fled to the kitchen.

Annie promptly appeared carrying a tray that held Boots' favorite deviled eggs and as she placed it on the table by his chair, said, "You gentlemen enjoy these while you get acquainted. Dinner is almost ready."

As Boots turned to sit, he found his chair, his sacred chair, already occupied and the deviled eggs disappearing at an alarming rate. He glared at the egg offered on Hal's palm and didn't miss the grin on his face.

Nodding his head towards Annie's rocker, Hal smiled and said, "Why don't you sit down, Pops, and let's get acquainted."

Striving to honor his promise, Boots smothered his seething rage that threatened to explode. *That cocky little bastard knows he has me over a barrel. How I'd love to break him in two with my bare hands.*

"Since you graduated last spring, I suppose you have a good job by now?"

"No, not yet, I'm still looking, of course. Dad would like to see me in law enforcement, but I'm not going to settle for being just another flatfoot walking a beat with free coffee." He didn't mistake the look in Boots' eyes, but he couldn't resist. *After all, what can he do about it?*

Hal leaned back in the big, comfortable chair, crossed his legs and reached for another egg.

"Say, you look really comfortable in that rocking chair, do you knit?" He gibed with a grin.

Boots turned the rocker closer to Hal and with a tight smile he answered, "No, but I can damn well use a nightstick effectively and I never miss with a .38. Do you go out much at night?"

The subtle threat was not lost on Hal. He was never so glad to see Susy as when she appeared in the doorway announcing "Dinner."

The table was set beautifully, the best china, the newly shined silver, the food delicious. Susy sat between Hal and her father, her happiness blinding her to the tension between them.

Well, of course, Hal is a little nervous and Dad is exhausted. I can't expect much conversation from them. After all, they've just gotten acquainted.

Annie and Marge tried to keep the conversation light for Susy's sake, despite their innermost misgivings.

Dinner limped by, Boots' plate untouched. Susy rose from the table. In a moment she returned with a three-tiered cake, elaborately decorated. "I did it myself, Hal," she said proudly.

The first slice went to him, then she turned to Boots. "Dad, you've hardly eaten a thing, don't you feel well?"

Boots stood to leave.

"Dad, sit down, wait. Don't you want to hear my surprise?"

She pulled Hal to his feet. Holding his hand, she announced ecstatically, "Hal and I are engaged. We're going to be married on my birthday next June, right after I graduate. Isn't that wonderful?"

A stunned silence followed. Boots pushed his chair back violently. "No, Susy. You're too young. Way too young."

"Dad, I'll be eighteen, and I know what I want."

That took the wind out of the old boy's sails, Hal gloated.

Annie interrupted quickly. "What a surprise. I don't know what to say. Are you both very sure?"

"Susy, you know we always want you to be happy, but it will take us a little time to think about it and . . . "

Hal tugged at Susy's hand. "C'mon, Blondie, let's go for a ride while the folks get used to the idea. Get my hat, Pops," he grinned.

Boots, still standing with clenched fists and eyes that narrowed into slits, made no move.

Marge rose quickly to retrieve the hat as Annie gave her a grateful look. Nudging Susy to the door, Marge whispered, "For goodness sake, don't be late tonight."

Boots' voice rose, "Susy, wait." But the sound of the door closing told Boots he had lost the battle.

Before he went on duty the next morning, Boots stood at Captain O'Malley's office. Before he could knock, the door opened.

"Come in, Malone, find a chair. I guess we'd better talk. Hal told me about the dinner last night and I want you to know I'm not any happier about it than you are."

"Well, I'm glad you feel that way, Captain, but what the hell are we gonna do about it? Susy is way too young to think about marriage."

"I told Hal to put it off for awhile, think it over. He's too immature and undependable to take that kind of responsibility. His mother died when he was ten, so he's pretty much done as he pleased and that sure as hell doesn't always please me. I've been too busy to have been a very good father. I think we'll have to go along with it for awhile and hope it burns itself out."

"I sure as hell hope so," Boots grunted as he turned to leave.

"Thanks for coming in, Malone."

The palm trees were wrapped in multicolored lights that spiraled high into the fronds that spread above elaborately decorated mansions; mansions that housed the rich with their imported wines and caviar, their Bentleys in the driveway and cardboard Santas complete with reindeer racing across velvet-green lawns.

Wealth insulated their world. As for the "other" world, Marie Antoinette couldn't have said it better: "Let them eat cake."

Beverly Hills announced the Christmas Season.

Downtown boasted no such Christmas joy. It was 1928; the depression had hit rock bottom. A man who had pursued his trampled dream to this land of "golden opportunity," fighting to keep his place in line, his pride shattered, lost in the dust of the never-ending breadline.

One man was holding an extra bowl to carry a morsel home for a woman who divided a three-cent loaf of bread, carefully cutting around the mold, as the ragged children never ceased their "Ma. I'm hungry, Ma."

Susy held on to her dream.

"Oh, Mom, I just know Hal will give me an engagement ring. Don't you think so, Marge?"

They continued to string the cranberries that would decorate their window frame and transform the poinsettia that masqueraded as a Christmas tree.

Hoping to ease the disappointment for Susy that Annie was sure to come, Annie said, "Susy, you know the times are awfully bad. A ring is probably an extravagance Hal may not be able to afford. Where is he working now?"

"Well, he's still looking. He quit that job because they wanted him to work overtime. Hal would never work overtime."

"Susy, your Dad is working double shifts because of all the trouble downtown, and he took a big cut in wages, too. Hal was lucky his Dad got him a job."

"I don't care. Hal is different. Someday soon we'll have our own home. He'll have a good job and I'll have such beautiful clothes. And no kids. Hal doesn't want me to ruin my figure."

Annie rolled her eyes at Marge. "Let's see if the coffee's ready." She hugged Susy as she left. "I hope all your dreams come true, baby, but I'll sure miss the grandchildren."

As Annie suspected, there was no ring for Susy, only a wilting bouquet of roses. *Bet he stole them from a graveyard*, Boots sneered privately. *I noticed he had a new hat though. Looked expensive, that cheap bastard.*

The New Year rang in.

Susy's head was in the clouds; she glowed with happiness. Her feet seemed to dance of their own volition while Mom and Dad prayed for the "burnout" that seemed to grow further away each passing day.

Her time spent with Hal, following his commitment, was both a joy and a struggle as he became increasingly aggressive.

"Damn it to hell, Susy. We're going to be married in a few months. What difference does a piece of paper make? C'mon, don't make me wait. Don't be scared. Hell, I'll be careful." His furious pleas were not placated by her tearful refusals.

It wasn't just her denials. *Hell, there were lots of girls who wouldn't waste my time*, he thought, but he was driven to win. He had to have what he wanted, when he wanted and he had tried every trick in the bag. *But someday* ... he knew.

Winter turned into spring seemingly overnight. Suddenly it was March in the City of the Angels.

The hazy blue-purple of the distant mountains, the muted green of the foothills, appeared as though God had laid the color with one swipe of His giant paintbrush. The soft beauty of spring seemed to dilute the sadness and ugliness that covered the land.

Hal phoned. "Susy, make some sandwiches. It's a perfect day for a picnic—be right over."

"Mom, what do we have for sandwiches besides peanut butter?"

"Susy, what about the homework that you've got to turn in tomorrow? You're way behind in your schoolwork."

"Oh, Marge will help me. I'll use her notes. This is the first time we've gone on a picnic, Mom. I hope Hal likes peanut butter."

The car pulled to the curb as she wrapped the last sandwich. The familiar honk sounded and she ran down the walk, her eyes bright with anticipation, her long golden hair swinging with every step.

Hal drove towards the foothills, then turned up a dirt road barely visible in high grass. He continued to a meadow spotted with oak trees and carpeted with wildflowers.

"Dad used to hunt deer here. C'mon, let's see if we can find one."

Whirling in a circle, her arms outstretched as she looked around her, she gushed, "Oh, Hal, what a beautiful place. How did you ever find it? Everything is so perfect and I'm so happy. Just think, only two months, three days, I'll be Mrs. Hal O'Malley. I can hardly wait."

Impulsively, she flung her arms around him. "Oh, Hal. I do love you with all my heart."

He kissed her tenderly, then removed her arms. "I love you, too, Blondie, but we need to discuss some things that I'm concerned about."

He carefully arranged the blanket in the shade of a big tree, then pulled her down beside him.

"Susy, I've been worrying. You know I love you, but I think you're too immature to understand what real love is. You only want to talk about it, you won't share it. I think you're afraid of the real responsibility of love. You're not ready to prove you're a real woman. I can't get married with this on my mind so I'm planning to join the Merchant Marines. The marriage is off."

He looked down at Susy's horrified face.

"But Hal, you can't. You don't mean it. We've set the date."

"I'm so sorry, Susy, but I do mean it. Let's go home. I'm going to enlist tomorrow."

"Hal, Mom is already sewing my dress. I've picked all my bridesmaids. Already there're planning a bridal shower."

Hal stood, "Let's go."

With hysterical tears flooding down her face, she reached blindly for his hand and pulled him down.

"Hal, please. Let me prove I love you. I'll prove I love you. Please, Hal. Please.

His kisses were bruising, his hands roughly exploring with no resistance now.

"Hal, you're hurting me. Please, you're hurting me."

"What the hell is the problem here? Your knees grown together?" He roughly knuckled his fist between her tender thighs. The pain was so intense Susy finally submitted to his brutal assault.

As he buttoned his pants, he looked down at her prone figure.

"You gotta stop that damn fighting and for God's sake stop bawling." He reached for a sandwich, then threw it down in disgust. "You know I hate peanut butter."

Susy lay with her arm covering her eyes, her torn dress tossed carelessly over her trembling body.

As she opened the car door, Susy was relieved to see her mother in the garden. She hurried quickly down the walk, opened the door, then moved quietly down the hall to the sanctuary of her bedroom. Marge looked up from her book in surprise.

"Susy, that was a speedy picnic. Did the ants get the peanut butter?"

Susy stood wordless in her rumpled, torn dress, eyes brimming with tears. Then her voice trembled, "Oh, I came home early because I have a terrible headache. I'm going to shower and go to bed. Tell Mom not to wake me for dinner, I'll be okay in the morning."

Marge felt an instinctive sick feeling in her stomach as she identified with Susy's "headache." There wasn't enough water in the world to wash away the hurt and shame, or the heartbreak of disillusionment.

Susy carried the hurt in her heart long after the physical pain had gone. Her disappointment came as a surprise. Those wildly romantic fables that Clara had embellished were nothing like the hurtful, frightening experience she had endured.

As the weeks sped by, her hurt faded into a bad memory that she finally convinced herself that she had overreacted to what was perfectly natural for a first-time experience. The excitement of her soon-to-be wedding crowded every other thought from her mind.

Now I am a woman. I've proven my love and soon we would be married. After all, we love each other, how can it be wrong?

The little yellow bungalow seemed to vibrate with the sound of the excited, chattering giggling girlfriends who seemed to come and go nonstop.

Graduation was all but forgotten in the excitement of the wedding plans. And, oh—the wedding dress. How beautiful it was.

Susy, of course, was on her own rosy cloud. Her happiness radiated to everyone around her with the exception of her father, who grew more distant with every passing day. Susy never realized the depth of her father's rage and frustration. She never doubted that given time, he would relent; she knew in her heart that he loved her.

Coming home later and later after a stop at the neighborhood bar,

Boots ate his cold dinner, skimmed through the newspaper, then slouched off to bed.

In the privacy of their bedroom, he stormed, "Don't you spend a dime of my money on something that's never going to happen as long as there's breath in my body. I'll die before I'll let her marry that son of a bitch," he snarled.

Almost fearfully, Annie pleaded, "Please, please, Boots. She will do it, don't spoil it for her. She will never forgive you and you will never forgive yourself."

"Will you stop this damned nagging and let me get some sleep?"

Chapter 7

The soft breeze of spring hurried over the San Bernardino Mountains, bringing the wondrous fragrance of the blossoming orange trees nudging the wildflowers into new life. The California spring was not even a distant cousin to the spring in North Dakota.

The spring thaw was late that year. It was early March when the unexpected blizzard howled down from the frozen Canadian plains into the Dakotas, venting its rage with great gusts of freezing sleet and blinding snow. The crocus, harbingers of spring, hid their colorful blooms, then shivered back to sleep.

Winter in North Dakota was not the winter that romantics would have it. The sleigh rides, the jingle of bells on old Dobbins' decorated harness, the laughter of children in their bright caps and mittens, the family in front of the fireplace. Not so. Rather, an exhausted, irritable mother worn out from a long day of refereeing the bored, housebound children, doing the heavy, dirty wash in a creaky wringer washer—if she were lucky enough to have one—then hanging the clothes to dry on anything stationary. Many times doing the outside chores by the flickering light of a lantern in the freezing cold because Pa held a winning hand at the club and couldn't make it home before dark.

Red Lake Falls, population 900 more or less, was a thrown-together town built on the shore of a large lake created by the converging twin forks of the Red River.

The residential section that huddled together on a low rise that overlooked the lake caught the errant breeze in the summer, the blowing sleet in the winter. A few trees, naked now, bordered the muddy streets that led to the business district.

Downtown boasted a dry goods store; a post office that hosted Dr. Tom's office above; a one-room schoolhouse with long wooden benches where the children sat to learn the three Rs; a church that doubled as a cultural center; a liquor store; a saloon; and a dilapidated, weather-beaten boarding house that housed only men—mostly old farmers who came to town for the winter. The exception was a stout blond Norwegian woman who, rumor had it, sneaked visitors in at odd hours to her upstairs room accessible by the back stairway.

The house was owned by a six-foot-tall half-breed Mandan Indian woman, who was known as "Injin Mary." She tolerated no profanity or drinking and it was a well-known fact that she needed no help collecting the three-dollar weekly room and board.

Then, of course, there was the Club, the most substantial structure in town and the most frequented.

The Club was sanctuary to men who wanted to escape the boredom of "honey-dos," or talk to a neighbor who knew the difference between a crank shaft and a blown piston, or discuss the price of hogs this year over a shot of Jack Daniels.

March was the month that farmers started to think seriously about spring planting, reassess the old John Deere, and speculate on the price of corn or wheat. Politics and local gossip flowed freely and loudly by the men at the bar— one muddy foot on the rail, their heavy winter clothing emitting the odor of wet flannel, a cigarette in one hand, the other shaking the dice to see who paid.

"Yeah, my old lady said last Saturday night I came home so drunk I scared the kids half to death. Said I smelled worse than a damned skunk. It's nag, nag, nag."

"Hell, I sure know about that, my missus was bawling her eyes out because a weasel got in and killed all her baby chicks. I told her, kill the son of a bitch but, of course, she wanted me to do it. She won't keep those squalling kids quiet. I can't stand all that noise and confusion so I just told her I'm goin' to town. Shit. She won't even make me a decent cup of coffee. It's getting so damn smoky in here, reminds me of home. I told her I'd fix the stove when I get home."

One man sat with both elbows on the bar, hunched over his drink, a week's whiskers showing above his turned-up collar, a stocking cap pulled low, his big rubber overshoes unlaced. He yelled at the barkeeper, "Hey, you. Can't you turn that damn nickelodeon down? That noise is gonna make me deaf as a post." He turned back to his companion. "I don't know what it is about winter that makes wimmen so damned uppity. The baby crapped his pants this morning while she was out slopping the hogs and she ast me did I change him?

"'Hell, no.' I told her, 'That's wimmen's work.'

"Well, I'll be damned." he interrupted himself. "Ain't that Helmer Nelson and Ed Garrity playing at the same poker table? They been feudin' for years. Hate each other's guts. That means trouble. That Garrity is a mean bastard when he's drunk, always lookin' for a fight.

Of course, he's a mean bastard sober, too."

"Hey, barkeep. Another round for me and my buddy here."

As the time passed, the large room, hazy with smoke, was packed to capacity, standing room only at the bar.

The poker table piled high with chips and overflowing ashtrays, the whist players seemingly oblivious to the scenes around them. Men were waiting in line at the pool table, the green felt worn from years of constant use. The crack of the cue ball. At last—a lucky hit.

The winner's ear-splitting whoop went unnoticed as pandemonium erupted at the far end of the poker table. Cards, drinks, and chips scattered like leaves before the wind as tables were overturned. A circle of cheering, cursing men packed tightly against each other, vying for the best view.

The bloodied combatants, punching, kicking, gouging, were oblivious to the passionate advice, the different strategies offered from the crowd. Breathing hard, they paused to trade insults.

"Garrity, you lyin', cheatin' old bastard. Did you ever play an honest game? You're so crooked they'll have to screw you into the ground when you die. Worn out, just like that piece of shit you drive," Helmer raged.

'Yeah? Well, you haven't put me on the floor yet, and that piece of shit can run that Hudson you're so proud of into the ground," Ed sneered.

"Put your money where your big mouth is. Have you got the guts for a race on the ice Garrity?"

The room quieted as the watching men held their breath. Everyone knew the danger at this time of the year. In his drunken bravado, urged on by his few supporters, Garrity sneered, "Hell, yes, you Norwegian loudmouth. What time and where?"

"Crow's Landing, one o'clock. Loser buys the house drinks. The good stuff, none of that watered-down soda. You old deadbeat. Probably the first time you will ever pay for a round," sneered Helmer.

"I'll be there, see that you are. Tomorrow I'll be drinkin' on yer tab," Garrity replied.

The word went out far and wide as if by wireless—"a race, on the lake." Excitement ran high. It had been a long hard winter.

On the way to the boarding house, Mac snickered, "Ya sure as hell got your tit in the wringer this time. Helmer's car is damn near new, only four years old. This old bucket of bolts is falling apart. Are you crazy or just plain drunk? I'm bettin' on Helmer."

"Well, you can go to hell, Mac. Ya wonna walk? It's carried your sorry ass for the last eight years. He don't know the river like I do. I know every twist and turn. Anyhow, I've got a few tricks up my sleeve. Wouldn't surprise me none if his brakes give out on a curve and he skids out on that thin ice. Tell you what, I'll bet my half of the farm—you got guts enough to bet yours? You wonna ride with a winner or are you too damned yellow? Speak up, Mac."

A moment's hesitation then, "Damn right I'll ride with you to hell 'n back. Just to see yer face when you buy that round. Helmer and I both know you're a loser an' he'll prove it. My money's on Helmer."

They spit in their hands and shook on it. Ed parked the Model T at the back of the rooming house. Throwing a heavy blanket over the hood, patting it fondly, he bragged, "This old buggy will do thirty miles an hour and that's fast enough on that slick ice."

"Well, that Hudson's just warming up at forty," Mac laughed.

Looking up, they saw Injin Mary, her hands on her hips, blocking the doorway, a dangerous glint in her black eyes.

"You better have the rent or you ain't comin' in."

Ed cursed but dug up some crumpled dollar bills.

"Mac, will you loan me a buck? I ain't got but two dollars on me."

"Hell, no. Ask Helmer."

"Ah shit. Mary, can I have until tomorrow?"

The lake, frozen over in wintertime, was the local playground for the young and daring. And it was a diversion for the elders who forced a hole in the thick ice to fish for Great Northern Pike. The deceptive thickness of the ice was caused by the channels of the river, which ran beneath and seemed to trace a different pattern every spring.

The morning dawned clear and cold.

The rivals met at the landing. After the usual insults and braggadocio, they walked the ice with their enthusiastic supporters. When the location of the course was finally agreed on, Helmer loudly complained that there weren't enough curves. Ed protested that there were too many or they were too sharp. A compromise was reached.

Metal rods adorned with bar towels and pounded into the ice marked the course, giving a festive appearance.

Despite the cold, the morning was clear. The sun shown down on the early arrivals, their breath vaporizing, fingers and toes numb even in their heavy covering, frost clinging to their beards.

As the morning warmed, they were joined by the nearby farmers in their bib overalls and engineer caps with red kerchiefs stuffed in their hip pockets. Wives and children, complete with barking dogs, rounded out the crowd. Families from the next township all merged into a great milling mass of people who swarmed over the once pristine snow, now trampled and muddy at the lake shore.

Empty beer bottles were tossed randomly, silently declaring the mood of the gathering that surged back and forth at the landing.

The strident voices of the excited men grew deafening as they gathered in smaller groups speculating on the winner, and wagering everything from a prime heifer to their seed money. Here and there a half-hearted shoving match was settled by the appearance of a bottle passed freely around. "Here. Take a slug." "Don't mind if I do."

Voices rose to a crescendo…

"Garrity hasn't got a chance in hell."

"I think he's still drunk or he wouldn't have the guts to take that old junker out on the ice."

"Don't under estimate him. He's a tricky old bastard and he knows the river. Born and raised on it, and I don't doubt he's got few tricks up his sleeve."

"If you're so damn sure, I'll be glad to take your money."

"Where in hell is Helmer?"

"Over there, talkin' to some old geezer."

"Helmer, you know damn well that ice ain't safe. This is the middle of March. You know Ed was drunk last night, give him a break."

"Hell, no. He ast for it, and he's gonna git it."

The crowd grew restless. "What time is it?"

"Not quite twelve."

"The hell it is. Yer damn ticker's stopped."

The excitement was at fever pitch.

"Let's go. Let's go. Let's go." the chant began.

The scene took on a carnival air.

Helmer swaggered over to Ed, blustering, "Well, old man, are ya ready to take your licking?" Turning to the crown he cupped his hands and shouted, "I'm buying a round for the house as soon as I run this pile of junk off the ice. We won't wait for that old lady to pull in."

The riotous crowd stomped and whistled their approval, and clapped their gloved hands.

"I've been waiting for you, you Norwegian blowhard. Let's go." Turning to Mac, "Git in, gutless, if you haven't already pissed your britches."

The cars proceeded in tandem, moving slowly over the ice to the starting line.

The whistle shrilled ...

The screaming mob surged forward as one man, jostling for the best view, pushed roughly, elbowing his way to the front as a roar split the heavens ...

"They're off."

The noisy crowd suddenly silenced as the sound of the engine sprang to life.

Helmer waved an exultant good-bye, then, before the last sound of the whistle dissipated, he was out in front, pulling directly in front of the old car, causing Ed to slam on the brakes.

Ed's face was furious. "That son of a bitch gonna get his, just wait."

Mac laughed, "He'll be the one that's waitin'."

The Model T labored to catch up, still two lengths behind as Helmer rounded the first curve. But on the straightaway, Ed gained and they were neck and neck.

Rounding the next curve, Helmer swung wide and Ed gained a length as he hugged the marker.

Speeding down the long stretch, Ed's car held the lead. As they approached the third turn, Helmer never slowed or turned, speeding past the marker.

The audible groans from the spectators turned to screams of delight as Helmer made a wide looping turn swinging back to safety, accelerating to overtake Ed.

Voices sounded from the crowd ...

"That damned fool. What's he showin' off for? Takin' them crazy chances, he's all over the ice."

Realization dawned. "Looks to me like he's havin' trouble with his brakes. Some son of a bitch must have screwed with his brakes."

The declaration swept through the crowd like wildfire. "He ain't got no brakes."

It was obvious to the onlookers on the landing that Helmer was trying to stay within the markers as the car accelerated on the slippery surface.

Ed grinned as Mac said dejectedly, "Looks to me like he's havin' trouble with his brakes."

"Sure as hell does. Wonder how that happened? You ready to sign off that half section?"

A sickening feeling swept over Mac as he grasped the meaning of Ed's mocking words. He tried to answer, but the words stuck in his throat.

"One more curve, then twenty yards to the finish line. I've beat that cocky bastard. Get your pen ready," Ed exulted.

Suddenly the Hudson shot past them in a desperate burst of speed, then skidded helplessly, smashing into the Model T, pushing it into an uncontrollable spin far outside the safety zone. The terrifying sound of the crushing metal rose above the sounds of the spectators. The Hudson righted itself, turned, then careened wildly down the last stretch. The crowd scattered for safety just moments before the battered car splintered the huge logs that supported the landing.

The jubilant crowd rushed to force the door and pulled Helmer, bloodied and cursing, to safety. One arm hung useless, but holding high the other, he gave a victorious salute to thunderous applause.

The last act of the drama played out as though on a gigantic stage. The backdrop was the faded blue of the horizon, the iridescent white of the ice, the dark form of the car as it stood motionless, fifty feet from the finish line.

Helmer's moment of glory was instantly silenced by the sound of an ear-splitting crack that sliced through the air like a rifle shot. Every eye turned toward the car on the ice.

The crowd watched helplessly as a widening black ribbon of water encircled the doomed car. It hung there for a breathless moment as though suspended by an unseen hand, then silently and slowly tilted downward to become only a shadow beneath the ice.

The rowdy spectators, so frantic with excitement only moments ago, were now subdued, numb with shock. They seemed to melt away, appalled to find the clammy fingers of death at their very elbow.

They hurried back to their homes as if to escape the sound of Ed's hoarse scream, the sight of Mac's terrified face as he surfaced for a brief moment, clawing at the unforgiving ice. The black frigid water closed over his head, deadly and silently. Ed and Mac—it was as though they had never been.

Helmer spit his chaw on the ground. Holding his injured arm, he nodded to his companions, "Well, boys, we may as well go back to the club. I can still hold a shot glass. We won't get Ed out until it thaws."

His companions added, "Well, he'll thaw fast nuf where he's goin'."

"He'll be playin' cards with the devil tonight."

"In that case, I'm bettin' on Ed."

A three-line obituary of the deaths was enclosed in a long letter from Ruth. Ironically, the land for which the men died belonged to neither. The Great Northern Bank held title to the heavily mortgaged section.

The land lay as it had since the world had been created.

Marge, too, endured, vibrant and alive. The memories of the two men were as dead to her as their bodies that lay frozen on the bottom of Red Lake.

Chapter 8

Already it was the middle of April. The bright sunshine filtered through the bougainvillea, lush with new growth and blooms. As it strayed across the window pane, Marge and Annie sat basking in the warmth, enjoying their first cup of coffee.

Their quiet was shattered as they heard Susy's lilting "Here comes the bride" as she danced down the hall, still in her nightgown. Annie hurried to pour her a cup of coffee. "Toast or muffin, Bride?"

Susy laughed. "One of each, Mom, thank you."

"Marge, you'd better be thinking about your dress. My maid of honor is special."

"I've already decided, Susy. It's bib overalls and boots. I don't want to outshine the bride," Marge retorted.

"See how Miss Perfect is, Mom? You always worried about me."

"On the back of Dad's paper last night was a big ad for fifty to seventy percent off at a big yardage store downtown. Don't you think we should start on the dress? You know how particular I'm going to be. Can we go today, Mom, please? My bridesmaids have decided on pale green and have already started their dresses. Won't that color look just beautiful with my pink orchid corsage? Oh, Mom, I'm so happy I could just die."

"Yes, it's going to take some time to make that dress. Let's make a list: a good grade of muslin…"

"Oh no, Mom." came Susy's anguished cry. "Not muslin. I want satin and lace and ribbons."

"Susy, you know we're on a very slim budget. We can't possibly afford satin. Dad hasn't been any help; I'll have to write Ruthie."

Marge interrupted. "You know, Dr. Tom sent me twenty dollars in his last letter. We won't scrimp on a thing; this is my wedding present to Susy. You will be the most beautiful bride. We'll be so proud, six bridesmaids, the church full of flowers. I'll wear my green dress with the roses that you gave me for the prom last year…for goodness sake, are you crying?"

Susy flung her arms around Marge. "Someday, I'll be your maid of honor and Mom can make your dress. Mom, let's hurry, what are you crying about?" As she rushed down the hall she called back, ". . . and gloves. Shoes. Veiling thread. Some decent scissors. Velvet ribbon. . ."

It was mid-morning when they stepped off the streetcar deep in the heart of the Los Angeles business district. It seemed nothing had changed since Marge's first shopping trip, how many months ago? The same aura of desolation hung over the city, shrouding the lines of the beaten, desperate men who shuffled helplessly in the long bread lines or drifted aimlessly past the empty storefronts.

"Don't look. Let's hurry." Susy whispered, "I'm scared, Mom."

"It's only three blocks from here," Annie answered reassuringly. "We're almost there—see the big sign in the window? *Going out-of-business—fifty to seventy percent off.*"

They stepped from the littered sidewalk into a large dimly lit room brightened by colorful bolts of material stuffed into large boxes that crowded every aisle. Huge displays of ribbon hung suspended from the walls; remnants piled high in a huge bin were a revelation even to Annie, who had years of sewing experience. Despite the inviting sales signs, the store did not have an abundance of shoppers.

They walked slowly, examining the contents of every box that looked promising, comparing quality with the marked-down price. Then Annie exclaimed, "Here is a very, very nice bolt of muslin, excellent quality, easy to work with, too. Only twenty-nine cents a yard."

"Susy, Susy?" She turned. Susy was nowhere to be seen.

"Where in the world did she go so quickly? I want her to see this. I think it's perfect, don't you?"

Marge nodded her agreement, then added, "It would be so pretty with that ribbon the on the wall, especially with that silk ribbon with the pink embroidered rosebuds."

"Oh Marge, it would. But I've got to keep the cost down."

"Annie, I've told you, it's my gift to her. We won't scrimp on a thing. Whatever she wants. Her wedding is a lifetime dream. Don't you dare cry. Aren't we having fun?"

Wiping her nose, Annie looked around. "Where in the world did that girl go? I don't see her anywhere. She wouldn't have gone outside. I'll ask the man at the cash register if there's a basement." Marge continued down the aisle, hoping for a glimpse of Susy when Annie hurried back.

"There's a small storage room where the more expensive material is stored. He said there was no demand for satin or the heavier brocades. Let's look there."

If a room could glow, it would have been lit with three-thousand-watt candle power.

Susy stood, her eyes clinging to a length of heavy white satin wrapped around her slender body, an ecstatic smile on her face. They stood, transfixed for a long breathless moment.

"Well, I guess we've found the material," Marge laughed. They carried the precious bolt to the cash register. As he measured and cut the exact amount, Susy's excited voice exclaimed, "Oh, the velvet ribbon with the silk rosebuds and that gorgeous imported lace; don't forget the four yards of that sheer veiling. Mom, which thread? Mom, you're not supposed to cry until I walk down the aisle. Wipe your nose."

Then Marge's magic words rang out. "Wrap it up."

Arriving home with their heavy packages, Marge and Annie collapsed on the sofa. Susy skipped down the hall, not stopping until all the precious bundles were deposited on the bed. "Guess we'll sleep on the floor tonight," Marge laughed as Susy unwrapped them all.

"Mom, can we make the pattern tomorrow?"

"NO, we cannot," Annie answered. "The graduation dress. What about that?"

"Oh, Mom, I'll wear my favorite— the prom dress Marge got me for my birthday last year. I'll try it on tomorrow, then you can start work on the pattern, okay?"

"Alright, I'm going to rest awhile before I make Dad's dinner. I'm tired."

"Me, too," Marge agreed, "but I've got a book review to finish. Susy, you'd better get busy, too, or you won't need that graduation dress."

"Miss Perfect, let's see your notes," Susy coaxed.

The peace and quiet of the following morning was disturbed as Susy, rubbing her eyes, walked into the kitchen still in her robe, her blue dress over her arm. Annie put her cup down.

"Susy, you're up early. That's a surprise."

"Well, I want to get this dress fixed so we can get to the pattern. I must have gained some weight, though. It zips terribly tight over the hips and it won't zip over the bosom." She dropped the robe and slipped the dress over her head and tugged at the zipper. "See?"

Marge laughed. "Susy, I'll bet you weigh a hundred and twenty pounds, that's five pounds more I do."

"Not funny, Marge. Mom, do something," Susy urged.

"Let me get the tape," then… "Susy, I declare. You've grown two inches in the bust and wider in the hips. You're going to be built just like your Aunt Ruth; she had such a beautiful figure. Stand still, I can let the seams out over the hips and two inches through the bust and it will fit perfectly. It won't take long."

A suspicious, fleeting thought pushed through Marge's mind. Instantly ashamed, she forced it back with the words, "Susy, you look more beautiful in that dress than you did a year ago."

A few hours later, the dress was finished to Susy's satisfaction and Annie was on her hands and knees laying out a pattern on the newspapers spread on the kitchen floor.

"Big puffed sleeves, Mom. A square neckline, fitted at the waist, and yards of material in the skirt and train, lace over the sleeves and all around the skirt and train. Trim the neckline, too. Won't it be gorgeous?"

Annie cut and re-cut the pattern. "Susy, stand still. I've got to pin this on you carefully if you want it to fit right."

"Ouch. Don't stick me."

"Raise your arm. There, that will work. I think that will do it."

Boots came home early that night to find Susy standing in a paper pattern, Annie on her knees adjusting the hemline, and Marge just starting dinner.

He stood in the doorway, his face twitched in anger. Annie scrambled to her feet. "Oh, Boots. I didn't expect you so early. I'll have dinner ready in a few minutes."

"Forget it," he growled. "I'll get a bowl of chow mein, good enough for a man who's just put in a ten-hour day. Don't let me interrupt you." The door slammed behind him.

Susy was the first to speak. "I'm getting damned tired of Dad's theatrics."

"Susy, don't you dare use that kind of language." Then she laughed.

"Me, too. Me, too." Marge added. The kitchen shook with the unrestrained laughter of the bride's mother, the maid of honor and the bride in her paper wedding gown.

The bars had long closed when Boots kicked the door open and stumbled down the hall, turning on lights as he went.

Startled, Annie sat up. He stood over the bed, his voice shaking with rage.

"What the hell do you think you're doing, encouraging her to ruin her life?"

"Boots, come to bed. Calm down, you'll wake the girls."

"You all need a damned wake-up call and I'm just the man to do it. No more of this bullshit. Do you hear me loud and clear?"

"Yes, and I'm sure the neighbors do, too."

"Don't get cute with me. I'll be as loud as I want to in my own damned house. You could get a taste of what that guy got down at the bar, so watch your mouth. No more of this wedding bullshit. You're a fool if you think that bastard will change just because some pompous old padre mutters a few words and says 'Amen.' I wish he was sayin' some words over lover boy's casket. If I could catch him alone some night, even the devil wouldn't recognize him, but he'd burn just as fast, what was left of him. Move over."

"Boots," Annie gasped as she sank back on her pillow beside her a man she had never really known.

The next morning they pushed all the furniture against the wall and everything pertaining to the wedding was contained in the girls' bedroom with the exception of the dress material.

Annie added two more boards to the kitchen table, then covered it with a sheet. She lay the slippery, shimmering satin down and pinned the pattern.

"Oh, girls, I'm terrified to cut into this gorgeous, expensive material. What if I make a mistake?"

"Start with a sleeve, Mom," Susy encouraged.

"You can do it, Annie. Pretend it's just a piece of cheap cotton," Marge added. "Don't be nervous."

"I'll pray."

"One, two, three, GO," the girls said in unison.

The new scissors shone as the cut lengthened exactly on the pattern. "Keep praying, Marge. Here goes the bodice."

In two days, the material was cut in precise pieces.

"Alright Susy, let's pin it on one more time so there will be no mistakes when we start basting. I'll lock the door so there will be no interruptions."

Carefully, each piece of material was pinned in place, adjusted and admired. Engrossed in their work, they did not hear the patrol car as it pulled to the curb. The front door rattled as Boots turned the knob with no results, then banged with his fist.

Annie's face paled. "You girls stay in the bedroom," she whispered as she hurried to let him in.

"I've lost my wallet, or did I leave it on the dresser?"

Then, "What the hell is going on here? Why is the door locked? I had to knock to get into my own damned house? Playing games again, huh? I ought to give you what I promised." Boots reached for her.

Annie stepped back, her arm flung protectively over her face.

In a second, holding her train up with one hand, the long sharp scissors in the other, Susy raced down the hallway to face her father, her face as contorted as his.

She stood, leaning forward on the balls of her feet, her eyes never leaving his. Her train fell, forgotten, to the floor as she held the scissors with both hands.

"If you ever touch my mother, I'll kill you," Susy screamed.

"You're no daughter of mine," Boots choked.

"You're right. And you're no father of mine. Don't you ever forget it."

Marge, with disbelieving eyes, stood transfixed in the doorway staring at the scene before her. She knew without a doubt, Susy was truly her father's daughter.

Boots came home long enough to pick up his clothes. The precinct gossip got back to Annie, via Hal, that Boots was staying at a cheap hotel just blocks away from the courthouse.

Tension at the little yellow bungalow dissipated into the warm California sunshine. The girls sat cross-legged on the floor basting as Annie did the big pieces, advised the girls, and occasionally took out a hem or redid a change.

As they worked, it was a wonderful, joyous bonding experience for the happy trio.

Great care was taken with the lovely satin. "So much love is going into this dress," Susy murmured, "I will save it for my own daughter someday, and her name will be 'Anne Margaret.' Mom, stop. Don't you dare cry on that satin. Do you want it to stain? Let's have some of that chocolate cake and a hot cup of tea. I absolutely crave that chocolate."

It was the fifteenth of May when the combined efforts of Marge and Annie lifted the heavy satin gown to slide it over Susy's slim shoulders. It fell in luxurious shimmering folds to the floor, its lace-covered top clinging to Susy as Annie painstakingly struggled with the tiny covered buttons that closed the bodice.

"This is what your bridesmaids are supposed to do for you." Annie groaned as she buttoned, one by one.

They stepped back to inspect their long hours of loving effort to make this the most beautiful gown in the world.

Susy, their most critical judge, declared, "It's perfect. Just perfect," as she preened herself and studied her reflection in the mirror.

Marge and Annie stood silent, spellbound at the sight of this beautiful young woman, magnificent in her wedding gown, teetering on the threshold of her new life.

Tears flowed down Susy's cheeks, "Oh Mom."

"Susy, stop. Don't you dare stain that satin."

"Let's take it off. I'm going to cry forever. Then let's go and celebrate, finish the cake and have a cup of tea."

The tears and laughter of the three celebrants flowed together. Then the wet tea bags and chocolate cake crumbs on the yellow Formica table proclaimed the celebration to be a success.

"Mom, we'll arrange for the church and the minister tomorrow. What was the name of that man who baptized me? Won't we need to order flowers and my corsage of pink orchids? We'll send Dad's suit to be cleaned, just in case, but I still want you to walk me down the aisle. Everyone should have their invitations by now. I even sent them to every man in the precinct. I think that pleased my new father-in-law.

"Isn't it lucky that lovely pale green dress with the pink roses you made, the one you gave to Marge for the prom last year, is just perfect for the maid of honor? She looked so much better in it than I ever did." Susy declared in a burst of generosity.

"Oh, Mom, Hal and I are going to look at a house. It's just perfect for us, only three blocks from here. I'm sure it's still for rent."

At the first honk of the horn, Susy flew out the door. She called back, "We're off to see the house, Mom. See you later."

As she opened the car door, she slid close to him. "Hal, I've found such a darling little house, just right for us. I made an appointment."

"Susy, we need to talk about some things I've been thinking about. Let's park for awhile."

They drove silently until Hal found a shady spot and parked beneath a tall Eucalyptus tree.

Susy's heart beat a steady refrain. *I just know he's going to tell me I'm going to have his mother's wedding ring.*

He turned to face her. "Susy, you know we're both young. We've got lots of time. I haven't even found a decent job yet. Why can't things go on just as they are for a few more months? Aren't we happy just the way we are?"

Susy's shocked, disbelieving voice, "Hal, you promised. I am happy that you love me, but now that you've gotten what you wanted, you make me feel cheap. You gave me your word we'd be married. Dad would say, 'It's a poor excuse of a man who doesn't keep his word.'"

The words flew out of her mouth before she even thought them. Shocked to hear them, "Oh, Hal, forgive me. I can't believe I said that. I'm so sorry."

Her innocent response came so close to his truth, he was momentarily taken by surprise.

His soothing reply, "Of course, Blondie, I know you're upset. I'm sorry, too, but we will have to postpone . . . "

"Oh Hal, we can't. The bridesmaids have their dresses, the invitations are out, the church and minister are reserved. Actually, all we need to do is send Dad's suit to the cleaners in case he comes, and decorate the church. We've been working on my dress for weeks, now it's finished. Hal, it's so beautiful, it even has a train."

"Susy, no. All that will keep." His voice roughened. "I'm not ready to settle down."

"Hal, you're just nervous..." She attempted to put her arms around him but he pushed her roughly away.

"No Susy. I won't do it."

The bottom dropped out of Susy's world. She heard the words but refused to accept them. *What can I do? What can I say? Now I'll have to tell him—I wanted to wait until after the wedding.*

"Hal. We have to do it; I'm three months pregnant." She spoke desperately.

Shock, rage and fear of the dire consequences screamed across his face. Caught in his own trap.

"I don't believe you. I've been careful. You're just trying to trap me. Well, it won't work."

"Hal, I haven't had my period for three months, not after the first time. I'm starting to show."

"You mean you didn't take any precautions?"

"I don't know about precautions. You know I didn't plan for this to happen."

"The hell you didn't. If I remember correctly, you are the one who begged me."

"Oh Hal, please, let's not quarrel. Dad will kill both of us."

"Have you told anyone?"

"No, who would I tell? It would break Mom's heart. I don't even dare to think what Dad would do."

Hal was very aware of what 'Dad would do.' There wasn't a man in the precinct who would dare Boots' wrath, including Hal's own father.

"Well, you'll just have to get an abortion. Clara can give you all the details. Nothing to it, no one will be the wiser. Do it the day after graduation."

"Oh Hal, I'm afraid. I'm so afraid. Will you go with me?"

"Of course not. Men don't do that. Take Miss Perfect. Just tell her you've got an errand. Clara will set it up for you. No one will ever know."

"Hal, please. I'm so scared, please come with me."

"Hell, no. Don't be a fool and spoil everything. Do it the day after graduation. I'll get you some money."

"Then we'll be married on my birthday? Promise?"

"Sure, Blondie, of course I promise. You know I love you. Everything will be alright."

Chapter 9

As a child would feel the air slowly leaking from a brilliantly colored balloon, which only moments ago was so burstingly full, Susy's exuberant feelings became less spontaneous. Annie's radar picked up the signals ... *This quieter, more restrained Susy worries me. But then, of course—she's exhausted, the finals yet to come. The stress of the wedding preparations is finally taking its toll. We're all tired. Thank heavens everything is ready except for the last-minute flowers.*

Her thoughts were interrupted as Susy entered the room quietly, standing behind her mother's chair, wrapping her arms around her mother.

"You know I love you more than anyone in the world, Mom. You have always been there for me. Even when it didn't show, I always knew."

Annie had known from the beginning that Susy was her father's daughter and had forced herself to accept second place in her daughter's heart, but now she gloried in her newfound status with no guilt. "Thank you, God. It's my turn."

In the short time before final exams, Marge had stolen every available moment for her schoolwork and had prodded Susy into some half-hearted efforts.

On graduation night, the fulfillment of her own and her mother's dream for her came true. Marge graduated with honors.

When Marge reached to accept her diploma, a strange, warm feeling flooded over her. She could smell the faint scent of lavender and feel the loving arms around her. She whispered, "We've done it, Mother."

Later, Mrs. Lowenstein pushed through the crowd. "Congratulations, my most extraordinary student. I am so proud of you. So grateful I have had a part in this."

"I haven't done it alone. I've had three strong women in my life who have made my dreams come true. I'll never forget it." Then to herself she added, *Dr. Tom, who saved my life then, made it possible for me to be here now. I thank God for the kindness of strangers.*

Susy, who had barely squeaked by and who could not have cared less, glowed in her favorite blue dress, escorted by last year's most eligible bachelor, resplendent in a rented tuxedo.

The graduation party paled by comparison to the anticipated wedding festivities less than a week away. It seemed everyone was saving the celebration for the main event.

Hal parked in the driveway, and for the first time got out to open the door for Susy. She clung to him as he kissed her good night.

With her voice trembling, Susy pleaded. "Hal, won't you please come with me tomorrow? I'm so scared. Clara's arranged it for eleven o'clock."

"Susy, it's been a wonderful evening, don't spoil it now. We've already discussed that. I'll see you tomorrow night." With a quick kiss he was gone.

Susy had been coaxing Marge to go with her, although she had secretly hoped that Hal would change his mind. But now that he had withstood her pleas again, she renewed her efforts with Marge.

Clara, too, had flatly refused to go. "Can't do it, the May Co. has a big sale on. Can't miss that. Don't be such a baby."

At breakfast, Susy enlisted the aid of her mother. "Clara had a fight with her mother and moved across town with a friend. I promised to bring her some stuff. I don't really want to go, it's a rough neighborhood, she says, but I promised." She renewed her efforts, "Will you go with me Marge, please?"

"Oh, Susy, I can't. I'm going to the movies with Tim. I've told you that. Let Clara come and get her own stuff."

"Alright, I'll go alone." The tears rolled down her cheeks.

Annie turned to plead Susy's case. "Oh, Marge, couldn't you postpone that till another time? I really don't want her to go alone. It would surely ease my mind."

Trapped, Marge tried to be gracious with her reluctant assent, but she added, "I don't mean to be nasty, but I've never liked Clara. Your Dad was right about her."

Susy, having gotten her way, just shrugged. She turned to Marge and spoke quickly, "I want to be there by eleven because I need to be home early."

"The earlier the better," Marge grumbled.

They caught the first car and had to change twice. It seemed to go forever. The car got hot and stuffy. Susy, for a change, sat quietly and nervously clasped and unclasped the closure on her purse.

"Stop that. For goodness sake, what are you so jumpy about? Let Clara run her own errands in the future," Marge complained.

"We've been on this car for an hour. This is a terrible neighborhood. I'm not surprised you didn't want to come alone."

Susy interrupted, "Watch for Ivy and Garden View Street. We must be getting close."

"Oh, there it is." She pulled the cord and the car jerked to a stop. Only the girls stepped out. Susy sat on the bench and dug in her purse, pulling out a crumpled paper with an address.

"We're right here—that awful looking two-story building. Looks like an old deserted apartment house—not even any curtains."

"Surely Clara can't live there, you must have the wrong address."

"No, Clara said it was brick. It does look awful, but I won't be long. Sit here or go across the street to that little store and get a Coke."

The feeling of unease escalated into a near panic as Marge watched Susy hesitate at the bottom of the stairs, then walked up the stairs to the door, opened it, and Boots' "baby" stepped over the threshold.

Two streetcars had gone by at fifteen-minute intervals.

She's been in there thirty minutes. What can she be doing while I'm roasting in this hot sun?

But worry overrode the irritation and her inexplicable premonition.

"Marge." The call was so faint, then, "Hey you, hurry up. You'd better help her down these stairs. She's a bleeder. Her own fault, she wouldn't lay still."

As Marge hurried up the stairs, she was horrified to see a crimson line creeping down Susy's white legs.

"Better get her to a doctor fast. Here's a towel."

Then the rough voice became threatening, "Ya don't know nothin' and ya better forget where yer at, ya hear, if you know what's good for ya."

The door slammed. Marge never forgot the rust-colored stains, now intermingled with the bright red of Susy's blood on the dirty white tennis shoes.

Susy trembled against Marge. "She hurt me, hurt me," she whispered in a dazed little-girl voice.

She slumped in Marge's arms. "Oh my God, Susy. What have you done?"

There was no need for an answer. The blood flowed steadily as Marge half carried her to the bench.

Susy's desperate little voice cried, "Call Dad."

Marge tried to staunch the increasing flow of blood but to no avail. The towel dripped red. She ran frantically to the little store, fumbling in her purse for a nickel.

The little Oriental woman behind the counter looked past Marge. As she saw Susy slump on the bench, the blood pooling on the sidewalk; she muttered, "Those bastards have done it again, will it never end?"

Marge dug blindly in her purse, finally dumping the contents on the counter to find the number Boots had given them so long ago.

"Give me the number. I'll dial for you," the clerk offered.

O'Malley stopped his agitated pacing long enough to stick his head out his office door and growled, "Bill. When Malone checks in, tell him I want to see him around noon."

He slammed the door. *I'll need that much time to find the guts to tell him,* he thought, as he sat down and re-read the letter.

"Somethin's eatin' the Captain—better walk easy today. I gotta feelin' heads are gonna roll. Wonder what shit Malone's stirred up now? He's been meaner than hell these last few months. It's that damned wedding. That O'Malley kid got more guts than brains. He's skatin' on thin ice. Can't say I blame Malone."

"What the hell you bitchin' about, Bill? Pour me a cup of that poison, too, will ya?"

The clock showed eleven forty-five when Boots opened the door to the Captain's gruff "Come in." He stood for several moments, staring out the window. Boots began to fidget. Finally, the Captain turned, thrust a crumpled paper at Malone. "Here, read this."

3:00 a.m.

Dad, by the time you read this, I will be gone. I joined the Merchant Marines last week. I will be at sea for five months. I don't want to get married, especially with that old bastard for a father-in-law. Ha ha. She's just a silly spoiled girl and she'll get over it. It was good while it lasted, but there's lots of others waitin' in line. Take care. Hal

Boots' feeling of joy struggled with the realization of the heartbreaking affect this would have on his daughter. With caution thrown to the wind, Boots let his anger speak. "That son of a bitch. I hope to hell he drowns. This will break Susy's heart. They've worked for weeks on that damned wedding dress plus six bridesmaids' dresses. The church, the flowers, all the invites are out. I saw her just once in that wedding dress and she looked like an angel." He gave a short laugh, "An angel packin' a scissor."

"Well, Malone, I can't tell you how ashamed I am, how terribly sorry. What else can I say?"

"O'Malley, you have till tonight to figure out what you're going to say and you damn well better get over to my house and say it to Susy's face. Am I clear? Answer that fuckin' phone. How long you gonna let it ring?"

"Captain O'Malley here."

Marge screamed, "Tell Boots Susy is hurt terribly bad. Hurry, hurry, Ivy and Garden View."

Marge dropped the phone, panting with terror as she flew back to Susy's near prostrate form. "Susy. Susy." Shaking her, "Talk to me. I called your Dad, he's on his way," her voice breaking.

Susy hung limp in Marge's arms, the red life blood encircling both girls as it colored the sidewalk.

The black-and-white had almost stopped when Boots leaped to the curb. His face changed from a furious red to a sickening white as it saw the blood-soaked girls.

He gathered Susy from Marge's arms. "For God's sake, what happened? What are you doing here?"

"I don't know. I don't know. She said she was going to see Clara."

Their bloody footprints followed them to the waiting car, the motor running, the door open. The driver didn't need instructions to head for St. Joseph's Hospital, siren screaming, and Boots' frantic voice, "Hurry for God's sake, hurry."

Boots held his daughter so closely it was as though they were one body. Barely audible, "I love you, Dad," she sighed as her head tipped forward against his massive chest.

Boots' hoarse cry, "Baby, baby, hang on." Then his great gulping sobs as she hung limply, her long golden hair lay twisted over his arm as he rocked her back and forth and groaned in agony.

"Hurry, in the name of God, hurry." His huge shoe banged the back of the driver's seat.

Boots knelt by the bed, his head on her bloodless outstretched arm barely visible against the white sheet.

"Help her, God damn you. Do something," he screamed.

"Will you please wait outside?" The doctor asked, but one look at Boots' demented face gave him the answer. A quick preliminary examination as Boots' great choking sobs, "Almighty God. Almighty God," wrenched from his kneeling body as though by a monstrous hand.

He never looked up as he felt the doctor's hand on his shoulder. He heard, but would not accept, the compassionate words. "I am so terribly sorry to tell you. She hemorrhaged from a badly bungled abortion. She was gone before she got here."

Boots' anguished screams that reverberated against the walls told Marge what she already knew. She slumped in the chair, her hand over her ears.

The doctor closed the door softly behind him. Frozen in her chair, Marge looked up as the doctor asked, "Is there anyone who can help you take him home?" She nodded dumbly.

As she approached the patrol car, the driver rolled his window down, leaned forward to hear her barely audible words. "Will you call Captain O'Malley to take Boots home?" The car sped away as she returned to her seat.

Captain O'Malley arrived so quickly that, for one brief moment, she thought he must have been waiting outside.

She pointed to the door, then heard the Captain's broken voice. "I'll never forgive him for this. He is no son of mine. Forgive me, Malone, in the name of God, forgive me."

From Boots came a guttural animal-like growl. "Tell him he'd better stay at sea for as long as I'm alive, or I'll kill him on sight."

The door opened and Marge watched the two men emerge. The deep, heartbreaking sobs of the two fathers as they clung to each other seemed to come from a bottomless well. A well that would never go dry.

"Why didn't you stop her? Why couldn't it have been you?"

"Boots, let up. It isn't her fault."

"C'mon, Marge, let's go home." The captain took her arm.

Boots followed, silence broken only by his muffled sobs. He turned to Marge. "You will have to tell her. I can't, so help me God, I can't." Again the massive shoulders convulsed with great heaving sobs.

"Oh, Boots, please, I can't do it either," Marge entreated.

The car pulled to the curb and Marge stumbled blindly up the walk. O'Malley called after her, "I'll be right back, Marge," catching a glimpse of Annie at the window. Boots' hoarse voice, "Let's go, let's go."

Annie was surprised to see the patrol car, and even more surprised to see Captain O'Malley. *What would he be doing here, in the middle of the day?*

Marge walked unsteadily, almost feeling her way to the door, where she stood wordless, numb, on the threshold in her bloodied clothing.

Annie's horrified face looked past Marge. "What's happened? Is Susy alright? Where's Susy?" Her nails dug into Marge's shoulders as Annie shook her. "Tell me Susy is alright. Marge, for God's sake, tell me Susy is alright."

Marge, speechless, could only shake her head. Annie shrieked as the unbelievable realization took root. She fell to her knees and when the floor rose up to meet her, she neither knew nor cared.

Later when Captain O'Malley looked in the open door, he saw Annie cradled in Marge's arms with her face pressed against her daughter's life blood that stained Marge's clothing.

"Let's put her to bed, Marge, and let her rest. Then you must shower and lie down, too." He patted her on the shoulder. "We must be strong. We're all she has left."

Marge heard his voice as though it came from another planet. As he drove away, she collapsed on the sofa and curled up with her arms around her knees. She lay there until the room tuned dark, then slid into a deep unknowing sleep.

She was awakened by her own happy laughter. She and Susy were doing the Charleston and Susy had forgotten the steps. Marge screamed into the rough fabric of the sofa pillow until she could scream so more.

Annie lay in bed with the blinds down. She would not eat, despite Marge's entreaties. She prayed for sleep that would numb her mind, allowing her to escape momentarily from the tragic knowledge that clung to her brain like a malignancy that would live forever. Her face to the wall, her eyes wide and staring blindly. Her mind churned with dreadful thoughts.

Boots was right. I never should have let her get so involved. I have failed so horribly as a mother. How could I have been so blind?

God is punishing me for my sin. Eighteen years I've been punished. God, will it ever be enough? God? God. There is no God, that is the ultimate lie. Of course, there is a God. Only a God could know this would be the crowning punishment and this is my hell. God, let me die. No, that would be too easy.

Her thoughts were interrupted when she felt a big warm hand tenderly turn her face from the wall and heard the Captain's strong voice. "Annie, Annie. It's been three days. You must get up and help me. We must think of the funeral. I've taken the liberty of choosing a simple white coffin subject to your approval, and some other arrangements with the church. I'll do everything I can to help. We haven't been able to find Boots. Now you must help me. What dress shall she wear?"

As Annie looked up, O'Malley said, "Here's Marge with a cup of coffee. May I join you?"

The silence in the little church was broken only by the sound of the minister as he thumbed through his notes and turned the pages in his Bible.

A golden ray of sunlight streamed through the elaborate lead-glass window to encircle the diminutive coffin draped with a blanket of pink rose buds. Susy lay in the casket Captain O'Malley had chosen for her, the deep soft velvet enfolding her slight body. Long silken hair covered the shoulders of her favorite blue dress; the pink orchids she had chosen for her wedding bouquet had been placed loosely in her cold hands.

Annie, leaning heavily against Marge, her eyes closed, prayed for closure of this nightmare.

Marge's eyes were fixed on the coffin. The forbidden door of her memory swung open. *I wonder what color Dr. Tom chose for my daughter's casket?* They sat, their bodies close, their spirits joined by a mutual agonizing grief.

The minister folded his hands, bowed his head, and the silence grew even deeper.

Suddenly the large double doors were flung open and Boots stood like an apparition in the doorway. There was a sharp intake of breath from the group of uniformed officers as they turned to watch, with disbelieving eyes, Boots' slow, deliberate walk down the aisle. The uniform he had always worn with such pride was now soiled and wrinkled. His shoulders sagged beneath the jacket that hung open to reveal his stained shirt thrust haphazardly into his trousers. A three-day stubble of beard was apparent and his bloodshot, swollen eyes never blinked. A holstered gun hung at his hip.

He stood beside the casket and gazed intently at the still form of his daughter. Reaching down, he wrapped a strand of her hair around his finger, then smoothed it back into place. He looked up at the man in the pulpit, then spoke, "Well, Padre, I don't know who this pretty girl is, but it sure as hell isn't Susy." As he turned away, he bent down and murmured, "C'mon, baby, let's go home." He leaned forward, his arm curved to fit around a little golden-haired girl who skipped beside him and gazed up adoringly into his face. He chuckled as his big hand tousled her flyaway curls. "C'mon, baby, let's you and your old Dad go for a walk, maybe an ice cream." He leaned forward to whisper in her ear as they walked down the aisle and out the door.

Captain O'Malley hurried to overtake Boots. "Malone, come back. Please. The service hasn't even started."

"What is that to me? We're going for a walk, maybe an ice cream before we go home." He attempted to push by the Captain, who blocked his way.

"What is that to me?" The Captain's shocked voice repeated. "For God's sake, Malone, aren't you even going to come to your daughter's funeral?"

"I don't know who you've got in that box, O'Malley, but my daughter is with me. C'mon, baby," he said as he held out his hand.

The black dirt, piled high from the excavation, was the backdrop for the small coffin. The pure white of the dainty casket shown through the heavy blanket of pink rosebuds encircled by a spray of orchids. A card read, "The Officers of Precinct II." The order had been given, "Flowers not to be removed."

It was a small, private gathering, seated on folding wooden chairs, who heard the brief eulogy. Four officers were pallbearers. One murmured, "The ink isn't even dry on the invite."

Marge held Annie tightly as she sat with her eyes closed, seemingly unaware of her surroundings. But as the minister paused with his last "Amen," she stood and stepped forward to look down into the deep dark hole that would contain her dancing, laughing daughter.

A blood-chilling moan escaped her lips as she fell to her knees. Captain O'Malley lifted her gently in his arms, his tears falling on her unconscious face as he carried her to a waiting car. Marge followed, never looking back.

As they pulled into the driveway, the bleak little cottage stood as though it, too, was lifeless. Only a few days ago it had pulsed with the sounds of laughter and music, the dreams of the young who had an entire lifetime to pursue their future.

Despite the fact that the sun was shining brightly and the bougainvillea still bloomed across the kitchen window, the house was cold, dark, and desolate. The silence was crushing as the Captain lay Annie down and turned wordlessly away.

Chapter 10

Marge's insistent voice pulled Annie back from her dream.

Baby, stand still. Those pins wouldn't stick if you'd hold still for one minute.
These big puffed sleeves with all that lace has got to look just right. Will you
please stand still.

Forcing her back to reality, Marge's intruding voice exclaimed,
"Annie. Annie. You've been in that bed for three days. You've hardly
eaten anything. Captain O'Malley says if you don't get up, you will have
to go to the hospital. I've fixed a nice warm bath for you, nice clean
clothes and I'll shampoo your hair. You'll feel so much better. Please,
Annie, please."

Annie rose stiffly. With Marge's arm around her, they walked
slowly to the bathroom. The air was permeated with Susy's favorite
bubble bath. Her towel had been flung across a hanger and long
strands of her hair were still caught in the brush that was tossed
carelessly in the open drawer of the dressing table.

Later, warmed and cleansed by the sweet-scented water, her hair
wrapped in a towel, Annie stepped into the hall. She paused at the
girl's bedroom, the door half open. The unmade bed, the scattered
clothing, just as they had left it, how many years ago? The day Susy had
urged, *"Hurry up, Marge, we've got to hurry. I can't be late."*

"Marge, I'm going to pack up Susy's things." Annie moved like an
old woman. "It's got to be done, the sooner the better. I'd like you to
have anything of Susy's that you could use."

"No, no, no. I never could. I'll keep the green prom dress she
gave me. I'll find some boxes." She hurried away.

She trailed behind Annie, hiding her face behind what containers
she could find. She did not want to see the beautiful satin gown that
hung on its padded hanger, suspended on the hook Susy herself had
pounded into the wall.

They worked feverishly. Drawers were dumped, clothing was

pulled from hangers, shoes were thrown in a heap.

"Oh, there is that high-heeled shoe Susy couldn't find, but I can't reach it." Silent tears flowed as clothing was sorted into piles.

Susy's "face paint" was tossed into a box marked "Goodwill."

Finally, as though she were a puppet and the string had broken, Annie crumpled to the floor, then crawled to the stack of clothing, laid her head down and closed her eyes. Susy's scent hung in the air and wrapped around her like a warm blanket. Susy would never be dead.

The satin bridal gown still hung as though invisible. Annie's eyes were dry when she closed the door.

The intolerable aura of grief so permeated the house it was almost visible. There was no need for spoken words. A loving pat, an understanding glance, a sudden hug—the message was unmistakable.

The days that followed were long and empty.

The house overflowed with so many relentless reminders. A slamming screen door that didn't slam anymore, the Victrola forever silent, the exuberant presence of Susy with her noisy fun-loving friends forever gone.

Annie took refuge in the garden that had always been her comfort. Because of recent neglect, the weeds had overgrown the once lovingly tended rows of vegetables.

Now she weeded with a frenzy that pushed her into an exhausted, dreamless sleep at night.

Marge was making coffee when the first rays of the sun turned the errant cobwebs that hung on the bougainvillea into iridescent threads. She knew Annie was already in the garden. *Thank God for that garden, it has saved her sanity. But what will we do with all the vegetables now?*

Then high-pitched, hysterical laughter. "Marge, come out and see."

Alarmed, Marge hurried out to see the garden plot that until recently boasted meticulously kept row upon row of vegetables. Now it was only a large area of black dirt, completely bare except for neat piles of both weeds and vegetables that lay wilted in the sunlight, the dirt still clinging to their roots in silent protest as if to give mute testimony to their reluctance to die so prematurely.

Annie's unrestrained laughter turned to sobs as she sank down on the back step and wiped her nose on her sleeve.

"Don't cry, Annie," Marge comforted. "We'll just replant."

Annie stood, shrugging Marge's arm away. "No need, let's have some coffee. I want to talk to you."

Marge sat, her mind in turmoil, her thoughts interrupted by Annie's quiet voice as the coffee was poured.

"Marge, I am going back to North Dakota to live with Ruth. I have thought about this for a long time, always planned to wait until Susy was settled," her voice broke, but then continued. "Now is the time. I plan to leave in two weeks. You will need to find a job and another place to live as I know you won't want to stay here with Boots. You should talk to Mrs. Lowenstein. She loves you and I know she will help you."

"Oh, Annie," cried Marge in a shocked, disbelieving voice. Marge, who had shown such strength and self-control throughout this hellish ordeal, put her head on her folded arms and wailed like a baby. Her tears intermingled with the coffee that spilled from the overturned cup that neither woman noticed.

"Oh, Annie, I want to go with you. Please let me go with you." She cried desperately.

"No, you can't." Annie's voice encouraged no protest. "Your life is here. You've made such a good start. You're young and strong with your whole life ahead of you. Stay here and make something of your dreams. North Dakota has nothing for you. You left behind what you never had, now I must do the same. Don't cry. Be happy for me. This is my only chance."

Marge raised her tearful face as a knock sounded at the door, then covered her face with her hands.

"Who can that be so early?" Annie murmured as she hurried to answer another insistent knock.

"Captain O'Malley. You're out early."

"Yes, may I come in?"

"Of course, you're just in time for coffee."

Too late to escape, Marge sat, tears trickling through the fingers that covered her face.

Immediately aware that he had interrupted at an awkward moment, the Captain looked questionably at Annie whose expression told him nothing. He pulled a chair close to Marge, and spoke gently, "Margie, Margie, don't grieve anymore."

"She's crying," Annie interrupted, "because I have just told her I'm leaving." As she spoke, she placed a steaming cup of coffee before him. He looked up, startled.

"Leaving, Annie? Why? Where are you going? If money is a problem, Boots was in this morning, asked me to bring you this." He thrust a roll of bills, contained by a rubber band, toward her. A shocked expression crossed his face as she roughly pushed his hand away.

"He can keep it. When I needed money for our daughter's wedding, I had to go begging. He'll need it for his booze. Keep it."

"Annie, Annie. Don't be so bitter."

"Don't play God with me, Captain."

"I've had to put him on indefinite leave, Annie. He looks terrible. I almost doubt his sanity. What about him, Annie?"

Her voice shook with sudden fury. "What about me, Captain? What about me? He's done what he wanted, when he wanted, all his life, so why should I interfere now? Is my life over? Has it no value, no meaning to anyone? I intend to remedy that. In two weeks I'll be on the train, heading for a new life where there will be happiness and love."

He stood and stepped toward her. "Oh, Annie, I have hoped," he stuttered, hesitated, then plunged in, "Annie, I've waited so long."

She rose on tiptoe to put her fingers over his lips. "Don't say it now, Captain. I don't want to hear what I've known for years. You and Boots are on the same time clock—you're both too late."

Her scornful, sad voice stated, "One needs me, one wants me. Aren't I the lucky one?"

His coffee still cooling in the cup, the Captain walked to the door and closed himself out of her life.

That night, as Annie lay in bed, her face to the wall, Marge's woebegone voice floated out of the darkness.

"Can I sleep with you Annie? That sofa is so lonely and the springs are poking through."

The bed squeaked as Annie moved over and threw back the blankets in a silent invitation. Marge slipped between the covers, cuddled up to Annie's back. She lay silent for a moment, then, "Oh, Annie, I'm so ashamed. How could I have been so selfish? I was thinking only of myself. Forgive me? I realize you have no life here and your new life is waiting. I pray it will bring you the happiness you deserve, the happiness you have given me. Eighteen years since you've seen your sister. Think of all the things you'll have to talk about. What fun you'll have with your old friends. Won't it be wonderful? Don't worry about me, Dr. Tom is still sending me money until I get a job. I'll start looking for a place tomorrow. I'm ready to leave the nest."

Annie smiled in the darkness as she listened to Marge's excited voice. *The young. How they bounce back. Well, I intend to bounce, too. There's no place for me but up. I think we're both ready to leave the nest.*

The room was still dark when Marge was awakened by an unfamiliar sound. She reached for Annie but found only the rumpled, disarranged covers thrown back, the indentation of her body.

"Annie, Annie?" She called softly with no response. She made her way down the hallway, her heart thudding against her ribs as she saw the light spilling through the doorway of the room she and Susy had shared.

Annie sat, her back against the unmade bed, holding the sharp scissors.

Compassion and distress chased across Marge's face as she watched, mesmerized by the shine of the scissors as it invaded the shimmering satin.

The thread that held this dress together was made of love, of hope, and prayer.

A prolonged cut, the skirt was slashed from hem to waist, then cut and cut again until it lay in the smallest possible pieces.

These big puffed sleeves. I did them over three times.

One cut, one strong jerk, and the sleeve joined the pieces that covered the floor. The buttons flew as the bodice ripped.

The day we covered those buttons we laughed because Susy got peanut butter on three of them. Had to do them over. She always loved peanut butter.

A quick jerk, the veiling was torn from the headband and lay in great drifts. The rosebuds that held the veiling looked forlorn.

I'll save it for my daughter, Mom.

Velvet ribbon wrapped about a stray high-heeled slipper, remnants of a dream.

Annie arose stiffly and looked about her. Marge, wordless, held her hand out. Annie clasp it, turned back for a moment, then spoke, "I remember when I wondered, why is it always 'his' and never 'ours'? So this must be 'his', too.

She closed the door.

Chapter 11

They sat at the table, the breakfast dishes pushed aside, the morning paper opened to the classified ads.

"I think it might be best to look downtown for a light housekeeping room in a nice neighborhood," Annie advised, then added. "There are better opportunities for work there, too. Let's start looking right away. Time is growing short, but I can't leave until you are safe and comfortable. I'll look for a city map. I know there's one around here somewhere."

They hurriedly caught the first streetcar, then transferred for the long ride to downtown. Seated together, their heads bent over the encircled ads, Annie laid out the route.

"Oh look. Large, clean room, light housekeeping, Twelve dollars a month. 117 Lawndale Street. Here's another …"

Annie interrupted, "One at a time, Marge."

Marge continued to read while Annie's mind wandered. *Susy sat beside me the last time I was in a streetcar just nine days ago. It seems almost incomprehensible that now there are only two where once there had been three, and soon there would be only one.*

Annie's voice broke up her thoughts. "The next stop is Lawndale Street. We'll walk the three blocks to one-seventeen."

As they approached the large two-story house, Annie examined it critically.

"Well, it's painted, the lawn's well-kept. It's a nice enough neighborhood."

A sign in the window read, "Rooms to Let."

Handing the map to Marge, she knocked. The man who answered the door did not meet Annie's approval—suspenders crossed over a dirty undershirt to hold up pants that sagged beneath his belly, and a three-day stubble of beard.

"We ain't buyin' nuthin'. We ain't got nuthin' to give and we don't want yer reading' stuff, now scat."

Annie pointed to the sign in the window.

"Oh, that. Well, we don't take no wimmens, especially young

ones. All they do is complain, 'no hot water, the lights don't work, the faucets drip.' They fight over the bathroom and don't pay their rent. Nope. No wimmens."

Annie's quick response, "The way you smell, you sure didn't use enough water on yourself."

"See what I mean? Always complainin'."

Exchanging looks, Marge and Annie broke into unrestrained laughter as his furious face disappeared behind the door.

"I didn't think I could ever laugh again," Annie said, surprised at her own reaction.

"1202 Elm Street, rooms to let. It's only six blocks. Perhaps we'll find something there."

They walked along, stepping around the few pedestrians they encountered, enjoying their jaunt away from the house with its memories that crowded every day.

The nearer the sounds, the downtown activity began to bring home to Marge the realization that soon she would be alone. She would become a miniscule part of this gigantic city. Her courage faltered. Impulsively, she reached for Annie's hand. Annie gave it a reassuring squeeze. "Lttle bird, our wings are strong. We can fly."

They turned a corner and came unexpectedly upon a house set back from the street, the peeling paint barely visible beneath the flowering vine that covered it.

A sign, "Room for Rent," hung on a stick that leaned precariously as though it were too heavily burdened.

"This wasn't in the ads, but as long as we're here, let's look at it."

Before Marge knocked, the door was opened and a little old man with a beaming, toothless smile, motioned them in. "Howdy. Come to see the room? Ma isn't here, but she'd be mad if I didn't show you. Come in. Can you set awhile?"

"Perhaps another time," Annie replied as the old man chattered nonstop.

"The bad times are awful hard on us old folks, so Ma and I decided to take in a roomer. We don't get much company. It would be nice to have someone young in the house." He paused, "We'll share the kitchen, of course."

Three large cats lay resting comfortably on the counter, a fourth on the table busily cleaning leftover egg stuck on a plate.

"Of course, you'll have to do your own dishes. Oh, them there's Ma's babies. She sets a heap of store by them cats."

He showed them down a narrow hall. "This here's the room. Feller died in here 'bout a week ago, but Ma cleaned everything, even turned the mattress."

As they looked at the rusty red splotches on the faded wallpaper, he said, "Looks like she didn't get all the bedbugs, don't that beat all?" He chuckled, "Oh, well, they don't eat much, but sure do make a mess when folks squash 'em."

"I don't think it's quite what we're looking for."

As they fled down the street, he called after them. "You won't find anything cheaper, only two dollars a week."

Marge didn't know if she should laugh or cry. "Poor, lonely old folks."

Annie said, "Too far to walk to the next one, we'll transfer on the next car. Hopefully we'll find just the right one. Then let's get a bite to eat and go home. I'm hungry." Annie fanned herself with the map.

The sound of a man's raucous laughter, then high-pitched giggles, and someone singing off-key made Marge hesitate at the partly opened door.

Annie gave it a determined knock, and the door swung wide. A heavily made-up woman, teetering on high heels, a garish robe tied tightly around her ample waist, stepped out pulling the door closed behind her.

"What can I do for you, ladies?"

Marge replied, "I found your ad and I'm looking for a room, a light housekeeping room. Do you have a vacancy?"

The woman spoke to Annie, "Is this your daughter?"

"Yes."

"She's a working girl?"

"She will be shortly."

The woman studied Marge appreciatively, then shaking her head in disbelief, said, "Times sure are tough, aren't they, Mom."

The woman turned, opened the door, then called in, "Hey you. Can we make room for a young, good-looking red-haired gal?"

A hoot of laughter, then a man's voice yelled, "Sure. Bring her in, let's get acquainted. You know we're a friendly bunch."

Annie, horrified, stepped protectively in front of Marge, as the sudden knowledge became crystal clear.

Hardly able to speak, Annie choked, "We're not looking for friendship. We're looking for a decent room. Obviously, we won't find it here."

The woman raised her eyebrows. "Well, you better move on then. Some folks might think we're a mite too friendly."

As they hurried down the walk they heard the laughter behind them.

"Well, Annie, we've struck out three times. But I did almost get a job."

"Marge," came the indignant response.

Reading as she walked, Annie spoke in a tired voice, almost lost. "We're not very far from downtown. We could catch a car here, then transfer to a car that would take us straight home. I'm hungry and tired, aren't you?"

They boarded the next car. Marge sank back in her seat and closed her eyes to the people who jostled around her, discouraged by the day's events. But it was not long before she was roused by Annie's excited voice.

"It's City Hall. Quick, pull the chain. Now I know exactly where we are." They were pushed along by the exiting passengers until they reached the sidewalk.

Marge looked up in open-mouthed awe at the giant structure; it glowed as the bright rays of the sun shone on its myriad of windows.

"It looks like a celestial stairway to Heaven." she whispered. "It's grown right into the sky."

Annie laughed. "It's the tallest building in the city. We're so close to Olvera Street, you must see it. We can have lunch there, too."

She smiled to see Marge walking backwards, her eyes still fastened on the building that dwarfed everything around it.

She bumped against a hurrying pedestrian. "Tourist," he mumbled.

Marge, still looking back, stumbled along behind Annie. "You know this is the first time I've been in downtown Los Angeles. These must be the tallest building in the world. And now Olvera Street? Tell me about it?"

"This is the oldest part of Los Angeles. Originally named Sonora Town by the Spaniards, the Mexicans claimed it as their own. They renamed Wine Street Olvera in honor of Agustin Olvera, a prominent local judge. Now, it is a very colorful marketplace called the Plaza. Everything happens here. Susy and I were here once. The food was so different and wonderful, Susy ate three tacos."

Nothing that Annie could have told her would have prepared her for the exhilarating sounds and sights of Olvera Street.

The red adobe archway that spanned the entrance intensified the vibrant colors. The green, red and white of the Mexican flag swung slowly in the soft breeze as though it, too, enjoyed a siesta.

It was a different world into which Marge stepped. Vendors' stalls lined the plaza, a marketplace with the culture of their people painted in the primary colors that dominated their lifestyle, music, dancing.

Annie walked beside Marge down the cobblestone street, guiding her through the crowd. The once red adobe brick was now worn to a soft gray-pink patina by the passing of so many feet over the years.

Marge's mind whirled before her. This was a world she never knew existed.

Annie laughed at Marge's amazement as she answered her excited questions.

The sounds and sights of the busy plaza were like no other. The soft laughing voices of the women who tended their stalls, the shrill voices of the children as they dodged among the shoppers playing hide-and-seek. Somewhere in the distance, one could hear the strident notes of a guitar, then the squeaking wheels of a vendor's push cart as he steered it along the crowded walkways and called in his tempting voice, "Hot roasted ears of corn. Melons. Lemonade. Tacos. Burritos."

"Oh, Annie. I'm starved. That smells so good."

"Yes, but let's eat at that stall with all those hanging baskets."

They walked toward a big umbrella that covered the eating area, but paused to watch a group of children, their big brown eyes squinted with laughter, their black hair flying. They danced barefoot on the warm tile bricks as they struck at a piñata, a huge purple papier-mâché parrot with orange ruffled wings just out of reach. Small scraps of paper floated to the ground. Someone had made a lucky strike.

"Oh Annie, how beautiful the children are."

"Yes," Annie echoed, her eyes brimming with tears. "How beautiful they are."

As they continued toward the big umbrella that shaded the table and its gaily painted chairs, they heard the coaxing, laughing voice of a young woman with a baby on her hip. His chubby body overflowed his diaper. His face was sticky from the lollipop he clutched in his little brown fist. His other hand was woven in his mother's long black hair. She struggled in vain to free herself as the baby clung tighter, his black eyes sparkling, his mouth open to show four new teeth and a busy tongue dripping with the sugary candy.

Marge stepped forward and held out her arms to the baby who

promptly reached his dimpled arms to her, holding tight to his lollipop and the strands of his mother's hair.

She hugged the sticky baby tightly for a moment, then relinquished him to his laughing mother.

"Oh Annie, this seems like such a happy place. I could never grow tired of this. Do you think there could be a rooming house anywhere in this neighborhood?"

Finally reaching the shade of the big umbrella, they sat at the little round table, delighted to rest their tired feet. In a moment a pretty young girl appeared, "Buenos noches, senoritas. We have enchiladas made from the finest cheese, burritos and tacos."

Turning to Marge, Annie interrupted. "Tacos. Susy loved them. Wouldn't you like to try the enchiladas? And flan, of course, and two lemonades, please. Lots of ice."

The order given, the girl stepped behind the hanging serape that served as a screen for the kitchen. They could hear the soft, rapid exchange of words. Soon the lemonade appeared.

While they waited, they sipped from the tall frosted glasses. Marge was entranced by the contents of the stall. A tall, thorny cactus contained in a large, wildly colorful pot stood guard at one corner. A string of hand-painted gourds hung above, clattering together, nudged by a passing breeze. Papier-mâché figures in their white peasant garb dangled from the long sweep of a bull's lavishly decorated horns. An elaborate wrought-iron cage held a large parrot so wondrously colored that Marge could not believe it was real. Handwoven baskets stacked against a wall shared a space that held oversized black sombreros, heavy with silver braid.

The mouthwatering aroma preceded the hot, spicy food, served high on sizzling platters.

"Can anything possibly taste as good as this smells?" Marge asked.

"Even better, wait till you taste the flan." Annie laughed to see how quickly and with such enjoyment the food was eaten.

"I could almost lick the plate." Marge groaned with contentment.

Annie sighed, "Oh, I've eaten too much. But wasn't it wonderful? Let's hurry home—I have some last-minute things to do and I'm tired, aren't you?"

"Yes, I can't believe the things I've seen today. I loved the food, the people, Olvera Street. Annie, I'll never forget this day.

"I've been thinking, do you suppose I could just stay at the house and take my time looking for a place? I know how to get downtown and it's fun to go slowly, see everything. I'll find my nest. Next week at this time, you will be in yours."

She flung her arms around Annie in a spontaneous rush of affection.

"Quick, here comes our car."

Annie was quiet, thoughtful, then spoke above the drone of the wheels. "If you'd like more time to look, that's probably a good idea. Although I did want to see you settled before I left, you surely could stay until you find something you feel is just right for you. The rent is paid up for another two weeks. I doubt if Boots will be back for awhile, then he'll probably leave, too. Tomorrow we will pack the essential things you'll need: bedding, cooking utensils and so forth. We'll get it all boxed up and leave it by the door and call the Captain. He will be glad to help you move.

"Pull the chain, Marge, the next stop is ours. I'll be glad to get out of these shoes and make a good cup of coffee."

Annie was about to slip the key into the lock when the door flung open violently. She was face-to-face with Boots, his huge body towering over her, his eyes mere slits in his furious bloated face.

"Where in the hell have you been all day? I've been waiting for hours."

Marge stood in the doorway, afraid to move.

"Marge and I have been looking at housekeeping rooms, not that it's any of your business."

Annie attempted to step by him but he grabbed her arm, his fist raised. "Don't do something you're going to regret, Boots. I'm leaving in a few days and you'll never have to wait for me again."

"Just watch your mouth, woman." he spat out. "I've just come from the Captain's office so I'm not in the mood for any more bullshit. After all that's happened, he dared to tell me I was on indefinite leave, to turn in my badge and gun. The badge and gun I've worn for almost eighteen years. I told him, among other things, to take it off me if he had the guts. I should have gone over the desk and given him the gun right over his head, and I may yet. He said he'd had complaints from the Commissioner. Said nobody wanted to work with me. To hell with them. Said I had to sober up and stay sober. Since when do I need some son of a bitch to tell me what to do?"

Giving Annie a shake, Boots exclaimed, "You see, it's not time to trifle with me. Don't ever, ever keep me waiting again."

Looking steadily up at him, she said calmly, "Take your hands off me, Boots. I'm going back to North Dakota to my family."

A disbelieving, bewildered look crossed his face.

"What? You can't leave. We'll find another house—I can't live here anymore."

"You don't understand, Boots. This marriage is over. I am going home to North Dakota. I'll be gone next Tuesday."

"Why would you go back to that godforsaken North Dakota? You have nothing there. Your family is here."

"Not anymore, Boots. I have a family there that loves me. It is here that I have nothing."

"How can you say that? Haven't I always been a good provider?"

"Yes, my belly was full, but except for Susy, my life was empty. Now what do I have? The crumbs you've given me are not enough to keep me alive."

He dropped her arm and stepped back. "Well, you can't leave me. Just forget it, I need you."

"Of course you do," Annie replied. "Who would do the laundry? What of my need? I need a man to love me and to hell with the laundry."

Boots' shocked voice barked, "Annie, have you lost your mind? You're a middle-aged woman. Don't make a fool of yourself."

"I'm a thirty-five-year-old woman, and I'm free to make a fool of myself if I please. You can believe I'll not do it alone. I'm filing for divorce as soon as possible."

Suddenly sober, Boots' crumpled. "I beg you, Annie, what will I do? What will I ever do?"

Marge stood in stunned silence as she watched a marriage in its death throes.

Boots stumbled against her as he walked blindly, his hands swinging loosely by his side. He paused in the doorway and looked back imploringly at Annie's unrelenting face.

Then he was gone.

Annie and Marge went to bed early, both exhausted from the excitement of the long day downtown. Marge was too excited to sleep, and tossed and turned.

Annie, torn in her plan to leave, the heartbreak of leaving Susy, rationalized, *Of course, I must go, there's nothing for me here. Ruthie sent me a ticket the day she got my phone call. We've always been in touch. And now she wants me to live with her. I need to go, but how can I leave Susy out there alone?*

Annie, she told herself, *you know Susy isn't there. She'll always be with you wherever you go. She would want you to be happy. You know you can't be happy here."*

Annie broke into great racking sobs. *I won't believe that I will never see her dance down the hall again or hear her call me "Mom."*

Too agitated to sleep, Annie got out of bed, slipped on a robe and paced back and forth. Marge sat up in bed trying to find the words to comfort or distract her. "You've told me so many times how strict your folks were, so how in the world did you ever get involved with Boots?"

Annie paused for a moment. "Boots was a migrant farmworker who traveled through the Midwest at harvest time with a group that went from one farm to another, threshing the wheat fields and bringing it to the graineries.

"That was always a frantic time because it seemed the weather was always threatening in late fall. When the rest of the workers finished and moved on, Boots stayed on as a hired hand with our nearest neighbor, two miles south of us.

"The sections were separated by a heavy stand of willows that hung over an old machine shed on our side and a cornfield on the neighbor's side.

"Boots was a twenty-nine-year-old man, six feet two, with black curly hair—he was a heartbreaker, alright." Annie closed her eyes and remembered. "He stood out like a beacon among the fair-haired Swedes and Norwegians. At every church bazaar that winter, girls buzzed around him like bees around a honeycomb.

"Dad complained, 'I thought those damned Irish were all Catholic, so what the hell is he doing at our church bazaars?' If he didn't know, the girls did. I was thrilled when he noticed me and winked.

"None of the locals liked him. 'Why didn't he move on with the rest of 'em.' Dad said. 'Heard he had a nasty temper and is a tough man in a fight, damned Irish. Don't you girls even look in his direction, hear?'

"'We won't Dad.'

"Well, he just happened to be hunting rabbits in the cornfield. I saw him out the window and just happened to remember something I may have forgotten in the machine shed.

"Ruthie begged me not to go. 'You know what Dad said.'

"So that was the beginning. I was crazy in love. At first I was scared, but he said, 'People who loved each other...' You know that old line. Of course, the inevitable happened...

"I don't know how mother knew I was pregnant. She knew before I did. I don't know how she had the courage to tell Dad. When she told me, I didn't believe her. 'NO. NO. NO. How could I be? I'm not even married.' Mother had always told us you had to be married to have babies. We were so innocent."

"'I don't want a baby,' I cried. 'What will I do with a baby? I'm not even out of school. I wish it were dead.'

"I'll never forget the horrified look on mother's face. Now, eighteen years later, God has granted my wish." Annie held herself with both arms as bitter tears washed over her face.

Marge tried to comfort her. "Annie, Annie. How many times did I pray for the same thing? Someday God will remember how young and innocent we were and give us another chance."

Steeling herself, Annie continued. "I saw him sneaking through the field, staying close to the tree line as he had so many times before, waiting at the machine shed.

"Dad walked out of the trees, carrying a pitchfork and I knew that Dad would kill him. I struggled with Mother as she tried to stop me. 'Stay out of this, girl.' But I fought so hard to break free and I ran, crazed with fear, to the shed. I saw Dad leaning on the pitchfork, Boots standing near the wall. Dad spoke so quietly I couldn't hear him, but I heard Boots laugh. 'Married? ME? HELL, NO. If she's knocked up it ain't mine. I ain't the only guy that knows the way to this shed.'

"When I realized what he said, I died. Not all at once, just a little bit at a time until I was numb.

"The pitchfork hit the ground so hard it bounced. Dad's fist came from nowhere, and the blood erupted from Boots' face like a geyser. He staggered back, fell to the ground, tried to get up, made it to his knees. Dad pushed the pitchfork into Boots' neck, the flesh of his throat bulged out, covering the shiny tines. Boots looked dazed, then puzzled. Dad was only five feet nine and one hundred sixty pounds— how could he pack a wallop like that? That look melted across his face like a shadow when he saw the death in Dad's eyes. Boots felt the wet warmth spread across his pants and he sank back against the shed and held his hands up.

"Those hands that had touched every part of my body; those hands I had loved.

"In disgust, Dad told Boots, 'God knows it's a black day when your mongrel blood runs in the same veins as mine, but what's done is done, so let's get to it. You be at the courthouse at one o'clock tomorrow or you're a dead man. It's just a matter of time. You may as well blow your own brains out; it would be a hell of a lot easier than what I'll do to you. You won't leave my girl with an illegitimate bastard in her belly. You be there.'

"'Now get up, you Irish son of a bitch, and get gone.'

"Boots pulled himself up the side of the shed. As he passed me, I could see his teeth through the split in his bloody lips. He stumbled across the field, a trail of blood tracking him through the snow.

"I ran to Dad, fell and wrapped my arms around his knees. I begged hysterically, 'Dad, Dad, don't make me go. I'm so sorry. Please, please, Dad.' He just shook me off and kept walking—didn't speak or even look down.

"I heard Mother calling and calling, but I just lay out there in the willows. Ruthie sneaked out with my heavy coat and a blanket. Mother came out with the lantern. 'Annie, it's no use, he won't let you stay. He won't let Ruthie or me say another word. He scares me. You'll have to pack a suitcase. He's taking you to town tomorrow.' Ruthie and I held each other and cried all night. I heard Mother sobbing, hiding out somewhere.

"Dad wouldn't look at me or speak to me as we drove to town the next day, my makeshift canvas suitcase, one end tied with binder twine, between us. My two uncles sat in back, my Uncle Vern holding a twelve-gauge shotgun.

"I wasn't a pretty bride, what with my eyes swollen shut. Boots wasn't pretty either. His lips were so swollen he couldn't talk, only nod.

"Dad handed him two tickets for Los Angeles and said, 'I'd better never hear of you mistreating her, ain't that far to California and I'm a travelin' man. You be on that three o'clock Great Northern.' He walked away without a glance.

"The last words he ever spoke to me were 'Good night, little girl,' barely forty-eight hours before. I was always his favorite, said I favored his side of the family, that I was a Bjornson through and through. I prayed someday he'd relent, but he got kicked in the head by a mule he was breaking and that killed him.

"Boots couldn't speak, or wouldn't, for the three days and four nights it took to get here. Finally, he said, 'Maybe this is for the best, I always wanted to see Californy.'

"He rented a room until his face healed, then he got a job with the police department. He loved it and told me, 'Your old dad did me a favor. Damn, but he did pack a punch for a little guy. C'mere, Mommy.' He spoke mockingly. 'I paid a high price for you.'

"That which had been a gift of love for me now became a meaningless household chore.

"Susy was a breach baby. I was thirty-six hours in hard labor and nearly died. When Boots dropped me off at the hospital, he said, 'Now, don't plan on me for anything with that kid. I'm busy earning a living and that baby will be your responsibility. Don't care much for kids anyhow.'

"The first time he pulled the blanket back to reveal the baby's face, he was shocked to instinctively know that it was he who was being inspected under his daughter's unflinching scrutiny, her lips curled at the corners in a tiny smile. He laughed to know that he had passed muster. Then his tears dripped on her indignant little red face as his face crumpled. 'My God,' he said almost like a prayer and held out his arms.

"He adored her. She was his only reason to come home. Her first words were *da da* and her first steps were to him. Of course, I adored her, too, but I knew, right from the start, she was daddy's girl.

"He was careful never to have another."

Marge lay sleepless until the first hint of daybreak. She got out of bed quietly, careful not to awaken Annie, who seemed to have cleansed herself of her early memories and now slept heavily. The housekeeping items that Annie had deemed essential for her were packed, the boxes stacked neatly by the door. Annie's lone suitcase was on top.

As Marge sat at the Formica table that had been the silent witness to the gamut of emotions that had known free range in that kitchen; the tears burned behind her eyes.

Now that Annie would actually be gone tonight, Marge thought, *I will sleep alone, among strangers.* Her hands trembled as she sipped her coffee.

As though sensing Marge's apprehension, Annie appeared, moving her chair close to Marge.

They sat silently, the air was charged with conflicting feelings. A vein of sadness pulsed just below the surface. Instinctively, they knew if just one tear escaped, it would release an uncontrollable flood.

"Today is the day," Annie said with forced gaiety. "Everything you need is packed." Then asked, "Captain O'Malley will meet you at the station and bring you back?"

Marge squeezed her eyes shut and nodded wordlessly.

"Everything is ready then. Let me get a cup of coffee and we'll see if we can find a bite to eat. We're ready to fly, little bird, and I want to get there early."

Carrying the suitcase as though it were weightless, they hurried for the streetcar that would take them to the station where the Great Northern waited.

"This suitcase is in better shape than the one I carried eighteen years ago. No binder twine," Annie laughed, but the tremor in her voice betrayed her.

Marge had forgotten how huge the terminal was. The rising crescendo of voices as the hundreds of hurrying people were all going, it seemed, in different directions.

No wonder I was scared to death. Ben had to almost push me off the train. How odd—Ben Olson? I haven't thought of him since then.

The big black engine stood, clanking and groaning, as though impatient to be gone, pushing the white smoke billowing into the blue California sky.

Then, at last, above the clamor of the crowd, the shrill whistle of the engine sounded, announcing its imminent departure.

Annie stood on the steps for a moment as Marge lifted the suitcase to her.

The last-minute piercing whistle of the Great Northern hung in the air as the porter called the final "All aboooard," then lifted the steps and Annie was gone.

Marge felt a tap on her shoulder as Captain O'Malley stepped from the crowd.

"C'mon Marge. I think we could both use a cup of coffee."

The tears in her eyes were reflected in his.

Marge sat silently as they traveled into the familiar San Fernando Valley. They pulled into the driveway of the little yellow house.

O'Malley opened the door for her and she fumbled for the keys as they walked to the entrance. The door stood open.

"How strange. I saw Annie lock the door just before she handed me the keys. What is that awful smell? I hope we didn't forget something on the stove."

The Captain knew before he crossed the threshold what he would find.

Boots' blood, splattered, smeared the satin remnants of the bridal gown that lay like a soft breast beneath his unknowing face. The brain that had always been so enraptured with his daughter now painted the wall behind his big slumped body.

Desperate little rivulets of blood chased down his cheek, dripped over the fingers that held Susy's high-heeled shoe. The other hand pointed silently to the gun, still warm, that lay beside him.

Marge heard the Captain's anguished cry, "Oh, my God, Boots. Boots." She ran down the hallway, terrified by the sound of his voice. The Captain met her in the doorway, blocking her view. She struggled to get past him.

"Is it Boots? Tell me. Tell me, is it Boots?"

"Yes, it's Boots. Marge, you absolutely cannot go in there. Where's the phone?"

Marge leaned against the wall, suddenly sickened by the smell of the comingled blood and gun powder.

She heard his agitated voice as she fled to the bathroom, dropped to her knees and retched until she collapsed, helpless, on the cold tile floor.

Moments later the Captain knelt to pick her up, then carried her to the car. "Promise me you'll stay here? Promise?"

Marge nodded dumbly.

In a moment the sound of sirens screaming preceded the rotating lights of a patrol car that led the coroner's wagon to the little yellow house.

Soon black-and-white patrol cars lined the curb as far as the eye could see. Curious neighbors crowded the sidewalk.

Marge watched with horrified eyes as the door was pushed open. The stretcher, supported by Boots' old-time friends, bumped against the doorjamb. One arm slid from beneath the covering sheet, hung limply, swinging with the motion of the stretcher as though in cadence with his comrade's hurrying feet.

The dark stain coloring his sleeve changed to a tell-tale red as it dripped sluggishly from the big lifeless hand that seemed to wave a final good-bye to his world as the doors of the coroner's wagon closed behind him.

In the background, the shocked murmur of voices.

"Boots was a hard man, but he was always there when you needed him."

"Yeah, he had the respect of every man in the precinct."

"When Malone was your partner, you never had to worry about your back." A choked voice cried "For God's sake, Malone," as if in anger or disbelief.

The tears that streamed unashamedly down O'Malley's face were wiped away with his sleeve. He didn't give a damn if anyone saw him tuck that high-heeled slipper in Boots' jacket.

Marge crouched on the edge of the seat, pillowed her face on her arms as she leaned into the dashboard. The shock had so numbed her mind that the tears seemed to have lost their way and crept out slowly.

She cried for the daughter she had loved and held so briefly. Her eyes screamed with tears for Susy's senseless death, Annie's unfulfilled life, for Boots, who would not live without the daughter who was his life, She mourned for them all.

Drained, she sat back, put her hands over her ears, pinched her eyes tight. *Life was too hard, was it worth the struggle? Would she carry it like the grief of a child or accept it with the strength of a woman?*

The words of Annie's father came back to her. "What's done is done, let's get on with it."

The police had scattered the crowd of curious onlookers and posted a guard when O'Malley finally closed and locked the door to the tragic scene within.

As he reached the car, he anticipated the painful disclosures that would surely follow. He had talked with his Chief, the coroner, and his men. He did not know if he had the strength or the courage to say another word. He forced the very thought of the afternoon's horror to the furthest corner of his brain and prayed that Marge would give him some time.

He paused momentarily with his foot on the running board, lay his head on the top windowsill and let his body relax. He felt like an old, empty, worn-out man who had outlived his ability to deal with life on any terms.

Marge leaned over and slowly opened the door. He stepped in, sat heavily, silently.

He drove slowly, aimlessly. The only sound was that of the passing traffic and the monotonous hum of his tires on the asphalt.

He chanced a quick look at Marge. He saw a composed young woman with her hair tied back, swollen eyes and a tremulous smile. He sensed she had made some decisions that would guide her and give her life meaning.

A startling thought flashed through his mind: *I wish she was my daughter.* Then her calm voice, "Let's find a cup of coffee, Captain."

They stopped at a small café, found a quiet booth and ordered coffee. When the hot, steaming beverage arrived, Marge thought she had never smelled anything so good.

"Ummm, this is just what I needed," the Captain said. "Tastes just as good as it smells, too."

They sipped their coffee slowly. "I know you and Annie had been looking for a light housekeeping room, but weren't you were planning to stay at the house until you found something to your liking? Annie didn't think Boots would come back for awhile." He paused to steady his voice, "But you can't go back now."

"I've been thinking of that, too. I'll have to find a place where I can stay temporarily until I can find a job.

"Annie had just shown me Olvera Street. I loved that area."

"That's close to Chinatown—not a very good location, Marge," the Captain interrupted.

"Well, I have to start some place and it will be easier to find a job downtown, but for tonight, I'm not sure."

He stirred his coffee thoughtfully. "There's a girl in the office who is getting married and moving to the Valley. She has only two more days with us. I surely wish that position wasn't already filled. Let me give her a call, she's a nice person. I'd guess she'd find a bed for you, and you might even like her place. She'll be getting off shift about now, so I'd better hurry."

As she waited for him to return, she leaned back and closed her eyes. Comforted by the quiet buzz of the impersonal voices and her third cup of coffee, she thought, *how different my life could have been if the Captain had been my father.*

He slid in beside her, smiling. "Well, we're in luck. She will be pleased to have you if you don't mind a mess. She's packing now."

A thirty-minute drive, it was quitting time and the streets were getting crowded.

They pulled up in front of a large two-story house that had obviously enjoyed better times, but now had been converted to a rooming house. It was shabby, but it was shelter.

The Captain shook his head. "I can see why she's moving. This is dead center between Chinatown and Olvera Street, and two stories."

The woman who opened the door had just gotten in; it was obvious she had hurried. A jacket thrown over a chair, packing boxes pushed out of the way, dishes in the tiny sink.

"Beth, this is Marge. Marge, this is our Good Samaritan, Beth."

Pushing some things off of a chair, Beth said, "Please sit down. Most everything is packed and I will move them out tomorrow."

"It's been a long day so I won't linger, you ladies have dinner on me tonight. It should be an easy choice." Smiling, he pulled some bills out of his pocket and dropped them into Marge's lap.

"Marge, I'll bring your things over tomorrow and you can decide what you want to do."

Walking to the door, O'Malley said, "Beth, your husband-to-be is a fine man. He'll go up the ladder fast. I wish you every happiness. Good night, ladies."

They heard his footsteps resounding on the stairs.

"Marge, if you will excuse me a moment, I'll freshen up. The bathroom is down the hall—seems like a mile way at night," she laughed.

Marge looked around the room. Though cluttered, it appeared large. In one corner a small kitchen had been sandwiched in. Past that, she could see a smaller room and the corner of a bed.

"I'm starving," Beth announced as she returned. "I haven't eaten since breakfast. How nice of the Captain to treat us. Do you like Chinese food?"

"I don't know, I've never eaten it," Marge replied.

"Well, I love it and there is a wonderful restaurant within walking distance. I'm sure you'll enjoy it. Aren't you hungry?"

Marge thought, *it's been a hundred years since breakfast, I should be.*

As they stepped into the hallway, Beth turned to close and lock the door. The click of the latch brought to Marge the instant reminder that only this morning the Captain had closed and locked the door on a whole year of her life. The tears trembled on her lashes.

Beth led the way walking briskly. Marge hurried to keep up with her and concentrated to avoid the pedestrians that seemed to be moving in every direction.

As they turned a corner, Marge looked up to see an incredible building. Although it was only late afternoon, the neon lights blazed the outline of the graceful, swooping roofline as it pointed heavenward at each corner. Lights twinkled at every window. Marge stopped to stare, jostled by the passing public, awestruck at the beauty of the unfamiliar contours.

She was momentarily distracted by the first sight of a fearsome, fire-belching dragon that wound sinuously in great serpentine loops about the building. All the burning colors of the palette painted his scales, including his huge head with the mouth that encompassed a gilded door.

Beth stepped back to her with a nudge, said laughingly, "C'mon, Marge, it's eat or be eaten."

A petite woman resplendent in a heavily brocaded yellow satin kimono seemed almost to have been waiting for them as they stepped into the softly lighted room. Her blue-black shiny hair piled high in an elaborate arrangement competed with the sheen of the satin.

Speaking in a melodious sing-song voice, she welcomed them in broken English as she escorted them to a splendidly decorated booth. Her jeweled hair sticks glittered as she motioned to the server.

Fragrant green tea steaming in a lacquered teapot appeared almost by magic, with two tiny teacups and the menus.

Marge looked at the menu. "Would you order for me?"

Beth replied, "I'm having chow mein, it's my favorite. I'll order the same for you. It's wonderful."

Marge looked about, fascinated by the exotic surroundings and the unusual language spoken so rapidly.

As they waited, Beth asked curiously, "What kind of job are you looking for? Have you made any plans? It's hard to find a decent job. The Captain only said there had been a death in the family and you needed a place to stay and a job."

"I had hoped to find an office job, but I can do waitress work. I need to find a place to live and then start looking. My finances are limited."

"Why don't you consider my place? It's really quite comfortable and larger than most. Originally I think it was the main bedroom, the smaller room probably for a baby. The rent is very reasonable, twelve dollars a month.

"The old lady who lives downstairs has probably been there all her life. As long as the rent is on time she never bothers anyone, although she has been unhappy with the Indian woman with the kids across the hall. The other two rooms are rented to the old lady's relatives. I hardly ever see them, but the Indian woman is very unfriendly when we happen to meet in the hall. That's fine with me," Beth said.

The food arrived. "Uh, oh. Chopsticks. Those take a little getting used to." She called for a fork.

Beth ate with gusto. Marge discovered that she, too, was hungry. The unfamiliar food was delicious. She watched with amazement at Beth's dexterity with the chopsticks and they laughed like two little girls when a noodle missed its destination and dangled from her mouth.

Beth was excited about her new home in the Valley. "Keith will be coming with his truck in the morning so I'll be completely moved out. Everything but the sofa. I'm leaving that as Keith says he has one with better springs. I hope you won't mind sleeping on it tonight? The Captain is bringing your things tomorrow?"

Marge could only nod.

Their hunger satisfied, they paid and the impressive golden door was opened for them. Marge paused on the threshold to look back and marvel at her first glimpse of the exotic oriental world.

Chapter 12

They walked slowly, Marge's knees trembling with each step. *I'm so terribly tired.*

The thought of the waiting sofa, Beth's comforting voice, "We're almost there, only another block," gave her the energy to go on.

Beth opened the door and kicked off her shoes, seemingly with one motion. Marge sank down in the nearest chair.

"I'm tired, too, and tomorrow will be busy. I'm going to bed early," Beth said. "I think this is the box with the bedding." She pulled out sheets and blankets, took a pillow from her own bed, then tossed Marge a nightgown. "See you in the morning."

Marge was surprised and grateful to find the sofa pulled out to make a double bed. A borrowed towel and washcloth over her arm, she walked down the hallway to the bathroom.

Returning, she stepped back to allow a young, dark-haired girl leading two reluctant, identical little boys, probably four or five years old, she guessed, coming toward her. Marge smiled, but the girl turned her head. Marge felt the unblinking stare of the twin's big black eyes as she continued to her room.

She undressed quickly, slid under the blankets, her body stilled but her mind racing.

She lay in a strange bed that night, insulated by the loneliness of the big city, knowing that tomorrow the sun would shine, the sky would be blue, and the uninitiated would still think Los Angeles was the "City of Angels."

Sometime in the night she heard a baby cry, then she slept.

She lay quietly, her eyes closed for a few moments when she woke, her mind disoriented, overwrought, trying to place herself back with Annie in familiar surroundings. She felt the presence of someone tiptoeing about.

She opened her eyes. Beth was laughing down at her. "I don't need to ask if you slept well. I could hear you breathing, I could say snoring. But, since you're my guest…"

Marge pushed the tangled hair out of her face, sat up and yawned.

"I don't doubt it. I don't know when I have ever been so exhausted." The events of the previous day scattered through her thoughts, but she resisted their intrusions. *No. I can't. I won't think about that. It happened yesterday, today is a new day. I guess Annie must be almost to Denver.*

Then, "I wonder when the Captain will be here. I surely need a change of clothes. Beth, I've been thinking, I could be very comfortable here, two rooms are more than I expected. I love the location and the rent is just right. Also, I don't want to move again. What do you think?"

"I think it's a wise decision. I've been very happy here. That Indian across the hall is the only problem, but if you work all day, you won't see much of her. Besides, I think her time here is running out. She and I had an understanding the first time we met.

"I wonder what time Keith will be here. I thought early." Almost before the words were spoken, a horn sounded. They stepped to the window and looked down to see a loaded pick-up and the Captain's car, three men waving at them.

"Oh my gosh, I'm still in my nightgown." Marge hurried to get into her clothes, grabbed her towel and washcloth and stepped into the hall.

The opposite door opened simultaneously; the Indian woman stepped out and bumped roughly against her.

"Excuse me," Marge stuttered.

"Would you look where you're going? Get the hell out of my way."

Marge stepped back in, leaned against the door, surprised and embarrassed. Beth looked at her curiously, "That was a quick trip. Come look, they're unloading the truck."

Marge stood silent. Beth looked puzzled, then, "Uh-oh, you must have met our neighbor."

"Yes, she bumped me, pushed me up against the wall and told me to get the hell out of her way."

Indignantly, Beth answered, "She tried that just once with me. I had just finished a ten-hour shift and was in no mood for pleasantries. I told her if she ever tried that again, I'd kick her skinny ass all the way downstairs. She's a bully—you have to stand up and fight for yourself in this town or you won't make it."

Marge laughed. "Well, she might kick my ass. But I won't make it easy for her. I can do it if I have to."

Beth grinned, "You're beginning to sound like a native already. I never knew an Irisher who wasn't hell on wheels in a fight. The dirtier, the better. I've got my money on you."

Their conversation was interrupted by the sound of heavy boot steps on the stairs, then the Captain, Keith and his helper plodded in, each carrying a heavy box.

"Whew. What's in these boxes? Rocks?" Keith asked.

"I didn't have any problem with mine. You young fellows aren't in very good shape," the Captain ribbed. Although the words were spoken lightly, the sadness in his eyes, the dejected slope of his shoulders, gave mute testimony as to his state of mind.

"Good morning, ladies. The Captain didn't think there was any point in bringing an empty truck, so we decided to do the move together." Keith smiled as he hugged Beth.

The Captain turned to Marge. "Did you ladies have a good dinner? Chinese or Mexican? I know Beth took good care of you. Beth, does Marge know where that little mom-and-pop market is? Close, isn't it?"

Since almost everything was in boxes, the moving proceeded quickly and efficiently; carrying Beth's possessions down, returning with a load of Marge's boxes, puffing up the steps.

Finally, the dropleaf table with two chairs, leaving only the old dresser and Annie's rocker to retrieve.

"Boots won't need this table and chairs, so I just brought them along," Keith said without looking at Marge.

She turned to see the old dresser with the mirror taped securely, resting sedately on the sidewalk, Annie's rocker standing guard.

"Ready men?" And the three men struggled upward with their heavy burden, the Captain cautioning, "Careful. Careful." Then it was deposited in the small bedroom.

"I'll bring up the rocker," the Captain said. "You poor fellows are worn out."

Marge ran her hand lovingly over the polished wood of the dresser. Annie's reflection in that mirror as she adjusted her hat was stamped irrevocably in Marge's memory.

Was it only yesterday?

"Thank God that's done," Keith exclaimed. "You ladies are moved. We've worn out those stairs."

The Captain added, "Keith, thank you for your help, and your truck. I'll see you later. Beth, thank you, too, for your kindness."

Turning to Marge, O'Malley said, "I'll look in on you from time to time. I've paid the landlady two weeks rent 'til you make up your mind. I've got to go, I've a heavy schedule today. Bye all."

Marge heard his steps go slowly down the stairs, as though the weight of the world rode on his weary shoulders.

"We're leaving, too," Beth added, "but I'll keep in touch. Remember what I said about kicking ass," she laughed. Then she, too, was gone. Marge envied their laughter as they descended the stairs.

For the first time in her life, she was really, truly alone. Her heart raced, she felt dizzy. She reached for a familiar chair and looked about the cluttered room.

Everything she owned in this world was contained in this room, this deadly silent room.

She closed her eyes. Where had the anticipation, the thrill, the excitement of the new adventure gone? She and Annie had planned their new life; now their "nest" seemed suddenly a mockery.

Then the familiar words, almost a mantra, ran through her mind. *What's done is done, get on with it.*

She got to her feet, pushed a smaller box out of the way and was surprised to find on the underside an envelope with her name on it. Annie's written message: "Just to get you started, Marge."

She discovered four eggs in a carefully wrapped carton, a half loaf of bread, paper plates, a cup, a jar of peanut butter, a fruit jar full of coffee grounds, a small enameled coffeepot and a jar of jelly. A knife, fork and spoon clattered to the floor as she shook the box.

She lit the gas burner and very soon the room gave up its silence to the cheerful sound of perking coffee.

The what-ifs, his son's involvement, the guilt and recriminations that had tormented him since Susy's death, waited at his bedside every night to collect their dues.

Yesterday's appalling experience had very nearly brought him to his knees.

As he neared the station, he hesitated, his steps faltered. It took everything he had to step within, nod hello, wave to his officers, then proceed to his office.

He sank into the battered, shapeless chair that had been in the office as long as he had, relieved that he did not have to present to the world a happy face; not in his environment.

His peace was broken by the loud declaration of his clerk.

"Malone just couldn't get past it. That girl was his whole life, he hadn't been sober since she died. Then his wife left him. Damn poor timing if you ask me. But who the hell ever figured he'd eat his gun? He was a rough old bastard, it won't be the same without him."

"Sergeant," the captain growled. "If you're finished with your public announcements, would you take care of this report that was due two days ago? If you could work it in between your other responsibilities in the coffee room, I'd sure as hell appreciate it."

"Sure thing, Captain. I'll get on it right away, Captain." As he hurried out, his voice trailed back over his shoulder. "Boots Malone. Whoever would have thought it?"

The linoleum floor was cold on Marge's feet. Apparently, the heat was controlled by the landlady. The radiator hissed and rattled as it slowly came to life and the room warmed.

Sitting in a familiar chair, drinking her first cup of coffee, she looked around the room, mentally arranging her few possessions.

Let's see . . . the dresser in the bedroom, of course. I'll have to find a bed somewhere, but the sofa will have to do for now. The table and chairs beneath the window. I'm so glad Annie sent those. I'll leave the sofa where it is, right there.

Another cup of coffee. *The shelves above the sink are more than enough for the dishes and cooking utensils. That little cupboard will hold everything else.*

Pushed down in a corner of the last box, Marge was surprised to find an old pair of kitchen curtains. She promptly retrieved some string from a packing box, threading it through the flimsy material. Standing on a chair, she hung it over the kitchen window on the two existing hooks. Leaning back, she admired her handiwork.

Oh, that looks so nice. The faint, sweet fragrance of lavender made Annie's presence seem real as Marge opened the box that contained the bedding.

She closed her eyes for a moment, but then folded the sheets neatly in the dresser's bottom drawer. She paused to survey her morning's work. *Now, this is beginning to look like home. Like my home, my very first home.*

As she flattened the boxes and carried them to the hall, she wasn't sure where they would go.

The opposite door opened and the Indian woman stood in the doorway, a cigarette dangling from her lips. Her small daughter stood behind her holding a baby as the twins pushed past her scrambling down the long hallway fighting and screaming.

"The trash goes in the basement, stupid."

Before Marge could answer, footsteps sounded on the stairs and the angry face of the landlady appeared at the top of the steps.

"Stupid. You're stupid if you think I'm going to put up with this mess. You said you had a baby when I let you in, now it's a baby that cries all night and three more. You damn Indian, you better be lookin' for another place fast because I want you out. I didn't want you in the first place, but I felt sorry for you. Get that cigarette out of my house this instant, damn you."

The small, thin girl handed the baby to her mother, then dragged the struggling twins within.

Blowing a smoke ring into the old lady's face, the woman spat, "Go to hell," her voice low and ugly. "Give me any trouble and I'll burn this shitty dump to the ground with you in it. And you damn well better not turn that gas off again." She slammed the door.

The old lady rolled her eyes heavenward. "That Indian slut. Too bad Custer didn't get her, too." Turning, she clomped her way down the stairs.

Marge had an uncontrollable desire to laugh. *If this is the City of Angels, which angel won that round?*

It's one o'clock, no wonder I'm hungry. Gathering up the flattened boxes, she located the basement door, then found her way out into the sunlit street.

Walking a few short blocks, she saw the sign "Fu Ling's Market" just across from the streetcar stop where a woman was waiting. Marge could hear it rumbling in the distance.

There stood the Indian woman with the usual cigarette seemingly grown fast to the corner of her mouth.

Both women, caught by surprise at the unexpected encounter, took the measure of each other.

Marge looked into the blackest eyes she had ever seen. The woman's hair, tied back with a band of string, was long, straight as a horse's tail, and raven black. The color duplicated the shine reflected in the glitter of her unblinking appraisal.

Her skin, bronzed by the sun, was a dusky, tawny color, slashed by a crimson mouth; the white of the dangling cigarette seemed almost to act as an exclamation point.

She was small, perhaps five-feet three, high-breasted, small-waisted, with rounded hips that tapered into beautifully formed legs.

Her feet were pushed into shapeless high-heeled shoes. Her short, tight dress revealed more than it covered of a body that gave no indication that it had once housed four children.

The streetcar slid to a stop. The woman sneered as she flipped her cigarette, Marge quickly stepping back to avoid the burning tip. She stood motionless for a moment, her rage building, then, with an angry shrug of her shoulder, she continued to the little market.

An unbidden thought spontaneously flared. *That bitch is going to bite off more than she can chew, and when she chows down, we'll see who spits up first.*

At the market, tables were heaped with vegetables she had never even heard of. Piles of oranges and golden bananas hung in great clusters. *Thank goodness they stock Maxwell House coffee.*

She bought as much as she could carry home, including the *Los Angeles Times*, a quart of milk, vegetables (the names of which she couldn't even pronounce), and two chicken thighs.

She was tired when she opened her door.

She made herself a quick lunch. Remembering Susy's fondness for peanut butter, she spread it thickly on her bread, reheated the coffee, and peeled an orange. After all the years on the North Dakota prairie, an orange still seemed a luxury.

Although she was certain a police report had been sent to Annie, she dreaded the letter she must write. She procrastinated, reluctant to relive the past horror.

Just as soon as I put on a pot of soup . . .

Soon, the delicious smell of vegetable soup was wafting through the room and into the hall.

She spent the rest of the afternoon writing on a piece of paper torn from Fu Ling's paper bag that still smelled faintly of the vegetables it had so recently held.

Completed, she folded it into an envelope that had contained the three dollars that Dr. Tom had sent, money she had just spent at the market, thinking *I must write to Dr. Tom also.*

The afternoon lengthened into evening. Comforted by a large bowl of the aromatic soup, she relaxed in Annie's old rocking chair, thumbing through the *L.A. Times* to the classified ads.

Help Wanted – Waitress. She circled three similar ads. She shuddered at the thought of, *Cleaning Woman - 20 cents an hour.*

She heard steps on the stairs and looked out the window to see the Indian woman walking down the dimly lit street. *Where can she be going this late? That's none of my affair.*

Making up the sofa, she lay down and was almost instantly asleep. A baby's crying woke her. *Surely that woman is home by now. Maybe the baby is sick. That is none of my business, but who keeps the children?* She dozed off.

It was after one a.m. when she awoke to stumbling steps on the stairs, drunken laughter, and the slurred words, "No, damnit, no. Get your paws offa me." The door closing.

She drifted back to sleep, only to be shocked to a sitting position by the loud BANG BANG BANG on her door.

Jerking the door open, she was confronted by the Indian woman, leaning drunkenly against the doorjamb, holding out a baby bottle. "Ya got any milk?"

Marge's first impulse was to slam the door, but the sight of the empty baby bottle unnerved her.

Filling the bottle, Marge said, "You've got enough money for booze and cigarettes, but not enough to buy milk for your baby?"

Reaching for the bottle, her black eyes narrowed as she backed away. "SCREW YOU." The ugly words were reflected in the gleam of her eyes.

Marge closed the door and went back to bed, but sleep eluded her. She could not forget the desperate, hopeless look that had surfaced momentarily and fought for equal space with the hate and disillusionment in the woman's black, black eyes.

The sun nudged Marge awake, but she was reluctant to leave the warm bed. Sleep had been almost nonexistent last night. She lay quietly for a moment, listening. All seemed quiet. Turning her back, she covered her eyes. *Just for a little while.*

Oh, I've overslept. Throwing the covers back, she tied Annie's old robe around her, quickly put the coffee on to perk, then hurried down the hall, toothbrush and towel in hand.

Upon her return, she fixed toast and sipped her coffee as she rechecked Annie's worn old map.

What to wear? Marge surveyed her meager wardrobe as it hung suspended from a wire secured by two hooks that spanned two corners of the wall. *Not much to choose from. This matching skirt and blouse should do.*

Pulling a comb through those riotous curls, she wrapped the heavy length around her head and secured it with long pins.

A dusting of powder to cover the freckles that seemed would be hers forever.

With the want ads, three locations encircled, tucked in her purse, she hurried out. Half an hour later, she was standing in front of an unkempt, shabby little building squeezed between a tire repair shop and a pool hall. The men leaning against the wall looked at her appreciatively.

She paused, nervously checking the address. The lettering on the dirty window declared it to be "Bill's Place."

I know what Annie and the Captain would say, but I've got to start somewhere.

She entered the near empty restaurant and stood uncertainly at the counter holding the want ads, looking around at the drab surroundings, and fighting her impulse to leave.

As though sensing her indecision, a man in a tall white hat, wearing a greasy, once-white apron mostly hidden beneath his overhanging belly, emerged from the kitchen.

"Hello, girlie, I own this joint. I'm the fry cook. I guess you're looking for a job? Any experience?"

"I worked at Lowenstein's Deli for a year."

"Well, I can tell you this aren't no deli, girlie, but I'll give you a try with the lunch crowd. Twenty-five cents an hour, maybe more if you work out."

Marge felt uncomfortable as his eyes slid over her and lingered.

"There's a uniform in the basement. Might be a little big, but it will be okay for now." He pointed to the stairs.

She hesitated for a minute, apprehensive. "Better hurry it up, girlie, the lunch crowd will be in …"

As she descended the stairs in the dim light, she could see a cabinet pushed up against the wall, a uniform hung haphazardly, and several overflowing trash cans.

I've milked cows in a better place than this. Smothering her gut instinct, she decided, *I've got to give it a try, I can always quit.*

Crossing her arms, she pulled her blouse over her head, tugged to get her arms out of the sleeves, only to discover she had not undone the tiny row of buttons on the cuffs. Her head imprisoned in the folds of her blouse, her hands above, held captive in the buttoned cuffs, she struggled.

She could sense his presence before she heard the scrape of the trash can as he bumped against it. Then his body pushing her back, her face against the cabinet, his rough hands covering her breasts, his ugly laugh, "Relax, girlie, it's twenty-five cents an hour."

Panting as he pushed, pushed, that hot mouth moving wetly across her back. She shuddered, screamed, her hair tumbling down around her shoulders.

He stepped back to slide a sweaty hand under her skirt. "C'mon, girlie, you know you want it." His hand slid farther up.

She whirled, her hands clawing at his face. He choked for breath as he retreated to the top of the stairs. "You red-headed bitch, you asked for it."

Tears of rage and shame burned in her eyes as she frantically tucked in her blouse. Still standing in the doorway looking down, he laughed at her. "You are a feisty one. Don't think you're right for this job."

Her legs trembled so, she could hardly climb the stairs, still arranging her skirt.

As she passed him, she drew her arm back and with every ounce of strength she had, rammed her elbow in his belly. He gasped for breath, his red face faded to blue as he stumbled back.

"You son of a bitch." Marge said through gritted teeth. "If I were a man, I'd kill you."

The words hung in the air as she smoothed her hair and stepped into the street. She was horrified to know she had used Pa's favorite obscenity, and she was glad. *And Beth would be proud of me*, she laughed.

She almost ran, the sidewalk hot beneath her feet, pushing her way through the pedestrians that crowded the street.

It seemed like a lifetime before she stood exhausted at her own door.

Standing in the middle of the room, with shaking fingers she ripped the buttons off the offending cuffs. She couldn't wait to get into the shower.

Stepping out of her remaining clothes that lay in a heap, she reached for the old robe, then with a new bar of soap and a large towel over her arm, she hastened down the hall to the bathroom.

She turned the worn old faucets on full force. The hot water steamed over her head as she scrubbed furiously, as though to cleanse each individual strand of hair. As she washed, the soapy warm water made her feel clean again. It was heavenly.

The small bathroom was foggy with steam, when fifteen minutes later the familiar BANG BANG sounded on the door.

"Hey, stupid. You've been in there a week, the rent's due."

Outraged, Marge flung the towel over her, holding it closed at the throat. She failed to notice that it covered only her back.

Marge kicked the door open with such force, the window rattled. Marge paused to confront the shocked face of the Indian woman who stared with such intensity.

Then, shrill laughter. "You dyed THAT, too?"

Marge reached for her, but the woman fled, Marge in full pursuit, the towel flowing like a cape behind her.

Marge could almost feel her fingers in that black hair when the door slammed.

Beyond reason, with her hair in wild disarray and the towel hanging limply over a shoulder, Marge pounded the door with her fists.

She raged, "You Indian slut, if you ever knock on my door again, I'll kick your skinny ass all the way back to the reservation." She silently thanked Beth for the quotation.

She heard the woman's unrestrained laughter as she fumbled for her own doorknob.

Chapter 13

Marge sat at the little table, holding her head on her arms. Tears of rage threatened to join the wet that dripped from her hair. She was almost frightened by the intensity of her fury.

What have I ever done that she should treat me this way? How dare she flip her cigarette at me and call me stupid. This confrontation, so soon after the humiliating experience of the morning, was almost unbearable.

She knew if she brought her problems to the Captain, Bill's Place would suffer some severe consequences and her Indian tormentor would be gone in the twinkling of an eye.

The nagging memory of that desperate, despairing look in those black eyes as she begged for milk made that action unthinkable.

I could pull every hair out of that savage's head. But I can't think of her out on the street with four kids. I don't want revenge, all I want is decent treatment. Ruthie always said, "Do unto others as you would have them do unto you."

Through her tears, Marge smiled, remembering their hysterical laughter as they had driven away down that old, rutted dirt road, looking back to see the fire shooting high above the roof. Ruthie's snort of laughter, "Well, it looks like you've done unto them as they've done unto you. Fair enough. You've made a good start. Then adding, "Don't look for trouble, but if it finds you, don't run."

Marge wiped her eyes. *I'm damned if I'm going to run. Since when have I started to use such language?* She answered her own question, almost defiantly. *Since I became a native. And I'm damned if I'm going to take my problems to the Captain. I'll take care of it myself, and I'll take charge of my own life.* She kicked the wet towel aside to join the pile of clothes on the floor, dressed and combed her hair.

A soft knock sounded at the door. Marge hesitated. *She wouldn't dare. Or would she? She'll get more than a bottle of milk this time.*

Marge yanked the door open so suddenly the Captain almost fell in.

"Marge." His startled exclamation, "You must really be glad to see me."

She flushed with embarrassment. "Of course, I'm glad to see you.

Come in, Captain. I'm just fixing a pot of coffee. The door must have stuck."

The Captain looked about appreciatively as he pulled out a chair. "You must have decided to stay, everything looks so nice. Everything okay? No problems?"

"No problems," Marge echoed. "Yes, I plan to stay, I'm very comfortable. I want to thank you again for all your kindnesses. I'm going to start looking for work tomorrow and I must write to Annie again. I'm sure you've contacted her?"

"Yes, of course. Just a quick cup, Marge, and then I must hurry."

Despite his "I must hurry," he lingered, making small talk, then reluctantly, as though the words were forced from him, said, "We buried Boots today, next to Susy. I don't know of a man who hasn't been in Boots' debt one way or another. He was a hard man, but a good cop. We'll never see another like him. He was one of our own. Well, as I said, I must hurry." Adding, "Busy day," as he rose to his feet.

He tipped his hat, then paused at the door. "Marge, if you ever need anything, call me."

Her coffee forgotten, she sat by the window and watched him drive away. *Well, it's been a long hard day I'll not soon forget. Boots is with his daughter at last. I pray Annie will find her peace, her happiness, too.* The tears slipped down Marge's cheeks, but she brushed them away angrily. *I'm done with crying, tomorrow is another day.*

Picking up her purse, she sat down in Annie's chair comforted by the sense of her benefactor's presence and love. She pulled out the wrinkled paper that held the encircled help wanted ads, then searched further to find the equally wrinkled map. Spreading it over her lap, the most appropriate locations, those within a reasonable distance, were underlined.

She closed her eyes, leaned back, dozed for just a moment it seemed; but when she awoke in the semidarkness she could see the city lights appearing as though the City of Angels was afraid of the dark.

Gathering up the papers she folded them neatly into her purse with the thought, *tomorrow, first thing, I'll be out looking. My money is disappearing and the rent will be due. Thank God the Captain paid for the first two weeks, but I won't let him do that again. What would I ever have done without him? He has been a true friend. I'll never forget all his kindnesses.*

She sat with her eyes closed in the growing darkness. She thought of the changes in her life brought about by the kindness of strangers.

Dr. Tom with his financial help and parental support. The loving association of both Ruth and Annie. Mrs. Lowenstein, her teacher and friend. Then added the Captain to the list.

She pushed away any thoughts of sadness or despair, dwelling only on Susy's fun-loving days and Boots' deep love for his daughter.

It's late, I may as well go to bed. I'll be up early tomorrow. She made up her bed and slept soundly, her mind at peace.

She did not hear the door across the hall as it opened quietly, the subsequent "Shhhh. Go to bed." Or the sound of high heels on the stairs.

The early morning found Marge walking briskly down the street. The sun warm on her back, reflecting her image in the tall windows of the storefronts. She smiled at her reflection and adjusted the band that held the torrent of red hair away from her face. Her face, alight with expectation and enthusiasm.

Today would be the day that "just-right" job would be just around the next corner. Of course today would be the day.

She walked, block after block, checking her map. As she rested momentarily on a bench, the sun grew warmer, tendrils of damp hair escaped the confining band and clung to her flushed face.

Then, as the day wore on, her enthusiasm faltered as the answers grew repetitious.

One gruff voice advised her, "Go home, girlie. It can't be any worse there than it is here."

Now it was late afternoon. The hot sun brought the perspiration trickling down her back. Her feet hurt like never before. She felt as though she had trudged over the entire city, answers always the same, "Sorry, miss."

A subtle change seemed to have overshadowed the city. The tall buildings that lined the sidewalks didn't look so glamorous in the failing light. The excitement, the expectations, tarnished as the shadows grew longer with the fading sun. People seemed to walk slower, a look of resignation clung to the defeated droop of their shoulders. Desperation and hunger seemed to make them all as one person.

I wonder if I look like that, too, Marge thought as she waited for the streetcar, relieved when she stepped up and deposited her nickel. She pulled the cord at the stop opposite the little Oriental Market.

Only milk, bread, and a few vegetables went into her sack. She knew it would get heavy as she carried it the eight blocks to her room.

How heavenly a hot shower would feel, some good hot food, the peace and quiet after the noisy, crowded streets. The anticipation made the walk go quickly.

Marge heard the shrill cries of the little Indian girl, the muffled screams and shrieks of the twins before she even started up the stairs. As she reached the hallway, she found the sobbing girl trying in vain to part the two struggling boys. Unable to pass, Marge put her groceries down, then grabbed a grimy little fist and, with a yank, brought him to his feet.

She shook him as she yelled, "You stop that right now. What do you think you're doing? Shame on you."

The girl stepped back, her eyes wide with fear, the other twin crawled behind her skinny legs, his shirt torn, blood and mucous smearing his face.

Marge released the hand she held. He ran to his sister who put a protective arm about him.

"Where is your mother?"

"I dunno. She didn't come home last night."

"Where's the baby?"

The girl answered sullenly, "Asleep."

"You dropped her and she cried." The boy shrugged her arm off as he tattled.

"DID NOT."

"DID TOO."

The black eyes of the three children stared wordlessly at Marge as she stared back. It was as though all four had grown fast on that dirty hallway floor.

What shall I do? Surely their mother will be home soon. I don't want any more trouble with that woman.

Conflicting thoughts raced though her mind. *Let her take care of her own kids. I can hardly take care of myself. This is none of my affair. Dirty, noisy little savages. They are nothing to me.*

She stooped to pick up her grocery bag. At her sudden movement all three rushed, pushing and shoving, squeezing through their own door, slamming it shut.

They close a door about as gently as they knock, Marge muttered silently as she set her groceries down.

You'd think I'd grown horns and a forked tail. But try as she would, she could not erase the picture of the three ragged children looking up at her with those big fathomless eyes.

She put the leftover soup on the gas burner, turned low. Carrying her toiletries, a towel over her arm, she headed for the warm shower she had been anticipating all afternoon.

The shower completed, she hurried back, the tantalizing aroma of the soup permeated the long hallway. In her hurry this morning she just had toast and coffee. Morning had been a long time ago.

Clad in Annie's old robe, her hair up in a towel, she filled a steaming bowl and sat down with a contented sigh. Picked up a spoon...a sound at the door.

Oh no. Please, no, Marge despaired.

Then a timid knock.

If I don't answer, they'll go away. I hope.

But the knock continued, resounded, three pairs of grimy little hands beat a pleading tattoo.

Marge put down her spoon reluctantly, her soup untasted. Tying her hair back, she opened the door. There stood the three Indian children, the baby balanced precariously on the girl's nonexistent hip.

She held out the empty bottle.

"Baby doesn't like crackers," one twin spoke so quietly Marge could only guess at what he'd said.

They huddled together fearfully, poised for instant flight, the girl still thrusting the bottle at Marge.

Resigned, Marge opened the door wider. "Have you kids had anything to eat?"

The girl shifted the baby to the other hip. "We got some crackers."

Again, the boy spoke. "Baby don't like crackers."

"We ain't got bread, too," the other twin added.

My God, they're half-starved and filthy. I've got to feed them. I hope I have enough soup.

"Come in and close the door. I'm not going to bite you. You kids sit at the table and I'll tend to the baby."

Fearfully, the three sidled up to the table, the girl standing to watch Marge as she ladled up three big bowls of soup and laid the spoons out.

Marge quickly heated the baby's milk and reached for her. The girl reluctantly released her hold on her little sister.

Holding the bottle as the baby sucked, Marge was revolted by the smell of the wet, dirty baby and the animal-like sounds as the children devoured their food.

Their spoons clattered against the empty bowls, but the children still sat, their eyes fastened on Marge with such hungry intensity she hurried to open the loaf of bread.

The soup was gone and most of the bread when they moved from the table to watch Marge as she undressed the baby and filled the sink with warm water. With an old soft cloth, she tenderly, carefully, washed the nonresisting baby, surprised to see the little hands and feet, both webbed, the strange little ears, the slanted eyes.

The girl spoke softly, "Ma says she's feebleminded, that's why she don't look like us."

The baby's little bottom was red and raw. Unchanged diapers and general neglect had written its own story on the tender skin.

Cornstarch, do I have any cornstarch? Searching the cupboards, she found it, mentally thanking Annie.

Marge applied it liberally, then made a diaper from one of Annie's old worn dish towels. Wrapping the baby in a towel, she sat in Annie's chair and rocked her to sleep.

The children, their bellies full, sat cross-legged on the floor at her feet and watched with curious eyes at this woman with the red hair who rocked Baby. They wondered at her tears, wiped away with a sleeve.

"Now kids, it's time for all of you to go to bed. Don't wake the baby for goodness sakes," Marge spoke softly.

She refilled the bottle, walked with the girl, the boys trailing behind as though reluctant to leave.

Marge stood on the threshold, the sleeping baby in her arms and surveyed the ravaged, desolate room.

A filthy mattress lay in one corner with a pile of equally filthy blankets twisted in a heap. A roll-away cot was tilted haphazardly on three rollers. The doors to a cupboard stood open revealing an empty cracker box, odds and ends of dirty dishes, an empty milk bottle. Leaning against a trash container, full and overflowing, lay a doll, all the stuffing scattered about. The one window that overlooked the alley was broken, stuffed with newspapers.

Marge shivered.

"She turned the gas off two days ago. It's cold, specially in the morning, at night, too." The girl spoke in a voice she tried to keep steady, her big eyes brimming with tears.

"Boys, go to bed," Marge ordered.

They crowded on the mattress, the girl untangled the blankets to cover them. They lay with their clothes on, their bare feet kicking at each other as they pulled at the flimsy coverings.

"Where do you sleep?" The girl pointed at the foot of the bed.

Marge laid the baby on the roll-away and looked for a blanket.

The door opened and the drunken Indian woman stumbled in. Her face blackened with rage when her bleary eyes finally fastened on Marge.

"What the hell are you doing in my room, with my kids?"

"Mama, don't be mad at her. We knocked on her door because the baby fell and wouldn't stop crying and there wasn't any milk. Don't be mad, Mama." The girl spoke quickly, pleadingly.

"We was hungry, too, Ma," one boy stammered. The other boy added, "She gave us soup, Ma, and washed the baby. Don't hit her, Ma."

The woman's angry glare intensified. "Snooping in my room, messing with my kids. Get out, stupid. And don't you ever come back or I'll have the law on you. I can take care of my own kids. GET OUT. NOW."

"Take care of your own kids? You've been gone all night and day. There's nothing for them to eat and they're filthy, almost as filthy as this stinking room. You're drunk and smell just as bad. I'm going to call the law myself."

"Listen, stupid, get the hell out of here before I pull every hair out of your head." She lunged, but Marge stepped back. The woman lost her balance, and fell to the floor.

Marge looked down. "Well, I guess my hair is safe for tonight," she laughed.

The woman, cursing and rolling about, was trying to get to her feet. Impulsively, Marge kneeled on her, pinning her flailing arms to the floor. Then her tone changed.

"Listen here, you drunken fool. I'm on top and you're on the bottom, flapping around like a fish out of water, so which one of us is stupid? Stupid and drunk."

"You and I are neighbors," continued Marge angrily. "Where I come from, neighbors don't act like you do. Let's introduce ourselves. You repeat after me, 'Pleased to meet you, Marge Reagan.'"

"You go to hell, you're nothing to me," the drunken voice declared.

Marge's hands on the woman's shoulders shook her until her head banged the floor. The boys sat up and watched with interest, but the girl tugged at Marge. "Please don't hurt my mama."

"Say it," Marge demanded.

The woman spit, but the spittle ran down her own chin as she struggled. Marge shook her so roughly that the black hair loosened, covering her face.

"Say it."

"Pleased to meet cha, Marge Reagan, SHITHEAD."

Marge bounced up and down. "You're makin' me mad, Pocahontas. Better say it or we'll be here all night." Marge's grip tightened.

Another shake, "Say it and I'll let you up."

Then a garbled, "Pleased to meet cha, Marge Reagan."

"That's better. Now what's your name?"

Sullenly, "Nina Vey Mahalaseah Johnson."

"And the girl is?"

"Dolly."

And then, "The boys?"

"William, Jr. and William Joseph."

"Glad to meet you Nina Vey," Marge laughed.

Marge stood and pulled the unsteady woman to her feet, guided her to the roll-away where she slumped beside the sleeping baby.

Marge bent to throw the dirty blanket over them when Nina's hands reached up and fastened themselves securely in Marge's hair.

"Is that red mess your own or is it Halloween?" Nina Vey laughed gleefully.

"Ouch. Damnit. That hurts. Let go." Marge gasped as she pried the clutching fingers loose. "Don't bite off more than you can chew, Pocahontas, or I'll have your scalp on my belt."

"Well, you wouldn't a got me down if I wasn't drunk."

"Oh, yeah? Want a give it another try?" Then mockingly, "What's my name again?" as she rubbed her smarting scalp.

Nina considered the alternatives for a moment, then, "Marge Reagan." But there was a hint of laughter beneath the words.

"Thank you, Nina. Now tomorrow, start cleaning up this pig pen. I'll help you. If you don't, I'm calling the law and you can put that in your peace pipe and smoke it. Get yourself and these kids cleaned up and I'll fix some oatmeal for breakfast."

"Pleased to have met you, Nina Vey Mahalaseah Johnson." Marge, laughing softly to herself, closed the door.

Marge shuddered at the thought of the room across the hall as she lay back in her own clean bed. She rubbed her still-smarting scalp and thought, *well, we haven't exactly smoked the peace pipe yet, but it was a good start.*

It seemed as if she had just gone to sleep when there was a tentative knock at the door, then a more insistent thump. Then the sound of muffled voices and a definite bang.

"Oh no. Not those kids again." Now wide awake, she hurried to the door, opened it just enough to stick her head out. There they were.

"It's too early, kids. It's hardly daylight. Go back to bed."

In the dim morning light the children looked anxiously up at her. Wedging as much of his unkempt little body as was possible in the doorway, Billy Joe said accusingly, "Last night you said you'd fix us oatmeal."

"Toast, too," added Billy Jr., the tears starting to form.

The girl stood silently, expectantly, behind her brothers. With a defeated sigh, Marge turned and pulled a robe over her nightgown.

"Have you kids washed up yet? Combed your hair? No breakfast 'til you're cleaned up, and I don't want to hear a sound when you go down that hall." As though she'd waved a magic wand, they disappeared.

Quickly she attended to her own face and hair, put on the coffeepot and prayed there was enough oatmeal left in the nearly empty box. She scraped the last remaining peanut butter from the jar, and spread it sparingly on the few pieces of bread that remained.

The water was still dripping from Billy Joe's rumpled hair as he pushed through the door. Billy Jr., wiping his wet hands on his shirt, was close behind him. Dolly brought up the rear, vainly trying to bring some order to her long black hair.

As the children devoured the food, Marge sat on her unmade bed, still in her robe, sipping her coffee and watching the children as they scraped their bowls.

"How come you boys are both named 'Billy'?"

The girl answered, "Billy Joe is named after his grandpa, William Joseph; Billy Jr. is named for our pa, William Junior. Ma and I just call 'em Billy Joe and Junior."

Billy Joe laid his spoon down.

"We don't know where Pa is. Haven't seen him for a long time."

Junior interrupted, "He's lookin' for gold out with the rattlesnakes, Ma says."

"You kids go home now and tell your ma it's time to get up. We're going to clean your room today, and you all can help. Tell her to come over and have a cup of coffee."

Marge dressed quickly. As she put away the sofa bed, the thought came to her suddenly. *Of course, why didn't I think of it before? Two beds and all those sheets, blankets and towels— where will it all go? Annie said I could have anything I wanted. I'm sure the Captain still has the key. He gave me his card and said to call if I ever needed anything. Well, we need those beds and I want it all.*

She walked quickly down the hall to the telephone and dropped a nickel in the slot.

"Fifty-second Precinct, Captain O'Malley here. Marge? How nice to hear from you. Are you alright? Of course. I'll come by the first free moment I have."

Congratulating herself for her wonderful idea, she pushed the empty cereal bowls aside and poured another cup of coffee. Her stomach growled and reminded her she'd had no dinner the night before. *I'm hungry, too, but what's to eat? That last bowl of soup sounds good.*

Marge looked up to see Nina's sleepy face at the door.

"Ma. She won't let you eat unless you're washed," Billy Joe informed her. "You gotta comb your hair, too," Dolly added.

Nina turned silently away, the children followed her. "Shhh, don't wake Baby."

Marge called after her. "When you're ready, come and have coffee."

It was a strange feeling that swept over Marge as she sat across the table drinking coffee with Nina, her hair neatly combed, tied back with a length of black ribbon hardly discernable in the blue black hair.

It was Nina who spoke first. "I want to thank you for the kindness you've shown my kids. I've been kinda crazy lately, drinkin' and raisin' hell. I've got to get a steady job and straighten up. I've got a part-time temporary shift, nine to eleven p.m. It's better than nothing."

"What about the kids? They shouldn't be alone."

"I can't help that. They'll sleep through if I can keep food in their bellies."

Fumbling in the front of her dress, she pulled out eight one dollar bills, crumpled und dirty. "Would you give three dollars to 'Old Hatchet Face' for me? That should buy another week, maybe.

"I need a dollar for the washing machine, water and electricity, you know. Thank God the sunshine is free. Buy food with the rest of it. Dolly will help you carry it."

"I'm down to three dollars myself, with no job in sight." Marge's shoulders slumped despondently.

"Are you scared, Marge?"

"Yes, I'm scared."

"Me, too. I've been scared all my life. When I was old enough to understand, I was scared I'd be stuck forever on that sandpile they call a reservation. I hated the ugliness, the sickness, the poverty. I hated the hopelessness that hung over the shacks like an incurable disease. I prayed to escape, and I did. Look how much better off I am."

The bitter words cut like a knife. "I escaped into the white man's world when we were forced from our parents and sent to a Catholic boarding school to learn your language and your customs. We were terrified of those black spirits from the afterworld, but they swung those willow switches like real flesh and blood. Indian kids, who had never even known a slap. But we learned more than just the language.

"The government paid for the Indians to go to college, and some of them did. It was a common sight on a Saturday night to see a drunken, blanket-covered Navajo holding up a wall with a bottle in one hand and a diploma in the other. Our white brothers called it 'going back to the blanket.' We never fit in, maybe some of the half-breeds did.

"One cold, cold winter, thirteen of our young men, boys, really, died from drinking antifreeze. Pouring it through a loaf of bread was supposed to filter the poison out. Sure didn't work for them."

Nina finished her coffee, pushed her chair back. "I'd better get that wash going."

A quick knock at the door and the Captain stepped in. He frowned as Nina hurriedly stepped past him.

"You shouldn't be associating with that Indian trash, Marge. What would Annie say?"

"She'd probably say I'm old enough and smart enough to choose who I want to associate with, Captain."

He was embarrassed, hurt by her sharp reply, and eager to make amends.

"Marge, how can I help you?"

"Captain, Annie said I could have anything I wanted from that house, now that we're all gone from there. I want the beds, bed linens, towels—everything that's usable."

"What in the world do you need two beds for?"

"The woman across the hall is sleeping on a filthy mattress with four children. She has no job, no money, the kids are hungry…"

He interrupted, "I'm not putting myself out for a damned Indian. I've got better things to do. Why doesn't she go back to the reservation where she belongs? That's why we gave those Indians a reservation, so they could live by themselves and not bother decent people."

"What of the children? Think of the children," Marge interjected.

"Not my responsibility."

"I'm sorry to have bothered you, Captain, may I have the key?"

"No, I can't give you the key for such foolishness."

"Then I'll break the damned window. I will have those beds if I have to carry them on my back."

He didn't misunderstand the cold fury in her voice.

"Margie, Margie." He laughed nervously, trying to divert her angry outburst. "Then I'll have to arrest you for breaking and entering."

"Then I guess I'll just have to take that 'dime-a-dance' job and buy the beds myself." Tears of rage stood in her big gray eyes.

The Captain threw up his hands in defeat, horrified. "Dime-a-dance?

"Please stop crying, please don't even think of that. I promised Annie I'd look after you, she'd never forgive me. Promise me you'll never do that and I'll have those damned beds here tomorrow. Promise?"

"I promise," Marge said wiping her eyes.

The Captain left, cursing under his breath. *Marge had always been so sensible. Unbelievable that she would get involved with some worthless Indian family. I knew it was a mistake to let her move into this miserable part of town. Now I s'pose I'll have to borrow Keith's truck.*

That night the family across the hall had full bellies and slept on clean sheets.

Marge went gratefully to her own clean bed, tired, but with a feeling of better things to come.

At one a.m., the phone rang and would not cease. Groggy with sleep, Marge finally groped her way down the hall, lifted the receiver to her ear. Nina's frantic voice nearly deafened her.

"Marge, Marge," she sobbed, "for God's sake, will you come down and see if you can get me outta here? Please, please, Marge."

"Where are you? Where? Where's that?"

"They've got me in the Los Angeles City Jail, next to City Hall, with a bunch of whores. They'll kill me," Nina whispered.

The line went dead. Marge looked out the window. It was so dark; the streetlights seemed so dim.

I can't just go out there. Nina will just have to deal with her own problems. Last night she was pulling my hair and tonight she wants me to get her out of jail. How does she think I'm going to do that? Why should I worry about her, I'm not her keeper. I absolutely will not go.

As she pulled her nightgown over her head, *I am not going. What does one wear to a police station in the middle of the night? City Hall. Annie and I were there once. It's got to be fifteen blocks and no streetcars. Where are my shoes?*

Dressed, she grabbed a sweater and her purse and tiptoed down the stairs. She opened the door to the dark, walking as fast as she could, stumbling into a half run. The streetlights seemed miles apart. At last she saw the brightly lit building in the distance.

She was trembling when she pushed through the heavy door of the crowded room.

Nina's small figure was overshadowed by a boisterous group of women, heavily made up, milling around in perpetual motion, their raucous laughter and traded insults kept the bored cops entertained.

Nina, uncaring of the consequences, shoved her way toward Marge, but was held back by the uniformed man who pointed his night stick at her. Despite the chaos and confusion, the long line moved slowly to the desk sergeant.

As the line thinned, Marge nudged her way in. *What am I going to say? I don't even know why she's here.* Desperately Marge searched for an answer. Her head was whirling, her throat was dry. *How did I ever, ever, get into this? What can I say?*

As last she stood in front of the desk sergeant.

In a tired, bored voice, "Name, please?"

"Marge O'Malley."

He looked at her curiously, then, with exaggerated courtesy, "Who brought this lady of the night in?"

The officers looked at each other blankly.

"Well, I haven't seen you before, girly, you must be new in town. A freelancer, huh?"

Outrage replaced Marge's fear as she realized his implication.

"Sir. I am Captain O'Malley's daughter, Marge. Captain O'Malley of the

Fifty-second Precinct."

He stammered an incoherent apology as the cops nearest him exchanged knowing looks, and hid a smile behind their hands.

"Miss O'Malley, what can I do for you?"

"You're holding my father's housekeeper here. It surely must be a case of mistaken identity. Dad will certainly be upset if breakfast is late." Turning, she pointed to Nina.

"That Indian? The sergeant looked shocked. "She's charged with assault, cut a fellow pretty bad, I don't think..."

Handing him the Captain's card, "Perhaps you'd like to call my father?"

"Call O'Malley at two a.m.? Not likely." He nodded to one of the nearby men. "How's that guy doing that got cut?"

"Okay. Lost a little blood, only eight stitches, so drunk he didn't even feel the needle," the officer laughed.

"Well, get that damned squaw out of here before we have a riot," the sergeant cursed.

He dismissed Marge with a disgusted wave of his hand.

Nina passed the cop holding the nightstick with a triumphant smile. Marge walked to meet her, and they stepped out into the night.

They walked in silence for a few blocks, then Nina asked, "What did you say to that desk sergeant? He sure backed off fast, thank God. I've never been in jail.

"When I got off work I took a bottle with me. I offered this guy a drink and he slugged down about half of it. Then handed me his empty bottle and just laughed at me when I wanted my own back. So I hit him with his own bottle. Lucky for him it wasn't full," Nina laughed. "He saw a little blood and ran cryin' to the cops. Eight stitches and he thinks he's dyin', stupid bastard. Then the cops pull me in."

"Well, you shouldn't have been out drunk, drinking with some man. You should have been home with your kids."

Nina's volatile nature surfaced instantly at the reprimand. She sneered, "Pleased to meet cha, 'Miss Goody Two-shoes'. I don't spose you've ever been drunk. Probably a virgin, too."

"I was drunk once and that was enough for me. When I rocked your baby, I thought of my baby. She would be about thirteen months old now, probably have most of her baby teeth, walking pretty good, I'd guess, curly red hair, saying 'mamma'...if she were alive. But she's in a homemade box, deep in the North Dakota prairie."

"Oh, my God, Marge. I am so sorry, so sorry. You are the only woman who has ever been decent to me. I'll never forget it. Forgive me? I know I can live without the men, and I'll try to leave the booze alone."

This was the start of a friendship that lasted through good times and bad for years to come.

Chapter 14

The boys crowded around Marge. "Oatmeal, Marge. We're so hungry."

"Is there any milk? I want some milk."

Baby seemed to have grown fast to Dolly's hip, rubbing her eyes with her little webbed fingers, whining for her bottle.

Half loaf of stale bread, no more milk, what will this baby eat? Marge was sickened by the ever-intruding thought, *will I have to ask the Captain for money?*

She spread the last of the peanut butter on a tired-looking slice of bread, cut it and handed each boy a half.

"Boys, hush. Your ma worked last night. Let her sleep. Payday tomorrow, then we'll have oatmeal and milk, but today...."

She couldn't bear to look into those pleading faces, and she turned away, unable to finish.

Nina appeared, a ragged sweater thrown over an equally ragged nightgown. Reaching for the baby, she handed Dolly a dollar bill. "Run down to the market and get a bottle of milk and a loaf of bread now. Hurry, we're all hungry." The boys were fighting over the last crust.

"Ma, Junior licked all the peanut butter off my toast."

"Did not."

"Did too."

"You kids shut up. As soon as Dolly gets back we'll have more toast and milk, too. There's no coffee?"

Marge shook her head, then, "I thought you didn't get paid until tomorrow."

"I don't. I lifted this dollar right out of that old drunk's pocket, passed out in the back booth."

"*Nina*," Marge exclaimed.

"If he can afford booze, he can afford a donation."

"Nina, that's stealing!"

"Hell. I'll steal before I'll beg. And I've done worse. Isn't there anything to drink? Tea?"

The boys raced to meet Dolly as her footsteps sounded on the stairs. Junior triumphantly carried the milk.

"Mr. Ching gave me bananas. He said they were too ripe to sell." At a glance Marge saw there were very nearly rotten. The boys ate ravenously, mashing their banana on top of their bread, then a glass of milk, mixed generously with water.

"Go play. Stay on this block, on the sidewalk, take your ball and don't fight. Dolly, watch the boys, don't let them in the street."

The baby, her diaper changed, her bottle empty, cuddled closer. Nina's arms tightened around the drowsing child as she studied the different little face. Resignation overtook the sadness in her eyes.

"Baby, Baby, whatever is going to become of you?" There was no answer.

"I've been out every day this week, always the same response. I don't think there's a job in this entire city." Marge's voice broke. "I can't stand to see the kids so hungry. They're like little animals. Have they ever been to school?"

"Well, the boys could start this fall, they're nearly six. Dolly has gone off and on. If we could ever stay in one place long enough I guess she'd have to start first grade again, but they don't have any clothes."

"Dolly ... that's a strange name for an Indian."

"Well, when she was born, Bill was just beside himself, he was so proud. He said she looked just like a little doll and the name stuck. He really was proud to show her off to everyone, except his mother. She wouldn't even look at her. When this last one came and I knew she wasn't right, I never even named her. So she's always been just Baby.

"She was born in an old warehouse down on East Main. The night watchman cut the cord and fed us til I could get on my feet. Then I learned I could make more money on my back. It wasn't an easy decision, but we weren't hungry.

"I got on the wrong corner, damn near got beat to death. So now I'm back to starving.

"Bill's mother, that old bitch. Sittin' in her fine house, her damn dogs eat better than my kids do. She promised Bill she'd send twenty-five dollars general delivery every month for the kids. And she did—twice. I wish I could have told her to stick it."

They sat in silence, sharing the tea bag.

"Oh, did I forget to mention I got fired last night? The boss caught me rollin' that old drunk."

Marge burst into tears. "Now what are we gonna do?"

Nina looked dumbfounded, then laughed. "Why is it you palefaces always cry when your feet are put to the fire?"

The tears ceased instantly as Marge glared at Nina.

"Well, if I rolled a drunk you can bet I'd get the damned billfold and not the pocket change."

She jumped to her feet. "Nina, I'll bet they haven't had time to hire anyone. What's the address? It's just ten a.m., I'm going right down."

"Well, take some of those old-maid pins out of your hair and wear something with some color. Don't do that 'Goody-Two-shoes' act. If he pats you on the ass, don't take it as a personal insult, it's supposed to be a compliment. He's Irish so you might get lucky. Walk in like you own the place."

"O'Hallahan's Irish Pub" read the sign in big, bold letters.

The bar had just opened and seemed empty except for the lone man behind the bar who was rearranging the bottles beneath the long mirror.

"Top of the mornin' to you, Missy. What can we do for you?"

Marge stood silent as she looked around, then she spoke with just a hint of disdain in her voice.

"I was told this was a high-class Irish establishment, but it isn't what I expected, not at all. Are you wiping glasses with that dirty towel?"

The man looked at her in amazement, as he quickly stuffed the towel behind the bar.

"Sean," he called back over his shoulder. "Come on out. I think we got a fresh one here, right off the boat."

A big, good-looking man sauntered from the back room, stood back and looked appraisingly at Marge. His eyes wandered from the top of her head to the toes of her shoes, not missing a thing. He raised his eyes, surprised to see her step back, her hands on her hips, her eyes passing over him so slowly. He flushed and wondered, *had he missed a button?*

A long tendril of the golden-red hair tumbled over her shoulder as she smiled, gray eyes fringed with black lashes, lowered lids with a sidelong glance slanted up at him.

"Faith and Begorrah. Is it a fairy from the Emerald Isle that's come to call? What is your name?" he asked with a smile.

"Mary Margaret Reagan. I'm looking for work. I won't take less than twenty-five cents an hour. It's little experience that I have, but I'm a hard worker and I'm honest. What is your name, sir?"

"My name is Sean O'Hallahan. I'm the owner and this is Timothy O'Leary, the best barkeep in this big city. Learned his trade in the auld country he did. Twenty-five cents an hour you say?" He paused and said, "I don't think so. No experience, it's twenty cents an hour. You're a long way from Ireland, lassie."

"It's sorry I am to have bothered you gentlemen. Mr. O'Leary, use a clean towel on those glasses. Cleanliness is next to godliness. I'm surprised you didn't learn that at your ma's knee."

She turned to go, her mind in turmoil. *How can I go out of here without a job? Maybe I should agree to twenty cents an hour.* She felt the bile rise in her throat. *No, I've stepped in it now, I may as well "hang tough," as Boots would say.*

"Just a moment, lassie, let me think a minute." The men stepped away, exchanged glances, and she heard their quiet laughter, a few murmured words, "...think she'd be honest... a looker, too...that never hurts the trade."

"Enough of this blarney. Do you need help or not?"

O'Hallahan grinned as he stepped toward her. "Can you be here by eight tonight so I can show you what this high-class establishment expects? Rule number one, no sassing the customers." *This red-haired lass looks fully capable of that,* he mused.

"I'll be here." She walked sedately to the door, but she wanted to dance and sing with joy, at last. At last. As she passed him, the barkeeper patted her familiarly. She slapped his hand away.

"You're buying my services, not my arse. Don't touch what don't belong to you." Over her shoulder she saw Sean explode with laughter. She laughed, too, and winked.

Her feet almost danced of their own volition down the sidewalk. Her happiness seemed contagious. The answering smiles of the passing pedestrians made her hurried walk seem like a leisurely stroll among friends. Even the palm trees seemed to dance in her shadow as she passed.

"Hey, girlie, you look so happy you must have seen a vision."

"Better yet, I've found a job." Marge threw back her head and laughed. Her hair, bereft of the confining pins, hung loose as it flowed like fire down her back.

Thank God, twenty-five cents an hour. Tears tangled on her lashes, then wet her cheeks. *Now we can eat.* She never thought to wonder when "I" became "we."

She rushed breathlessly up the stairs, banged on Nina's door.

"Nina, I got the job." The red hair entangled with the black as the two women embraced and whirled around the floor. "Thank God," they exclaimed in unison.

"On second thought, thank God? Thank Nina. Look what I had to go through so you could get that job."

"Yeah. You had to go through his pockets, right? Thanks, Nina."

They giggled like two school girls. But then Nina's volatile mood shifted.

Anger and despair blazed in those big black eyes.

"I've been thinking all morning about that money I'm supposed to be getting. Bill's been gone three years and I've never seen a penny. He's never seen Baby. All I ever got from Bill was four kids, two miscarriages, and a chipped tooth when I mentioned it. He's out there prospectin' in that damned Mojave Desert for gold. He's crazy for gold. He says he knows it's there and some day he's gonna find it. I hope the rattle snakes and tarantulas don't get him first. His mother always grubstakes him 'one more time.' I think she just does that to keep him away from me. I'm gonna call that rich bitch and tell her me and the kids are comin' to visit and we'll sit on her front steps til she pays. I'm gonna raise so much hell in that fancy neighborhood she'll be glad to pay up. I am legally Mrs. William Johnson after all, and I'm not beggin'. I'm gonna call her right now, she's in the phone book, if I can find a nickel … I'm in the right mood."

Her chair toppled backwards as she pushed to her feet, then her steps pounded down the hall. The sound of the nickel dropping, then the explosion of her enraged voice.

"Bill, you son of a bitch. Where in hell am I? Where in hell are you? Home with mommy for another grubstake? Where have you been for three years while me and the kids have been starving? What money? We're at 506 Crenshaw Boulevard, first slum hole at the top of the stairs. Bring money." Her voice screamed down the hall. Marge stood dumbfounded.

Nina yelled for the kids and they scrambled hurriedly up the stairs at the urgency of her voice.

"You kids get cleaned up. Comb your hair, find something clean to wear. Your Dad's coming.

Pandemonium broke out, the kids all trying to use the bathroom at once.

Baby crying, her little face as red and wet as her bottom. Marge lifted her tenderly, bathing her in the sink. Nina searched for a clean diaper. Baby was finally pacified with an extra bottle and an old worn shirt pulled securely around her.

"Marge, I don't have a damn thing to wear," Nina lamented. Without a word, Marge pulled the green prom dress from the wire hanger. "Put a belt around it and you can pull it up if it's too long. Let me help you with your hair."

Nina slipped on the old, run-over shoes, her legs bare, then found her lipstick. "How do I look?"

While they waited, Nina stormed, "Things are gonna be different this time, real different. No more kids, and he's gonna get the money to provide for these kids before he goes if he has to kill that old bitch and collect her insurance. This time is different, you'll see."

A big car slid up to the curb. The horn sounded and Dolly ran, her face alight with joy and expectation. The boys followed slowly, casting anxious glances back at Marge, waiting for their mother who walked slowly, carrying Baby in her makeshift diaper and ragged shirt.

The boys waved to Marge as she stood in the window then they were out of sight. A vague, empty feeling crept over her. She sank weakly into a chair. *Oh, for a cup of coffee. I wonder, do I dare to ask the landlady if I could borrow a cup? Well, all she can say is no. It's worth a try.* She walked quickly down the stairs and tapped on the door. It opened a crack and one suspicious eye peered out.

'Oh, it's you. Been meaning to bring this letter up…came a couple days ago…but I didn't want to meet up with that Indian slut. I see she just drove off in some big fancy car. Wonder what she's up to now?"

Marge waited until the old lady rummaged through a pile of papers, finally producing the letter.

"Hope to God she stays gone." As Marge hesitated, "What do you want?"

Marge stammered, "I wondered if I might borrow a cup of coffee? I just got a job today, but I'm short of money. I'll pay you with my first check."

A long pause, then, "You promise to pay it back?"

"I promise."

Another pause, then a gnarled old head emerged, holding a cup. The door quickly closed, but suddenly reopened.

"Don't make me come and get it." With that, the door slammed shut.

As Marge climbed the stairs, the enticing smell of the rich coffee grounds and the comforting feel of Annie's letter seemed a fitting celebration for a memorable day.

She sat in Annie's chair holding a cup of coffee in her hand, the room warm with the afternoon sun. Her tears blurred the ink as she turned the pages of the open letter in her lap.

My dearest Marge,

Hope this letter finds you well and happy in your new home.

I can't say how sorry I am to tell you Dr. Tom died last week. A heart attack, so he went quickly. His funeral was last Thursday. People came from everywhere. He was a much-loved man. He has always referred to you as his adopted daughter. I know he loved you dearly and was so proud when you graduated with honors.

His will has not been read, but I understand there is a new, young doctor in town who wants to buy his house. We need a doctor here, but no one will ever fill Dr. Tom's shoes. I know how badly you will feel, but life goes on.

Ruthie and I are having a grand time. I've gotten reacquainted with so many of my old friends. My high-school sweetheart lost his wife several years ago and he is raising his two adorable little girls alone.

I miss you and remember our happy days, how Susy laughed when you danced the Charleston at the prom. How can I ever forget. I am happy here and feel I made the right decision. I pray you are happy, too.

Love from both of us, Annie

O'Hallahan's was crowded on Saturday night. "'Tis a poor time to be teaching you, but Maurine will help you. Tim will handle the money." He called an older woman over. "Maurine, this is our new girl. Can I call you Marge? Maurine, will you show her the ropes. Give her a hand if she needs it. I think she's a quick learner." He grinned at Marge and added, "You remember to be polite to my trade, lassie. They're paying our wages. Look lively now."

He needn't have added that as Marge's excitement was obvious in her sparkling eyes and flushed cheeks. Her natural friendliness, quick smile, her saucy repartee soon made her a favorite. A fact that O'Hallahan was quick to note.

It was nearly two a.m. when the door closed on the last customer. Tim asked, "How are you going to get home? Someone going to pick you up?"

"No, I walk."

"Walk. In this neighborhood? Are you daft? I'll run you home if you don't mind riding in my old flivver."

When Tim returned, he said, "Sean, it's a wise choice we made in that little lassie. She is a decent woman, has a natural way with the trade and she's a hard worker. Where's the keys? My feet are killing me. Hurry up. And don't hog the covers tonight."

Four days passed without a word from Nina. The upstairs was so quiet Marge was nervous. *I can't believe I want to hear those kids in the hall. I hope everything is alright.* She was apprehensive, remembering Nina's determination…her declaration regarding changes. *I hope that old woman will survive Nina in case they meet,* Marge snickered to herself. *That insurance is a big incentive to Nina. I wonder if she's coming back.*

The loud, prolonged honking of a car boomed through Marge's sleep. Startled, she threw back the covers and ran to the window. The big car sat idling at the curb, Billy Joe on his father's lap, the steering wheel in his hands. Junior, fighting for the horn, met her startled look, Nina waved to Marge, standing in her nightgown.

Suddenly the hall was crowded once again with the noisy group. Marge's eyes opened with amazement. This was not the ragged, down-at-the-heels family that had stood in this same hall only four days ago.

The boys' hair was cut and combed neatly, new clothing, new shoes, their faces so clean. Big, happy smiles as they hugged Marge enthusiastically. Tears came to her eyes as she saw Nina, dressed beautifully in lovely shoes, sheer stockings, her hair cut in the latest style, holding Baby. Baby, her funny little face framed in a big pink bonnet that matched her pretty dress. Her little feet boasted black patent-leather shoes nearly covered by the ruffle on her socks.

Dolly, reluctant to leave her father, came last, wearing a white dress with long pink streamers hanging from the big bow that fastened in the back. Proudly, she held her foot out to show Marge the soft leather sandal.

Billy Joe took Baby from his mother and held her toward Marge. He said delightedly, "Smell her, Marge, just smell her. Don't she smell good?"

Nina laughed. "I told you things were going to be different this time. His ma grubstaked him one more time. He's leavin' Wednesday, so we'll be home early. Like my hair? Just came by so the kids could show you their new clothes. We've been stayin' in the gardener's apartment over the garage. She don't want me in her fancy house. Guess she thinks I'll pee on the carpet. I just might, too.

"She's sure fussin over the boys, though. Wants to send them to that same school she sent Bill to. Thinks they look like Bill. Fat chance. She can forget that. I'd send them back to the reservation before she'd ever get them. Bill says my worries are over, he'll take care of everything before he goes." Pressing two twenty-dollar bills in Marge's hand, she said, "Look for a decent place to live, close to school. Let's get out of this rat hole. You got a job and I got money," she laughed. "Ain't life just a bowl of cherries?"

The horn sounded impatiently. "Gotta go."

The children clattered down the stairs, but Billy Joe ran back and wrapped his arms around Marge's waist. "I wish you wuz goin' with us. We miss you."

Nina hugged her. "See you Thursday. Things are gonna be better, real different."

With a wave of her hand they were gone. Suddenly Marge felt alone.

Thursday came and went. Another Thursday passed, and still another week was gone. Nina's rent was far in arrears. The old landlady insisted that at least one bed should compensate, but Marge moved Susy's bed in her bedroom and all the linen she could carry.

Susy's bed stood as a mute reminder of the pretty, golden-haired girl who had danced and laughed, who had found such joy in being alive. A girl who would dance and dream no more.

Marge worried. Then she was angry. *She's livin' high- on- the-hog now. Guess she's forgotten who got her out of jail. She could at least call and say she's having fun. I miss the kids, wonder if Baby will ever learn to walk? Dolly sure looked pretty in that white dress, looks just like her mother. I suppose the boys are still fighting. Guess Bill must have decided not to go back prospecting. Hope they're happy. Nina deserves it, she's had a hard life. Maybe she found the gold.*

Finally Marge was resigned to the thought that Nina was gone for good.

"Sean, I think we ought to put Marge on full-time. Maurine is getting old and tired. What do you think?" Tim asked.

"Good idea, let's get her a decent uniform, too. Something green and short. Show off those pretty legs and give this establishment a little class."

"I suppose you'll be wantin' to take the measurements?" Tim gibed.

"Well, it might be I'd hold one end of the tape," Sean grinned.

A full-time job. Marge was delighted. But it was too quiet and lonely in her room.

The two men became like family to her and filled the void that Nina and her brood had left.

To her surprise she enjoyed the camaraderie of the regulars, the give-and-take of the general public, the flattery of the young fellows vying for her attention.

"Faith and begorrah." Sean whistled. "Did you ever see the likes of that lassie? Tim, you got a good eye, that uniform is perfect for her."

Marge blushed with embarrassment. "It's the wrong size, it's too short. I'll take the hem down."

"Don't touch what don't belong to you I once heard a lassie say. But if you drop anything, just let it lay."

The men roared with laughter.

Chapter 15

"Now seriously, there's a party of eight coming in later tonight. 'Tis the new Councilman we've elected, he's coming in for a bit of relaxation. So be on your toes, lassie, he expects the best and I know you'll give him your full attention."

The prior festivities piously attended to, the noisy group arrived late at O'Hallahan's for some serious celebration.

Sean welcomed them at the door and showed them to the lavishly decorated table with cardboard shamrocks and dancing leprechauns.

"'Tis happy I am you won, Mr. Fitzpatrick." Then pulling out a chair for the stout lady beside him, Sean added, "I'm sure your lady is proud of you." She gave him a frosty stare, but Fitzpatrick boomed, "'Tis happy I am to be here, O'Hallahan, with my own kind. That sanctimonious bunch down at City Hall has given me a powerful thirst, they have," as he waved t the barkeep.

"What will be your pleasure, Councilman?"

"The biggest, coldest pitcher of beer you've got, and keep 'em coming."

As Sean turned to leave, he nudged Marge forward. "This lassie will be your waitress, and there's none better in the whole of Ireland." Marge blushed.

Mrs. Fitzpatrick turned to look at Marge. "Didn't they have a uniform in your size? No decent woman would show herself like that. Why, I can see your knees plainly."

The Councilman quickly interrupted, "My dear, what can I get for you?"

"You can get me a taxi. This is no place for a lady." Her chin quivering, "I'm giving you half an hour, and then you'd better be ready to leave."

A silence had fallen over the celebrants, the party mood was dissipating.

"Half an hour is what I'm giving you...you hear?"

Fitzpatrick's soothing, embarrassed voice murmured, "Let me order you a cocktail, dear."

"Waitress. A double shot of bourbon, no ice, and make it snappy."

Marge hurried back with the tray heavy with platters heaped with pickled pig's feet and the bourbon. Fitzpatrick beamed with delight, his followers reaching over each other, not waiting for a platter to be passed.

Sean followed with three pitchers of beer, the froth trickling down the sides of the sweating containers, the heavy mugs crowding the tray. "Cheers" were said, then clapping as the mood lightened and the party gained momentum.

The irate woman asked, "What is this horrible smell? I can't believe you're eating that disgusting thing." She downed the bourbon with a quick toss of her head.

"O'Hallahan knows pickled pig's feet are my favorite. You know, my dear, I haven't had the likes of these since I left the auld country." He motioned to Marge, "Bring my wife another drink and put some whisky in it, on the rocks."

Marge could smell the cheap perfume and carefully placed the drink in front of the irritable, complaining woman.

"What the hell is this ice? If I want ice water I'll order it. Take this back to that dumb barkeep and give me a straight shot. Make it a double—he probably waters it down. And speed it up—are you always so slow?"

"Now, dear, I'm sure this little lassie is doing just fine," the Councilman said as he patted her. She tried to remember Nina's advice: "If he pats you on the ass ... it's supposed to be a compliment," but inwardly she raged and tried to evade his groping hand.

Tim snarled, "If that glass comes back again for ice or no ice, it's going back a Mickey Finn."

Marge had brought several more pitchers of beer plus the bourbon. The party grew louder, more demanding. The Councilman's wife was leaning back in her chair, gently snoring.

Tim complained, "I wish they'd go home, it's past closing time. You must be exhausted, Marge, I am. I'm glad tomorrow's Sunday."

The pub was empty, except for the happy party at the corner table. Sean was standing at the door, talking earnestly to a uniformed man, who was pointing to the clock with one hand, holding a beer in the other.

Fitzpatrick raised his glass in a silent salute with a happy grin.

"One more and then it's home we go, me laddies," he shouted, pounding the table.

"Bring it here, lass, this mug has a hole in the bottom." As she bent to fill his glass, he leaned against her and his hand slid under her skirt.

Surprised and furious, she stumbled back. The tray tilted precariously, then to her horror, the pitcher fell, drenching both the Councilman and his dozing wife.

His companions watched incredulously, then roared with laughter as Fitzpatrick tried to shake the beer from his hair and stem the flow that streamed down his flushed face then over his clothes. His wife, awakened so abruptly by the ice-cold beer cascading over her, screamed.

"Where's the proprietor of this rotten bar? I demand that this trollop be fired right now. Attacking my husband and pouring beer all over us . . . she must be drunk."

Marge stared into the Councilman's furious face. "You reached way up under my skirt and you . . . "

"You're a liar," he shouted.

Without a moment's hesitation, she swung the tray. A sudden thud as it connected with the side of Fitzpatrick's sodden head, then a thin trickle of blood showed at his eyebrow.

"SEAN. SEAN. QUICK. We got a riot goin' on out here," Tim yelled, and scrambled from behind the bar as Sean appeared from nowhere.

Fitzpatrick stood, holding his handkerchief to his face and looked with disbelief at the red stain.

Sean glowered, but Fitzpatrick would not meet his eye.

"I didn't touch that little tart," he declared.

"If she said you were under her skirt, then you were. Better you go home and fondle your own wife. I think that's what she needs, a good, thorough fondling, if you know what I mean." Fitzpatrick's outraged look told Sean he understood.

Mrs. Fitzpatrick was trying to stand, speechless with rage, while the last of the celebrants whooping with laughter found their way to the door.

"I'll have you closed, O'Hallahan." Fitzpatrick stood with an effort.

"Do that. I'm sure the *L.A. Times* would love to publish the story, Councilman. It's sorry I am that I voted for such a damned fool."

Marge laughed through her tears as Sean comforted her with his description of Mrs. Fitzpatrick's face as the beer raced down her ample cleavage.

"I'll be drivin' you home, lass, as soon as I clean up this mess."

Tim spoke over his shoulder as he stacked the chairs and swung the mop. "Get your things together."

Tim drove quickly. When the car pulled to the curb, the beam of the headlights outlined a small, unmoving figure huddled on the lower step of the stairs, half in the shadow of the doorway.

Marge's heart leaped. Instinctively she knew Nina had come home.

Her arms wrapped around the little pile of rags that was Nina and she half carried her, one step at a time, up the stairs that seemed endless. The uncared-for body odors, mingled with the filthy smell of the streets, the hacking cough, painted a vivid picture of Nina's past month.

"Oh Nina, Nina. What have they done to you? Where are the kids?"

"Gone."

"Gone? Gone where?"

In a desperate, defeated whisper, Nina said, "Away. I don't know where."

Marge bathed Nina's unresisting body, burning with fever, as tenderly as she had bathed Nina's Baby. The long hair hung dull, lifeless, as Marge washed and brushed the mats that clung to every strand. For three days she never left Nina's side, except to re-wet, then apply the cold, wet towels to Nina's feverish, malnourished body. She raved in her delirium, but nothing coherent came from her cracked, dry lips.

Oddly enough, it was Tim's old country remedy that broke the fever.

Sean weakly complained of Marge's two-day absence.

Tim promptly retorted, "Monday and Tuesday are our slow days. We can cover for her. She'll have that time come hell or high water, that lassie will, so plan on it. 'Tis a grand thing she's doin', for a damned Indian, too."

"Well, there's a lot of people that think more highly of Indians than they do of the Irish, especially the Irish that share the same bed,"

Sean retorted.

"There's no one in the world I'd rather share a bed with, but I confess, it's worried, I was, when that bonny little red-headed colleen pirated your black heart for twenty-five cents an hour."

"And well you should have been," he teased. "For sure, I do love that little lass, and when she gets back, it's tellin', I am, that you're wipin' glasses with a dirty towel."

With a flip of the towel in Sean's general direction, Tim, laughing, retreated behind the bar.

For three weeks Nina lay weak and exhausted. The days and nights were one as she lay in Annie's old worn robe, willing herself to die.

Marge pleaded, coaxed, almost forced the food she had mashed into a soup-like consistency through Nina's tightly closed lips, ignoring her feeble attempts to avoid the persistent spoon.

Then, another week, Nina lay with her face to the wall, silent, her black hair covering her face. Her only movement was a walk to the bathroom.

"Alright, Pocahontas. Time's up. I'm not getting nurse's wages here. I'm tired of waiting on you. In fact, I'm just plain tired. A man I never knew, but whose words I'll never forget, said, 'What's done is done, now let's get on with it,' and that's very good advice. Now get your skinny ass out of bed and make the coffee, not too strong either. I've been lonesome for you and you've been damn poor company lately," she said, patting Nina gently.

Nina gave Marge a look that would have stopped an elephant, but she swung her feet over the bed, then stood on her shaky legs. One tentative step at a time, she moved slowly to the kitchen and reached for the coffeepot, Annie's old robe dwarfing her frail body, trailing on the floor behind her.

Marge continued, "For heaven's sake, get out of that miserable old robe and get dressed. You can wear something of mine, I burned yours. I'll make some toast, then we'll talk...is the coffee ready?"

Dressed in Marge's clothes, Nina looked like a stick figure. Marge turned her head to hide the tears that dimmed her eyes.

Curled up on the sofa, with a piece of toast, Nina spoke, an edge of disbelief clung to her words.

"I didn't see it comin'. Bill was so happy to see the kids, even Baby. So loving and the kids were crazy for him. He bought them anything they wanted. He had all that money accumulated from his trust fund and he couldn't spend it fast enough. Money that old bitch was supposed to send us, starving' on the street.

"He said he'd made the right arrangements this time, it would never happen again. Everything would be different. He asked me how I felt about putting Baby in the state hospital for the feebleminded. I said NEVER. We love her and we'll take care of her. He didn't bring the subject up again.

"I wouldn't go in the big house, even if she would have let me. We stayed in the little guest house, way out in back. It was a palace for me and the kids. We ate and drank and romanced the nights away. I've paid a high price for that good wine.

"The old lady really doted on the boys. Bill said they had to carry on the Johnson name, he was the last of the line. Of course, they look like Bill, too, lighter skin. One night he said, 'Maybe it would be a good idea to let her send them to the same schools I went to,' those damn fancy schools for rich kids. I don't see where it ever did anything for Bill. It don't take no fancy education to kick around in the sand with a pick and shovel, talkin' to the rattlesnakes.

"She didn't cotton to Dolly. My girl looks too much like me, all Indian. I told Bill, 'Forget it. I'll never let them go.' He said, 'She could do so much more for them, it isn't fair to them.' I got really mad. 'Bullshit. All she ever gave you was money, were you ever happy? Why are you out there on the damned desert by yourself, what have you ever done with your life?'

"Well, we had a pretty loud fight, then his mama's chauffeur took the kids to the movies. Bill and I went to some expensive restaurant, I think the Brown Derby, for dinner. He ordered a bottle of wine that would pay our rent for a year, and then another one and then we took a couple with us. 'Celebrating,' he said. 'I'm leaving for the Mojave tomorrow, my equipment is loaded.' A pick and a shovel is 'equipment'? I asked, and he laughed, wasn't mad anymore. We finished another bottle and I guess I passed out, didn't wake up 'til late afternoon the next day.

"The place was quiet. Bill was gone, the kids were gone. Nothing but empty bottles and full ashtrays. Found a note on the table, propped against a bottle of imported whisky.

"*Nina, the kids are off to boarding school. They said to tell you good-bye.* "The lying bastard." Nina said as the tears started to flow.

"*It is for the best. They will never lack for anything. What can you give them?*

Try to see it my way, Nina. I will be back someday, then we'll see them. Don't look for them, you'll only cause yourself trouble and grief. Take this three hundred dollars and look out for yourself. Mother left this morning, too, for her Palm Beach house, so don't try to cause trouble. Bill

"I been drunk and on the streets 'til my money ran out. Didn't take long, some guy stoled most of it while I was asleep. If I could find Bill, he'd go out the hard way. I'd show him how the Indians do it. He'd lose 'em, one at a time, while he was tellin' me how different he was going to be."

She paused and looked at Marge imploringly. "How was I to know? He was like quicksand. It looked, felt, so safe. Bill was so loving, the kids were so happy, the better life he promised seemed real. I believed because I wanted to believe."

"Baby, Baby, Baby," the cry was torn from her heart. "How can I live without my kids?"

"Who will know that Baby chokes when she gets scared? That she falls down so easy, that she wakes at night and calls for Dolly? Who will know? Who will care? If there is a God, let me die."

She crumpled the uneaten toast and slumped back against the cushions. She sat silently, wiping the tears away with the back of her hand, then continued.

"And what will happen to my Dolly? She won't fit in your world. She won't go back to mine, unknown, unknowing of her own people, used and rejected by your people. She will float between the two worlds as I have. Always on the outside looking in."

The long day passed. Despite her obsessive desire to die, she lived and slowly regained both her mental and physical balance.

Nina was out looking for work the day the landlady puffed up the stairs, handing Marge a letter. She said accusingly, "I know you got somebody up here, ya think I'm deaf? That's two dollars a week more for as long as he stays. He can't be any worse than that damned Indian."

The return address stamped on the envelope read "E.F. Scottvold, Esquire, 104 Main Street, Red River, North Dakota."

Dear Miss Reagan:

This is to inform you that Dr. Tom O'Reilly, deceased, has named you the sole beneficiary of his estate: Twenty-one thousand dollars on deposit in the Liberty Bank of Red River, and a house valued at two thousand dollars.

Dr. Holmsby has offered that amount.

Please advise at your earliest convenience.

Yours sincerely,
Ernest F. Scottvold, Esquire

Tears welled in Marge's eyes as her mind slipped back to Dr. Tom's loving care and financial aid, when never in her life had she needed it more.

Folding the letter, she stuck it in her pocket and walked to the nearest telegraph office. *"Sell house. Open account for me, deposit funds. Marge Reagan."*

She hugged the secret to herself, luxuriating in the rich sense of security that it gave her.

A mission had donated some clothing to Nina, a far cry from what she would have chosen for herself, but served her purpose until she could find a job. Marge paid for the shoes—good, sensible walking shoes.

"No heels?" Nina complained, but with a smile.

Work was what hundreds were looking for, but finally Nina found a night job for twenty cents an hour cleaning the offices at City Hall. She slept on the sofa, always aware of Marge's house rules: No drunks and no men here.

Their social life was scant, due mostly to long hours of hard work. Marge enjoyed flirting with the men who always seemed to have enough money for a few beers.

The flirtations dwindled out due to the intimidating gimlet stare of either Sean or Tim. It always stopped with a wink, a whispered suggestion, and a grin,

Nina's discreet absences centered around a man who came to Los Angeles twice a month to haul supplies for the Army Corps of Engineers, who were building a large dam on the North Fork of the American River near a small town in Northern California.

Both women looked forward to the Sunday afternoons they often spent at the Mexican Bar and Grill on Olvero Street. They loved the spiced food, the ambiance of the little neighborly gathering place and a glass of cold beer.

As they walked arm-in-arm down the cobblestone street, they were a study in contrasts. Nina was a petite five-foot three, with long hair swinging across her shoulders, eyes that would dance with merriment at an off-colored joke, could burn black and cold in an instant rage.

Marge was well aware of the volatile nature that lay close to the surface of that beautiful exterior and the periodic deep depressions that made Nina unapproachable.

Marge was slightly taller with blue eyes that had lost their innocence on the prairie, centuries ago, it seemed. The wide, smiling mouth, always quick with a wisecrack, covering a friendly, outgoing nature; slow to anger, but as Sean said, "When she gets that Irish temper up, hell's comin' with her."

Her red-gold hair, now cut short, fell in curls clinging to her head and spilling to her shoulders. Heads turned and eyes followed the two women, each beautiful in her own way.

The street was a riot of color and crowded with enthusiastic celebrants. The Cinco de Mayo celebration was gathering momentum. A Mariachi trio, accompanying themselves with their guitars, was stomping out the rhythm with their elaborately decorated boots.

Nina, her voice tinged with bitterness, said, "You know, my people were never happy like this. I never saw my mother smile. I guess they didn't have much to be happy about on that godforsaken reservation."

Marge answered, "Nina, you've never told me how you ended up in Los Angeles. Is that where you met Bill?"

Nina paused, "That's a long story. I guess it would take about a fifth of tequila to get through it."

"Couldn't you settle for a few beers?" Marge joked. "You know how you get when you drink tequila."

Juan saw them come in. Almost before they were settled in their usual booth, he appeared with two bottles of beer and glasses. "Buenos dias, Senoritas, welcome."

Marge smiled up at him as she inspected the glasses, then wiped them with a clean napkin. Nina sat silent for a moment, filled her glass, leaned back and laughed, "You wanna hear the story of my life?"

"I was born and raised on the Navajo Lone Pine Reservation, that hell-hole that hugged the Panamint Mountain range on one side, Death Valley on the other. Three hundred acres of prime sand that," a bitter laugh interjected, "produced lots of cactus and rattle snakes." Nina added, "I never really appreciated it until I was learning how to be civilized in that Catholic school. But, I did learn there was something more and whatever it was, I wanted it.

"I lay awake nights, listening to the wind as it tumbled the sand against the tin and cardboard walls that separated us from the intruding desert and the things that crawled in the night; hearing my parent's and my brother's breath an arm's length away.

"I was the oldest of four kids. 'Too pretty' for my own good, the nuns said, and my father watched me like a hawk. But there was no need. I knew I would never settle for what my mother had, or didn't have. I dreamed of the day I could escape to the other world where I would never see the sand again.

"With what little spark my father had left, he built a little three-sided stand along Highway 395 where it crossed one corner of the reservation. He caged up some rattlesnakes and lizards, put some signs out that attracted an occasional tourist who bought a soda pop and asked dumb questions.

"I had just turned fifteen the day I was alone in the stand. I swept up the sand that drifted in at night with every breath of wind. As I finished, I leaned on the broom and gazed off into the distance. I saw a glint of light bounce off the chrome of a fast-moving car. As it passed, the breath caught in my throat. It was so beautiful. A long, sleek, red convertible with a single occupant. Impulsively, I waved and the car slowed, hesitated, then turned back. Idling for a moment as he looked at me, he smiled as he stepped from behind the wheel.

"He was young, later he told me he was twenty-two. As he walked toward me, I thought my heart would break. I knew the likes of him were not for me.

"He asked me, 'Got anything ice-cold to drink? Nothing is even damp in this desert.' He grinned at me and I felt a warmth I had never known before flood over me. I trembled as I handed him the lukewarm soda. He smelled so good.

"He held out a nickel, but then raised his hand to my face and slowly slid his hand down my arm, so dark against his white fingers. The faint sound of the nickel fell on the floor as I grasped his wrist. Instinctively, every part of me knew what was happening. I must have been radiant with joy.

"'Wanna go for a ride?'

"I heard my father's despairing plea, 'Neva, Neva, no.' He rounded the corner in time to see me scrambling into the car. Then there was only the sound of the big car's accelerating motor, the wind in my hair.

"'How old are you?'

"'Eighteen . . . keep drivin'.' I knew I'd never go back."

Nina paused, put down her empty glass. "Marge, I feel like it must be my birthday. Juan, bring us a couple of shots of tequila. You'll drink to my birthday won't you, Marge?"

"You know me Nina, a couple of beers is my limit. The last time you had a birthday, only a few months ago, it took Juan and I plus two others to carry you home, kickin' and cussin', and the landlady ran us off."

"What the hell. I'll drink 'em myself. I get thirsty tellin' you my life story. *True Confessions* would probably buy it from me."

Two shots of tequila later . . . "Where was I? Oh … we got down the road about a hundred miles and stopped at some little town for gas. He asked me what my name was."

"'N e v a V e y M a h a l a s e a h.'

"'What the hell does that mean in English?'

"'Little-Bird-That-Sings-in-the-Night.'

"'I'll just call you Nina. If you don't mind.'

"He didn't seem to give a damn that people stared at him walking down the street with a ragged, barefoot Indian girl holding tight to his hand.

"It was later in the afternoon when we drove into Barstow.

"'Guess I should get you a toothbrush or somethin'. How about a new dress, shoes? C'mon, it'll be fun to dress you up. You'll look like a little doll.'

"He didn't have to coax me. He picked out everything. Even my first lipstick. And high-heeled shoes that I couldn't walk in. I felt like a princess. He checked in at a little rundown hotel, I followed, my new clothes pushed in a paper sack held tight in my arms. A bottle of wine and a carton of cigarettes in his.

"I was drunk before he ever opened the wine. Drunk with happiness. I modeled all the dresses for him as he lay propped up on the bed, drinking wine from a paper cup and watching.

"'We forgot a nightgown,' I said. We laughed. He pulled the dress over my head; my hair got caught in the buttons, his breath was hot on my skinny shoulders as he worked to free me. I stood there, naked, in my high-heeled shoes."

Nina paused, her eyes dreamy, as she relived the moment.

"Well, we got pretty well-acquainted that first night. When he realized I was a virgin, he was really easy with me. For sure I wasn't his first, nor his last, either. He's never deprived himself.

"He was my whole life. In the beginning, I was just a new, different toy for his pleasure, but then, as time went on, I think he learned to care for me. When he really knew I loved him for himself, wasn't after his money like the others.

"We laid up in Barstow for awhile. Eatin', makin' love, talkin', sleepin' . . . wakin' up to do it all over again. Bill said he'd been gallivantin' all over the country in that pretty car, raisin' hell and spendin' money. Told me where he lived and talked about his father.

"'Dad was a millionaire, made his money with government contracts during the war,' Bill said. 'He died a couple of years ago. I loved him, he was all I had. My mother got it all but my trust fund. That's when I hit the road. She's high society and rotten to the core. I despise her. Private schools, expensive camps in the summer, was the closest I ever got to her, and later, as I grew older, closer than I wanted to be. I lived in the guest house, way out behind the tennis court.'

"I could tell Bill was gettin' itchy feet again; he was tired of Barstow.

"'Let's go someplace,' Bill urged. 'Wonder what they're doin' down in Texas, besides rustlin' cows?'

"By that evening we were headin' for Texas. We had to cross that damned desert again, but he loved it.

"'Someday I'm gonna go prospectin'. I know there's gold here and I'm gonna find it.' There was never a doubt in his mind.

"I didn't think much of Texas, although I liked El Paso. I wasn't feelin' good and I was scared I had TB like so many of the Indians on the reservation.

"'Hell,' Bill said, 'I'll bet you're pregnant.'

"I didn't want to be pregnant. None of those pretty dresses fit and my feet swelled so I couldn't even wear my high heels. Bill was tickled silly. He would lay his head on my belly and say, 'Talk to me, Junior.' and when the baby kicked, Bill would just whoop, 'Yeah, it's a boy, alright.'

"I liked El Paso and I didn't want to leave, but Bill was restless, said there was somethin' he needed to do in Los Angeles, then we'd come back.

"I wasn't sixteen yet and six months pregnant.

"When we got into Los Angeles he bought me a pretty white dress I could get over my belly. Didn't ask me, just took me by the hand, walked me into City Hall and we were married by the County Clerk, the same City Hall I'm cleanin' now. Ain't that a kick."

Nina stopped and leaned back, closed her eyes. "If you want the rest of this story, pour me a double," she demanded.

Juan stepped forward, but Marge covered the glass and the tequila slid over her hand to the table. Nina raised the glass and swallowed.

"Damn you, Juan. You've watered this shit down. Don't think I'm too drunk to know the difference. Bring a towel, you've slopped it all over," Nina complained.

"Well," she continued, "we drive through this residential section with houses I've never even dreamed of, then up a long windin' driveway to the biggest house I've ever seen, all lit up like a Christmas tree.

"'Home sweet home,' Bill sneered as he tossed the keys to some guy that was parking cars.

"I didn't want to get out of the car but Bill took me by the hand and said, 'C'mon, this is gonna be fun.' I was scared to death, hung on to his hand for dear life. The place was packed with people dressed to kill...eatin' and drinkin', a band playin'. Someone was singin' 'Happy Birthday' to this woman that was standing in front of the musicians, holdin' a glass and smokin' a cigarette. She had a ring on her finger, a stone as big as a nickel that about blinded me.

"Bill walked up to her, cool as a cucumber, waved the band quiet. 'Hello, Mother. Didn't think I'd forget your birthday, did you? Surprise.' Pulling me forward, 'Your birthday present. Your brand new daughter-in-law.'

"She choked and dropped her drink. I thought she would have a heart attack. She stepped back as though I was contagious, then forced a little laugh. 'Bill. How nice to see you.' She turned to the suddenly quiet guests, her voice shook. 'You're such a practical joker, Bill. Such a sense of humor. Why would I be surprised?'

"Bill put his arm around me, turned to the orchestra. 'Play something pretty for my bride, Mrs. William J. Johnson.' We waltzed around the floor, the guests started to clap. His mother cut in and hissed like the worst snake my father ever had. 'Get that squaw out of my house.' I never saw Bill laugh so hard.

"'We'll be staying at the guest house, Mother, if you'd like to rock your grandchild.'

"He surprised us both when he scooped me up and carried me through the door of the little guest house, my arms around his neck, loving the feel of him.

"Dolly was born three months later, a quick, hard labor. The doctor was there. He handed the baby, wrapped in a towel, to Bill. Wild with delight, I'll never forget Bill saying, 'He looks just like my father.' The doctor laughing, 'Better look again,' pulling back the towel. Didn't matter to Bill.

"'She's beautiful. Just a little doll.'

"She was always Bill's favorite, although we had twin boys who did look like his father.

"He got that prospecting bug when the boys were three. It was a quick kiss, a wave good-bye and 'Be good.' How the hell could I be anything else? Three kids and pregnant with Baby, plus two miscarriages and I wasn't even twenty.

"He put the convertible in storage so his mother couldn't touch it, made arrangements, he said, for me to get half of his monthly check. How that old bitch queered it, I'll never know.

"Two days after he left, a cop knocked on the door and said I was being evicted for trespassing. I banged on the door of the big house. His mother yelled through the window, 'Go back to the reservation where you belong, you Indian whore. I'll keep the boys, but that girl can go to hell.'

"So I'm on the street with a hundred twenty dollars in my pocket. I've seen him once, when he stole my kids. ONCE IN THREE YEARS.

"I hope to hell he fries out there with the rattlesnakes in that damned desert. He's been prospectin' for that gold that he knew 'was right there' all these years. All he's ever found was sand and cactus. I hate that thievin' bastard."

Marge put her arms around the now openly sobbing Nina. "C'mon, let's go home."

"Juan, I think you'll have to call us a cab. Drinkin' makes us awful tired."

Marge was considered "family," not just "help" by the proprietor's of O'Hallahan's Pub, and her name had become synonymous with the Pub over the last five years.

She came to work one day and was met at the door by a jubilant Sean who pounced, whirling her around and around. Puffing from the exertion, he spoke, the words tumbling over themselves with excitement.

"Lass, time seems to have flown by like magic. You've been here almost from the start, and it's lucky we were to have had you. Now it's good news I have to share. My grandpa, God rest his weary head, has passed on, left the auld family farm to me. We'll be celebratin' Tim's birthday dancin' with the leprechauns. 'Tis my grandpa's gift to both of us.

"How grand 'twill be to see the auld house with the sod roof and crooked windows waitin' for us in that green meadow where the shamrocks grow. That auld house that sheltered three generations of O'Hallahan's. Faith and begorrah. 'Tis the good life for us gentlemen farmers."

"And when might all this be happening?" Marge asked, caught up in their joy, but knowing what a large part of her life they had become. How she would miss their easy camaraderie and love.

"Just as soon as some lucky devil comes up with the greenbacks." Tim declared.

O'Hallahan's pub had been established for years on a choice corner of the City. It was a benchmark of the architectural standard of the times. The City seemed to have grown around it. They had no difficulty finding a buyer in a few short months.

Marge dried her eyes as she stood on the pier knowing that part of her life was finished when they waved from the deck of a large ship, bound for the Emerald Isle.

Tenants had come and gone but Marge and Nina still lived at the same rooming house. Nina did not want to move, hoping against hope that Bill would come back and she would see her children again.

As the years passed, she resigned herself to the very real possibility that it wasn't going to happen. When she allowed herself to think of them, she dropped into a bottomless pit of depression that frightened Marge.

Nina would lay motionless for hours, hours that lengthened into weeks. She once sunk deep into her own cold, dark, pitiless world for several months.

Her cleaning job at City Hall was terminated when she physically extracted an apology from some person who rashly commented on her ancestry. After weeks of desperately searching, she found a job that paid twenty cents an hour in a rundown Chinese restaurant bordering Alvarado Street.

"The gal that's leaving says his waitresses had to 'put out' or 'get out.' He can't keep his kimono buttoned," Nina snickered. "I can stall him for a little while until I can find something better. He's got a young indentured Chinese kid workin' fourteen hours a day, seven days a week in the kitchen. The kid can hardly speak any English, scared to death. He got six more years to work, the boss says, to pay off his passage. Hell, the kid will be dead by then, worked to death."

"Indentured?" Marge questioned.

"Yeah, that old chink has got a slave for as long as the kid lives, I'd bet. Most of the Chinamen come over that way. Workin' for somebody who paid their passage.

"Of course, everybody takes advantage of them, poor devils. They live like animals. At least us savages got a reservation from our white brothers." With a bitter laugh, she added, "Now ain't that blind luck?"

She fell silent, a faraway expression crept across her face. Then, "Cody wants me to move to Auburn, that's a little town up North, not far from Sacramento. Said I could work at his brother's place. But now his brother wants to sell and tramp through the hills lookin' for gold. Cody says they've found some good spots and now there's a big rush. The government is building a big dam up there, too, so the little town is growing. He says it's a good opportunity goin' to waste. Of course, I can't. Bill might come back. Then how would he find me? I'd never see the kids again. They're getting big. Dolly will be fourteen, almost a woman. I wonder if Baby ever learned to walk." She closed her eyes and groaned, "Oh, my boys. My boys."

"You aren't going to get in one of those moods again, are you Nina?" Marge asked anxiously.

"Hell no. I never felt better. I gotta get to work, see you later." She left, despair stuck tight to her like a second skin as she fled down the stairs.

A few weeks later, on Nina's day off, they were seated in their usual booth at Juan's Hideaway when, for the first time, Marge met Cody. He was on one of his semimonthly trips to Los Angeles to buy supplies for the crew working on the Ruck-A-Chucky Dam.

Marge was impressed with his good nature and quiet, courteous treatment of Nina. It was obvious he was more than a friend.

Juan hovered over them.

Nina spoke hopefully, "I think we ought to celebrate, Cody's back. Bring us a bottle of tequila."

"Three beers." Marge interrupted, turning to Nina. "You just had another birthday if you can remember, and I can't forget."

Nina pouted through several beers, then excused herself to go to the door marked "Senoritas."

Cody made small talk as they waited for her return. Marge's eye wandered to the bar. Caught in the act, laughing, Nina raised her glass in a giddy salute.

"Well, how's the job going, Nina?" Cody asked when she returned.

Nina's face flushed with instant rage. "If that old bastard says 'No tickee, no washee' one more time, I'm gonna split his head with his own cleaver. One more 'cop-a-feel' and he's a dead man. I hit him upside his pigtail with a bag of rice last night in the kitchen. His slanty eyes crossed like this…" She held up two fingers. "So time is limited and it's back to poundin' the sidewalk." Her black eyes mirrored her frustration.

Cody couldn't help his laughter. "Hey, take it easy. Marge is supposed to be the hot-headed Irish gal; you're the stoic Indian, remember? Bet he outweighs you by a hundred pounds. I doubt you could hold him down long enough to scalp him."

"I'm gonna cut off more than his pigtail the next time he puts his hand on my ass." Nina retorted.

Then in a serious voice, Cody coaxed, "Sure wish you gals could find somebody to grubstake you so you could buy my brother's restaurant. It's even got a little two-story shack that's livable. He bought a claim up on the American River and can't wait to start diggin'. He'd sell cheap. It's a wonderful opportunity."

"C'mon, Nina, let's go home and get you sober. Tomorrow is another day." Marge urged.

"I'm ready," Nina answered as she rose unsteadily to her feet, one hand enclosed in Cody's big calloused hand, the other tucked securely under Marge's arm.

The seed had been planted. It sprouted and came to full harvest as Marge lay awake that night.

One month later they were on their way to Auburn. Tucked among the month's supplies for the Army Corps of Engineers were Annie's dresser, her rocking chair, and a terrified but determined nineteen-year-old Chinese boy, whose name was Ah Sing.

It was late Saturday afternoon when the truck pulled up a narrow street on the outskirts of the little town of Auburn, population fifteen hundred, a gathering of buildings held captive by the low sloping foothills that hugged the rugged Sierra Nevada mountains.

"I sure as hell hope you know what we're doin', Marge, this ain't nothin' but a stopover for mountain goats. You're gonna be buyin' me a ticket back to civilization if things don't look up pretty damn soon. Cody, what the hell are we stoppin' for?"

He swung the door open and with a sweeping motion of his arm, he pointed to a long, low structure crouched up against a vast sea of weeds and vines that crawled over it, nearly obscuring the faded, hand-painted sign that declared it to be "NICK'S EMPORIUM."

"C'mon girls, get out. This is home," Cody announced happily.

Neither woman moved. Nina snickered, "So that's an 'emporium'. I always wondered what an emporium looked like. Now let's go home."

"Well, Nick was always one for big words. He's the one with book learnin' in our family. C'mon girls."

Marge's first glimpse of her purchase—sight unseen, but encouraged by Cody's glowing description—was utter disbelief. *How could I?* The panic-stricken thought pounded through her brain. *How could I have wasted three thousand five hundred dollars of Dr. Tom's money for a shack in the middle of nowhere. I've trusted a man I've hardly known. What a fool I am.*

They were parked in the shadows of massive steel skeletons that outlined the sky and seemed to push into the clouds. Steel pipes for penstocks, six feet in diameter, to take water from forebays to turbines in huge, noisy dynamos in the power stations, owned and operated by Pacific Gas and Electric, that squatted beneath them.

"What is that horrible thing?" Nina asked. "It looks like a giant spider and it's right on top of us."

Cody tried to explain. "It's transporting water for power." Nina interrupted sarcastically, "Sure distracts from the beauty of the Emporium."

Marge stepped down from the cab, shaking with rage. "Cody. How could you lie to me like this? How could you? How could I have been such a fool?"

Nina got out to stand with Marge. Ah Sing, alerted by the tone of Marge's voice, crawled fearfully from his nest in the back of the truck and stood beside them.

"Now Marge, you listen to me. I didn't lie to you. I told you it was a golden opportunity to get out of that hell hole, own your own place, be your own boss, and make a good living. And you're lookin' at it. There's nothing wrong with this that a little paint and a lot of elbow grease won't fix. I'll get you some cheap labor and you can make it anything you want. It's yours. Look at this parking lot. It's packed and it's only five o'clock. Beer has just been legalized and business is booming, as you're smart enough to see. Don't be comparing this to O'Hallahan's Pub. Let's go see the rest of it."

They followed behind him, chastened and silent, as he opened the door to the packed, smoked-filled room. Noisy laughter and the wailing voice from the nickelodeon were bouncing off the walls.

Cody shouldered his way to the front, the women and Ah Sing in his footsteps. The music stopped suddenly as he pulled the plug, then rapping his keys on the bar, he announced in the abrupt silence:

"Listen up boys. I want you to meet the new proprietor, Marge Reagan, her sidekick, Nina, and Ah Sing, the answer to a cook's prayer."

Dead silence. Then the riotous clapping, foot-stomping and wolf whistles rocked the room until Marge, in spite of herself, laughed and waved.

Nina, not to be outdone, did the same.

Ah Sing disappeared into the kitchen.

Nick, his face wreathed in smiles, stepped from behind the bar, wiping his hands on his apron before offering them to the ladies.

"You can't know how glad I am to see you. Cody, you sure can pick 'em."

Again, the room was in an uproar.

"Show the ladies Marge's new home. Please excuse a bachelor's messy quarters. See you later Cody, it's a busy night," as he hurried behind the bar.

As the door closed behind the trio, Nick grinned. "Well, boys, don't say I didn't leave you in good hands. Won't those gals be an improvement around here? My new address will be at the 'For Sure' mine, upper Cow Creek Canyon. If you visit, bring a bottle and your own shovel."

The voices muted behind them as they walked up a winding overgrown path behind the bar, then crossed the shaky footbridge that spanned the gully below.

Marge looked up at the little cabin that hung precariously on the hillside. A crooked stovepipe at a slanted angle to avoid the tiny room that perched like an oversized sparrow on the patched roof. Heavy blackberry vines, now in bloom, gave the cabin a soft, misty aura and clung tenaciously to cover a wall. Two apple trees, long past their prime, bore pristine white flowers promising the fruit yet to come.

Nina, reluctantly, gave it her stamp of approval. "I've lived in a hell of a lot worse."

It was so blessedly quiet, so peaceful. Marge stood back and looked at the little cabin—it seemed to welcome her. Remembering Cody's caustic words,

"It ain't L.A., you know." Marge spoke fervently to herself, *Thank God.* Then, *I think I've come home.*

She pushed open the doors and stood on the threshold, surveying a large room. Obviously it was bachelor's quarters. Rough-sawn plank floors, no curtains, denying the presence that any woman had ever lived here. Yet there was that faded, peeling, rose-covered wallpaper in the room adjoining, a bedroom, judging by the sagging, unmade bed and clutter of clothes.

In the back corner, a sink full of dishes, wooden shelves holding miscellaneous pots and pans, a wood-burning stove, a table with two benches indicated a kitchen.

Short, steep steps pointed to the room above, snugged to a sharply pitched roof.

"Well, it doesn't leak and it's got to be steep because it snows pretty hard up here. The snow would crush it if it couldn't roll off," Cody explained.

"Guess I'll sleep downstairs," Nina said.

"Guess you won't," replied Marge.

The front window overlooked the bar. Gazing out, Marge was surprised to see saddled horses tied to a rail beyond the parked cars.

Cody explained, "Many of the miners live near their mines way up in the canyons where there are only trails. There's still enough gold in these hills to make a good living."

What Cody didn't say was that the lucky strikes that made some men millionaires overnight were in stark contrast to the many who labored and endured incredible hardships for the occasional nugget they found that fueled their passion and held them tight in a golden web.

"Let's get something to eat, I'm starved," Cody complained. "C'mon, I'll show you some of the town before it gets dark."

As they drove down the main street he pointed out various buildings. "There's Star Theater, showing a new picture with Tom Mix called "The Lone Ranger." There's the barber shop, haircuts fifty cents, a new JC Penney store opening next week, and the foundation for Montgomery Ward. Gonna cost forty-five thousand dollars, they say. That's the Placer County School over there and that big building up the hill is the Court House, built in 1914. That's where you'll go tomorrow to get the paperwork done for your new property, Marge."

Cody guided them into the Shanghai Restaurant. They lingered over the tasty food.

Nina leaned back and questioned, "If this is Chinese food, I wonder what we were servin' back in Ah Chung's joint? Bet his pigtail stood straight out when he came in Friday morning and found his boy gone and his cash drawer empty." She smiled devilishly. "I figured it all out, for every time he copped a feel, I charged him five dollars. Odd how quickly that counts up." She added, "This ass don't come cheap."

When they stopped laughing, Cody said, "Lots of Chinese up here. They get treated pretty rough. They work too cheap and that annoys the white people. Lots of Indians around, too. The U.S. government gave them the American Indian Rancheria, a fancy name for reservation land adjoining the south side of Auburn."

He yawned, "It's been a long day and I gotta get this load up the hill. I'll drop you off at the Traveler's Hotel. It's old, but clean. Marge, I'll help you with whatever you decide to do."

Marge lay awake unable to sleep.

Chapter 16

As she reviewed the long day, the plans whirled in her head. The opportunity that the little town offered became clear to her, and she could hardly wait for the morning sun to rise.

The next morning when the doors were open, Marge was there.

"It's mine. All mine." She exulted, "It says so, right here on this paper." Standing on the courthouse steps, she kissed the notary's signature.

"I've never had anything of real value before and now I own an acre of land, a restaurant and a house." Marge's face was radiant. Her red hair, grown long, swirled about her shoulders as she flung her arms around Nina in a wild surge of joy.

"Nina, it's a new start. A new life. It can be anything we want it to be. Thank God."

"Stop dancing around like that, or you'll make it rain," Nina said as she righted herself.

"Now, where's the bank? We saw it last night. Oh, there it is." Marge turned, Nina hurried to keep up with her. No longer able to contain her curiosity, Nina asked, "Who grubstaked you, Marge? O'Hallahan?"

Marge paused on the narrow street, her eyes misted as she almost felt the loving presence of the old doctor in the faint breeze that caressed her flushed face.

"The man who saved my life and made it possible for me to be here was Dr. Tom. He grubstaked me, as Cody would say, from the grave."

The good Chinese food, the cold beer, the two good-looking women made the little bar on Almond Street a gathering place. Not only for the locals, but an irresistible draw for the two-hundred- plus men who worked on the Ruck-A-Chucky Dam. They promptly claimed it as their own.

President Roosevelt had appropriated one million, five hundred thousand dollars for the construction of dams on the Middle Fork and the North Fork of the American River. The first work that was ordered, on the hydraulic dams by the Army Corps of Engineers, was the Ruck-A-Chucky on the Middle Fork of the American River.

The bar was uncomfortably crowded, the old scattered tables did not provide adequate or comfortable seating. It was obvious they needed to expand. The cabin too, with its outside plumbing, smoking oil lamp, and small misplaced windows were far from Marge's dream. She voiced her plans to Cody, who, true to his word, assembled a work crew made up of local Chinese laborers. He assisted in every spare moment; he felt responsible for both women, and was overjoyed at their success. He regarded Marge as a little sister, but he loved Nina with a dog-like devotion. She was an indifferent lover. "Too many, too late," she laughed.

Marge's attempt to understand the fractured English that the crew spoke made them smile, but they were in awe of this small woman with the flaming hair who often worked beside them and knew the difference between a saw and a hammer.

Cody was shocked with her easy rapport with the crew, but amazed at how quickly the dining room rose out of the ground. He advised, "The best place to buy your supplies is Olsen's Lumber and Hardware. He's honest and sells good materials. He's only been here a couple of years, and already bought out his competitor. He's done real well. I've heard he also owns outlets in Truckee and Nevada City. He was awarded the Civilian Conservation Corps Camp bids, already had Bear Creek and North McCann. Rumor has it he made his fortune without leaving town."

Cody continued, "Marge, you girls are workin' overtime, you're both lookin' a little peaked. I think you should hire a bartender and I know just the man."

Nina spoke up. "Ah Sing has found a little Chinese girl who would be a tremendous help to me. I'm tired. What do you say, Marge?"

"I say, wonderful."

The sing-song voices of the Chinese men, the steady hum of the saw, every slam of the hammer was like a song in her heart. From the bare earth, the dining room grew and took shape.

Then the floral-covered oilcloth was spread over the tables and touched the bench tops; the ruffled curtains, tied back across a large window that Cody direly predicted "would let all the heat out in the wintertime." A large sign enclosed by twinkling lights read "MARGE'S PLACE."

Cody had hired the Chinese for fifty cents a day; white men were paid seventy-five cents. When Marge became aware of this, she was furious at the unfairness and increased all workers' daily wages to seventy-five cents. She was informed that feelings ran high against the Chinese. They were assaulted, robbed, murdered and had no recourse because they had no voting power. She was disillusioned to learn they had no voice in the courts.

Cody was disturbed by her views. "You'll get yourself in a big mess of trouble doin' that. You're ruinin' them Chinamen."

The word passed throughout the townspeople and the locals boycotted her. She didn't notice or if she did, it was of no consequence.

The sound of loud, angry voices floated up from the parking area to awaken Marge just after midnight. She looked out the window to see a large group of men pushing and shoving her two Chinese cooks, a man with a knife was attempting to cut the squirming Ah Sing's pigtail, while another man held Ah Sing's arms behind his back.

She was half-dressed as she rushed down the path to confront the mob. "Don't you dare. Let them go. Get off my property." she screamed. Her heart sank as she saw the display of guns; a man with a bullwhip whirled, then cracked it like a rifle shot. He growled, "We're the 'Miner's Anti-Chinese Association.' We're getting' rid of all these damn chinks takin' jobs from the white man. Go tend to your knittin', little lady. You mind your business, we'll mind ours. Now, git."

Marge turned back into the bar, her knees shaking, and picked up the shotgun that stood behind the door of the storeroom. A gun Cody had insisted she have, "just in case." The door slammed behind her as she stood on the steps and brought the gun to her shoulder. A murmur ran through the crowd, then a voice laughed.

"Lady, that gun would knock you on your pretty ass if you were fool enough to pull the trigger. Bet it ain't even loaded."

The last word hardly sounded when the ear-splitting boom of the big gun thundered through the canyon, the echo dancing off the walls. Marge staggered back against the door, but her voice was calm and collected as she stepped forward.

"Where do you want me to put the next one?"

"Son of a bitch! She'll kill us all with that damned artillery."

Ah Sing and the older cook suddenly appeared beside her. "Now get the hell off my property and if you ever come back, I'll know where to put the next shot. Now git."

The word spread far and wide, enhanced by the crew of the Ruck-A-Chucky who pledged instant retaliation for anyone who annoyed the proprietor of Marge's Place.

Cody was horrified. "My God, Marge, be careful with that gun. You could have killed somebody. If you're goin' to run around totin' a gun, you gotta know more than where the trigger is. At least let me show you how to shoot."

"Seems to me that I didn't do too bad," Marge retorted.

Cody had to fight for his turn with other "instructors" to teach Marge the fine art of shooting and cleaning a gun. He confiscated the shotgun, replacing it with a rifle and a small pistol that Marge kept in the cabin. Marge's volunteer instructors from the dam each took full credit for her near-perfect marksmanship and bragged loudly and shamelessly to each other of her achievements.

It seemed like most of the men at the Ruck-A-Chucky were in love with Marge and she loved them all; once again, she had acquired a family.

Nina asked, "Marge, don't you ever get lonely for a man?"

"I will when I find him."

"Yeah, but you ain't lookin'."

Most of her work crew had drifted back and camped out in a secluded area not far from the cabin. Renovation began with indoor plumbing, then electric lights replaced the smoky oil lamp.

Mindful of Cody's predictions of the cold winters, Marge bought a new stove that served both for heating and cooking.

Rose-patterned wallpaper to cover the wall's imperfections was ordered from JC Penney's catalog. That paper was nearly Marge's undoing. All day she struggled to hang the paper straight, and there was paste everywhere but on the crooked strips of paper.

She was rescued by the smiling man who was installing the stove.

"Missy, let me."

By evening the paper was hung beautifully and Marge was washing the paste from her hair.

Then the new furniture arrived, which was in stark contrast to Annie's dresser and old chair. At home in Marge's bedroom, they brought back memories of a different time, a different place, a different Marge.

Cody's sensible advice fell on deaf ears. Marge, in a burst of enthusiasm, had additional windows installed that gave her a view of the hills covered with apple trees and the faint outline of the mountains beyond. She added window boxes, heaped high with the riotous red of geraniums with their heady fragrance that paid for their audacity with the first winter snow.

As she wrote the checks that paid for it all, she remembered Tim's oft-repeated words, "Ah, lass, money. 'Tis a wonderful thing to have, it is." Looking at her handiwork, she gloated, *it's mine. Every board. Every nail. My home.*

She paid the men in cash.

Summer had passed too quickly and the winter Cody had promised was here. Marge played in the snow like a child, a snowman with a hardhat and hob-nailed boots decorated the parking area. She had fun in the snow that she'd never had in

North Dakota. She shuddered as she remembered the winters in the snowbound house that would never know snow again.

One morning as they lingered over breakfast, a cup of coffee at her elbow, a cigarette in her hand, Nina complained, "I get bored with all this damn snow, Marge. Don't you ever want anything more?"

"More? More than what? I have my home, a good business, good friends, what more do I need?"

"You need a man, of course. Don't you ever want the feel of a man between your legs, holding you so tight you can't breathe, even if you wanted to? The smell of him, the taste of him, so what if there's only the wrinkled sheets in the morning. Tomorrow there's another night. What's holding you back? There must be something lacking in your make-up, it ain't normal. You're like that second batch of geraniums you planted so late—the frost got the buds before they came to flower."

That arrow found its mark and Marge flinched. The instant flashback, would Ed's face always hide in the dark of her brain? Her doubts rose up to challenge her. Was she damaged too deeply to ever love a man? *Yes, the geraniums do remind me of myself, all used up before I came to bloom.*

Her coffee cold in the cup, Marge rose and walked to the window. She gazed silently at the snowy landscape. Her glance dropped to the window box, lifeless in its soft white blanket. She looked again—could it be? Her breath caught a flash of color in the snow, a small sprouting of green leaves, defiantly alive, growing from the rootstock.

Turning to Nina, she spoke in a sure voice. "I want a man in my heart, in every cell of my body. Yes, I do. I want him in my arms, but before I want him between my legs, I want to know with every part of me that this love will be forever."

Nina laughed as she stubbed out her cigarette. "Marge, you're such a dreamer. In this world it doesn't happen that way. Life is a roll of the dice, don't waste it all on one man. Life is short."

Changing the subject, "Guess it's time to open up," Marge said as she cleared the dishes. "We need to go over the supply list, we ran short last week."

As they walked down the winding path, Nina commented, "At least this snow is good for business, even the miners are coming in for a little hot food and socialization. Poor devils, it must get awful lonely up there, sloshing around in all that mud, living on hardtack and hope. Always the 'big one' is just around the corner."

"Seems to me, you and that Jack what's-his-name, are havin' a pretty good time weighing out his gold dust. He must be doin' pretty well?"

"Well, we'd be doin' a hell of a lot better if Cody made a few more runs to L.A.," Nina laughed. "Jack gave me some gold nuggets. Sure are pretty, wish I had a ton of 'em, make that two tons."

"Seriously, Nina, what would you do with it?"

She answered without hesitation, "I'd buy a dozen fur coats, the biggest, fanciest house in Beverly Hills, a baker's dozen of those big, gorgeous automobiles, the Auburn Cord, in every color, enough pretty clothes to cover a tribe and I'd live forever."

Said Marge, amused, "Now who's dreamin', Nina?"

"Well, Ah Sing's dreams have sure come true, haven't they? He's his own man, has his own kitchen, and a pretty little wife. That was a good move Marge, when we stole him from that ass-pinchin' old bastard. Wonder if he's still lookin' for us?"

Their laughter was cut short as the sound of screaming sirens startled them. With one hand on the doorknob they turned to see two police cars flashing by, followed by an ambulance turning up the torturous road that led to the dam. They stood frozen in the doorway, watching 'til the cars were out of sight.

"They've been lucky so far. No serious accidents, only Big Ed's broken leg and he was fallin' down drunk when that happened." But the premonition of disaster hung heavy.

Much later, small groups started quietly drifting in. The mood was somber, then the murmured voices.

"How the hell could that have happened?"

"They were all experienced men, they'd been drillin' through that rock for three days, almost finished."

"And what the hell was the boss doin' down there?"

"Just in the wrong place at the wrong time," and turned to hide his face.

More and more men collected, clustered in groups, seeking comfort from each other and the forbidden bottles that seemed to materialize from thin air.

The liquor half filling the drained beer glasses, Marge pretended not to notice.

Nina asked, "What happened?" Wanting to know, but dreading to hear the answer she knew she'd get.

"The boss, John Wilson, down checking the job, when a blast went off prematurely. Killed him, Jack Avery and Mickey Mahoney. My God, what a horrible sight, that dynamite damn near moved the whole mountain. Blew concrete chunks to hell'n gone. I don't envy the guy who'll have to tell their families. Mickey got back from San Francisco yesterday, his wife just had a baby girl—and who's gonna replace Wilson?"

The men came in, mourned as only men can. A furtive tear, a muttered curse. "Jack's best friend took refuge in the cab of one of the big tractors and stayed drunk 'til we pulled him outta there. He would'a froze to death."

The work went forward, but slowly, while the men waited for John Wilson's replacement to be found.

"Won't be easy, he was top of the line. It takes brains, and guts, to run a job like this, and that's just for starters." The men talked among themselves.

"Jack Wilson was a good man, you could go to him for anything. He always had time to talk to you. I've seen him with a stack of paperwork on his desk a foot high. But he always got the job done. It'll take a real man to fill his shoes."

"Are you crazy? No man will ever fill his shoes. There will never be another man like Jack."

Two weeks later, a battered, mud-splattered pick-up drove up that mountain with a lone occupant. The word spread like wildfire.

"I'll be a son of a bitch. If he ain't an Indian."

"An Indian with white hair? Someone been screwin' with you. There ain't no such thing as an Indian with white hair. What do you take me for, a fool?"

"Well, for sure, he ain't no fool. He's got a wall covered with degrees in engineering with his name in big black print, 'Cotton Eeagle,' spelled with two Es. But I doubt he'll be able to handle this crew. I'm surprised they didn't send a damn Chinaman."

"Well, I hear he's six-feet-two of solid muscle under that white hair. I'm not sure he'll have any trouble; not from me, for damn sure. I like my hair right where it is. Hear they brought that Cherokee up from Texas. Wonder if they're still takin' scalps."

The next morning there was a general meeting. The new Chief of Engineers introduced himself. There was a lot of commotion in the back rows, almost drowning out his introduction.

Then, a ribald voice, "Hey, is that Cotton Eeagle related to the shit bird? Can it fly?"

The crowd held its breath.

"Would you come up here please and repeat your question, I didn't quite get it all."

A big, burly man with shoulders like a buffalo pushed through the waiting men and stood before the new boss. His body half crouched in a fighter's stance, his big beefy fists clasped at the ready, he sneered, "Eeagle, is it? That's first cousin to the shit bird, I've heard. Can you fly?"

Like a striking snake, Cotton's fist blurred out and connected unerringly with the man's jaw. He staggered back, then fell like a sack of cement and lay unconscious.

The room was dead silent.

"Oh, for anyone else who is interested, I can't fly." His swarthy face was impassive as he looked about the room. "We've got a dam to build, let's get down to business. Somebody haul this asshole out of here."

The crew talked among themselves.

"An Indian. A goddamn Indian. But he's a rough son of a bitch for all that book learnin'. He didn't take no bullshit—there ain't a man here who could stand up to him. But I don't get my jollies takin' orders from no damn Indian."

"Well, learn to love it. He ain't going no place. He knows his business; he runs this job smooth as glass. Give the devil his dues."

"Been here a month and hasn't been off the premises, hasn't even been down at the bar for a beer."

"Well, who's made him feel welcome around here? What the hell do you expect, war whoops and tomahawks? You're just jealous. He's got brains and he's a damn fine lookin' man, all man, I'd say. I got no complaints, I don't care what color he is."

"Oh, go to hell, Murphy. You always was an ass-kisser."

Spring was late April. The apple trees were in full bud, Marge's new geraniums were flourishing, and the hills greening.

"What the hell's goin' on with you?" Nina asked peevishly one night after Marge had snapped at her.

"You've been so damned irritable and restless, you're a real pain in the ass."

"I'm sorry, Nina, I don't know. Must be spring fever. Guess I must be bored now that everything is finished."

Looking out the big window, her gaze followed the winding path that led to the newly shingled bar and adjoining dining room.

"I think I'll add a wooden floor outside, where the bar connects to the dining room. It makes a perfect corner for outside eating. We'll need that this summer. As Cody predicted, business is better than I ever dreamed. I'll add benches and tables, then I'll string some of those Chinese paper lanterns from the eves and every night will look like Saturday night. Won't that be pretty?"

"Why don't you buy a car and get out of here for awhile? You never get any farther than the bottom of the hill. You can afford it. Think of the freedom it would give you. This place will exist without you. You're so damned cranky you're gonna drive the trade away. Buy a Cadillac. Do us both a favor."

Marge bought a Ford coupe with a rumble seat for twenty-five dollars. Cody was aghast.

"A coupe. What in hell can you haul in a coupe?"

"Oh, shut up, Cody," Marge said rudely. "This ain't no damned truck. This is a pleasure car and I don't intend to haul anything heavier than a screwdriver."

When the salesman took her for a trial spin, he explained about spark plugs and the carburetor and different gears and the clutch until her head spun.

"Let me drive awhile," Marge said.

With grave misgivings, he moved and she slid behind the wheel.

"Slow down. Slow down. Are you trying to kill both of us?" he cried as they careened down the twisty, rutted road. "No. No. That's the gas, there's the brakes. I'll drive back; move over." His voice shook.

Marge just laughed as she turned the car around. After the location of the gas and brakes had been established, Marge needed no further instructions.

Marge toured the countryside at every opportunity. She loved to explore the little twisty roads, sometimes no more than a trail. The sweet blossoms from the flowering orchards dropped their painted petals into the little streams made agitated by the melting snow. Occasionally a hurrying squirrel or curious butterfly caught her eye as she daydreamed of the wood fairies floating downstream on the fragrant petals.

As she drove in the surrounding hills one morning, she was surprised to see the large skeleton of a building standing high on a hill, overlooking the valley and a large part of the town. The overgrown road indicated there had not been any traffic for a long time.

The little Ford chugged determinedly upwards. At the top, Marge got out and surveyed the huge structure. The view was breathtaking. That evening she asked Cody about the house.

"Oh, that's Jake Colburn's place. 'Colburn's Folly,' the locals call it. Over six thousand square feet. Colburn built it for his wife. He hit a good vein and it made him rich. His wife came down from San Francisco, but hated the country and, after she got his money, she hated him, too. So there it sits, too close to the reservation, too big for the locals, too far from San Francisco. He'd sell it cheap, just for the lumber, but who's got any use for it?"

Marge teased Nina, "You wanted a big house, Nina. Here it is."

"Not me. Too close to that reservation. Some day I'm going back to civilization. Thanks, but no thanks."

Chapter 17

Every table was full, the bar crowded with men who were glad it was Saturday night. Marge and Nina sat, for a brief respite, at the end of the bar joking and laughing with the men who swarmed around.

Marge felt his presence before she looked up to see him standing in the doorway outlined by the wooden frame. She heard Nina's sharp intake of breath, then hissed, "I saw him first." As though, instinctively she had somehow seen into the future.

Marge seemed to drown in the depth of his black eyes, her eyes held fast by his naked gaze of wordless speech, by the golden glints that flickered, almost hidden by the thick black lashes. His nose, sharply defined between the high cheekbones that declared his Cherokee heritage, the generous curve of his mouth, the sensuous line of the lower lip that almost blatantly announced the passionate nature within. His face overshadowed by the striking whiteness of his hair that looked whiter still in shocking contrast to the red-brown skin, darkened even more by the sun's hot rays.

Nina hurried to greet him, but he nodded indifferently. The broad shoulders and slim-hipped body moved with feline grace. There was something primeval in the thrust of his stride, the hob-nailed boots almost soundless on the worn floor.

He stood before her. Marge rose and slowly put one hand in his, their fingers clung as though fused. It was obvious to the gawkers that he had marked his territory.

It had been a long, busy day when Marge locked the door. Both women were exhausted. Nina was uncharacteristically quiet as they walked up the path to the cabin. She stopped suddenly, turned to face Marge and spoke in a low, ugly voice.

"There are two hundred men working on the Ruck-A-Chucky, you could probably have any of them. It was obvious tonight that you've made your choice. You've waited for the only man I've ever really wanted. I wonder if you're willing to pay the price."

Nina had verbalized what Marge had yet to acknowledge to herself. Surprised and angered, Marge answered, "It seemed to me that he did the choosing, Nina. You know I've never interfered in your private life. How dare you tell me how I feel, when I don't know myself." Sarcastically, she added, "I don't have your vast experience with men. I'm sorry for Cody."

"Save your sympathy, you'll need it for yourself."

When the lights went out in the cabin that night, both women dreamed of the same man.

Confused, untrusting of her exploding emotions, Marge did not go down to the bar when she saw Cotton's truck in the parking lot.

Nina was relieved. She was obsessed with Cotton. Other men suddenly had only been a stopgap for her. Cotton seemed oblivious to her none-too-subtle overtures, a fact that only fueled her efforts. *It's just a matter of time*, she thought, *when he gets hungry enough and I'll be there.*

"I miss old Jack. He wasn't standoffish, like this Indian."

"Well, I'd guess there's parts of him still around."

"That's a helluva thing to say."

"Yeah, guess so. He always had a good joke."

"You mean a dirty one. This Indian ain't one for much conversation, but he's a helluva worker, I'll give him that. This dam is really startin' to come out of the ground, already has over two hundred thousand yards of gravel in it. I read in the *Sacramento Bee* the brass said it was 'highly satisfactory' and Congress has approved six million for work done on the site. Should be completed in '38 or '39."

"And to think it's ramrodded by a noble redskin. Wasn't that long ago that hair woulda been hangin' in two braids, decorated with beads and feathers. I'll bet if you scratched the surface, he's still not civilized."

"Yeah, well, if you want that surface scratched, have at it. I'll scratch my own."

"Hey, barkeep. What the hell does a feller have to do to get a beer around here?"

"You got the last one, I'll get this one."

The early morning sun streamed through the window, warming Marge in the chill of the restaurant, quiet now, except for the faint sounds coming alive in the kitchen.

The soft closing of the door went unnoticed as she concentrated on the open ledger before her. He lifted the heavy hair from her neck, bent to slide his lips slowly across her flesh.

Startled and furious, she drew back her arm, only to find it captured in Cotton's restraining hand. As she relaxed, he released his grasp and her hand moved up, her fingers anchored in his hair. Pulling his head down, she fastened her mouth to his in a kiss that seemed to drain every need from her body.

Nina unexpectedly appeared from the kitchen and stood frozen with shock that instantly blazed into rage. The violently slammed door screamed reality as the moment shattered.

"I was beginning to think I had only dreamed you, so I came to make sure," he murmured.

"And are you sure?"

"I've never been so sure of anything in my life," he answered.

The door closed as softly behind him, as it had opened.

Silently, Ah Sing appeared with a cup of coffee. Marge's hand trembled so, she could hardly raise the cup to her lips. She dreaded the confrontation with Nina that she knew would follow.

She put the ledger away, knowing concentration was impossible today.

Walking slowly up the path, she recalled those never-forgotten words, "What's done is done, get on with it."

Nina was waiting, her face flushed with anger. They sat across the table from each other as they had for so many years, when they had shared the good times and the bad.

"Nina, you know we've been like sisters for how many years?" Marge's voice shook. "I don't want to hurt you. I have a war going on inside me. My reason and my emotions are driving me in opposite directions. My reason tells me he and I are strangers, we are of different cultures." She paused, adding, "Perhaps I am just a challenge to him, I'm sure he's had his pick. My emotions seem to be beyond my control. I wanted him the moment he stood in the doorway and looked at me." Then her voice rose passionately. "I wanted to feel his arms around me, his body so close to me. I've waited my whole life for him. I'm overwhelmed by what I've never felt before.

"You said once that I was like my own geraniums, the bud frozen before it could flower, but remember the bud that pushed up from the root stock? I want all of what I've never had."

Nina ground out her cigarette, pushed her coffee cup away.

"Somewhere in the back of my mind I've known, sometime,

somewhere, it would come to this, and now it's knocking at the door. I feel sorry for you, Marge. You've got just about as much chance for happiness with him as I had with Bill. Stick to your own kind. You won't find what you want with an Indian, no matter how educated or how handsome he is. He is what I've always dreamed of. We're two of a kind and it goes deeper than skin color. I can wait for him. You've won the first round, but the game's just started. Let it be."

The enduring friendship that had existed between the two women disappeared the moment Cotton had walked through the door. Gone was the lighthearted banter, the shared confidences over morning coffee. The tension lay dormant between them, pushing at the restraints.

Nina was biding her time. Marge, caught between her own desires, was trapped by her reason, wavering between delight and despair; but at what cost? She dreamed of him in her sleep and imagined his presence in her every thought.

A strong current of uneasiness ran beneath the seemingly pleasurable surface of the bar where tired men sought a few hours of respite from their hard day's work. Something was not quite right, but what? The tension grew each day.

Cody, in his usual place, covered his forlorn look with an indifferent expression. Nina was sullen. Seated beside Cody, her eyes were tracking Cotton's every gesture. Cotton's eyes always on Marge; her every nerve tuned into him.

It became increasingly apparent to the regulars that there was a love triangle burning hot and ready to explode. Rumors ran wild.

"I feel sorry for Cody, that poor son of a bitch."

"Yeah, he gets his nose rubbed in it every time he comes in. I wouldn't put up with that for a minute."

"Why doesn't he just tell her to go to hell?"

"Well, that's love for you. They've been together, must be close to three years, since the dam started."

"Looks like Cotton's gonna take the red scalp."

With a shrug, "Maybe yes, maybe no. I ain't makin' no bet."

The days were getting shorter. The apple trees that had bloomed so beautifully such a short time ago, now hung heavy with fruit.

The colorful papier-mâché lanterns that lit the patio at night cast a rosy glow over the table pushed back against the wall. The climbing wild honeysuckle scrambled over the trellis and lay its heady perfume above the exotic aroma of Ah Sing's kitchen.

Marge sat facing Cotton's smiling face.

"What is that wonderful smell coming from Ah Sing's kitchen?"

Marge laughed, "I have invaded his sacred domain and taught him how to make an apple pie. The trees are loaded and I can't bear to see the apples go to waste. Ah Sing is becoming very creative with apple dumplings and apple cake, and I don't doubt apples in the chow mein. 10 Mile Road ends at an old abandoned apple orchard that the deer and I share, although they get more than I do."

His hand reached for her, his fingers curling a strand of her hair. She moved away, her face flushed, feeling Nina's hostile stare. Seeking to divert his attention, a ploy he was perfectly aware of, she asked, "Who named you Cotton? Surely not your parents."

He laughed. "A Catholic nun who was raised in the south, Sister Agatha. She called me 'Cotton-head' the first time I was herded through the door of the Catholic boarding school. There were thirteen of us—four of my nine sisters and eight other boys. I was twelve that fall. They were going to teach us the real, true religion and to eat with a fork. We were terrified, especially when they cut our hair. I prayed mine would grow back the right color but I guess I prayed to the wrong God. My sisters were all separated. After four years the only thing different about them was the length of their hair. After the shock wore off, I learned to love the learning. I was lucky. Sister Agatha saw something in me that I never understood. She taught me the joy of reading, the challenge of numbers. I became a top student. Of course, I was held up as a perfect example of how well their program was working, and it was, with me.

"I went back to the reservation just once, for my father's funeral. I was more of a stranger there than I had ever been in this world.

"I went on to Texas A & M with Sister Agatha's help and encouragement. I was the only Indian enrolled. It was rough, but not rough enough. I came out with top honors and my degree. A framed diploma to prove it. It has been my life's ambition, all I ever wanted, until you." The naked longing in his eyes made her look away.

"Cotton, we've only known each other such a short time. You're the first man that I've ever been physically attracted to, but that's not enough. How can I be sure? I want love to last a lifetime. Nina says that's only a schoolgirl's dream, but is it?"

"Marge, I'm thirty-six years old. I've known many women, but I've never known one I wanted to marry, to spend the rest of my life with, a mother for my children. I have a different feeling for you, one that overrides the physical that God knows burns night and day. Yes, I want you to be sure you love me. I wouldn't build a dam on sand; I won't build a marriage on doubt."

Nina sat with Cody at the end of the bar, her brooding gaze fixed on Cotton as he leaned closer to take Marge's hand, his barely audible voice whispered, "Let me take you home, Marge." Her murmured reply. Both Cotton and Nina knew he'd get no farther than the door, even as they both knew his passion was at fever pitch.

Marge clung to Cotton as he kissed her good night, her body pressed close as he trembled against her.

Nina urged Cody to go home. "It's late and I'm tired." With a hangdog look that said it all, he drove away. As she watched his taillights disappear, she followed, walking in the moonlight. When she came to the turn in the road that led to the dam, she stopped to light a cigarette. She knew it wouldn't be long before the next sound she would hear would be Cotton's truck.

It slowed for the curve. She stepped forward and, in the glare of the headlights, she was clearly outlined. The pick-up ground to a stop. As Cotton slammed the door behind him, he knew the answer before his rage-filled voice demanded, "What the hell are you doing here?"

She moved to him, her arms outstretched, but he pushed her away so roughly she stumbled back. Instinctively he reached for her to break the fall, but she fastened herself to him, pulled him off balance and they fell together. She arched the full length of her body against him, her mouth everywhere, her hands caressing, wise in the ways of seduction. He closed his eyes and his passion burned with hers in the raw, all-consuming, primitive coupling of animals. Her mouth searched for his, but he turned his head.

Afterwards, he stood and walked to the truck. Nina picked herself up, brushed the grass from her clothing as she walked toward him, reaching out as he stepped back.

"I love you, Cotton. I've waited for you."

"It's immaterial to me who you love, you're nothing to me. You've got what you've been wanting and that's all you'll ever get from me," his voice thick and ugly.

"Cotton, you know we're two of a kind under the skin."

"Don't put me in your class, you two-bit whore. That's all you are to me. Don't pull this trick again or you'll just be a bug on my windshield. Forget this happened or you will live to regret it. You found your way here, now find your way back."

Then he was gone.

She laughed triumphantly as she walked back, knowing it wouldn't be the last time. She wouldn't be a bug on his windshield, but a stain on his upholstery.

Marge can play the lady, but I've played the fiddle and he's danced just the way I like it, rough, she thought with a triumphant smile on her lips.

As she slipped up the back stairs carrying her shoes, she was careful to avoid the third step, the squeaky one.

In the following months, tranquility seemed to have been restored. The women were speaking again and actually having coffee together. The tension that had been so apparent seemingly dissipated. Nina was her happy flirtatious self again; Marge's smile was one of relief.

Thank God she's paying some attention to Cody. I wish Cotton would go easy on the beer. Do I just imagine it, or is he drinking more than he used to? But that dam is such a tremendous responsibility, he needs a little relaxation. She smoothed her worry away.

Cotton seemed resigned to wait for Marge's decision. He had banked the fire, but the coals burned hotter than the flames.

Except for a few forgotten apples that clung, as though afraid to fall, the trees were near naked. Red and yellow leaves covered the ground beneath dark branches; the hills turned muted brown from the hot summer sun, and over it all, the blue, blue sky.

It was nearly October and fall had definitely arrived with its crisp, cool mornings and sunny afternoons. Ah Sing lamented the shortage of apples. Marge was restless and needed no urging. *Perhaps the deer have missed a few. That old orchard at the end of 10 Mile Road would be the best possibility and besides, the drive would be beautiful.*

Ah Sing carried the baskets to her car, then waved a cheerful good-bye.

As she drove through the secluded countryside, ablaze with fall colors, her heart overflowed with happiness as she reflected on her life. *I own my own home, I have financial security, I'll never leave this beautiful country. I have good friends and now my best friend and I have regained what so nearly we lost. I love and am loved by a wonderful man. Life is truly beautiful, thank God.*

Cotton, from his vantage point, high upon the crest of the great dam, glanced down. A flash of something. What could be down in that secluded canyon? He raised his binoculars to his eyes and was amazed to see the little coupe, standing at the end of 10 Mile Road. He turned to his foreman, "Go ahead as planned, I won't be long. I've forgotten something."

Marge heard the sound of a motor, looked up to see the familiar pick-up. A conflict of emotions raced through her mind as she saw him park and stand for a moment, a smile on his bronzed face.

It seemed as if a mysterious force pulled her forward as she ran to meet him. An unseen hand had directed them to this spot, at this time. Destiny had set the stage.

She walked into his arms. His lips covered hers in a slow, draining kiss that hurt with joy. The pressure of his face moved her slowly backwards until they lay together amidst the scarlet leaves. He looked down into her eyes and saw himself reflected there. His hands moved to the buttons on her blouse. He kissed each spot as it opened to him. She tried to say no, but couldn't form the word against his lips. Then she needed no words as her body answered his perfectly. She held him fast, and moved against him, her face buried in the male smell in the curve of his neck. He shuddered as her lips touched his bare skin. She closed her eyes as he moved, slowly, tasting her with every kiss.

The tide came surging, rose, lifting high, then receded and rose again higher. She whispered, "Please," but his mouth covered hers, silencing the word. The tide came rushing, wave after wave, then nothing could stop the flood as it swept over her and carried her to another world.

His seeking mouth kissed the sweat from her face, his fingers traced away the tears. The choked voice murmured, then repeated, "Marry me, Marge. Marry me."

He picked the leaves from her hair as she whispered, "When?"

Later, propped up on his elbow, he said, "Today is Friday. Let's go to Sacramento, we can be married in the State Building and come back Sunday."

Marge smiled at his intensity. "Yes, I don't want anything fancy. I'll need to find something to wear and tell Ah Sing to get some extra help."

He grinned. "Well, you won't need to pack a nightgown or a hairbrush."

The hour was late, the crowd was big and noisy as usual on a Sunday night.

Marge and Cotton walked to the front, unnoticed. Cotton put his hand on the bar and with one lithe movement lifted himself.

Standing erect with his head thrown back, he gave a piercing, drawn-out war whoop. The boisterous crowd silenced in an instant.

Cotton laughed. "Hang onto your scalps, men. I want to announce the marriage of Marge Reagan and Cotton Eeagle that took place at three o'clock yesterday at the State Building in Sacramento. Wish us happiness." With one graceful leap, he was among the whistling, clapping crowd.

"The beer is on me, but you all better show up for work tomorrow." Laughing, he swept Marge up in his arms and carried her over the threshold, her radiant face showing over his shoulder as she waved.

Nina crumpled against Cody. Heartbreak struggling with disbelief was followed instantly by a murderous rage.

"I think we ought to find a place in town tonight," Cody said as he slid a protective arm around her. "Better still, why don't you drive down to L.A. with me for a few days? We could go dancing, take in a few shows. I know a wonderful steak house. You could buy some pretty clothes. You've been working hard, you need a little time off. I'm leaving first thing in the morning. C'mon, you need some fun."

She followed him silently, then, "Wait a minute, I need to get my purse."

Cody came back four days later, alone. Tears stood in his eyes as he told Marge, "I got a room at the best hotel in L.A. I had dinner sent up with a bottle of wine. She said, 'Just a minute, I want to get some cigarettes.' I'll have them sent up, I said. 'No, I want to get them myself.' And that was the last time I saw her. I've looked everywhere, even went back to that place you used to live. Oh, Marge, I've loved her for so long."

Marge's joy was put on hold as she tried to comfort Cody. Cotton's outspoken opinion, "He's better off without her and so are you. She was no friend to you, a troublemaker. I'm glad she's gone," as he breathed a sign of relief.

Marge and Cody mourned together.

Chapter 18

To awaken in the night and feel his warm body close, an arm flung lovingly, carelessly, about her, wrapped Marge in a sense of boundless security. Their love flamed strong and steady—the union was everything Marge had dreamed it could be. Minor differences were quickly solved by mutual consent. Cotton showed his love with every word, every gesture. He was an ardent lover that awakened feelings in Marge that she had never even imagined.

He teased, "This honeymoon is never going to be over."

"I surely hope not," she laughingly replied, as her arms held him closely.

Cotton grinned to himself. "I think I've met my match."

Marge spent more time at the cabin as she depended more and more on Ah Sing, who had long since proven his honesty and loyalty, his culinary art was exceptional. He had adapted quickly to the customs of the western world and the English language, although he had kept his pigtail and Oriental philosophy. The dining room and kitchen had always been his pride and joy and, now that Nina was gone, his undisputed domain. Marge was surprised to learn that he and Cotton shared the same sentiments regarding Nina. Marge managed the business end and Ah Sing was happy to be second in command.

She and Cotton spent less time there, and it wasn't "Marge" anymore, it was "Mrs. Cotton" from the men at the dam.

Cody didn't come in as often. When he did, he sat at his usual place, a sad and lonely man.

Now it was December and the weather brought snow and punishing wind to the workmen on the massive dam. Work slowed, but was still ahead of schedule. The crew marveled at Cotton's transformation. His once-strong reserve seemed never to have been— now, he was "one of the boys." His quarters stood empty as he came home to Marge.

There was a gossamer dusting of snow, like powdered sugar on a festive cake, that danced over the mountains and transformed the tall pines into ghostly sentinels. The lights from the little hillside cabin that held his world glistened on the snow. He stood at the window for a moment, gazing at the vibrant red-haired woman who had come into his life, so far from any other existence he had ever known.

If I die tomorrow, I will have had everything this world has had to offer.

When he opened the door, Marge moved into his arms and knew she would never want to be anywhere else.

The room was dominated by the fragrant tree that claimed the entire corner. The intense green of the boughs was colored only by the wide swath of red satin that hung from the top and cascaded in great looping swirls, wrapped about the trunk and spilled on the floor. Concealed in the satin folds was an oblong velvet box, a jeweler's stamp on the satin interior. A smaller box, wrapped in green, lay hidden deep in the branches.

Christmas morning they seemed to be encapsulated in a white silent world that belonged only to them, the quiet broken by the crackling fire and the sound of perking coffee.

Marge, her hair tumbling around her shoulders, her robe tied loosely, watched as Cotton fumbled in the folds of the satin ribbon to retrieve the velvet box. He sat, pulled her in his lap, his arms around her as she opened the lid.

A pearl necklace with a diamond clasp encircled a wide gold wedding band that lay on the satin. Cotton moved her hair to the side, then slid the lustrous pearls over her head. The tears flooded down her face wetting the pearls as he placed the ring on her finger. Wordlessly she kissed him until his cheeks, too, were wet with her tears. Gently she pushed his arms aside.

"Let me up, Cotton. I have a surprise for you—actually, two surprises." Quickly she found the small box and presented it, her face flushed with anticipation at his reaction. His black eyes shone with pleasure as he adjusted the wristwatch with the wide gold-nugget band.

"Nothing could have pleased me more. I've needed a reliable watch forever and this is almost too elegant to wear." He held out his arm to admire the watch.

"Don't you want your other present? You'll like it better," Marge teased.

"I couldn't." He warned, "I won't like it as well as this beautiful watch." Marge moved closer and opened her robe to place his hand on her naked belly.

"You'll have to wait until June for this present."

He stood instantly, his arms around her. Hiding her face against his chest, she could feel the beat of his heart as it thudded against her face. But he was silent, silent so long she looked up anxiously. His eyes blurred with tears that left a shiny trail down his dark face, then, he too, was wordless.

They hugged their secret to themselves until Marge's condition became obvious. It was officially announced at the restaurant amidst deafening cheers and congratulations. Happiness seemed to weld the Ruck-A-Chucky dam workers into Marge's extended, delighted family. The men respected her as a fair-minded, hard-working business woman who tolerated no nonsense, but they loved her as a sister. Many would have loved her differently had she given any encouragement. There had been those who had been reluctant to accept the mixed marriage, but now their doubts melted into the background when they saw Cotton's utter joy as he made the announcement and Marge's happiness in her marriage was unmistakable.

Cotton's exuberance spilled over the job site like syrup on a hotcake; morale among the crew was high. Occasionally he would overhear—as he was meant to—a member of his crew refer to him as "Daddy," a familiarity he accepted with a euphoric grin.

One cold, clear night Cotton sat in the big chair, his belly full. Stretching his feet to the fire he gazed about the small cabin as Marge finished the dishes. Suddenly the thought occurred to him, "Where will *she* sleep?"

Turning, she dried her hands and laughed.

"*He* will sleep in a crib at the side of the bed—my side, of course."

"The room's too small."

"Yes, but I want our baby close."

"But when she's older?" Cotton questioned.

"Marge, let me buy a house with big rooms. You know I can easily afford it—how wonderful to have room to turn about in without bumping into furniture."

"No, no, no." Marge was adamant. "I love this cabin—my first home."

The quiet hung between them for a moment, then "Let's build a big bedroom on the back, with big windows—just imagine. We could lie in bed and look at the mountains, watch the trees turn color, what do you think?"

"I think it's odd I've never noticed you looking at the view when we're in bed," he answered, his long fingers strolling through her hair, laughter in his eyes as he looked down.

"Yes, and see what happened when I wasn't looking," Marge retorted, a smile tugging at the corners of her mouth.

"Well, you better keep your eyes open, or it could happen again." As she snuggled in his arms, they planned the room.

"I'll hire a few good carpenters and it will go up in no time..." He was interrupted by her "No, Ah Sing will find the men I need. This is my project. You can take care of the bill at Olson's Lumber, fair enough?"

Cotton threw his hands up in surrender, and they sealed the contract with a kiss.

"Four a.m. comes early. Let's go to bed—you can admire the view," he grinned.

When the men on Cotton's crew saw the Chinese carpenters, they ribbed him.

"Hey, who's chief in that little teepee?"

"Believe me," Cotton answered, "the chief sure as hell doesn't have white hair." Then he added softly, "Anything she wants, gentlemen, anything at all." His voice roughened. "Now get to work."

Construction started at once. The ground too frozen to dig, the foundation went up on cement piers. The sound of the saw, the hammers pounding, was music to Marge's ears. The men worked steadily, six days a week, fortified by Ah Sing's hot soup and gallons of tea. The men at the dam suggested to Cotton that some hot tea would be nice. He assured them that as soon as they worked as hard as Marge's "crew," he'd have the tea sent right up.

Seven weeks later Marge was at JC Penney's newly opened store.

A beautifully colored braided rag rug to accent the new oak floor caught her eye, then the sheer blue gray of the curtains that almost captured the soft misty sheen of the mountains in the early morning, an oversized chair for Cotton and then, on impulse, an extravagant spacious bed made to order to accommodate his large frame.

How wonderful to shop—money being no object. Her mind flashed back to her first shopping spree with Susy and Annie, how she had agonized over the purchase of two pairs of shoes. *I think I still have those D'Orsay pumps somewhere. Annie's pleasure, later disappointment, with the pretty nightgown—Susy's joy as she preened herself in front of the mirror as she twirled about in the blue prom dress—the dress that she was buried in, all too soon.*

I haven't heard from Annie in ages. I must write.

Marge moved into the children's department. *Oh, what lovely baby things—so tiny, so soft, so, so, so perfect.* She shopped until she could shop no more, then suddenly remembered the old worn dish towel she wrapped around Nina's Baby. Momentarily she was distracted, Nina's memory still clung. Marge could not—would not—remember what Ruthie had wrapped her baby in, but she would never forget Ruthie's care and kindness, or how they had laughed as they drove down the rutted dirt road and looked back to see the old house burn. *All that life is past. I won't, I won't remember. God has blessed me with a fresh start. Life is so wonderful.*

"Please put a rush order on the bed and mattress—and the linens," then gave directions for the delivery of her purchases.

It seemed forever before the bed arrived.

Cotton's big chair sat close to Annie's old rocking chair. The mirror on the much-traveled dresser reflected the magnificence of the oversized bed.

Marge's pregnancy was uneventful, without even morning sickness. She grew more beautiful in the months that followed. Her skin radiant, the soft gray of her eyes seemed to sparkle with an inner joy, the long red-gold hair glowed like fire. Cotton pampered her shamelessly. He insisted she have the baby at the hospital in Sacramento—eliciting the now familiar response, "No, no, no." Marge chose an old doctor in town who would be with her at the birth. Ah Sing brought an old Chinese woman Mai Ling, who spoke very limited English, but there was no need for words. She anticipated Marge's every thought and lived out her life in the safety and warmth of the little cabin.

Marge had searched, but without success, for the perfect crib. She expressed her dissatisfaction to Cotton while cuddled close to him in the big chair. "I guess we'll have to look in Sacramento—they probably have a larger selection . . . "

"I'll build the crib myself," was Cotton's instant reply.

He labored every spare moment to produce a crib made of the finest oak. A majestic eagle, carved deep into the wood, the involved spread of the great feathered wings as it soared above the treetops, each feather so intricately formed one could almost feel the pull of the wind. On the opposite side, the nesting mother, as the father circled above, standing guard over all that he held dear. Cotton's love shone through with every cut of the knife.

The crib stood at the foot of the bed, the down-filled mattress heaped high with soft blankets. Marge studied the baby bed, entranced by the awesome beauty and Cotton's silent show of love.

The days grew short and seemed to fly. Marge spent less time at the restaurant as she enjoyed her home and counted the months, the days, the hours.

The bar seemed to run itself, aided by the two dependable bartenders. Ah Sing ruled his domain with an iron hand in a velvet glove. "Marge's Place" was a landmark, known for excellent food and good fellowship. Locals vied with the workers from the Ruck-A-Chucky, and the out-of-towners soon became regulars.

Marge's pride in her establishment knew no bounds.

One morning as she curled up in Cotton's big chair, still in her robe and nightgown, her coffee cup balanced precariously on the arm, Nina intruded in her thoughts. Marge laughed to herself when she remembered how she had sat on Nina's prone body as she had forced her to say the words, "Marge Reagan." And Marge wondered how she had ever found the courage to refer to herself as "Marge O'Malley"— the name that had kept Nina out of jail. Marge missed the intimacies that they had shared over coffee in the past but knew that Nina had chosen the best way out of a conflicting situation. She prayed Nina would find her own happiness along the way.

As Marge's pregnancy progressed, her breasts became large and full, her body thickened with its precious cargo. As she grew, so did her happiness. In the evening she listened for Cotton's fast steps on the wooden bridge, now blurred by the sound of rushing water, urged on by the melting snow. The apple trees had donned their greenery, the buds bursting from their winter sleep.

Sunday mornings, they lay in the big bed where they had their most intimate conversations and gazed out the picture window at the beautiful view as Marge had predicted. Cotton nudged her, "What will it be Marge—a girl or a boy?"

"Do you want a boy, Cotton?" watching his face for a clue.

"No, I want a red-haired girl."

"Well, I've got inside information and it's a boy. I've even chosen a name."

"What name?"

She laughed. "I won't tell you—it's a surprise."

Cotton complained, "I thought I'd ordered a girl."

The day began as an ordinary day. Cotton, as usual, left for the dam at four o'clock. For Marge, stabbing back pains graduated into great waves of agony. Mei Ling, who had known such excruciating pain as a child, hobbled on her crippled feet to Ah Sing, who sent for Cotton and the doctor simultaneously.

The doctor had just finished his exam when Cotton burst through the door.

"Don't worry, she'll be fine," he assured a shaky Cotton. "Childbirth is something women do very easily you know. I'll be back in a few hours."

Cotton sat at Marge's side, their hands joined as she strained. She comforted his obvious distress between her contractions. "Stop worrying—this will soon be over." She panted as she pulled hard against his hands. The contractions continued with torturous regularity but no results.

Cotton called for the doctor to return. Peevishly, he examined Marge again.

"She's a little slow, but it's only been six hours. She's doing just fine—don't worry. Let's give her a few more hours."

Mei Ling wiped Marge's face with a cold wet towel and smoothed her hair back. Cotton held water to her lips.

Mei Ling's little toothless face was set in an angry scowl as she watched the doctor leave. Marge groaned as she fell back on the pillow. "Please, God. Let this baby come."

Unaware of any difficulties in the cabin, a celebration was building at the bar.

"A toast to Marge."

"A toast to Daddy." Then the innumerable toasts to the baby.

"I got five dollars says it's a boy."

"Hate to take your money, but I got ten dollars says it's a girl."

"Cotton says it's a red-headed girl—here's my ten dollars."

"Sure seems to take a long time . . . "

"Yeah—hope every things okay."

"Saw the doctor go up there a couple times——there he goes now."

Now late afternoon, Marge writhed on the bed. "For God's sake, doctor—can't you give her some thing for the pain?" Cotton begged.

"Well, I could but it will slow the labor down. Don't worry.

Women are built for this. She will be just fine. Why don't you go and get yourself some dinner?" He wilted under Cotton's wrathful stare.

"There's nothing we can do but wait. These things take time, you know. I'll be back after dinner."

Cotton paced and inwardly screamed. *Can this be right? I've never seen a human birth. The doctor must be alright—she chose him.* His pleading eyes met the black shiny eyes buried in the wrinkles of the Chinese woman's face. She shook her head negatively.

It was after midnight when, with a great bloody gush, the water broke and a tiny hand reached out.

The doctor paled, "Oh my God, it's coming breech. I'll have to go back to my office and get my forceps."

With murderous fury, Cotton opened the door and screamed at the terrified doctor, "I'll kill you if anything happens to my wife." The look in his eyes told the doctor to hurry.

Mei Ling appeared with a brown bottle, the contents unseen, the Chinese writing on the wrapper unreadable. She patted Cotton on the shoulder and with a surety born from years of experience, she pantomimed her request and intent.

Cotton felt the confidence of Mei Ling and an inner peace quieted his fears. Marge gave a desperate nod.

Mei Ling quickly washed her hands and liberally applied the contents of the bottle. She placed Cotton's hands on Marge's shoulders, then slowly, surely, she inserted her little yellow hand. With her eyes closed, she pushed and turned, paused, then resumed her gentle manipulations. The baby's hand disappeared. The head, a shoulder appeared, followed quickly by the other shoulder. She spoke one word sharply to Marge, and with one last agonizing push, the baby slid out.

The door opened, the doctor hurried in.

"Well, well, well. What do we have here? See, I thought it would right itself." He quickly cut the cord, held the baby up by the feet, the sex obvious, a light slap on the tiny bottom brought a lusty cry of protest. Mei Ling smiled as the doctor handed her the boy.

Cotton fell to his knees to hold Marge, who spoke barely above a whisper. "I want to see my baby."

Mei Ling lay the bloody baby on Marge's naked stomach, but her eyes were so clouded with tears she could only feel the soft white hair as it curled wetly around her fingers.

Chapter 19

Cotton knelt, his arms around them both. Marge reluctantly surrendered the baby to Mei Ling's waiting arms and she carried him triumphantly away. Cotton lifted his face.

"What is his name?"

"Cottu."

Cotton, wordless with pride, his black eyes shone with an inexpressible joy. He stood to receive his son, now cleaned, that tiny replica of himself, the little face showing above the blanket, sucking hungrily at his fist.

Mei Ling turned her attention to Marge's comfort, then Cotton lay the baby in her waiting arms. Marge's breasts were full and overflowing. The baby nuzzled blindly, seeking the nipple, his wee fingers kneaded the soft warm flesh like a kitten as he sucked greedily. As he nursed, Marge studied every part of him: The cap of white hair atop his perfect little head, his body long and slender. The high cheekbones that guarded that snub of a nose, the curve of the lips. He was so like his father. But the large gray eyes of his mother dominated his face.

Marge drank the nourishing broth that Mei Ling urged, then fell into an exhausted sleep. She didn't hear the happy cheers that reverberated throughout the canyon from Marge's Place when Cotton made the long-awaited announcement.

Cottu was a strong baby who grew vigorously. All too soon, it seemed, he had his first tooth. Cotton was utterly entranced and was certain there had never been or ever would be, another like him. Marge teased him about the red-haired girl he had "ordered."

"No, never again." He was adamant, "I'll never let you go through that again. Anyhow, I could never love another one as I love Cottu, it wouldn't be fair."

That Cottu was an extraordinary child, there was no doubt in the minds of the three people who loved him most. Mei Ling sat for hours by his crib and crooned lullabies in her foreign tongue and Cottu kicked his chubby legs and his big eyes sparkled at her entrance.

He sat at six months, then took his first unsteady steps at nine months. He bypassed his parents, who waited breathlessly with outstretched arms, and reached for Mei Ling.

Cotton looked disconsolate, then grinned. "I'll bet he can speak Chinese, too. I'll have to learn another language."

In rapturous delight, Mei Ling's eyes disappeared in the wrinkles ear to ear.

Cottu was a joyous child who laughed at everything, yet he was not a demanding baby. His first words were "Da-da," which had sent Marge into spasms of laughter at Cotton's ecstatic response. Marge indulged herself, cuddling him close. She rocked him to sleep at nap time and gloried in this perfect man-child who faded the memories of the baby girl that had been hers so briefly.

Marge kept her books, and conferred with Ah Sing at her usual table secluded in the back of the restaurant. Cottu played among the customers. He was utterly fearless as he investigated every nook and corner.

The awkward love offered by a grizzled old miner as Cottu clung to the calloused, work-worn hand, brought tears to Marge's eyes. The family men from the dam played with him as with their own. Marge laughed to see the amazement on the second cook's face as Cottu pulled and played with Ah Sing's revered pigtail.

Suddenly, it seemed, it was June again, and Cottu's birthday celebration fell on a balmy Sunday afternoon. His party was attended by the miners' wives and children, the families of the Ruck-A-Chucky dam workers, and many of the local townspeople. Ah Sing and Marge had decorated the restaurant with gaily colored balloons that danced in every passing breeze and fascinated the children. Cottu bravely poked a chubby finger through each balloon that he could reach, then shrieked with delight when the expected bang resounded. Cotton appeared with a shaggy gray donkey, happily donated for the day from an old prospector. The children were enchanted and stood in line to ride as Cotton coaxed the reluctant animal to accept the rambunctious riders. Cottu rode first, insisting that his seat be backwards. His eyes were wide, questioning, and fastened on his mother.

"A trick rider," Cotton enthused. "A natural-born horseman."

The children played. Their contented mothers sipped lemonade and regaled each other with the latest antics of their noisy offspring.

The birthday cake Ah Sing had so painstakingly decorated was a work of art. The one big candle that stood on top, balanced precariously as the children crowded around, all hoping for the first piece. Cottu, secure in Marge's arms, stuck a finger in the frosting and then in his mouth. With a blissful smile, he wiped his finger in his mother's hair.

The festivities over, a sleepy Cottu was carried up the winding path in Cotton's arms, Marge hurrying to keep up. In her hands was a plate with a generous slice of birthday cake for the little smiling woman standing in the doorway.

Cottu's little hands relaxed around the sticky strings of the balloons he had refused to relinquish. Now they floated away above the treetops. Mei Ling held out waiting arms for the sleeping boy.

Later in the week Marge went early to the restaurant for her usual meeting with Ah Sing. Intent on checking her supply list, she was surprised to hear the sound of a motor so early. She looked out to see Cody's truck. *He must have driven all night, his supplies are still loaded. He must be exhausted, and probably hungry, too.* She called to Ah Sing to prepare Cody's favorite breakfast and waved to him as he walked wearily through the door, a newspaper under his arm.

"Cody, you look so tired. You must have driven all night. Are those supplies a rush order?"

He sat down heavily and wordlessly handed her the *L.A. Times*.

"PROSPECTOR STRIKES IT RICH," the headlines read.

"BIGGEST LODE OF SILVER EVER RECORDED"

Local man Bill Johnson, after searching for the elusive gold for over a decade, finally struck it rich with the discovery of the largest deposit of silver ever found in America.

The days were hot, the nights were cold for eleven years. Bill Johnson lived a solitary life on the lonely Mojave Desert searching for the gold he was sure he'd find. His only companions, rattlesnakes and cactus. What he found was silver. He named it "THE SILVER SLIPPER."

"I earned it and I'm going to enjoy it." he declared as he pointed to the mansion that stood proudly on two acres in Beverly Hills. His wife Nina, resplendent in a gorgeous mink coat, drove off in a baby blue Auburn Cord convertible.

Cody pushed his breakfast away and spoke with a catch in his voice. "I guess I won't ever have to worry again about her sleeping on the street or if she has enough to eat. I hope she gets everything she ever wanted. I'll never forget her."

"I'm happy for her, too, Cody. Now she'll get her kids back, that will be her happiness."

Nina's good fortune was the main topic of conversation for a few weeks, but soon talk resumed about the usual current events at the dam of the little community.

The summer flew by and once again the family lazed away on Sunday mornings to watch the trees turn color and drop their leaves, and eventually the snow that drifted down to wrap their happiness in a soft white coverlet. Cottu wrestled fiercely with his father in the big bed, while Marge built a protective wall about herself with the soft feather pillows.

Cottu, a robust, mischievous child of nearly two, disdained his beautiful crib to cuddle between his parents, only to be removed to his own bed as soon as he was safely asleep. His white hair had the slightest curl as it lay against his tawny skin. He walked with a gracefulness unusual in a child, one foot slightly toed in, an inheritance from his Cherokee grandfather.

"Cottu should have his own bedroom," Cotton insisted. "We need to build a bigger house, and he's almost outgrown that crib."

"I love this house, Cotton," came Marge's instant, predictable response. "Let's build two more bedrooms and one for Mei Ling. Those stairs are almost impossible for her. Please. I want to do it," she insisted.

Cotton swung a feather pillow, "Okay, chief. It's your teepee."

Once again the air was filled with the sound of hammer and saw, the chatter of the Chinese workers. Mei Ling's toothless smile and twinkling black eyes expressed her happiness with the room next to that of her adored Cottu.

Two weeks before Cottu's second birthday, Marge was awakened by the boy bouncing on her bed, tugging at her hand. The house was still. *How odd, Mei Ling is always up at daybreak.* With Cottu still tugging at her nightgown, she hurried after the boy who finally ran ahead. Mei Ling's door was open and Cottu, with a puzzled look, stood holding her lifeless hand.

Marge's grief was overwhelming. Cottu cried because his mother cried and because his beloved playmate had disappeared. Cotton held them both.

Ah Sing took charge of the funeral plans, but discussed their foreign procedures with the local Chinese elders, many of whom thought her remains should be sent back to China, as was the old custom, but Ah Sing insisted, "Let her bones lay where she has lived, close to the people who loved her most."

Five different kinds of food, wine, and tea sat on a table in the restaurant patio to feed her spirit in the other world beyond. Against a steady background of Chinese funeral music, the body was carried to a quiet grave site near the house where she had lived and loved a little boy.

Cottu's birthday party this year was not the riotous party of last year. An aura of sadness clouded the small gathering and there was no one waiting at the door to take the sleepy child.

Cotton had worked a twelve-hour shift at the dam that day. Tired, he hurried home to relax in a long, hot shower. Marge had dinner prepared, waiting on the back of the stove. Cottu was sitting on the floor, amidst his toys, banging loudly on a battered pie tin with a wooden spoon. Marge made a mental note to hide that spoon.

Above the clatter Marge heard the unfamiliar deep-throated growl of a powerful engine drifting up from the parking lot.

It was just dusk, but looking down she could barely see the large car with the top down parked at the bar. Then a faint outline and the sound of steps on the foot bridge.

A knock at the door and Marge opened it to an almost unrecognizable Nina, a baby in her arms, leading a little unkempt barefoot girl whose swarthy face and black eyes, smudged with tears, were hardly visible under a cap pulled down to her ears.

Marge laughed with delight. "Nina Vey, after all this time! Where have you been? I've missed you. What baby is this?"

As Nina stepped into the room she handed Marge the baby.

"You're lookin' good, Marge. Looks like married life agrees with you. Oh...this baby? Bill thinks it's his...maybe it is, if he don't look too close." Nina stumbled to a chair, obviously drunk.

"Oh Nina. You're not driving that big car drunk, are you?" Marge worried.

"Why the hell not? I already rolled one but we've got three more. I wrote to you, didn't I? Maybe I forgot to mail it. Ma Johnson's sittin' up there in Beverly Hills in that big fancy house, happier than a pig in shit...all those people to wait on her."

"Where are the kids, Nina?" Marge interrupted.

"She put Baby in an. . . an institution. . .for the feeble-minded....Dolly...she's out on the street turnin' tricks. I don't know why, we've got more money than God...guess she likes it. She hates me because I'm the old bitch that deserted her.

"The boys don't have anything to do with me, passin' themselves off as Spanish…Billy Jr. has run off someplace again, Billy Joe is in reform school.

"Bill's drunk most of the time, got some floozy knocked up. She thinks she's gonna get a big settlement—over my dead body." She paused, "Whatcha lookin' at? Yeah, I've put on a little weight, all that good food ya know."

Marge was looking at a once petite, beautiful woman, now a bloated caricature of what she once had been.

Cotton, alerted by the voices, looked around the door, a towel around his hips.

"Well hell-lo Cotton," Nina slurred. "Long time, no see. You're lookin' good but I liked you better naked. Still got that birthmark? I brought you a present. She was just two years old a month ago." Nina stood unsteadily, holding the back of the chair. Disengaging the girl's clinging fingers, she gave her a push toward Cotton.

Turning to Marge, she laughed, "You missed the good part, Marge. I took the fire out of him for you in the bed of that old pickup. Rough on my back, rough on his, too, sometimes. Rough anyway we played it. Don't know that it was worth it, I've had a hell of a lot better. All I got out of it was a bruised ass and this damn kid. Bill hates her."

Marge sat as if paralyzed, her stricken eyes looking mutely at Cotton, begging him to deny it. The sick look on his gray face told her he couldn't. Then his face purpled and he stepped toward Nina.

"You drunken slut. Get out or I'll kill you," Cotton's threatening voice raged.

"Don't come any closer, Cotton, or I grab the towel." She taunted, "Let's see if you're as big as you wish you were."

She laughed as she took the baby from Marge's suddenly lifeless arms. Still laughing, she pushed the terrified child toward Cotton— "Go to daddy"—then pulled the cap from the baby's head. Freed from its confines, the pure white hair stood like a dandelion gone to seed.

There was a stunned silence, then Nina's mocking laugh floated over her shoulder as she paused at the door, trying to disengage the little girl's frantic hands that clung tenaciously to her skirt. The sobbing child stumbled barefoot beside her drunken mother into the night.

From far, far away Marge could hear Cottu screaming with fright. She could hear Nina's footsteps on the bridge, then the roar of the big engine, the squeal of brakes as it fishtailed through the parking lot. She felt as if she were falling down, down, down, into the bowels of the earth and knew she'd never come out again as long as she lived.

Her impulse was to hide from this ugly devastation, but hiding was impossible. She rose to comfort Cottu as he stretched out his arms to her, frightened by the loud voices.

She looked up and saw the truth indelibly stamped on Cotton's impassive face.

Why doesn't he say something? Her mind screamed but he stood silently, then disappeared into the bedroom and dressed.

Holding Cottu closely against her shoulder, she moved blindly to the sofa and lay down. His fear vanished and he slept. She closed her eyes, her mind sifting through each detail of this nightmare.

Cotton walked to her, looking down, his mouth opened, his lips moved but no words came. Marge jerked upright as she heard the sound of the door closing and the sound of his footsteps fade into the unreality of this night.

She was still awake as the first light touched the mirror of Annie's old dresser. There was a hesitant knock. Carefully she nudged Cottu aside and moved silently to open the door to Ah Sing who was holding a grimy, tear-streaked little girl with white hair.

Guess I raised some hell up there, Nina laughed. *I hate that Cotton son of a bitch. I hate myself more. We've done Marge twice, and she's the only truly decent person I ever knew. I know Cotton will give her a hard time about the kid. Every time I look at her, she reminds me of him. Bill told me not to bring her home if I had to dump her along the road.*

Where in hell is that bottle? That whisky up there is just as bad as it always was. This damn thing is empty. Guess I'll stop in Bakersfield for gas, get some milk for this bawling kid and pick up a bottle of somethin' fit to drink. If I step on it I can be back with dear old Ma Johnson tonight. I love rubbin' her nose in it, now that it's my fancy house. The old bitch. How in the hell did it get to be six o'clock already?

Back on the road, she drove steadily, the big car weaving wildly, as she tipped the bottle to her lips.

I shoulda been in L.A. by now. Where in hell am I? Barstow? Musta took the wrong turn when I stopped for that bottle in Bakersfield.

She pulled into the first motel she came to, an old wooden building that showed six windows to the world.

She gave the night clerk a hundred-dollar bill, and he pretended not to see the big car parked carelessly, partly on the driveway, the rear wheels digging into the grass; pretended not to notice that the Indian woman was drunk as she stumbled back to the car, to return with a crying baby and a paper bag under her arm.

Kicking the door shut, she muttered, "This baby is driving me crazy. What in hell does he want?" She propped him between two pillows, stuck a pacifier in his mouth, and tossed a blanket over him.

She tore the bottle from the sack, and with shaking hands tilted it to her lips and drank greedily, the liquor trickling out the corners of her mouth.

The baby whined with little mewling sounds. *Damn it to hell, if I never see another cat it will be too soon. I thought I dumped that kitten at the liquor store. That yowling is like a knife in my head. My head is bursting. If I could find that little bastard, it would never yowl again. Probably hiding in the blankets.* She tugged the bedclothes together and piled them high on the little heap that squirmed between the pillows. At last, the sound was quieted. *I'll get rid of it in the morning.*

She sank down on the worn chair, lit a cigarette, closed her eyes as she inhaled, then laid it on the tray and reached again for the bottle, her body screaming for the peace that only oblivion could give her.

She groaned. Pain stabbed through her head like a sharp knife. Her body whirled as the walls moved against her, crushing her in their deadly embrace. What was that thing that came twisting through the floorboards, crawling up her body, that thing? That writhing slimy horror that covered her face and sucked at her mouth. It tightened against her throat, slithered over her shoulders, then returned, again and again, sucking, pushing . . .

Her fists beat against her face until the blood ran red as it colored the heavy strands of hair caught in her fingers. She pounded her head against the wall again and again, screaming silently with her mouth tightly shut. Anything. Anything to dislodge this hideous thing as it screwed its way to her brain. Blinded by her blood as it ran down her face, she fell, rolling on the floor, screaming soundlessly, then crawling to a corner of the cushioned chair.

She lay her head back, her arms dangling, the bloody hair still clutched between her fingers, smothered into unconsciousness as the thing exploded into her brain.

The ash glowed red as it fell from the shallow lip of the ashtray, the smoke rose lazily at first from the worn cushion. Then, like a hungry animal sensing prey, a spark licked along a shabby seam. A taste, then hungrily the smoke parted like a curtain to reveal the ravenous red mouth of the outreaching flames.

Nina lay, curled back against the corner, her mouth open, snoring, indifferent, uncaring to the world, to the muffled bleating cry of her baby.

Speculation and gossip flew wherever the men gathered.

"She was drunk as a skunk when she staggered up there, thought she might fall off that bridge. She looked like hell warmed over. Marge sure musta been surprised."

"Yeah, Cotton sure as hell took a dim view. Draggin' that poor white-haired little girl up there to rub his nose in it. He's been gone a week. Guess he's layin' low."

"Wouldn't you? 'Bout broke Marge's heart, I'd guess. Sure is a sight—them two white-haired kids."

"Ah Sing said Nina left that girl and told him to take her up to the cabin as soon as it got daylight and then just drove off. Called him a 'damned chink,' too."

"I s'pose Marge will keep her. Poor pitiful little thing. The barkeep said Nina was spoilin' for a fight. You know she always was feisty. Thank God she didn't stay long."

"Gawd-a-mighty. Did you see that car? An Auburn Cord—top of the line, and a convertible, too. I'd trade my place in heaven just to drive it for an hour."

"I don't give a damn about Nina, but I hope to hell she didn't wreck that beautiful car."

Three days later, it was early and the bar was empty. Cody walked from the loaded truck, the motor running, the door swinging open. He looked like an old beaten man. He leaned against the threshold, his eyes blindly seeking Marge. His ashen face was tear-streaked, as he thrust the paper at her, then collapsed on a stool at the bar, his head in his hands.

Marge sickened as she read the glaring headlines:

Wife and infant son of millionaire, Bill Johnson, owner of the "Silver Slipper Mine," dead in motel fire.

Her arms wrapped around the sobbing man, her voice gentle. "The Nina we knew was dead a long, long time ago."

The tears left their tracks down the little girl's swarthy face as she struggled in the bathwater, her long coarse hair impossible to comb.

Marge's thoughts traveled back to that hot, crowded little room in the big city, where she had bathed Nina's other Baby in the kitchen sink, wondering if there was enough soup to feed three hungry children, or if there was enough milk to fill Baby's bottle. Her heart ached for that baby who had reached her final destination—the state's institution for the feebleminded.

This little girl cringed at any sudden move, and Marge well remembered Nina's sudden violent tempers.

At last, the child quieted, comforted by Marge's soothing voice. She was wrapped in a big soft blanket, her large eyes wide with wonder as she watched the knots that had defied the comb fall to the floor. Cottu, as he watched, entranced, imitated with his two chubby fingers the snip-snip of the scissors and laughed with glee. When much of the girl's hair lay on the floor, Marge stepped back to observe her handiwork.

How pretty she is. And how she looks like Cottu—they could be twins.

Despite Cottu's every effort to play, the little girl turned away. Her sad cry as she wandered about echoed the cry in Marge's own heart.

Poor little girl. You cry for a mother you never had; I cry for a man I never knew.

A few days later, as Marge rocked Cottu, a little hand from beside her reached slowly and lay tentatively on her knee. Marge reached down and gathered the girl to her lap, holding both children, she rocked.

The two children regarded each other complacently, then the girl stuck a stubby thumb in her mouth and went to sleep. Both children fit snuggly in the crib.

In the coming days the girl's fears receded slowly as she adjusted to her new environment. She held up her arms to Marge, and echoed Cottu's "Mama." Marge's pity turned to love and she knew out of the destruction of her marriage, she had gained a daughter.

What to name her? She knew Nina could never reclaim her, that Cotton would never accept her. *I'll name her Mary Margaret Reagan. She's my daughter, mine alone.* Cottu promptly shortened it to "Maryem."

Marge busied herself with the two active children during the day, keeping her inner feelings at bay, but at night the tormenting thoughts crowded sleep aside. Alone in the big bed, her mind thrashed about in a riot of turmoil, seeking the answers that wouldn't come.

She fought for her dream, her marriage. Her heart searched for reasons to exonerate Cotton. Her mind nagged.

Perhaps I was too prudish. After all, I wasn't a virgin.

Nina was a beautiful woman and she intrigued him. She warned me she was "still in the game," her very words.

Yes, but I trusted him and he said he loved me.

He's been a faithful husband, yes, but Nina was gone.

The pain cut so deep that she wanted to run and hide.

I'll take the children and just walk away and start over. I have the money to do it. But where will I go? This is my home. Cottu adores his father and Cotton will never give him up.

Run away from it all her heart cried. Her reason knew there had to be another way, but there was no way out but to stand. *I pray the future holds the answer.*

The chains of responsibility pulled tighter and finally Marge accepted the grasp of the old adage, "What's done is done. Get on with it."

But she knew the root stock of her love from which the bud had grown and bloomed, had died on that dreadful night, and she wept for the waste of it.

It was after midnight, eight days later, when Marge heard the door open softly. She stood and switched the lights on as a disheveled Cotton entered the big bedroom, the unaccustomed odor of liquor preceding him. They faced each other and Marge waited for him to speak. The prolonged silence became unbearable. She stepped forward, looking up. Her voice shook. "Say something, Cotton. Surely you have something to say—I want to hear it from your own lips." In her heart a flicker of hope fighting for her dream, she pleaded, *Make it like it was before.*

"Cotton, make it right. Please make it right."

"What do you want to hear? The truth? You've heard the truth. Now forget it happened," came his overpowering voice.

An instant flash of rage swept over Marge. "Apparently that has been easier for you than it will be for me. Now what will we do?"

"That will depend on you." His voice ugly, "If you hadn't been such a holdout, this wouldn't have happened." Nina's drunken face floated between them.

"If you wanted a whore, you should have married Nina. Maybe you shouldn't have been so rough on her the other night. Oh, I forgot, you like it rough." He raised his hand as if to slap her. Her gray eyes blazed into his. As she stepped forward, his hand dropped to his side. Suddenly Marge felt very small and vulnerable as she stood before him, barefoot in her nightgown.

"Marge, this is the end of this conversation and there will not be another."

"I guess we don't know each other at all. I am not a squaw you'll order around. Don't waste your time and don't waste mine."

The black eyes glittered, not with the love and desire she had once known such a short time ago, but with a deadly intensity that made a finger of fear run up her spine.

He never knew he had broken the window of opportunity she had offered, and now, the window would never open again.

Cotton walked past her to Cottu's room. Switching on the light he saw the two white-haired children sprawled together. Her fear deepened as she heard his rage-filled voice.

"Get this whore's brat out of this house or I'll put her out."

He reached for the girl but Marge was there before him, holding the sleeping girl close as she retreated to Mei Ling's room. She covered the child, closed the door and stood in the darkness.

Instantly the door was shoved open so violently it banged against the opposite wall.

"When I come home tomorrow, it will certainly be in her best interest if she's not here. Go to bed and never close a door to me again." His voice was low and ugly.

She looked at this stranger who stood before her, Nina's laughing face blocking her view, Nina's words resounding in Marge's ears... *You are of two different cultures, stick to your own kind.*

She lay cold and removed beside him in the big bed where they once had their most loving, most intimate moments together.

Awake, acutely conscious of the man beside her, whose irregular breathing told her he also lay awake, her mind raced. *What shall I do? What can I do? Where would I go?*

She thought of the two children, how happily they had played together. Cottu's gray eyes dancing with mischief, teasing Maryem with a toy as she shrieked with laughter, both of them with the same foot, toed in, their mutual inheritance from their Cherokee grandfather.

I will not let her go, I will not. I will not. I'm all she has and I love her.

Morning came and Cotton had gone. Her mind struggled all day for a solution.

Marge tensed as Cotton's footsteps sounded, but she

continued with the dinner preparation. She could hear the water running in the bathroom, and knew he would be ready to eat. He walked into Cottu's bedroom, smiled as he stoked the little hand as it lay outside the coverlet. Turning to Marge, "You got rid of her, I see."

"No, I didn't get rid of her anymore than I would have gotten rid of Cottu. I don't understand you—she has as much of your blood as he has. She is an innocent child. How can you be so cruel?"

"I told you to get rid of her or I would." Then his sudden realization: "She's in Mei Ling's room. I won't have her in this house."

"Aren't you forgetting whose house you're in, Cotton? I love her as I love Cottu, as I once loved you, and I will not give her up. Do you hear me? I-will-NEVER-give-her-up."

"Then choose between us. She goes or I do."

"That will be your choice, Cotton. She isn't going anywhere."

He looked down at her incredulously, his eyes wide with disbelief, his voice hoarse with rage.

"I'll take the boy then."

"Over my dead body," Marge blazed back. "I'll kill you, one way or another, if you try."

He laughed, then seized her by the upper arms and shook her like a rag doll. She never flinched as he dropped her.

"Never threaten me, Marge." She stood straight before him, her eyes never left his.

"Don't mistake me, Cotton. That was a promise."

He looked into her eyes for a moment, as though searching, a twisted smile on his face. He walked out. The door closed behind him as quietly as it had opened.

Cotton never spent another night in that cottage. His visits were usually on Sunday, when he spent the time in Cottu's room. Marge could hear Cottu's delighted laughter as he pinned his father to the floor, and Cotton's undistinguishable murmur. But as time went on Cotton's drinking became more noticeable, his actions more erratic, his play rougher. He never asked Cottu what he wanted to do anymore, always it was a lesson in wrestling. His voice loud, "Not that way. This way. See?" A yelp of pain from Cottu.

Marge confronted Cotton as he left. "Don't come here when you're drinking. You scare Cottu."

"I'm teaching him to be a man, not a mama's boy. He needs to be toughened up—at least the Irish part."

"He's barely past two years old, he doesn't need to be tough."

"He's my son and I don't need your opinion or your permission. You remember, I intend to take him this summer."

"You remember what I promised."

His visits became a nightmare for Marge, and eventually even Cottu's joyful expectations turned to fear.

Finally, Cottu met his father at the door with the words, "I don't want to play today."

"Are you sick?"

"No."

"Then go to your room. I want to show you a new hold."

Reluctantly Cottu led the way to his room, then the door shut. A moment later, a loud thump and Cottu's outraged cry, "I won't play with you anymore. You hurt me. You don't smell good, go home."

The sound of a slap, then Cottu's angry "I hate you. Go away."

Marge pushed open the door to see Cottu defiantly looking up at his father, his hand on his smarting cheek, the tears trickling through his fingers. He moved to his mother.

"Cotton, leave, you're drunk and you've hurt Cottu. Don't come back again unless you're sober."

"I'll come when I please. Don't get in my way or that red hair will be on my belt." He gave a short, ugly laugh.

Three days later, Cody brought up a little Christmas tree. Marge and the children strung popcorn and the tree was wrapped from top to bottom. A few homemade decorations, colored with fanciful designs, were tucked among the strands. Two little socks hung close, and letters to Santa Claus addressed in Marge's hand were conspicuously arranged in the branches.

It was later than usual when the children went to bed, tired from the extra activity. When the lights were turned out, Marge lay awake, remembering past Christmases.

She smelled him before she saw his shadow standing over her as he shed his clothes.

"Cotton." She forced the word out, her throat tightening with fear. "What are you doing? Get out of here."

"I've come for my Christmas present and to give you yours. You used to love it, remember?"

She rolled to the opposite side of the bed but quick as a cat he grabbed her foot and twisted her to her back.

"Don't. Don't. Don't." She didn't want to wake the children. She fought furiously; he laughed.

"I'd forgotten what a little hellcat you could be. But then, you know what Nina said, I like it rough. Rough . . . and ready."

She bit and scratched and one flailing arm knocked over the bed lamp with a loud bang. "No. No. Please don't." He slapped her and put his hand roughly over her mouth. Suddenly her mind flashed back. It wasn't Cotton anymore, it was Ed's big beefy hand, the same hard, hurting knuckles between her thighs and the same pounding, driving, insulting pain.

Unexpectedly, the room was flooded with light. Cotton paused, turned his head to see his son in the doorway, screaming, "You're hurting my Mama."

Cotton pulled away, turned and put on his pants, picked up his shirt. Cottu still standing, frozen with fear in the doorway.

Without a backward glance, Cotton brushed past the boy and walked out into the night.

As the children played hide-and-seek among the tables one early morning, Marge looked up to see Cody approaching, precariously balancing two cups of coffee.

"Marge, haven't seen you for ages. I'd guess we're just two ships that pass in the night," he joked. Cody settled himself and sipped his coffee. His gaze followed the playful little girl.

"She looks like Nina, almost. She's got her eyes," he said. He held out his arms and she slowly approached, but then backed away and ran laughing to Cottu.

"We're off to a bad start this year, Marge. Everything seems to have gone to hell. Nina gone, you and Cotton. Things are not going well up at the Ruck-A-Chucky, either. I s'pose you know Cotton's drinking heavy and he gets mean when he's drunk. Makes me heartsick—you know those Indians can't hold their liquor. The work at the dam was goin' so great, it was almost fun to work there. Now the morale is so low it's nonexistent. Used to be Cotton's decisions were right on the money, now they've accumulated in a mish-mash of expensive mistakes and downright dangerous procedures. His belligerent attitude has alienated most of his loyal friends. He's drinkin' on the job. The men are tense, waitin' for the other shoe to fall. Oh, damn near forgot. Ah Sing told me to give you this, just came in yesterday." He handed her a letter.

Marge's eyes fastened to Cody's face, her mind processing his words. She dropped the envelope among the papers in her lap.

"I don't know what to tell you, Cody. There's good and bad in all of us. Hasn't been that long ago I threatened to kill him, but for the first three years no woman could have asked for a better husband. Nina, I loved like a sister, and she destroyed my marriage. Her life was shaped by our society. It was a white man who introduced her to that which destroyed her. It wasn't Nina, it was the evil spirit within her, just as the same evil spirit is destroying Cotton. Some part of us will always love them, Cody, and as we will confront our own demons, perhaps we will understand what made them who they are."

There was a hoot of laughter from the kitchen. Marge paused, "Where are those kids?" Another burst of laughter led her to the source. Ah Sing was teaching the two white-haired children to manipulate the chopsticks—Cottu trying to suck in a dangling noodle, Maryem trying vainly to catch it with her sticky fingers, the young Oriental girl Ah Sing had sent to replace Mei Ling, laughing helplessly.

The icy snow came down in little gusts on a bitterly cold, late afternoon a week later. Marge heard the piercing blare of the police cars as they sped past, lights flashing, turning at the corner that led to the dam. Her heart sank and instinctively she prayed it wasn't Cotton.

The waiting seemed like an eternity, then the first men stamped the snow from their boots and filed in. Marge met them at the door, the freezing wind slamming it shut behind them.

Gripping the nearest man by his arm, "What happened? Who was it? Tell me," she demanded.

"Big Sam Michaels." They wouldn't look at her as they headed for the bar. She ran ahead, and four glasses appeared as if by magic and just as quickly a bottle was produced. The snow melting on their rough clothing, they drank in silence.

"Tell me. Tell me," Marge implored.

"Kelly can tell you, he was there."

The words seemed pulled out of Kelly's mouth at first, but then they came in a gush.

"Big Sam was a high-scaler, the best. The high-scalers had to be a special breed of men and they were the highest paid men on the job because it's such hard, dangerous work. Hanging on a rope, on the side of a canyon, sometimes eight hundred feet in the air, loaded with tools, picking their way through the line air hoses, electrical lines and bundles of drill steel. Forty-four pounds of jackhammer lowered on a steel cable to drill the holes in the rock and pack with dynamite," he interrupted himself.

"Marge, I s'pose you know all this. Hell, Cotton must have told you about the high-scalers." He continued, "Well, something went wrong. When the jackhammer swung down, it hit Sam dead center, broke the rope, and he fell."

The tears ran unashamedly down his bearded cheeks.

The other men turned their heads, perhaps to hide their own tears, or not to see his.

Marge shuddered as the picture came clear, and refilled the glasses from the bottle that stood brazenly on the bar.

The man on the end downed his drink with a single gulp, wiped his lips with the back of his hand, and spoke. "Big Sam, he's been foreman on that crew before the first rock was blasted. He was the best in the business, and he loved knowing it. He was a prideful man, Sam was."

"Yeah, but we all knew sumpthin' was gonna blow sky high. There's been bad blood between Cotton and Sam ever since the first day when Cotton cold-cocked Sam and broke his jaw."

"Heard they damn near came to blows a few nights ago. Cotton was drunk and Sam sure wasn't far behind, wasn't that right, Jake? You was there." The other man nodded.

Kelly continued, "Well, it was gettin' to the end of the shift. It gets dark early you know, especially up there in them canyons. The lights were on, of course, but the shadows reflect offa them steep walls. Cotton told Sam to get his gear and swing over and finish the job, needed two more holes. Sam looked surprised, he didn't think much of that idea."

"Hell, no. It'll be dark in half an hour."

"You are a yellow-bellied son of a bitch, aren't you? I'll do it myself and show you how to do it right. Gimme your gear."

"Yeah, Sam took the bait. I doubt they'll ever find his body."

"Of course, there'll be a big investigation, but it won't do Sam a hell of a lot of good."

They finished the bottle silently, each man lost in his own particular hell.

Marge shuddered as she visualized Sam's dangling body, then only the frayed rope as it swung wildly from the impact.

It was daybreak when the silence of the cabin was broken by a knock on the door. Marge pulled on a robe, half asleep. *What now. It's too early.* Covering her yawn with one hand she reluctantly opened the door. Silhouetted against the sun's bright trays, Cody stood, flanked by the sheriff and two other official-looking men in their suits and ties. Cody stumbled forward, as though pushed by an unseen hand. "Marge . . . Marge . . . " He tried to speak and tried again. Then the sheriff stepped to the front. His voice faltered, "Mrs. Eeagle, I'm sorry to bring this bad news. There has been an accident at the dam. Your husband is presumed dead, the body has not been recovered, so terribly sorry."

The blessed numbness that descended crowded out any further words that might have been said. Blindly, she watched them until they got into the car with the official lettering, then turned to Cody who led her to the sofa and sat with his arms around her.

"What happened, Cody?" Her voice choked as she trembled against him.

"I knew he'd gone crazy when I heard that big four-ton earth-movin' machine start up in the middle of the night. I knew it had to be Cotton, who else would dare? I didn't even grab my pants, I just run out in my longjohns to see what the hell he was doin'. That machine was goin' just as fast as he could push it in circles, just in circles. I tried to wave him down, but he kept comin'. I moved fast or he'd a run me over. He smashed through the barricades, blinked the lights and went straight for the edge. It seemed like an eternity before I heard it hit on the spillway, seven hundred feet down.

"The noise woke everybody up, everybody runnin' every which way, then ran to look over, but not me. I'm not gonna be in line, tomorrow is my last day. Here, I snitched this offa his desk, I didn't think the whole world had to know it." Cody handed her a single sheet of paper. It was Cotton's termination papers, effective tomorrow.

Work slowed to a standstill at the uncompleted dam, already seven hundred feet high. Thirty million tons of concrete and a million dollars worth of equipment stood idle. The dam swarmed with officials and the investigation dragged on.

Word from the grapevine went out. Cody assembled the entire crew on a meadow overlooking the dam. The men, restless, openly curious, quieted as Cody, balanced on a large flat boulder, held up his hand for their attention. He spoke plainly, "Who the hell says it was suicide? You all know time didn't mean nuthin' to Cotton. If he got a notion to get that machine out of the way so we could get an early start in the morning, he wouldn't give a damn if it was dark or daylight. It was an accident, pure and simple, wasn't it?. The insurance company don't pay for suicide, think about it. Who's gonna help Marge raise them kids if there's no insurance?"

"Suicide, my ass," a voice from the background yelled.

"Any damned fool know'd it was an accident. I saw the lights flicker and go out on that machine two weeks ago. A malfunction in the electrical system, it shoulda been in the shop then. Ain't that right men? Anybody here say different?" The clapping and whistling began.

Before leaving town, their investigations nearly completed, one government official offered his opinion to the sheriff.

"Accident, hell. That was one damn smart Indian. Did you see all those degrees and diplomas on the wall? All them awards? Ain't no way in hell that could have been an accident. He knew exactly where those barricades were and what he was doing. Heard he was having trouble with that good-lookin' red-haired wife and, of course, the booze. My God, what a mess. Nothing left of anything."

The sheriff spoke. "You damned well better keep your opinions to yourself if you want to get out of town alive. There's two hundred men or more up there that'll make you a liar. People get lynched in these parts. Just a thought, of course."

Cottu and Maryem were older now, already in school. They were her whole life, but Marge knew she had to start weaning herself and let them belong to themselves.

As Maryem grew she resembled her mother more and more. A tilt of the head, a sidelong glance, the lightening quick response to Cottu's teasing, brought vivid memories of Nina. Days when they had laughed, the hard times when they had agonized together, pushed through Marge's mind and seemed to take up permanent residence there.

Ah Sing managed both bar and restaurant so well that Marge felt like an extra thumb. She decided to lease him the business and started the necessary procedures.

Sorting through the paperwork, she was surprised to find the unfinished papers and the envelope tucked between the pages that had fallen in her lap the day Cody had told her of Cotton's heavy drinking on the job and the resulting difficulties. Curiously, almost fearfully, she opened the envelope, a letter from the dead, and found Nina's familiar scrawl and prestigious Beverly Hills address. As she withdrew the single sheet of paper, a check made out to her in the sum of one hundred fifty thousand dollars dropped out. It was dated two weeks before Nina's death. A quick intake of breath, she sat stunned, almost afraid to touch that small piece of paper. Her hands shook as she held the letter and her tears blurred the words as she read, whispering to herself.

Marge, I feel like hell this morning, but while my head is as clear as it's going to be, I want to get this off my mind. I'm sending you this check for the favor you are going to do for me, although you don't know it yet. There isn't any doubt in my mind that you will.

I know money can never compensate for all the good things you've done for me and mine, or compensate for what I've done to you. I don't know why, you were always my 'North Star,' but I guess I've been wandering in the dark so long I lost sight of that, too. Use this money anyway you like. Nina

The check lay on the old dresser for two days, held in place by Marge's heavy gold wedding band, Marge's mind struggling with the significance of the check and the pathos of the accompanying letter.

She drove to the bank, asked for the manager and, to his great delight, opened another account. Leaving, she drove aimlessly into the countryside. The fearful events of the last few months had left her despondent and lonely, frightened by the sudden ambush of life, apprehensive of the future.

Money. I have more than enough of my own. What shall I do with all that money? What do I need? Inner security? I feel like a leaf floating on a wind, going nowhere. Life is passing me by. I'm out of step with the world. When I was poor, life was full of challenges and I felt vibrant and alive. That's what I need, a challenge.

She drove on. *I don't want to go home. The house is too quiet, too empty. The children have each other, but who do I have?*

She found herself on the road that served as a boundary for the Indian Rancheria, "A fancy name for a reservation," Cody had said.

Looking ahead, high on a hill adjoining the reservation, Marge could see the skeleton of "Colburn's Folly" still standing, its unfinished wooden fingers pointing to the sky.

What an incredible waste, her practical mind lamented. *What could a person do with that? I believe Cody said there was fifteen acres, but it's worthless; nobody wants to live next to that Indian Reservation. Surely the Indians could find a use for it if they owned it but, of course, they are so dirt poor they hardly survive, especially in the winter.*

Suddenly, as though a curtain had been drawn open, a thought flashed through her mind. *Of course, what a perfect spot for an Indian School! I will build a decent school for the little ones, and add a trade school for the older ones who need to make a living outside the reservation. Nina's money will give them what they've never had, an opportunity to learn a better way of life. She will leave a better mark on the world, a world that surely left its mark on her.*

Marge had caught the vision. Her eyes sparkled with excitement. A clear, unmistakable picture came perfectly into focus. She could see the finished building, standing proud against the skyline, built of red rock, of which there was an abundance, and local timber.

Dormitories for both boys and girls, a large well-equipped kitchen and dining room, bright cheerful classrooms with new books, buildings where the trades will be taught, tools and other equipment, the best that money can buy. Oh. And generous scholarships for those who follow their own dream. She could see it all with her eyes closed.

Carved high on the stately front of the massive stone face:
NEVA VEY MAHALASEAH MEMORIAL

Marge bought the property the next day from a grateful Mr. Colburn for eleven-thousand five hundred dollars.

She lay awake that night in the lonely big bed gazing into the darkness as the full realization of the magnitude of her plan took hold. The first doubts crept in, nagging relentlessly at her dream. *What if? What if? Lord, I've prayed for some direction in my life, a challenge, but this? This?* Her heart faltered. Still refusing to budge, impatiently waiting, lay the dream. Her imagination ran riot. Mentally placing every stone, every structure. *Should the dorms be here? Or the kitchen there? And then, of course, the classrooms facing south.* Her thoughts soared from the possible to the impossible as she reviewed and discarded the ideas that flooded through her brain.

As she lay in bed that night, she planned. *I'll go up there as soon as it's daylight and walk every inch of that property.*

She dressed in the semidarkness. Boots, jeans, an old worn shirt. She tied her hair back with a colorful scarf then picked up a denim jacket; even in June the mornings were chilly. As she walked toward the kitchen she could see the back of the chair with a crown of inky black hair barely showing above it, a small hand holding a cup of tea resting on the table, and Marge knew her coffee would be waiting. As the kitchen warmed by the early morning light, she spoke softly.

"Take the kids to the restaurant for breakfast, it's a treat. Don't let

Ah Sing spoil them." The little Oriental woman laughed as she poured the coffee.

Half an hour later the optimistic little Model A Ford had struggled up the narrow winding road. As Marge stepped out to gaze at the panorama below her, a grandiose thought intruded, *I'd have paid double, just for the view.* She threw her head back and laughed with joy, her entire being soaked in the beauty of the scene.

She could see the outlines of the distant town and hear the muted sounds as another day began in the Sierra Nevada foothills.

As she picked her way through the aborted beginning of the elaborately planned mansion, she thought, *surely some of these heavy timbers are salvageable and that rock foundation can't have deteriorated. Of course, most of this subfloor is gone,* and so, methodically, she took inventory.

"Six-thousand square feet of nuthin'," Colburn had muttered as she signed the papers that made "six-thousand square feet of nuthin" the foundation for Marge's dream.

As she trudged over the land, so much grown over with scrub oak and weeds, she was thrilled to find the hill sloped back, giving acres of useable land. Then the sun rising high over the eastside to unveil an old abandoned apple orchard, vibrantly alive with the sweet scent of the white and pink blossoms that promised a bountiful harvest. She clapped her hands and laughed. *Ah Sing will be so pleased. It will be chop suey and apples again.*

Suddenly she was exhausted. She had tramped up and down and around it seemed for hours. She sat quietly leaning against a rock that formed part of the foundation. The foundation that would validate her dream. Her mind sorted through this sudden new twist in her life while her fingers played in the red dirt.

Now, I must make this vision a reality. This will be no small undertaking. A skilled, knowledgeable architect is a must and that's where I will start. A man who can plan and design these buildings to be both beautiful and functional, buildings that will stand the ravages of time. Where will I find him? Who would know a man with the best qualifications?

Her head in her hands, she concentrated. *I heard the men talking about a house, a very big house. They laughed and said it was nearly as big as the Ruck-A-Chucky. Some local guy, that guy at the lumber yard, doesn't even have a wife they said. Now surely he had the best architect in Sacramento, what was his name? It was familiar, I shouldn't have forgotten it. There. Of course, I should have remembered it, the Olson Lumber Company. I'll stop by on the way home. Hope I can catch him before he goes to lunch, I'm certainly not very presentable.* As she brushed the dust from her jeans and tried to scrape the red dirt from her boots, she pulled the scarf off to wipe her sweaty face, leaving her hair to curl, heavy and damp in careless disorder. She tucked in her shirttail and tossed her jacket on the worn seat beside her. *There, that's the best I can do.*

The little coupe left a trail of dust as it sped down the road, as if happy to be going down instead of up.

She hurried back to town, her mind bursting with ideas. Intent on her thoughts, she missed the entrance to the lumberyard and had to turn back. *That's what happens when I'm day dreaming,* she muttered under her breath. She pulled into the crowded parking lot and squeezed the dusty little Ford next to a luxurious, immaculate Packard.

I hope I haven't missed him, combing her hair with her fingers. *I want to get home and get cleaned up.* She walked quickly to the impressive storefront reaching hastily to open the door, but it was opened more quickly still, from within. Thrown off balance, she stumbled, a strong arm extended to steady her and she looked up to see a tall man with an embarrassed, apologetic smile. "I'm so sorry to have barged through that door so carelessly, I hope I didn't hurt you. Are you alright?" Marge nodded and he smiled as he held out his hand. "My name is Ben Olson, may I help you?"

She extended her hand to meet that of this stranger, yet he didn't seem like a stranger. Even the spoken name seemed vaguely familiar.

She withdrew her hand, still without speaking. Her eyes were questioning what instinctively she knew was true, and yet incredible. She recognized this stranger with the thick dark hair that still fell over his broad forehead, those blue eyes that she had once seen fill with tears as he helped her off the train. She even remembered his words, "Don't worry, Miss Marge, this is where our new life begins." She looked at the good firm mouth with its lines of humor and tolerance. She felt he had depths of sternness in him, but justice tempered with mercy. He would always be in command of the immediate moment.

Is this handsome, well-spoken, well-dressed man the Ben I knew?

It is Ben. Of course—it's Ben. He's not the hungry boy that I took to the dining car on the Great Northern train how many years ago? Not the boy whose father's wedding suit hung on his skinny frame as though it were hung from a wire hanger. The gangling, awkward and frightened boy had become a man.

"Ben," she said softly, "did your grandma ever get the firing pin fixed on that old shotgun?"

"Marge? Marge Reagan. Can it be you?" His question was laid

waste by the surety of his heart. "I've thought about you always and wondered where you were all these years. No one else in this world ever had hair that indescribable color."

As he took her hand, something flowed from him to her, something reassuring, steadfast, something forever.

She said quietly, "You've changed, Ben."

"Yes, I have." He wanted to hold her to him. He saw her breast swell as if drawing a heavy breath.

Again, silence between them, like the knock of an old friend on an old forgotten door.

He went to her then, and held her, and his voice broke. "You don't know how your memory comforted me all these years. Just the thought of your courage, your lovely generous spirit, has kept me afloat so many times."

His arms were warm and firm, and his feelings seemed to surge over her like an ocean wave. She smiled at him sadly. "Ben, there's been so much water under the bridge. I've changed, too. I'm not the Marge you knew."

"Nor am I the Ben you befriended those many years ago. I cried when we went our separate ways, but now the tears I feel are tears of joy. I've found you again. Marge, will you let me see you again soon?" His voice shook.

He could see her gray eyes darken, the gold-tipped black lashes shadow her suddenly flushed cheeks, the soft, full lips parting. He felt her body lean into his.

"Yes, oh yes," she whispered.

They embraced each other gently.

Marge thought, *if he takes his arms away, I will surely fall.* Her heart sang. *I'm home at last.*

A Note From Dolores Durando

Now the prairie grasses cover the old North Dakota homestead where the blacksmith shop, with the housekeeping room in the back, once stood. I lived the first five years of my life with my loving grandpa in that back room. I played among the muddy boots of the farmers who sat around the pot-bellied stove, spitting Copenhagen, watching it sizzle as my grandpa worked the bellows and hammered the plowshares.

Now, at 90 years old, I live comfortably and enjoy painting with water colors, sculpting in alabaster, earning a few blue ribbons at juried shows, and for the first time, writing.